SCENERY
OF THE
CRIME

A RETRO BROADWAY MYSTERY

FRANK "FRAVER" VERLIZZO

CAMEL
PRESS
Kenmore, WA

CAMEL
PRESS

A Coffeetown Press book published by Epicenter Press

Epicenter Press
6524 NE 181st St. Suite 2
Kenmore, WA 98028.
www.Epicenterpress.com
www.Coffeetownpress.com
www.Camelpress.com

For more information go to: www.epicenterpress.com
www.FRAVER.com

Scenery of the Crime
Copyright © 2025 by Frank "Fraver" Verlizzo

ISBN: 9781684923106 (trade paper)
ISBN: 9781684923113 (ebook)
LOC:2024952535

Cover art by FRAVER

To Susan L. Schulman
Press Agent Extraordinaire
Who Loved Her Life in Theatre
As Much As We Loved Her

Acknowledgments

So many of my friends and family have shown their support for the Retro Broadway Mystery series. They are the first-readers, commenters, suggestion-makers who have helped me shape this book.

Craig Burke, Jon Bierman, my agent Susan H. Schulman, Barbara Dhyne, Jim Dhyne, M.R. Ligammari, Janet Ligammari, Nick Verlizzo, Bryan Andes, Caitlin Blot, Helene Krasney, Dean Ravosa, Anne Trites, Phil Garrett, Jennifer McCord and

Joseph Ligammari

and

My Broadway colleagues and friends whose inspiration can be felt within these pages. They gave me indelible, cherished memories of my career in theatrical advertising, which began in 1974.

Nancy Verlizzo, who taught me to love books.

Helena Baxter Is Dead; Famed Broadway Actress

By IAN LEIGHTON-CROSS

Legendary Broadway, Hollywood, and Television actress, Helena Baxter was killed this afternoon in a freak stage accident. Miss Baxter was rehearsing for her new play, *Don't Hang Up*, which began previews at the Helen Hayes Theatre last evening. Part of the elaborate scenic design, a mechanized trap door, was accidentally kept open. It has not been established how or why Miss Baxter was alone on the stage set when she fell nearly thirty feet into the cavity. The actress toppled head first into a pile of empty trash cans, metal folding chairs, and percussion instruments kept in storage in the trap room below. More details to follow.

This tragedy comes directly on the heels of another calamity involving the late actress just two days ago, as several guests at a cocktail party she hosted at her apartment at the Dakota were poisoned - one fatally. That case remains under police investigation, and it's unclear whether these two incidents are related. More as the story develops.

Famous for a sparkling personality and warmth of character in her private life, Helena Baxter came under intense scrutiny several years ago when she reportedly bashed a foreign tourist on the head with a ten pound exercise dumbbell, killing him instantly.

Over time, the incident has entered Broadway folklore guaranteed to illicit awkward laughs in the retelling.

Wed to British actor/producer/director Rex Merchant—after a somewhat tumultuous break-up with Hollywood movie-mogul Earl Quick—Miss Baxter recently returned to the Broadway stage in the new thriller, *Don't Hang Up*. The highly anticipated show was scheduled to open next week after a brief period of low-priced preview performances.

Helena Baxter's exact age was unavailable at the time of this report.

Friday – March 7, 1975

Scenery of the Crime

CAST OF MAIN CHARACTERS (In Order of Appearance)

VIC SENSO .... Advertising Art Director at Thompson & Co

TOBIN KLEIN .... Partner and Creative Director at Thompson & Co

MARK RHODES .... Assistant Theatrical Press Agent

CAL LOCKHEED .... A Familiar Broadway Actor

HELENA BAXTER .... Star of Stage, Screen, and Television

BETTIE BALBOA .... Advertising Account Executive

GUY ANDERSEN .... Sardi Building Lobby Attendant

MIZZ MITZI .... Society Clairvoyant

REX MERCHANT .... British Producer/Director, Married to Helena Baxter

EARL QUICK .... Hollywood Producer, Married to Celeste Farris

AVA CHASTEN .... Broadway Press Agent Extraordinaire

ARNE ENGELS .... Broadway General Manager of *Don't Hang Up*

MARSHA DAVENPORT ..... Receptionist at Thompson & Co

VITO LANZETTA .... Her Protective Italian Boyfriend

CELESTE FARRIS .... Broadway Diva and Hollywood
Superstar

TERRY HAGEN .... Theatrical Photographer

SIMONE CALDWELL .... Understudy/Secretary to Helena
Baxter

RODNEY CLEMENTS .... NYPD Mounted Policeman

DR. PATRICK WHEELER ... NYPD Medical Examiner

CAPRICE FOURNIER .... Housekeeper of Helena Baxter, and a
Budding Chef

PERRY CHAN .... Scenery Designer for *Don't Hang Up*

VENUS PLUTO .... Former Actress, Secretary to Celeste
Farris

OSKAR LINQVIST .... Editor at Simon & Schuster
Publishing

RENNY CLEMENTS .... NYPD Detective, Officer Rodney
Clements' Brother

JD .... Celeste Farris' Driver

Act One
Scene One

Tuesday - March 4, 1975
Three days before the murder at the Hayes Theatre

There are few inanimate objects as deceptive as a theatre seat. At once, seemingly snug and inviting in all its plush velvet glory, it can quickly become an instrument of torture for anyone other than the most elfin of audience members. Given the quality of the production being scrutinized from your assigned location, the level of discomfort endured while sitting can be easily measured based on the brilliance—or dullness—of the program being offered. Some productions can transport you to a place that obliterates all awareness of lumpy cushions and lopsided postures. Certain other entertainments invariably draw your attention to insufficient legroom, all the while announcing every squeaky spring in your restricted, upholstered confinement.

E105 may be considered a good seat, but that is entirely subjective.

Although Vic Senso was not a fan of airports or flying, at least Pan Am has the capacity to offer a long-legged patron an upgrade from standard economy class. Unfortunately, all theatre seats are created equal (aka cramped.) Since uncontrollable crying is typically frowned upon by theatre managers—as well as by everyone else seated around you in the hushed environment—

suffering in silence becomes the only civilized option available. Some find solace in emitting muted coughs or subdued sneezes to ease the pain. A furtive glance around the audience will reveal a few bobbing heads belonging to a select minority, who've been blessed with temporary relief from leg torment by falling asleep during the performance. If one doesn't really care to extend consideration to the other people in their row, another surefire alternate escape route is to scurry past knees, pocketbooks, and souvenir shopping bags in order to dart up the theatre aisle toward the restrooms.

That's precisely the choice Vic made, and instantly regretted, as his legs became trapped between an attache case and an obstinate umbrella. Relief for his crushed knees was a short-lived reward when confronted by the wall of cigarette smoke that blasted him in the face upon entering the downstairs men's room. A non-smoker himself, Vic hadn't seen that much cloud cover since watching a Bette Davis movie on late night television. A quick survey of the hallowed lavatory revealed two press agents, three casting assistants, and what seemed to be a good percentage of the staff from the theatrical advertising agency that employed Vic. This evening was, after all, the first preview of a new play. The audience was typically populated by the inner circle: those who worked in some capacity on the show but will not be invited to opening night. Friends and family of the performers, who may or may not be invited to opening night. Also included are avid fans of the arts willing to invest up to $15.00 for a prime orchestra seat to an unreviewed stage vehicle. This guarantees bragging rights in the event the production doesn't last until opening night.

The new play being performed for the audience upstairs, entitled *Don't Hang Up*, is neither particularly bad nor good. It is the type of entertainment that would probably have been assured a decent run before the phenomenon of television reared its ugly head. Unless you were feasting on the likes of Frederick Knott or Ira Levin, suspense thrillers were plentiful on the tube and could be viewed in your living room on any given evening. And—this is the major plus—you could watch in total comfort while dressed only in your underwear. Vic was warned early on in his career by his sage boss, Tobin Klein, that whenever attending a first preview you should appear to be having a good time, keep smiling, and never look at your wristwatch during the performance.

One should expect to be surrounded by stealth clients, or friends-of-clients (aka show-spies), who are anxious to report back to those check-writing producers any bad word-of-mouth they may have overheard between acts. Heaven forbid it gets traced back to you. The last thing Vic needed at the next advertising meeting was a crowded conference room table loaded with stink-eye.

It's insensitive to judge a first preview. The playwright, the cast, the producers, the director, the general manager, the press agents, their assistants, the folks manning the box office, the ushers, and usherettes—everyone wants the production to be a hit. After weeks and weeks of grueling rehearsals, massive rewrites, creative differences, and sudden cast changes, no one wants to hear your constructive criticism on how to fix their show. All anyone really wants to hear is, "Congratulations."

"This bathroom is more crowded than the mezzanine." observed Mark Rhodes, a relatively new press assistant, zipping up his fly. Mark was young, well-built, and spoke in a soft, soothing tone that could have earned him serious money doing radio and television voice-overs if his career focus hadn't settled on theatrical publicity. "Is it always like this?"

"No, young man. Sometimes there's a long line out the door just to get in here."

This utterance was projected in a booming voice trained to be heard from the last row of the balcony. It emanated from Cal Lockheed and was accompanied by one of his trademark sweeping stage gestures encompassing the smoke-filled toilet. A familiar Broadway actor, and a classically disciplined graduate of old-school dramatics, Cal was currently between projects. After taking a breath, he added, "Lillian Hellman, Tennessee Williams, Clifford Odets—they all smoked like bloody chimneys while working. I'll never understand how any of those self-respecting playwrights could expect their actors, fellow smokers mind you, to function without a cigarette for over an hour. It's totally inhumane."

"What do you do when you're starring in a production and performing on stage for over an hour?" Mark asked.

"I never do Shakespeare or any play that takes place before the advent of Lucky Strike. Years ago, I hired Babe Butler to write an adaptation of *The Legend of Sleepy Hollow* for me as a touring one-man show. It was a tremendous success across the country, darling. Since I portray all of the characters from Ichabod Crane to Katrina Van Tassel, I asked that Babe intersperse the action, which takes place in 1799, with a modern day narrator. As such, I could spout my lines and light up a Lucky intermittently throughout the evening."

"I'm sure Washington Irving would simply have loved that idea," commented Vic.

Cigarette hanging from his bottom lip, Cal was studying his swarthy reflection in the mirror above the sink as he spoke, "It's the reason why I fail to work as much as I should. Most directors cannot fully understand the artistic motivations for having my characters using cigarettes."

"Well, smoking like a chimney would certainly put a unique spin on your portrayal of Mahatma Gandhi." Vic chimed in. "I'd pay to see that."

"Pay? Who are you kidding, darling?" Lockheed snapped, "You would never step foot inside a theatre unless you'd been comped."

Grinning, Vic asked, "May I inquire just how much *you* coughed up to sit in the audience tonight?"

Cal winked, "I was invited, darling. Chalk it up to a personal appearance."

"Well, if you're going to be embracing fans and signing autographs, you should at least wash your hands," Vic advised.

In a huff, Cal pumped the soap dispenser while his cigarette smoke curled up into his eyes. "Don't you have to get back to your seat? Your clients might quiz you on the contents of the play."

"Don't laugh." Vic grimaced, "It would be just like them to do that."

"Besides, you certainly wouldn't want to end up on the leading lady's hit list," said Cal, coyly. "Could be dangerous."

"Don't go dredging up that old scandal." Vic was either waving away lingering cigarette smoke or the ghost of past headlines. "I was obsessed with that godawful incident as a teenager. It's been at least fifteen years."

Mark's interest was piqued, "What old scandal? Remember guys, fifteen years ago, I was in seventh grade and living on a farm in the hinterlands. I'm a sponge for vintage Broadway gossip. That's why I'm working in publicity."

"The lovely star of tonight's play is a bona fide murderess," announced Cal.

"She went through a hell of a horrible period. The press hounded her mercilessly," Vic said, "The poor woman wasn't even in the same state when it happened."

Mark lit up a new cigarette. "Well, now I *gotta* hear the story. Helena Baxter killed somebody? Who was it?"

"A foreign tourist. Yes, really!" smirked Cal. "But, I'm leaving out the best part. You'll never guess what the murder weapon was."

Gray eyes wide, Mark inhaled, and held his breath.

"Death by dumbbell!" Cal crossed his arms for dramatic emphasis.

Vic was quick to amend the dramatic response, "If you're going to tell the story, at least get the facts straight. Like I said, as a kid, I was a theatre and movie nerd, and still remember the details— obsessed by all the sordid hoopla. Our Miss Baxter was having her bedroom air conditioner reinstalled after much delay. When the appliance had originally been removed for repair, a temporary screen was set up to replace the vacant window space. Helena Baxter temporarily propped two ten-pound exercise dumbbells on the sill to hold it tightly in place."

"So far, this sounds more like a bad DIY project than a murder." said Mark, finally releasing his mouthful of smoke.

"Fast forward a few weeks," Vic continued, "Her housekeeper decides to clean the window ledge in preparation for the reinstallation of the air conditioner. The maid asked the secretary to help her with it. The two started to remove the screen from the seventh-floor window. According to my memory of the press coverage, one of the dumbbells suddenly began to roll across the window ledge. They both reached for it but neither was quick enough. A Norwegian tourist happened to be strolling by—talk about being in the wrong place at the wrong time—as the dumbbell came hurtling down, hitting him directly in the head. He was killed instantly. The press had a field day. Helena Baxter was branded a cold-blooded killer until all of the facts finally came to light a few days later. It turned out that she wasn't even in New York at the time, but out-of-town in a show."

Mark laughingly admitted, "Death by flying dumbbell—that's infinitely more exciting than the play being performed upstairs. Poor Miss Baxter. She's so sweet to everyone, even to an underling like me."

"You can attribute that to her training from the Old Hollywood studio-system," said Vic. "1) Always appear in public dressed like a star, 2) Be charming to your fans, and 3) Ingratiate yourself to those who make you look good on stage and screen."

"I was once told a funny story about Lana Turner," interrupted Cal, "She was attending a movie premiere and emerged from her limo dripping in jewels, full makeup, and wearing a dazzling gown. One of her fans broke through the line and ran up to her babbling, 'Oh, Miss Turner, you always look so stunning.' To which, Lana replied, 'Thanks honey, the studio forces me to wear all this crap.'"

Mark guffawed as Cal continued.

"Helena Baxter could teach a Master Class in deportment, elegance, and grace under fire. Compounding that awful calamity, there was her scandalous romantic breakup which was front-page tabloid fodder for weeks. It took Helena Baxter a few years to recover from the avalanche of terrible articles written about the dumbbell incident. Fortunately, all the publicity gave the lady a boost at the Hollywood box office with two blockbuster films back-to-back in the early 1960s. Her next Broadway show was a sell-out smash hit.

The ratings on her television appearances went through the roof. Critical and financial success make little things like sudden death take a back seat, darling. Life seems to have gotten even better for her now that she married…um…much, much younger British director, Rex Merchant." Cal added.

"I'd better get back upstairs to the show," said Vic, "I've missed quite a bit of the action."

"That's right, one never knows if this is the evening that Helena Baxter will commit another crime," winked Cal. "You know, a prop knife that's been switched for the real thing—a sure cure for having upstaged the headliner. Perhaps, a random stage light cut loose from the wings will come crashing down on an irritating co-star. A bit of poison discreetly dropped into a prop cocktail—bye, bye, pretty ingenue! The stage can be a creative playing field for a killer with chutzpah and a fertile imagination."

"Well, it's been a pleasure, gentlemen. Let's do it again soon," said Vic.

Mark Rhodes ran his half-smoked cigarette under the cold-water faucet and tossed it into the trash bin. "Wait for me. I'm going to stand at the back of the house for the rest of the performance. With any luck, my boss'll think I've been working all this time."

Vic said, "Bettie's meeting me after the curtain call. She watched me sneak up the aisle. She knows I cannot tolerate sitting in theatre seats for too long. We're going back to the office for last minute prep on our presentation for tomorrow."

"Good luck with that," said Mark. "I'll be there. It'll be a first for me."

Although the plot of *Don't Hang Up* hadn't captured his interest thus far, Vic greatly admired the scenic design. The entire play is set in a warren of theatrical agents' offices. The stage scheme prominently featured three office doors, which when opened, revealed each particular character's private workspace. It was extremely voyeuristic and fascinating. Helena Baxter was portraying a publicist whose life was being threatened by an unhinged actor. To give the production a cinematic touch, when the action was centered on Miss Baxter (which indeed it was most of the time), the scenery moved forward on a track to give the equivalent of a screen closeup. The interior of her office was composed of a desk, two lamps, a typewriter, various desktop supplies, and a mountain of papers, presumably resumés. Behind her workspace chair, there was a wall covered with glass-framed 8"x10" actor and actress headshots photographed in black and white.

Headshots were a mandatory tool every Broadway hopeful needed as a leave-behind at an audition. They could be found in stacks in any publicist's office. It made for a hypnotically clever backdrop—having all those faces staring back at the audience. Hung in a perfectly configured grid, ten frames across and ten rows down, the effect was slightly unsettling. Vic was certain that that was indeed intentional on the part of the brilliant set designer, his friend Perry Chan.

Don't Hang Up was chock full of nifty stage tricks including a trap door and two side turntables that were used to heighten suspense and effectively scare the audience at various points during the play.

Before turning his full attention to the rest of the performance from his location at the rear of the darkened theatre, Vic couldn't help but wonder—while scanning the impressive set for a myriad of potentially life-threatening hazards—if there'd ever been a stage-related accident that was, in actuality, a cover-up for murder.

Scene Two

Bettie Balboa was stunning. Vic finally spotted her walking up the aisle among the throng of theatergoers heading toward the exits. He was struck by how the jarring house lights complimented, rather than criticized, her fragile beauty. Bettie was intelligent, witty, creative, and happened to be his co-worker at the advertising agency. She was reliable even in the harshest of circumstances. Vic knew he could always count on her support and hoped that she believed the same of him. Bettie was a dynamic force at Thompson & Co. Vic admired her utter control and diplomacy in handling sticky client situations, only once witnessing a glimpse of her smoldering Cuban temper, which she gracefully kept in check. He decidedly did not want to be on the receiving end of that tsunami when it was ultimately unleashed.

Now safely distanced from the theatre, Bettie discreetly asked, "What did you think of the play?"

"I've seen worse, and definitely have seen better. It'll be a tough one to advertise for sure unless it receives fantastic reviews." Vic kept looking over his shoulder in the event of a surprise ambush by a stray client. "What's your take on it?"

"The box office has a bit of an advance, so that might hold them until the critics get in to see it. Unfortunately, the production falls off a cliff financially after opening night, which is scheduled two weeks from now. Helena Baxter will probably work her magic in terms of getting good word-of-mouth on the streets. The audience clearly loved her performance. I thought her costumes were gorgeous. The scenery was amazing. How was the men's room?" Bettie asked.

"Packed." Vic said, "I saw your boyfriend, Mark Rhodes."

"Future boyfriend. Maybe," mused Bettie. "I've only met Mark briefly a few times in crowded conference rooms. He's still new to the Broadway scene. I'll bide my time and monitor how he handles himself under pressure. Dog-eat-dog and all that. He could be ground mincemeat by next month. Besides, Mark hasn't even been around long enough for gossip to catch up with him. I'd like to do some research before taking a serious interest."

"He's awfully easy on the eyes," said Vic, "There's a lot to be said for that."

Their walk from the theatre back to the office involved a brief trek down Broadway from 46th to 44th Streets. Late at night, Times Square has a certain sleazy allure that can never be duplicated. The blindingly bright lights of the movie marquees clash and blend with neon reflections both on the concrete sidewalks and on the gawking tourists that crowd them. All this, while the athletic-looking Winston cigarette man blows his smoke rings over and across the wide thoroughfare from his advertising billboard erected three stories above ground level.

Turning the corner on 44th Street, one could always tell final curtain time by the masses elbowing their way through the entrance doors of Broadway's most famous restaurant. A chic mob of theatergoers often spilled out onto the sidewalk while waiting to gain admittance. Bettie and Vic walked briskly past them and headed into their building, referred to as The Sardi Building, by those whose businesses were located there. Few out-of-towners ever suspect that the unassuming set of doors, a few steps away from the eatery's main entrance, not only gave one access to several floors of active office suites, but to Sardi's restaurant and its hallowed private rooms above.

They signed in at the lobby attendant's desk. Aristocratic, with an ever-grumpy demeanor, Guy Andersen, former character actor in daytime soap operas, was on duty.

Before beginning his second career as Sardi's lobby doorman, he'd played everything from judges, doctors, and scientists, to cab drivers, waiters, and bartenders in his long television career. Guy knew just about everybody in the business, and always kept his eyes and ears wide open for any current gossip involving the entertainment industry.

"Any good star encounters tonight, Mr. A?"

Andersen always perked up whenever he was in close proximity to Bettie. "Tony Perkins was here earlier, and I spotted Chris Plummer sneaking in. Deborah Kerr came for dinner with her family after her show. What a class act she is. Big doings, big doings," the elegant, retired actor said, enthusiastically.

Vic walked ahead while Bettie heard the rest of the latest celebrity low-down from the door attendant.

Guy Andersen typically ended his litany of current gossip and star-sightings with a blind item. For those in the know, a blind item consisted of gossip—which hopefully included scandalous details—while the identities of the people involved were hinted at, but not revealed.

"Tonight's headliner: Which famous Broadway star is currently sleeping around with someone who's not her producer husband?"

"That could end up being a rather lengthy list, Mr. A." Bettie laughed.

The small, marbled lobby led to two elevators. Both were extremely busy during the daytime and pre-theatre hours. In the late evenings, one was kept dormant while the other was held for freight. The inactive car was designated out-of-service and remained inactive on the seventh floor with the switches off, until early morning. With a touch of the up-button, Vic rang for the elevator on the ornate wall plate. Bettie caught up just as it arrived.

The brass doors opened to reveal the highly polished oak-paneled interior. The operator's smiling face appeared front-and-center as well.

"Working late again tonight?" the uniformed gentleman casually asked, as the car leisurely climbed its way to the seventh floor.

"Presentation tomorrow. There are always last-minute details," said Bettie.

The operator brought the elevator to a stop, shimmying the control lever up, then down again, for closer alignment with the floor rail outside. "Don't work too hard, you two," he advised, while pulling open the brass inner gate followed by yanking wide the outer sliding door. Vic believed the manual elevator was one of the most charming features of leasing office space in the Sardi building, but the antiquated contraptions were fast becoming a vanishing part of contemporary New York City life.

The lights were still ablaze throughout the office suite as Bettie and Vic headed toward the empty art department located at the extreme back area of the expansive layout.

"Did you connect with the psychic lady today? You said she sounds a bit flaky. Without her, our new-business pitch won't be nearly as lively." Vic was already sitting at his drawing table to put the finishing touch on a poster comp using a T-square and a few select magic markers.

In the spirit of friendly competition, the three major theatrical ad agencies often vied to procure the same new clients with their media and art proficiency. All things being equal, any one of Thompson & Co's rivals could possibly nab the account. The advertising firms were expected to pull out all of the stops in order to impress the producing partners with their unique creativity, deft media planning, and expert spending savvy.

The upcoming art and campaign strategy presentation was being held for the impending Broadway revival of Noel Coward's classic comedy, *Blithe Spirit*. Helena Baxter's husband, Rex Merchant, would be billed as producer above the title in association with his incredibly wealthy west coast backer. Merchant was currently working (in the capacity of stage director) with Thompson & Co on his wife's new thriller. As far as Vic could tell, everything was moving along swimmingly. He was banking on Rex's familiarity with T&C to tip the decision on agency selection in Bettie and Vic's lap.

Bettie rifled through some papers she'd picked up from her desk on the way into the art department. "This clairvoyant person has a great reputation in high society circles. My former college roommate, who often travels in those circles, knew all about Mizz Mitzi. It seems she's been hired to hold séances for some of New York's most prestigious families from the Astors to the Ziegfelds. At least a few times a year, high profile doyennes schedule readings with the psychic medium as an offbeat entertainment for some of their more eccentric lady friends.

"At first, when I learned of Mizz Mitzi's popularity, and sensing a high price tag, I hesitated to contact her. It was a pleasant surprise to find that a celebrity mystic would deem our lowly ad agency worthy of receiving her presence," Bettie quickly added, "for a handsome fee, of course."

"I'd guess Mizz Mitzi could forecast that this gig would be a great networking opportunity. What more appreciative audience is there for smoke and mirrors than theatre people? Especially theatre people such as these producers, who have a lot of money and Hollywood connections." Vic said while squinting at one of the poster sketches. "Besides, why shouldn't clairvoyants have to hustle to make a living along with the rest of us?"

Vic continued, "Among her other gifts, I suspect Mizz Mitzi must possess marketing savvy and a great sense of humor. The spelling of her name is extremely clever. It's only been a few years since the word "Ms." has entered into our public's conscience at all. Probably a highly creative women's libber advised Mizz Mitzi on her branding. Some rather famous feminists launched *Ms. Magazine* a few years ago—coining the new word to offset marital status. Using the terms 'Mrs.' and 'Miss' today totally renders a person uncool. Unless, of course, you're an Old Hollywood movie star. Joan Crawford has it built into her billing contracts that she must be credited on screen as 'Miss Joan Crawford' to denote lofty celebrity status. Not only is 'Mizz' extremely sophisticated, it's memorable, too."

"You're babbling, but I appreciate the current events lesson," muttered the account executive snidely, as she reached for the nearby phone, "and I'm thoroughly aware of the feminist movement, thank you very much."

Vic realized he'd been rambling aloud in stream-of-consciousness mode while sketching and finished with, "Just saying."

Bettie already held the receiver to her ear as she dialed. Vic could hear the call ringing on the other end of the line followed by the strident tones of Mizz Mitzi's voice as the medium answered by saying, "Are you there?"

"Of course I'm here, Mizz Mitzi. I called you. This is Bettie Balboa from the Thompson & Co advertising agency."

"Mizz Mitzi was expecting you to phone. You just wanted to remind me about the presentation tomorrow. I've memorized the script. There will be ten people at the table."

"Yes, we're expecting about ten in attendance," repeated Bettie.

"Mizz Mitzi is telling you," emphasized the psychic, "there will be ten people for certain."

"Okay. Stay calm. We'll be sure to order enough bagels," Bettie assured her facetiously. "If you'd arrive here fifteen minutes early, we can get everything comfortably set up. All of us at Thompson & Co really appreciate your help with this."

"Well, you are paying me, aren't you?"

"You tell me. You're the psychic." Bettie added, "Sorry, I couldn't stop myself."

Mizz Mitzi, utterly dead pan, answered, "Yes, it's the first time I've ever heard that line before. You're a regular Fanny Brice."

"Uh, thank you again. We'll see you here tomorrow." Bettie hung up.

"She sounds exactly like Eartha Kitt," Vic said, while collecting the proposed poster designs for the visual portion of their pitch. "Let's hope she's a hit."

"Did you catch that accent? It's part British, part Caribbean, and part Middle Eastern by way of an alien planet. Mizz Mitzi, who usually refers to herself in the third person, assures me that there will be ten of us at the meeting. There's myself, you, Tobin, raging pothead Rex Merchant who'll be wearing multiple hats as director and first-time producer. Let's not forget his new business partner, what's-his-name again?"

"Earl Quick," Vic said. "He's from Hollywood."

"With a name like that, I'm not surprised." Bettie giggled, "Ava Chasten is the publicist, so Mark Rhodes will probably tag along to carry her pencils even though her office is just one floor above ours. Arnie Engels is the general manager. If Mizz Mitzi is a true psychic, we should be expecting a wild card attendee."

"And, if she's a fraud, we can wrestle over the extra bagel," Vic carried all the posters into the conference room, which was the first office outside the art department. He began placing the poster sketches facing the wall, to ensure a dramatic reveal during the pitch. The recently installed poster railing was constructed to display the proposed ad campaigns to great effect under museum-style lighting.

"It's hard to believe there hasn't been a major revival of *Blithe Spirit* since it played at the Morosco in the 40s," Bettie was a veritable encyclopedia of Broadway theatre history. "Say what you will about Rex Merchant, but he certainly has an innate sense of good taste. That play is quintessential Coward at the top of his game."

"Now, you're talking like a quote ad headline," Vic smiled, "Nabbing Celeste Farris for the lead is a real feather in his cap, too. I would love to have been a fly on the wall when he made that announcement at home."

"Oh, my god, yes!" Bettie screeched, "Helena Baxter has been squabbling with Celeste Farris for years. Those ladies have publicly battled over stage roles, over film roles, over agents, over men and, well, pretty much, over everything. In comparison, Merman and Martin seem like a pair of Anglican nuns."

The office phone rang. "That's probably Tobin checking up on us and advising us to go home for some rest," said Vic.

Although Bettie put the receiver close to her ear, Vic could still hear the voice of Mizz Mitzi piping in loud and clear over the phone connection.

"Are you there? Just one thing I must tell you, Bettie Balboa," the medium said hurriedly, "The spirit world sometimes takes over during a séance and cannot be controlled. I could sense some shadows when we were talking earlier, just enough that I feel I should warn you."

"Does this mean you're trying to notify me in advance that we're not going to win the *Blithe Spirit* account?" Bettie asked.

"Mizz Mitzi is certain that you *will be* representing the production—thanks to my participation—no problem. But once the séance begins, although Mizz Mitzi will be following your script, it's possible other voices might demand to be heard."

"Uh, okay." Bettie didn't want to be the one to tell the medium that all of Thompson & Co thought psychic readings, mediums, and séances were equivalent to dusty old vaudeville routines. "We'll take our chances."

"Do not hold Mizz Mitzi responsible if the séance goes awry."

"You'll still be paid, don't worry." Bettie assured her. "Are you sure you haven't been, uh, smoking weed or something? You're suddenly sounding paranoid about the job."

"Mizz Mitzi felt compelled to tell you this. That is all. I will see you tomorrow." She hung up while Bettie was still staring at the phone receiver before nestling it back in the cradle.

"What a crackpot!" Vic laughed, having overheard the entire conversation, "She'll add just the perfect touch for our meeting."

"According to her crystal ball, it's a done deal," Bettie said.

"You have to admit, making that phone call was a bit creepy on her part. It's sort of the equivalent of a horror movie character screaming, 'Don't go in the basement!'"

Bettie suddenly felt a slight chill. "I normally look forward to new business pitches, but I can't wait for this one to be over. Mizz Mitzi's line of work is too unnerving for my taste. It makes me feel anxious. I don't like scary situations."

Vic played with different combinations of the room's lighting, turning switches on and off, "This presentation is going to be funny, not frightening."

The conference space was configured as a perfect square. There were no windows. With the door closed, you were plunged into pitch-darkness. Naturally, once the overhead bulbs switched on, it morphed into a comfortable, calming place to meet. When utilizing the additional museum-style lighting positioned above the poster railings, it became positively posh-looking.

"Tobin knows how he wants this séance to proceed, so we'll leave that for him to direct when we convene in the morning." Vic looked around the room. "Chalk it up to all this psychic mishegoss, but I'm having a vision. I predict we will soon be guzzling big, fancy cocktails at Sardi's second floor bar. Drinks are on Thompson & Co."

"Nothing scary about that," Bettie sighed with relief.

Scene Three

Wednesday - March 5, 1975
Two days before the murder at the Hayes Theatre

It was a bright, chilly March morning. Unfortunately, the bracing Fahrenheit scale outside the Helen Hayes had little effect on the rising heat inside the theatre. Blood-boiling body temperature was responsible for the reddening hue that was beginning to discolor Rex Merchant's otherwise milky complexion.

The director of *Don't Hang Up*, who rarely lost his cool British exterior, was angry at himself for having had agreed to an interview for a high-gloss, celebrity-driven publication called *Intervista Magazine*. Ava Chasten, the show's publicist, had coerced him into meeting with the reporter at the theatre citing the journal's high-profile reputation among the glitterati. Other distinguished and glamorous show business personalities the publication had covered ranged from Liza Minnelli to Alfred Hitchcock.

Abruptly putting an end to the infuriating session moments before, Rex was now briskly wending his way from the Broadway house on 46th Street down toward the offices of Thompson & Co located in the Sardi building on 44th Street.

Upon reflection, Rex had been unprepared for the correspondent who sat down with him in one of the empty backstage dressing rooms. The unkempt interviewer possessed all the style and professionalism of a freshman frat-boy and was constantly pushing his thick eyeglasses up the length of his sizable nose to keep them from sliding off his unpleasant face. The writer garbled a rushed, unintelligible introduction. It was immediately apparent that the young man appeared to be totally unaware of the existence of Broadway, or live performance, or the artists behind the stage magic. Merchant made a mental note to strangle Ava at the first available opportunity.

The reporter met him with a blank stare when Rex referred to his internationally famous wife, actress Helena Baxter. Merchant knew any ensuing conversation would be a lost cause.

"What's the difference between being a producer and being a director anyway? I always thought it was basically the same thing," barked the imbecilic correspondent as he carelessly leafed through scribbled notes.

Fortunately, Merchant had once spent a few weeks with John Lennon in Maharishi Mahesh Yogi's ashram during The Beatles' trip to India in 1968. Rex tapped into his Transcendental Meditation training as he replied in a completely composed manner, "The main difference between a producer and a director is that the producer will handle the business components of the stage production—for instance, raising the financial investment, hiring the advertising agency, and finding the proper theatre. The director is mostly concerned with the creative aspects of the play—working with the actors and the scenic, costume, lighting, and sound designers."

Merchant, speaking rapidly to make quick work of the ordeal, continued, "I am a seasoned theatrical director in Great Britain, credited with numerous West End stage productions. I've recently become interested in trying my hand across the pond as well. When the opportunity arose to direct a thriller for the Broadway theatre, starring my wife, Helena Baxter, I jumped at the chance. *Don't Hang Up* will mark my directorial debut on Broadway. Our show started previews last night and will open in two weeks."

The remainder of the interview was a complete blur. Rex mechanically responded in curt sentences and frequently looked at his wristwatch.

"Well, I'm afraid that's all the time I have. I'm expected at the advertising agency for a meeting on a new production for next season, which I'm not at liberty to discuss."

The journalist had stared vacantly at Rex Merchant as if he was speaking Swahili.

On his brief walk down Broadway, Merchant looked surreptitiously over his shoulder as he lit up a joint. Marijuana helped soothe the director's riled nerves so that by the time Rex entered the Sardi building, he had calmed down considerably.

Things definitely began looking up when the lobby attendant recognized him and flashed a smile, "Thompson & Co is on the seventh floor, Mr. Merchant." Guy Andersen beamed.

Earl Quick had just left his wife.

Not permanently, mind you, since they'd just tied the knot a few weeks ago on the west coast after living together for a mere nine years. He'd left her with a representative from Cartier who'd come to their suite at the St. Regis toting several diamond bracelets. Quick's new bride, actress Celeste Farris, was considering them for purchase as part of her wedding gift. The recent groom reminded his far-from-blushing bride that they were both due quite soon at the advertising agency for a presentation. Rather than waiting around the hotel suite, Earl decided to take the short crosstown walk to Thompson & Co, leaving the car and driver at his wife's disposal.

"Don't be late, darling," he called over his shoulder, "Our meeting's at eleven."

Earl Quick (born Peter Argent) was a major player in Hollywood. He was easily identifiable at any smart Hollywood gathering by his incredible mane of wavy silver hair, which served to frame a rich bronze tan. His famous follicles led to the creation of his movie studio's moniker, Quicksilver Productions. Earl had carved a profitable niche for himself in the movie industry.

Following the trend of casting mature actresses on the tail-end of their careers in steamy screen vehicles that Variety christened "women's pictures," the distinguished gentleman had had a string of commercial successes. Producer Ross Hunter had started it all in 1960, when he invented the lucrative cinematic formula by featuring Lana Turner in *Portrait in Black*, Susan Hayward in *Back Street*, and Doris Day in *Midnight Lace*. It turned out to be a winning combination— big budget films with melodramatic plot lines where the glamorous leading ladies could swan around in celluloid splendor, decked out in incredible designer wardrobes, all shot in dazzling Technicolor.

Shamelessly shadowing Hunter's footsteps, Quick had similar success with *Hotel Luna* (1961), *Widow's Weeds* (1963), and *City of Shame* (1965)—all starring his highly-publicized lover at the time, Helena Baxter.

During the early part of the 60s, Quick had been living with raven-haired Helena Baxter while filming *Hotel Luna* and *Widow's Weeds*. Three years had passed since Baxter's notorious dumbbell accident had made major headlines around the world. However, the public's fascination with everything "Helena Baxter" was more intense than ever.

In 1965, Earl cast actress Celeste Farris to play Helena Baxter's sister in the romantic melodrama *City of Shame*.

Production on the *City of Shame* project had just begun when blonde and beautiful Celeste Farris bulldozed her way into Earl Quick's life and turned it upside-down.

A symbol of glacial beauty, Celeste Farris was the epitome of upper-class British gentility. This facade was muted somewhat by the little-known fact that she grew up as Cora Bumstead of Flushing, Queens.

Swedish in heritage with the bone structure to prove it, she worked as a fashion model to support herself while attending NYU. She wisely changed her name early in her career on the advice of her agent. Shuffling from audition to audition, Celeste came to the realization that she was just one of the countless tall, sultry blondes vying for the same roles. She needed "a special something" that would set her apart from the rest of the peroxide crowd. Over time, she practiced and perfected a British accent—and it was an immediate success for her. Celeste began to win more and more parts that called for a cool, glamorous, "British" blonde.

Helena Baxter's intuition told her from the outset that the seductive actress was going to be trouble. Earl was clearly lavishing more focus on the blonde rather than on her. To prove her point one morning during shooting, Helena Baxter emerged from her dressing room wearing a blonde wig.

"What do you think you're doing?" Quick asked.

"It seems that blondes get much more attention around here. I thought I'd join the club for a day to see what the magic's all about."

A photo of Helena Baxter casually sporting a blonde wig on the set of *City of Shame* made the front page of nearly every tabloid newspaper the following day. Celeste Farris was furious and unleashed her rage on hapless Earl Quick.

There were endless on-set arguments. Helena Baxter suspected that Earl was screwing around with Celeste Farris, but still wasn't quite certain—until the night of "the" phone call, that is.

"Hello, dear. This is Earl's latest…um…bedfellow," said Celeste in a casual tone of voice suggestive of ordering a pizza, "I've been waiting for over an hour. He's normally very punctual. Where the hell is he?"

Typically reserved, Helena's outrage was apparent as she tightly gripped the receiver, "Listen, you. Everyone in Hollywood's well aware that Earl Quick and I have been a happy couple for some years. You have the unmitigated gaul to complain to me because my live-in lover is late for a dinner date with a cheap tramp like you?"

Celeste Farris cooly replied, "Oh, you're always such a lady. Perhaps if you got down off your high horse and put a little more spice in your sex life, the other half of your 'happy couple' might not be banging every available piece of ass in Beverly Hills."

"How dare you?" Helena Baxter sputtered.

Celeste took a deep, dramatic breath. "If your man doesn't feel that he needs to respect your relationship, why should I?"

That—as they say in the columns—was that.

Following an insider private screening of their new picture, *City of Shame*, at a celebratory cocktail bash at the Beverly Hills Hotel, it was obvious to the general public that Earl Quick and Celeste Farris were an item.

Quick's distinguished good looks matched with Celeste Farris' regal demeanor and killer accent ignited the Hollywood social scene.

After a much-publicized breakup, which included Helena Baxter's dramatic suicide attempt, the Baxter-Quick-Farris love triangle came to a head with an explosive red-carpet altercation at the 1966 Academy Awards.

Quicksilver Productions' movie mogul, now linked to golden girl Celeste Farris, went on to become part of a tabloid power-couple as well as a veritable hit machine with three cinematic box office blockbusters in a row: *Forbidden Past (1968)*, *Sins of the Daughter (1969)*, and *Dark Overture (1972),* all starring Celeste Farris. The Hollywood bigwig was hoping the press release announcing his Broadway plans to present *Blithe Spirit* on stage starring his illustrious wife would stir the public's interest and translate into a box office smash.

It was guaranteed to generate some publicity fireworks since his co-producer would be none other than British wunderkind Rex Merchant. Of course, that young gentleman was now married to Quick's ex-lover, Helena Baxter.

And, speak of the devil, Earl could spot Rex walking just ahead on 44th street and into the entrance doors of the Sardi building. Earl Quick thought the young Londoner appeared perpetually stoned whenever he saw him regardless the time of day or night.

It wasn't the first time that Ava Chasten burst into general manager Arne Engel's office, from her suite next door, requesting a neck massage. In point of fact, it wasn't even the first time this week. The feisty redheaded publicist shared a mutual attraction with Engels of which she presumed to take full advantage. They'd already been colleagues on a number of past Broadway shows before they each took on the Helena Baxter vehicle, *Don't Hang Up*.

As press agent and general manager respectively, Ava and Arne spent countless hours together at various meetings and conference rooms. It was just a happy bit of karma that their separate offices were located adjacent to each other on the eighth floor of the Sardi building. It made daily communication easier, and saved money on their phone bills—not to mention the immediate accessibility to said quickie massages. It was a win/win proposition. Stressed-out Ava would achieve several moments of sensual relaxation while it afforded Arne plenty of vantage points in which to check out her ample cleavage as his talented hands worked their magic.

"A-choo!" sneezed the brawny hunk, interrupting a particularly erogenous juncture.

"You know, Arnie, they sell a variety of drugs to take care of allergies nowadays," said an annoyed Ava, "You might try investing in some."

"I have a desk full of them," he sniffled, "I've tried them all—sprays, capsules, and vitamin pills. My condition's chronic and appears to defy medication."

Ava sighed and leaned into him, "How much time do we have before the start of the advertising presentation?"

"We should head downstairs shortly. Will Mark Rhodes be joining us?" Arne asked referring to Ava's newly hired assistant press agent.

"You bet your sweet beefy ass. He's never been to an ad presentation before, so I invited him. I want to get Mark indoctrinated as quickly as possible, especially with *Blithe Spirit* preparing to go into production for next season. Thanks, by the way, for getting me hired on the show. I know your strong recommendation sealed the deal for Earl Quick from Quicksilver."

Arne dug his thumbs deep into Ava's shoulders, "Speaking of the upcoming *Blithe Spirit*, has Rex Merchant been behaving himself? Cooperating with you and your press proposals?"

"He's been an absolute dream so far. Honestly, I think he's overwhelmed with his directorial duties on *Don't Hang Up*. Helena Baxter might be as sweet as pie as a wife, but she's an incredibly demanding actress as far as her performance is concerned."

Arne said, "If all goes as planned, Helena Baxter will not be involved with *Blithe Spirit* next season in any capacity. She'll be too preoccupied with *Don't Hang Up* running its limited engagement, and her television commitments resuming in the fall. *Blithe Spirit* will then move into the Hayes. Hopefully, Rex Merchant and Earl Quick will be co-producing the Noel Coward piece without any interference from her."

"It's hard to believe that Rex was able to convince the Missus that casting her rival and nemesis Celeste Farris was a good thing. Those ladies hate each other." Ava snarled with glee.

"Helena Baxter may be a lot of things, but she's not dumb. Of all people, she understands the value of a strong performance and a marquee name at the box office. There's lots of money to be made from having a star of Celeste Farris' caliber in any Broadway show. Besides, Miss Baxter would want her young hubby's foray into producing a Broadway play to become a huge success. Having Rex co-produce in association with a Hollywood heavyweight like Earl Quick has certain advantages."

"The opportunities for tabloid press are astounding. Celeste Farris has secretly tied the knot with Mr. Quick. His ex-lover is Helena Baxter. She's now married to young Mr. Merchant. If I can't get an avalanche of newspaper articles out of that situation, I should retire right now." Ava wriggled in her chair, "Oh, Arnie, that's the hot spot right there. Really dig your fingers in deep."

The office door swung open. "From outside, it sounds like you two are watching a porn video." Mark said, popping his head into the room. "We have to hightail it downstairs to Thompson & Co for their advertising presentation *tout suite*."

Reluctantly rising from her chair, Ava purred, "I've read somewhere that frequent neck massages can lower heart rate and blood pressure."

Arne grabbed a manila folder from his desk and held it below the waist in front of himself before attempting to walk. He blushed a bit when admitting, "I believe those same massages have the absolute opposite effect on me."

When stepping off the elevator into the reception area of Thompson & Co, there sits the glorious vision of Marsha Davenport at her desk. Twenty-six years old, guileless, and gorgeous, she set the tone for an agency whose aim was to promote Broadway glamour and allure. However, upon opening her mouth, all illusion was shattered by a voice that was the choral equivalent of nails-on-a-chalkboard topped by a thick Brooklyn-Queens accent. Marsha was escorted to the office every morning by her staggeringly virile mobster-type Italian boyfriend, who came equipped with gold rings, neck chains, and strong cologne. The very same Vito Lanzetta also promptly picked her up at the end of the day to drive her back to Staten Island, where they now lived together. Apparently, there was no trusting Marsha—or no trusting any self-respecting male who drew breath in her vicinity during office hours. In actuality, she was a delightful, unpretentious young woman, who was nice to everyone. She just happened to look like a scorchingly sexy pin-up centerfold torn from the pages of Playboy magazine. The entire office staff loved her.

While awaiting the arrival of their psychic guest, Tobin, Bettie, and Vic were chatting with the receptionist when the lift doors were opened by the chipper daytime operator, with a rattle and a clang.

"Here we are, seventh floor," the elevator jockey announced. "How nice. It appears you have a welcoming committee. Please watch your step."

It came as shock to everyone when Mizz Mitzi stepped off the elevator. Not only was she prompt, but she made quite an impression on the group who'd lined up to greet her. Vic hadn't really known what to expect. Mostly, he'd had visions of her looking stylistically similar to a gypsy fortune teller at a side show, equipped with flowing robes, rings on every finger, and a turban.

The lady who stood in front of them was wearing a chic, simple black dress, and fashionable black stiletto shoes. An oversized pin, made of beaten metal in the shape of a lion, was her only adornment. She was sporting a rather large black leather Mark

Cross tote bag. Mizz Mitzi's most extraordinary feature was the contrast between her dark skin and the massive mane of white hair that was brushed back from her forehead. It was as if a sudden gust of wind blew into her face, creating a perfect frame by pushing her coiffure back, and widening her saucer-like eyes, clearly her most prominent feature. The medium's amber irises were accented by gold glitter eye-shadow and black eyeliner. If it were not for her Chanel outfit, she could have easily been cast as a voodoo priestess in a 1940s Maria Montez movie. She appeared ageless.

Tobin Klein, Thompson & Co's dapper creative director, stepped forward with obvious stars in his eyes. "It's a pleasure to meet you, Mizz Mitzi. We really appreciate your help. I believe you've already met our account executive, Bettie Balboa, over the phone."

Bettie stepped forward to shake the psychic's hand. "Welcome, and thank you again for coming today. I'd like to introduce you to Vic Senso, our art director. Let's head over to the conference room where Tobin will take us through the presentation. Oh, and this is Marsha, our receptionist."

Mizz Mitzi looked over at the stunning blonde and raised an eyebrow. "Your man loves you, honey girl. He's a sketchy character but will always be true to you. Convince him to stop wearing the Paco Rabanne cologne. It'll lead him into trouble one day."

Clearly puzzled, Marsha grunted and smiled, "Wha?"

As they strolled through the busy office, the medium was noticeably turning heads, eliciting broad smiles along with shy glances. Vic could hear Mizz Mitzi softly humming the music to *On a Clear Day You Can See Forever* as they sauntered through the office.

Tobin explained as the group walked, "*Blithe Spirit* is by British playwright Noel Coward. It's a comedy about a man who is haunted by the ghost of his first wife, Elvira." Tobin opened the conference room door, "Her spectral presence will not leave their house, so Charles and his second wife, Ruth, hire Madame Arcati, a local medium to help them. Of course, circumstances get more complicated and humorous as the story progresses."

The psychic tossed her head, "Mizz Mitzi's familiar with the piece. I majored in film studies at NYU and the classic David Lean version airs many times on late night television," the medium surprisingly declared. "Mizz Mitzi adores Rex Harrison. Now, please reveal what your setup is going to be for the reading."

Bettie and Vic watched as Tobin lead the chic psychic to the farthest side of the table and, with a gentlemanly gesture, pulled out the chair. "If you would please sit here? When the others arrive, we'll usher them into the room. Just casually greet them with a nod of your head as they enter and take their seats. They'll assume you work here, so act as if they should know who you are. Did you bring the, uh…"

"The orbuculum, yes." Mizz Mitzi said as she reached down into her Mark Cross bag and pulled out a crystal ball.

Tobin continued, "I'll ask you to keep that globe out of sight and in your lap until the appropriate time. The first order of business is to introduce you as Broadway's ultimate psychic medium. When the time is right, you will look towards the door, and point to it. It will suddenly close and all the lights will go out. That's when you will take the crystal ball out of hiding and place it on the table in front of you. Wait for the room to be totally pitch-black before you do this. Then, a single overhead canister will illuminate over your chair putting you in the spotlight. That's when you can begin reciting the script you've memorized."

"How will the door close by itself when Mizz Mitzi points to it?" asked the medium.

"In addition to his many talents as creative director, Tobin's an amateur magician and well-versed in the art of misdirection," Bettie chimed in, "He's great at special effects and sleight of hand. He has rigged the door with invisible wire, so the instant you point to it, Tobin can pull it shut from wherever he's standing in the room."

The intercom system suddenly came to life with the raspy-throated receptionist trumpeting office-wide in her thick New York City accent, "Oh, mah gawd! The *Blithe Spirit* people are awl here at the reception desk. Awl of them at once." Marsha made every announcement sound as if it were an exciting event. You'd swear the husky, disembodied voice had come from a Lauren Bacall or Brenda Vaccaro female impersonator.

"That's our little Marsha!" Bettie rolled her eyes. "Vic, let's greet them and herd them back here."

The entire *Blithe Spirit* production team indeed stood huddled in the confined reception area off the elevator, seemingly in good humor, with lots of chatting and laughing. Bettie and Vic wrangled them all and started to lead the way toward the conference room.

"We're expecting one more from our group," said Rex Merchant, who motioned them to stop, "By the sound of that noisy lift coming back up, our mystery guest should be making an entrance any minute now."

Indeed, the opening of the elevator's brass inner gate followed by the rolling of the metal doors revealed none other than luminous star of stage and screen, Celeste Farris. The ravishing blonde, who appeared as if she'd dressed to meet Queen Elizabeth for afternoon tea at Buckingham Palace, stepped into the reception area to approach her adoring entourage. Silver-haired Earl Quick, the Hollywood producer, was her first target. "What an utter delight to see you again, Mr. Quick. It's simply minutes since we've been (she pronounced it as 'bean') together." Celeste draped her arm around his.

Laughingly, Arne Engels informed the group, adding a wink, "Celeste and Earl were married last month in Los Angeles."

"Oh, Arnie! It's still a big secret. I haven't given the exclusive to Liz Smith yet," said Ava Chasten, ever the publicist. "I plan on breaking the news when we announce *Blithe Spirit* for the first time."

Heartfelt congratulations were extended all around as they moved toward the inner recesses of the Thompson & Co offices. Spontaneous applause from surprised staff members followed Celeste Farris as she leisurely made her way to the conference room.

As expected, when entering and taking their seats around the table, each person nodded and smiled when first setting their eyes on the imposing Mizz Mitzi. Tobin made quick work of getting them settled in.

"Thank you all so much for coming here today. I'm Tobin Klein, partner and creative director here at Thompson & Co. We are thrilled to give you our advertising presentation for your upcoming production of *Blithe Spirit*. As with all 'meet and greet' occasions, let's begin by going around the table introducing ourselves. Rex, will you please start?"

"It's a pleasure seeing you all. I'm Rex Merchant, the co-producer and also the director. I'm extremely excited to be here today with the team. We're looking forward to reviewing the campaigns you've created for our show."

Rex spoke with a charming British accent. He was young (at least an eighteen-year difference between himself and his esteemed wife Helena Baxter), possessed boyish good-looks, was slightly fleshy, and enjoyed all the perks that one would expect from marriage to a bona fide Television, Hollywood, and Broadway superstar. The weed he'd smoked on his way to the meeting furnished him with a mellower-than-usual demeanor as he gestured to the next-in-line to speak.

"Hello, everyone. I'm Earl Quick. This will be Quicksilver's debut production on Broadway," said the distinguished sixty- year-old gentleman sitting to Rex's left. The producer wore a bespoke suit that emphasized his apparent wealth. Sporting a healthy-looking salt-and-pepper mustache framed by his deep California tan, topped with a gorgeous mane of wavy silver hair, Quick cut a dashing figure. "Ordinarily, I work out of Hollywood. This is a new adventure for me. Uh, I don't think the lady sitting beside me needs any introduction. Miss Celeste Farris."

"Mrs. Earl Quick, please!" The room laughed and applauded. "It's going to be such fun working with Earl and Rex on *Blithe Spirit*. I'll be playing that most glamorous ghost, Elvira Condomine. I cannot wait to meet the other theatrical spirits inhabiting the house at the Hayes!"

Tobin Klein turned his attention to the frenetic redhead, "I believe we're all familiar with this human ball of fire."

"I'll tell you kids, Celeste Farris is a tough act to follow. Ava

Chasten here, press agent. I just want to ask if anybody has an aspirin because my head's pounding. No, alright! I'm…uh…intimate with pretty much everyone at the table since my office is located upstairs." Her brief speech encapsulated the outspoken attitude that helped make Ava a vital force among Broadway publicists. "This is my assistant, Mark Rhodes, who is soon to be a familiar face on the street."

Mark signaled a salute and uttered a modest, "Hello," as he turned to the clean-cut, muscular man seated to his right.

"I guess I'm the guy responsible for getting this illustrious team together. I'm Arnie Engels, general manager of *Blithe Spirit*," said the golden-haired, rugby-built, thirty-something man seated beside Bettie. He was attractive and perfectly proportioned. Many young women would have considered him a near-perfect catch if it were not for his annoying habit of sniffling and sneezing periodically due to numerous allergies.

Next at the table, "Bettie Balboa, I'm an account executive here and thrilled to meet all of you. Also, a huge Noel Coward fan."

Vic quickly chimed in, "Vic Senso, art director. This is indeed a real pleasure."

"I suppose you are wondering who the lady at the end of the table is?" Tobin asked the guests. "It's my honor to introduce Mizz Mitzi, Broadway's premiere society psychic."

All eyes were now on Mizz Mitzi.

On cue, the medium abruptly stood, bowed slightly, and pointed towards the door. Courtesy of Tobin's trick wire, it slammed shut as the lights went out, and the conference room was plunged into total darkness. There was hardly time for anyone to register surprise at the sequence of events before Mizz Mitzi and her crystal ball became illuminated by a single overhead beam.

The room filled with the buzzing murmurs of oohs and ahhs as the medium exclaimed in her purring Eartha Kitt-esque voice, "Everyone, please join hands. Remain seated, and do not break the chain regardless of what may happen during this séance. Mizz Mitzi has gathered you here today to announce that the revival of

Blithe Spirit will be a tremendous hit on Broadway in the coming season. The critics across all media—the newspapers, magazines, on television, and on radio—will heap praise upon this theatrical venture. Celeste Farris will be lauded for giving another Tony Award-winning performance in her starring role. I see a Best Director of a Play Tony Award being presented as well. The Theatre Wing will even institute a new award category for Best Revival of a Play." Mizz Mitzi paused here, seemingly to take a breath as her saucer-eyes widened, and her teeth assumed a chattering grimace. "Acceptance speeches, gowns, publicity, standing ovations! Outer Critics Circle Awards, Drama Desk Awards. The box office will explode with ticket sales. Limousines will be lined up and down 46th Street every evening. An avalanche of accolades for *Blithe Spirit*. Mizz Mitzi sees the details as clear as day. It will all be set in motion today, at this meeting, with this creative proposal at Thompson & Co. Let the presentation commence!"

With that, the lights were turned back on. The room erupted in laughter and applause. Vic immediately launched into revealing the artwork campaigns and poster concepts. Tobin then read the announcer copy written for a sixty-second radio commercial to be recorded in a studio. This was quickly followed by Bettie distributing a media-buying schedule that explained how they proposed to introduce all the disparate elements of the ad campaign to the theatergoing public in a timely rollout blitz.

Having already attended the presentations at two other rival ad agencies, Rex Merchant and Earl Quick, after a brief tete-a-tete at the table, immediately awarded Thompson & Co with handling the Broadway-bound *Blithe Spirit* advertising account. Celeste Farris couldn't have displayed more exuberance over the decision.

"Bravo! That wasn't a presentation, it was a real show!"

"Clearly, the best presentation was saved for last!"

"How in the world did you get that door to close on cue?"

"Having a medium hold a séance at the meeting was a stroke of creative genius."

Deemed a resounding success all around, everyone in the client group made their exits after congratulating the psychic and the advertising staff on a job well done. It wasn't until things quieted down that Bettie noticed something odd.

"Mizz Mitzi, are you alright? Do you need some water?"

The medium, frozen in her seat at the table, seemed breathless and tried to stand. Once on her feet, the psychic headed toward the door. She reached out to Vic's arm for support. He caught her as she attempted to gain her balance.

"Mizz Mitzi wanted to ignore the signs. The spirit voices would not stop." The clairvoyant said, breathlessly, "Please forgive...if the speech was rushed...but the vision was overpowering...awful... bloody...Someone in this room today...the entire time...had only murder in mind."

Scene Four

"Murder?" Bettie repeated, "Murder? What are you talking about? Murder?"

Mizz Mitzi, having taken a few sips of cold water, was now slumped in a chair. She turned ashen while speaking slowly. Vic was kneeling beside her. This was not the dynamic clairvoyant persona, full of bravado, who was talking now, but a badly shaken lady who had been given a real scare.

"Listen, people, I realize you do not take my gift seriously. That's alright. I myself, on occasion, treat my capability as an amusement, a commodity. I admit sometimes what I am hired to do is scripted and manipulated. Several of my society ladies love all the embellished astral predictions and a bit of harmless occult fun to fill an afternoon and the money's good."

Vic reached out and put his hand on Mizz Mitzi's trembling shoulder. "Clearly something startled you today. Drink some more water. Tell us what happened if you can. What's frightened you?"

"Someone at the table has a screw loose in the head…possessed by violent inclinations…murder and death always top of mind. I have worked with law enforcement on finding missing persons, solving tricky problems when the cops feel they've exhausted every other avenue. The local police department has consulted with me as an extra resource on many difficult criminal investigations. They have been pleased with the results of my participation. I can handle the specter of violence…it sometimes can be traumatic work. Maybe today, it was the proximity, but I have rarely experienced the intense malice I felt in this room. Something bad is going to occur, and most likely…soon."

As the clairvoyant relived her distressing experience, Bettie paced the room like a cornered cat. The beautiful ad executive never took her eyes off Mizz Mitzi as she listened intently, all the while absentmindedly collecting the pads and sharpened pencils that had been distributed earlier on the conference room table.

"I started it all when I called my friend for a recommendation, didn't I? It's my fault that this awful thing has happened to you today."

"That's foolish, Bettie," Vic chided her, "Nobody's to blame."

"Mizz Mitzi felt something was wrong last night when speaking to Bettie Balboa. Often there are premonitions when working on an official case. But…can sometimes be mistaken," admitted the shaken medium, "Yes…sometimes mistaken."

"You're really working with the police on solving crimes?" asked Tobin. "Honestly, we had no idea. Could this be something like mixed messages? Maybe you were getting a vibe from another criminal case in which you are currently involved, and it crossed over into our little séance?"

"Like a wrong number, you mean? Unlikely," muttered the exhausted psychic.

Vic said, "You need to go home and get some rest. Can we call you a car service? Will you be okay to stay in your apartment on your own? Can you telephone a friend or relative to meet you there?"

The medium stood up, now much steadier on her feet. "Vic Senso, if you would be so kind as to escort me downstairs to a taxi, that would be sufficient. Mizz Mitzi sadly will not be able to fly back to Murray Hill on her broomstick," she smiled weakly.

Bettie thought it was a good indication towards a speedy recuperation that Mizz Mitzi was once again referring to herself in the third person and making an attempt at humor.

After they ushered the rattled clairvoyant and Vic onto the elevator, Tobin turned to Bettie and said, "Holy shit, that was creepy!"

"If Mizz Mitzi was trying the scare the bejesus out of us, she sure did an effective job of it. Shall we promise not to never speak of this again? I'd be happy to forget the entire experience."

"At least the presentation was a big success," said Tobin, gleefully.

"Sure, if you can ignore the eerie forecast of violent death," added Bettie with a distinct shiver. "Really, Tobin?"

He shrugged, "The whole thing's crazy, Bettie. Can you actually imagine anybody in this conference room today being a killer?"

"I suppose everyone's capable of murder under the right circumstances. You have to admit, having a leg in both the theatre and advertising worlds, our group has all the necessary qualifications for extraordinary histrionics."

"Unfortunately, Mizz Mitzi didn't include any specifics in her premonition. Come on, we all thought she was a phony anyway. That's the way it works. It's probably how she gets repeat business. She relies on her clients' curiosity to learn more about unspecified events. Anyhow, that's my theory and I'm sticking to it, otherwise I will totally freak out." Tobin was speaking over his shoulder, walking toward his office, as Vic reappeared.

The art director sounded both excited and anxious, "What a way to start the day, huh? It's going to take me a while to process what happened here."

"That's the understatement of the year." Bettie arched her perfect eyebrows.

"Don't forget, we have our meeting with the photographer at the theatre in a half hour. It shouldn't take too long," said the art director. "For god's sake, please don't mention Mizz Mitzi's prediction to Rex Merchant and Helena Baxter—or to anyone— for that matter."

"Not a problem, believe me," Bettie said emphatically as she watched him amble back toward his office.

Vic Senso was tall and walked with a languid stride. He seldom stood fully erect, and had a habit of leaning against a desk, a storage cabinet, or whatever stationary furniture was conveniently positioned within reach. He often slouched, draping himself on the arm of a chair to easily stretch his long legs. Vic gave the impression of having little vitality to waste and wishing to sustain that which he had.

Senso stepped into his private office to gather his wits for a few moments before the next task was at hand. The strapping designer sat in his chair, legs extended, elbows planted on his drawing table and, with fists under chin, closed his eyes. Earlier, he'd had the presence of mind to study the faces gathered around the conference room table during the meeting. It was standard practice for him to attempt to 'read' a roomful of clients and decipher their reactions to the various elements that comprised a presentation while it was in progress.

Everyone seemed genuinely tickled when Tobin introduced Mizz Mitzi. There were smiles all around the table as everyone laughingly joined hands. The medium then launched into her rehearsed reading. Vic observed newlywed Celeste Farris excitedly tap Earl Quick's manicured fingers when the psychic predicted multiple Tony Award wins for *Blithe Spirit*. The legendary star of stage and screen looked exceptionally alluring enveloped in the warm golden glow cast by the clairvoyant's crystal ball. Acting as if this were the most fascinating experience of her lifetime, Celeste leaned forward and stared into the prop orbuculum, perfectly aware of its flattering lighting effect.

Based on her body language, it was clear that publicist Ava Chasten was anxious to commandeer the nearest telephone in order to feed Liz Smith or Cindy Adams an 'exclusive' scoop about the society psychic who was predicting Broadway's future. Vic watched as the animated press agent nervously twitched her dialing finger during the reading. The jittery redhead, massive curls haphazardly piled on top of her head, was seated diagonally across from him on the far side of the table.

Rugged Arnie Engels continually elbowed the equally attractive Mark Rhodes in the ribs as both men savored each entertaining moment of the orchestrated séance. Vic was still trying to determine if Arnie's sexual orientation was straight or gay. This was sometimes challenging given the nature of the industry that employed them. The hunky general manager also managed to keep a low profile and had a proven tendency to shy away from rumormongers and the gossip mill.

Ever the sophisticate, Rex Merchant maintained his cool British exterior throughout, obviously transfixed by the vision that was Mizz Mitzi. He seemed to be held in an hypnotic state as the dynamic medium gathered steam. Or maybe, it was simply the effect of all the cannabis kicking in.

Enlisting the bizarre accent she'd perfected, blatantly patterned after songstress Eartha Kitt, the clairvoyant brought her equally outrageous predictions to a smashing conclusion.

Fast forwarding to the art presentation, Vic witnessed a sea of deadpan poker faces. This was typical when revealing posters for the first time to any group. No one wants to be the first to give an opinion, so blank stares are generally put to use. Vic always finds the vacant expressions rather unnerving, but after years of experience, it was now the expected norm.

Eventually, someone will venture an initial critique (in this case, Rex Merchant) which then gives everyone else license to weigh in on the art at hand—for better or worse. This is generally the most time-consuming portion of the presentation since the critical skirmish to select the perfect poster can go on and on ad infinitum. The art director was able to move on from the posters with the suggestion that it was always best to have the images gestate and return to the discussion later.

During Bettie's media-schedule presentation, it was compelling to watch how the other males in the room took full advantage of their opportunity to stare openly at Thompson & Co's most beautiful account executive. As she employed words like 'allocate' and 'implementation' to express her buying strategies, one would've thought she was spouting Shakespeare sonnets by their rapturous attention. Vic routinely felt somewhat envious of the power that possessing overwhelming physical beauty held for Bettie.

The art director glanced over at Celeste Farris, who couldn't have been any-too-thrilled, either. However, the stunning actress was more than capable of holding her jealousy in check, maintaining a frozen smile, during Bettie's number-crunching, businesslike proceedings.

Regardless of how many times he ran through the presentation in his head, Vic could not imagine that anyone at the table had been contemplating homicide while Mizz Mitzi was revealing her scripted predictions.

An avid reader of detective fiction since his early teen years, Vic was well acquainted with the "big three" motives for murder: 1) sex, 2) money, and 3) revenge. He was also fully aware of the fact that he knew so little about most of the people involved, it would be impossible to hazard any guesses as to the 'why' factor. Obviously, the 'when' and 'where' remained to be seen. Undoubtedly, the 'who' would be fun to speculate, based on the scant personal information at hand—sort of comparable to guessing the outcome of The Tony Awards in any given season.

Of course, this was much more a serious concern—if only he could fully buy into the legitimacy of the clairvoyant's abilities to foretell future events.

Scene Five

Their next scheduled meeting of the day was over at the Helen Hayes Theatre on West 46th Street, site of where *Don't Hang Up* performed its first preview the evening before. Vic and Bettie were to have a brief chat with Helena Baxter, Arne Engels, Ava Chasten, and photographer Terry Hagen to outline the photo shoot scheduled for later in the week. The pictures were to be 'set-ups' which were used for advertising and publicity purposes in advance of having actual production photography. This basically amounted to various posed shots of star Helena Baxter reenacting scenes from the play along with the rest of the supporting cast. It would send the visual message to likely audience members that *Don't Hang Up* was not a one-person show (typically a difficult sell at the box office) and to hopefully intrigue said potential ticket buyers to want to learn more about the new Helena Baxter vehicle before any critical reviews hit the streets.

Entering the theatre via the stage door always held a certain thrill for Bettie and Vic. Both native New Yorkers (she-Brooklyn, he-Manhattan) they grew up worshipping Broadway and its stars. Despite already having spent a few years working in the entertainment industry, even a simple meeting like this provided a 'pinch me' moment for each of them.

Lester Potts, the surly gentleman on guard at the Helen Hayes stage door, looked them over and indicated recognition from their previous visits. "You can't take pictures in there," he grumbled at Vic, who always carried his Canon camera with its case slung over his shoulder. "Union rules."

"Yes, I know. Thanks. No worries, I'm not the photographer."

"Miss Hagen is already setting up on stage." Lester pointed to a makeshift passageway behind a curtained area. "You can go through that way."

The path led them directly onto the brilliant set for *Don't Hang Up*, which was even more impressive upon closer inspection. "That wall of framed headshots is pure genius," Vic remarked, stepping back a bit to admire the full effect. "Perry Chan has really knocked it out of the park. It's totally disconcerting having all of those faces staring back at you during the entire show. It really serves to emphasize the playwright's running theme of nagging guilt."

Bettie took a sideways glance at Vic. "Um, didn't you have a dinner date with Perry recently? I never did hear about how that went."

"It was fun, lots of laughs, and tons of unprintable theatre gossip. He is a great guy." Vic had a dismissive tone in his response. That was clearly the end of that discussion.

Stagehands were busily hammering and generally bustling around them as Terry Hagen, the theatrical photographer, spotted Bettie and Vic. The tall, cool blonde, poured snugly into a black turtleneck sweater and khaki slacks, walked toward them.

"Hello, you two. It's been a while. So happy you're handling this show."

Perfunctory hugs and kisses were shared all around. Vic peripherally spied Helena Baxter approaching from a darkened area backstage.

He sprang into ad agency executive-mode as he broke from the group and held out his hand saying, "It's a pleasure to meet you, Miss Baxter. I'm Vic Senso, the art director from Thompson & Co…"

"…and I'm *not* Helena Baxter," the attractive lady laughingly informed him. "Don't worry, it happens all the time with the right lighting. I'm Simone Caldwell, Helena's secretary and her understudy. She'll be along in a few minutes. Just finishing up a phone call."

At that moment, both Arne Engels and Ava Chasten stormed down the theatre aisles from opposite sides of the house in unplanned synchronized entrances. Ava, in true chaotic fashion, was laden with several press kit folders tucked under her arms. In addition, she carried her standard accessory, an oversized Gucci tote bag.

Vic marveled at her sheer strength as she maneuvered her way towards the stage. In a gentlemanly gesture, Vic ran down the rehearsal stairs and took the tote bag from her. He carried it the rest of the way onto the set and was relieved to put it down.

"My God, what do you keep in this thing? It's heavy."

"Are you kidding? What *don't* I keep in that bag? I could fit a three- year-old child in there."

Vic grimaced, "I'm afraid to ask how you would know that, Ava."

The press agent had her massive red curls arranged on the top of her head held tentatively in place by several Ticonderoga number two lead pencils.

"Bufferin…Tylenol…Aspirin…anything. Anybody?" This was the pale publicist's greeting to the assembled party. "What a banging headache. How're y'all doing, kids?"

Ava was wearing a white ruffled blouse, crisp pleated plaid skirt, and penny loafers. The entire ensemble would've been reminiscent of a Catholic school girl's uniform, that is, if the skirt hadn't been four inches too short and the blouse nearly transparent. She would certainly be identified as one of the sluttier girls in any parochial classroom gathering. Strangely, Ava still managed to look salaciously sweet in the outfit.

Polar opposite, fashion-wise, wearing conservative shirt, silk tie, and sport jacket, Arne Engels certainly couldn't take his eyes off her as he signaled their meeting to begin.

"Not yet, please, Arnie. We're waiting on Helena," announced Simone, dramatically. "She won't be long now, I'm sure."

Arne responded silently with an irksome scowl aimed in her direction.

SCENERY OF THE CRIME • 43

Vic pulled Bettie aside. "After this meeting, remind me to tell you an old story I remembered about Helena Baxter and a dumbbell—it's hilarious!" the art director whispered to his co-worker. "You won't believe it."

Vic was intrigued by the attractive stand-by actress, especially given her possible involvement with all the undesirable notoriety fifteen years earlier. "Can I ask how you juggle the two jobs—being both understudy and secretary?"

"Helena's a terrific boss," she smiled, "the secretarial position's full time and pays all my bills, while the understudy gig is pretty much gravy since the-one-and-only Miss Baxter never misses a performance. I've been doing it for almost eighteen years now and haven't gone on once yet! When she's doing work on a film or television, I'm always credited as Helena's stand-in."

"That has to be some kind of world record." Vic marveled.

They were joined by Terry Hagen, who held up her camera as a signal, "Simone, let's take some shots of you on set before Miss Baxter gets here. Sit there behind the desk with the headshot wall for background."

As the actress moved into position, Terry turned and asked, "Hey, Vic, would you mind terribly if I borrowed your Canon? The F-1 system is terribly impressive. My old Nikon is starting to wear thin, and your lens looks more advanced."

"Be my guest." Vic handed it over and watched as the expert photographer framed and snapped numerous pictures of the understudy in rapid succession.

Arne was restlessly pacing the boards, sniffling, and checking his wristwatch. He suffered a sneezing fit and finally walked off stage in search of Helena Baxter. It wasn't long before he returned with her arm-in-arm, escorting the famous star of *Don't Hang Up* onto the set.

Helena Baxter was radiant with charm. She walked forward gracefully, hand outstretched, as she introduced herself to Bettie, Vic, and Terry. "I apologize for my tardiness, everyone. Let's begin, shall we, Arnie?"

"Okay, we have two weeks of previews to get through before opening night and the critics. Every waking moment should be used for rehearsal. We're at somewhat of a disadvantage as our esteemed playwright has decided to take a Transatlantic cruise rather than subject himself to the grueling preview period. He'll be staying far away from the show until well after opening and critical responses. Let's map out the photo shoot so we will not waste any time deciding set-ups on Friday. We'll need shots to fill the front-of-house display cases, and to use for advertising and publicity. Helena, how many costume changes do you have during the show?"

"Three, but we're still making alterations on the structural design for the last outfit," said the actress. "It has to withstand being torn and frayed during a bit of stage fighting in the course of the dramatic climax."

Ava jumped in with, "Tell me, which is your favorite costume? The one you look best wearing?"

"My entrance outfit, the mauve suit." Helena answered without hesitation.

"Let's concentrate on using that look, then. Until we have production photography."

The rest of the meeting involved discussing the number of camera setups, how each would be lit tapping into the electrical scheme available, and which scenes should be covered. Vic's chair was positioned with his back to the theatre orchestra. He sat facing the headshot wall, allowing him additional time to admire Perry Chan's brilliant scenic design.

With his attention fading in and out of the conversation at hand, Vic once again became entranced with the framed grouping of black and white faces that dominated the stage set. The meeting was over in about twenty minutes, after all the logistical questions had been asked and answered regarding the upcoming shoot.

Terry Hagen, still using the borrowed Canon F-1 camera, requested that the group huddle together for several quick informal shots. Helena Baxter, Simone, Ava, Bettie, Arne, and Vic jockeyed into position as the photographer began snapping away. Terry was backing up to take in more of the atmospheric scenery when Helena Baxter screamed, "Stop where you are, or you'll fall into the orchestra pit!"

The ice-blonde shutterbug froze in her tracks and pivoted around. Looking down into the dark abyss of the shaft, Terry blanched, and quickly jumped away from the edge of the stage.

"Oh my god, thank you for the warning. I wasn't aware at all. I was so intent on taking pictures," she breathed, "that could've been an awful accident for sure."

Clearly having a tale to tell, Helena Baxter took hold of Terry's elegant shoulders.

"Allow me to reveal a little backstage anecdote about safety on the stage." The actress led the shaken photographer over to a chair and guided her into it. "I started my career in musical theatre and was lucky enough to have been cast in a Broadway production choreographed by Jerome Robbins. I say 'lucky' because it looked great on my resumé, but it was hell working for him. He was terribly condescending and ran the company like an army drill sergeant. One afternoon, Mr. Robbins was relentlessly working with us onstage during a rehearsal. He was stern, he was nasty, he was cruel—as he gave us numerous reprimands and personal critiques. During this process, he was ever-so-slowly walking backwards. All of us dancers were frozen in place as he kept yelling, yelling, and stepping closer and closer to the edge of the stage. We'd been strictly trained by him never to speak out of turn without being spoken to. We were so incredibly intimidated that we all watched in utter silence as he finally reached the edge of the stage, lost his balance, and toppled over into the orchestra pit. No one uttered a sound…no one laughed… we were horrified. It happened because he was so wrapped up in his tirade that he was unaware of the impending danger."

This reminiscence was followed by several seconds of dead silence.

Helena Baxter concluded with, "Jerome Robbins' fall into the pit illustrated a lesson in theatre safety. One must always be alert while on stage. For example, our show employs a trap door. Rex was most insistent on our using it for the play. It's incredibly dangerous, but great for getting a scream out of our audience when it's put into effect. While the distance from falling into the orchestra pit is about fifteen feet or so, the drop through the trap door is probably double that. I'm telling you this because it's terribly easy for a mishap to occur if you're not paying attention to your scenic surroundings. I cannot repeat enough times, one must always be alert while on stage."

Ava was holding her fingers to her temples, wincing in facetious pain. "Well, Helena, that rather long story did nothing to relieve my pounding headache. But you did deliver a riveting monologue."

"For a publicist, you have no sense of drama," chided the stage star humorously, "and now, I'm heading home to husband and hearth. I'll see you all at the shoot in a few days."

Arne put a friendly arm around Ava's shoulder, "Let's walk back to the Sardi building together. I'll even treat you to a couple of Excedrin along the way."

The publicist smiled weakly as she picked up the pile of press kits she'd been carrying for no discernible reason. Ava briskly nodded her head in agreement, knocking a few pencils out of her hairdo in the process, "You're a fucking saint, Arnie," Ava sighed, as she tossed Engels her oversized Gucci tote bag to carry. "Play your cards right and I'll treat *you* to a couple of antihistamines."

Arne nodded and sneezed in appreciation.

Vic called after Simone as the understudy had begun wending her way backstage. "It was a pleasure to meet you,"

Bettie added, "We'll see you on Friday," to no one in particular.

Before leaving the theatre to return to the office, Vic and Bettie looked around to say goodbye to Terry. The lovely photographer was nowhere to be found. She was probably off and running to her next assigned stage shoot.

"Well, what do you know?" Vic hissed in frustration, "Terry still has my camera."

Scene Six

Numbered high on the list of Vic's favorite experiences growing up in Manhattan was catching site of galloping NYPD Mounted Policemen patrolling the Times Square area. The friendly officers would always allow him to pet and talk to the horses, asking their names and ages. Indeed, part of the mission of the Mounted Unit, along with crowd control, traffic guidance, and prevention of street crime, is community relations.

Truth be told, even now, Vic felt a certain flutter of excitement when watching one policeman in particular making his rounds in the theatre district. There couldn't be a better representative for NYPD public relations than the toweringly handsome presence of Officer Rodney Clements. Originally hailing from the small town of Hooker, Oklahoma, Rodney was fond of explaining to new friends, "It's a location, not a vocation." This was ironically apropos, especially when horse and rider were stopped in front of any of the lurid burlesque establishments located near and around 42nd Street.

Bettie once asked Officer Rodney why he preferred this equestrian unit over other, more standard assignments. His charming response was, "Nobody ever tried to get acquainted with my police car, but they line up to meet my horse, Fiona."

You couldn't argue with that statement, especially when it was coming from a small town country boy, who just happened to possess the angular face and muscular physique of a classic Greek statue.

"I'll guarantee, it's not only Fiona the horse they're clamoring to meet," observed Vic, as an aside to Bettie.

Officer Rodney was galloping east on 44th Street just as Bettie and Vic reached the entrance to the Sardi building. Bettie waved enthusiastically as Fiona, the chestnut mare, and her rider pulled over for a friendly chat.

No slouch in the looks department himself, Vic suddenly felt like the least attractive person on the planet while conversing with Bettie and the policeman. After exchanging a few pleasantries, the conversation invariably turned to celebrity sightings. It was something to which Rodney still hadn't grown accustomed. He would visibly blush whenever confronted by an illustrious personality during the course of his daily appointed rounds.

"Have either of you seen anybody famous lately?" the stage-struck cop asked.

"Celeste Farris was in our conference room this morning. We've just come from a meeting with none other than Helena Baxter." Bettie told him.

Rodney Clements beamed, "Really? Is she as nice in person? I just watched her on that game show of hers." He was clearly a fan.

Assuming that Rodney was referring to Helena Baxter and not Celeste Farris, whose reputation was less than angelic, Bettie answered, "Oh, she's extremely elegant and gracious. An absolute doll. If you'd like to see her new play, I can get you a pair of comp tickets."

During the preview period of most new shows, complimentary seats were readily available as a courtesy to those working in the biz. Posted daily on the Thompson & Co office refrigerator, there were sign-up sheets to just about any show beginning performances or already in previews. Producers and cast members alike were invariably anxious to play to full houses (or even half-full) for morale purposes, to gain some audience feedback, and generate early word-of-mouth.

Rodney smiled, revealing perfect white teeth behind his perfect lips. "That would be awfully kind of you, Bettie. Is the show any good? Have you seen it already?"

"We went to the first preview yesterday." Vic said, "But Bettie has to go back to see the play a few more times before it opens. Perhaps, you could go with her one night."

Bettie involuntarily emitted a flustered laugh and tossed Vic a panicked look.

"Holy cow, that would be wonderful," responded Officer Rodney Clements without hesitation. "Can I let you know later? After I've checked my duty roster back at the precinct?"

"Of course," said Bettie, smoothly, "You know where to find me."

"Would it be alright if I stopped by your office today after my shift? I'll know my schedule by then." Rodney was clearly thrilled to pieces and didn't want to pass up Bettie's generous offer. "I've never been inside the Sardi building before."

"I look forward to it," Bettie smiled. "We're on the seventh floor."

As Rodney signaled goodbye, he and Fiona trotted eastward, heading for a crowd of Broadway tourists visibly anxious to greet them.

Vic turned to Bettie and smiled, "You can thank me now."

"How embarrassing. You dope, that could have been a disaster." She punched his arm. "Honestly!"

Vic winked, "But, it wasn't, was it? I could tell he's smitten with you. That's probably because he really doesn't know you." Bettie punched his other arm as the art director continued, "Ouch! The most challenging part of the deal is that you have to sit through *Don't Hang Up* one more time before opening night."

"And just how did you profess to know I'd be interested in Rodney Clements at all?" she asked.

"I took a shot in the dark," said Vic, coyly. "You could always come up with an excuse and back out of it. I'd be more than willing to take your place."

"Over my dead body!" Bettie laughed as they entered the building.

Vic wondered aloud, "Maybe that's what Mizz Mitzi had in mind with her murder prediction. I'd venture to guess that there are lots of us who would kill to spend some 'alone time' with that magnificent Copcake."

"Oh, I like that nickname." Bettie cooed. "It really suits him—it's sweet."

"Let's not forget edible, too. It's settled, then. I hereby dub Officer Rodney Clements as Copcake. And he shall be so called from this day forward," Vic announced with a sweeping theatrical gesture, quickly adding, "Never to his face, of course."

Stopping at the front desk, Bettie smiled and approached the typically sullen lobby attendant, Guy Andersen, and asked about his lunchtime celebrity sightings. His demeanor changed instantly.

"It was a busy afternoon. None other than Mr. Tennessee Williams himself was here. That was a real thrill, I'll tell you. Lordy, that man was already drunk as a skunk and it was barely lunchtime. Lena Horne popped in. She's the nicest lady. And we even had a rare visit from Charles Aznavour and his entourage." Andersen, usually deadpan in his delivery, appeared duly enthusiastic as he gave his report. "Tonight's blind item: what Broadway heartthrob was caught snatching a gold wristwatch from a Tiffany counter?"

Bettie was pleasantly taken aback. "Wow, forget Tiffany's—that is an incredible lineup of star power for a weekday afternoon, Mr. A.—even for Sardi's!"

"Well, they might've been going to the second floor restaurant, but who can tell? They could also have been heading to your offices, or any number of press agents' and general managers' offices upstairs. The building's lousy with them."

"Lousy might be a bit too harsh, but it's not far from accurate." Vic chimed in as he grabbed Bettie's arm and led her over to the awaiting elevator.

As the time-worn car clanged and climbed upward, a thought passed the hungry account executive's mind.

"If we're lucky, they'll be some leftover bagels from this morning's presentation. We failed to pick up any lunch," said Bettie. "I blame it on all the distractions by psychics, stage stars, and the Mounted Police."

"Not even sure I'd have a minute to spare for a stale bagel. I've got to do some research in the art archives this afternoon." Vic was visibly antsy as the elevator reached the seventh floor. "But I will definitely find time to pee…right now." He raced toward the restrooms.

While Bettie strolled back to her desk to catch up on phone calls and paperwork, Vic headed directly into the art archives after his brief bathroom break.

Thompson & Co's art archives were sacred ground for Vic. The agency had been in the business of theatrical advertising for over 40 years. It had accrued a wealth of artwork created by talented folks from both the commercial and fine art worlds, who'd been hired to design speculative concept posters for various Broadway productions. All of this discarded art-for-hire was kept in both vertical and horizontal racks, as well as in paper drawers, file cabinets, and most recently in a modular system that could be expanded to any size at any time. The storage shelves secured the illustration boards, canvases, and masonite-mounted artwork in their position to prevent slipping or bowing. Although the room was temperature-controlled, little else was done to ensure the safety of what had turned into a valuable stockpile of creative output for the Broadway theatre. This was the artwork that had fallen by the wayside in the first half of the Twentieth Century.

It was a dream-come-true playroom for Vic, who was an avid admirer of commercial art. He always took advantage of spending any time he could spare among the long-forgotten sketches, paintings, collages, and etchings created by some of the most remarkable artists working throughout the past four decades.

Just as a point of departure for his research, the art director wanted to check out any posters that may have been rejected for the 1941 Broadway production of *Blithe Spirit*. This was more challenging than one might have expected given that the archive was not arranged in any particular type of order. The sizes of the boards and canvases submitted varied greatly since the artists were never given any parameters in terms of proportion. That fell under the art director's job description. It was his or hers assigned task to create the title design, position the artwork to compliment the traditional 14" x 22" window card format, and to leave ample space to accommodate the massive amount of billing credits that were contractually required to appear on the poster.

During his time thus far at Thompson & Co, Vic was learning where to root around for certain pieces in the archives. On the whole, it was a matter of painstakingly hunting through the tremendous amount of accumulated artwork until you found what you were searching for, or finally gave up the ghost.

He had totally lost track of time, which was easily done when surrounded by the brilliant collection of poster comps to be found in the archive's racks, shelves, and drawers. Bettie popped in.

"Oh, you *are* still in here." She handed him a plain bagel with a schmear of cream cheese. "What're you looking for anyway?"

"My trusty intuition tells me that the artwork we presented today might need to be rethought. It helps to look through the archive to fire up the ole creative juices." Vic explained, as he took a healthy bite of his paltry lunch.

He had placed some of the rejected sketches he'd discovered on the recently installed poster rail. The railing ran the length of the room and had been installed at the same time the Thompson & Co conference room improvements were completed. As in the conference room, the sleek shelving served to highlight selected poster sketches and comps under museum-style lighting. Vic had uncovered a few beauties, which he'd propped up on the display rail during his search.

"I just found these poster concepts drawn by a cartoonist who was often featured in *The New Yorker* magazine throughout the 1940s. I can't read the artist's signature because it's basically a scrawl. I don't think they're right for a contemporary production of *Blithe Spirit*, but I wanted to get Tobin's take on them. What do you think?"

Bettie looked them over briefly, "I'm not the right person to ask. You and Tobin are the artistic geniuses around here. What are these other posters for?"

"I hadn't come across these before. They're a real find. Obviously, those two paintings were created by Tom Morrow for the original Broadway production of *Cabaret* in 1966. He did a wonderful series of paintings in the style of artist Georg Grosz."

A blank stare from Bettie lead Vic to further explain, "Georg Grosz's watercolors exemplified Berlin before World War II. His favorite subjects were wounded soldiers, prostitutes, fat businessmen, orgies, and sex crimes. Harold Prince thought the Dadaist style perfect for the musical he was producing and directing. These are the rejected paintings—and they're gorgeous. Same story here, I'm guessing," said Vic as he brought Bettie's attention to the last poster in the row, "Mr. Prince is always focused on a particular style of art for most of his shows. The only markings or signature I can find on this painting is an "M" in the corner of the canvas. Unfortunately, it's gotten somewhat beaten up and worn in that particular area. I strongly suspect it's another Tom Morrow piece, probably created for *Fiddler on the Roof* in 1964. I actually think it has possibilities, with certain revisions, for use on *Blithe Spirit*. This time around, Morrow must've been asked by Mr. Prince to paint in the style of Marc Chagall."

"I recognize that name from Art History classes," said Bettie with authority.

Vic continued his impromptu lecture, "Marc Chagall was a Modernist painter whose brilliant use of color was admired by none other than Pablo Picasso. Morrow has successfully tapped into Chagall's lively imagination which often depicted dancing figures or floating bodies, flowers, and animals."

The vibrant painting indeed showed a man holding a woman's hand while another woman floated above them, showering flowers down upon the couple.

"I can imagine adapting that artwork somewhat for *Blithe Spirit*, yes? The only thing missing is the Madame Arcati character."

Bettie was typically reluctant to make any creative suggestions.

Vic finished his bagel with one healthy mouthful. "I'll show it to Tobin later. I think he's still in touch with Tom Morrow, if we want to hire that artist to further adapt it. In recent years, Morrow's been making headway from the commercial arena into the world of Fine Art galleries where there's bigger money to be made."

"I'd imagine he could make a real killing in the fine art of forgery," said Bettie as they made their way back to their respective offices.

"Oh, before I forget, we're in for a genuine treat this evening. The charming Rodney Clements, aka Copcake, plans on stopping by to let me know his availability regarding being my date for a preview performance of *Don't Hang Up*. Let's offer to buy him a few cocktails downstairs at Sardi's bar. He's never been there before."

"I suppose we can all use a drink," Vic joked. "Especially after Mizz Mitzi scared the hell out of us this morning."

"I'm sure a few martinis will help soothe our shattered nerves." Bettie said.

"…and perhaps even lift our spirits?" added Vic, wincing at his own bad pun.

Scene Seven

The bar located on Sardi's second floor was always hopping during pre-theatre hours. Bettie had asked her waiter friend, Julio, to reserve a table for them near the window overlooking 44th Street. Bettie and Vic, with an awestruck Rodney Clements in tow, were ushered directly to their prime location amidst the noisy crowd of thirsty Broadway-types who were just beginning their night on the town.

"This place is a madhouse!" yelled Rodney over the din. "It's so exciting."

They ordered cocktails and dove into the small plate of crackers and pub cheese the waiter had delivered to their table.

"Working in theatrical advertising certainly sounds thrilling," Rodney said, "I've always had an interest in The Arts. Fine Art, especially. I didn't have too much formal exposure to it in school, so I studied it on my own at the library. I've a well-worn volume of Jansons' *History of Art* on my coffee table at home."

"I know you hail from Hooker, Oklahoma—that's a difficult detail to forget," Bettie said lightly, "Do you come from an artsy family?"

"Dad's basically a farmer, although some of our neighbors might more accurately describe him as a landowner. Our mom belongs to the local community theatre company. She's always been interested in performing. I believe she's actually a good actress. I used to help her learn her lines and would do double duty as her rehearsal partner. That's how I became interested in the stage—but not as a performer, as an audience member—and avid fan."

"How did you get involved with law enforcement?" Bettie asked.

"I studied for the Police Officer exam when I moved here. I passed. I was given an offer to join the NYPD Mounted Unit for the Broadway community. Being a theatre-loving country boy, I couldn't very well say no to that. It was a perfect convergence of my interests in fitness, horses, The Law, and The Arts."

"Not a typical niche to fill. Seems as if it was kismet," laughed Vic. "Sometimes lucky chances just drop in our laps. It's up to us to make the most of our golden opportunities. I feel the same way about my career."

Bettie added, "I was always told I should become a model or an actress. But I was never terribly interested in those fields. Theatrical advertising—now, that spoke to me!"

"Here's to happy careers," said Vic.

The three of them clinked glasses and sipped their cocktails just as a voice broke through the barroom commotion, "Well, if it isn't our fantastic ad agency!"

The trio turned to see producer Rex Merchant, who had just stepped out of the lone phone booth, discreetly located in the corner of the immense restaurant space near the men's room. He had spotted them in the bar area and approached.

"I'm meeting Helena and Simone for a quick bite before the show. Drop by our table and say hello when you're through here." Merchant said, his hazel eyes red-rimmed, betraying the massive quantity of marijuana he'd just smoked.

Bettie took a bit of wicked pleasure in introducing their guest. "Rex, I'd like to introduce you to Rodney Clements, one of NYPD's finest Mounted Policemen. You may have seen him making his rounds in Times Square on his horse, Fiona."

"Well…yes, of course…it's a pleasure to meet you." Rex muttered, nervously blinking his eyes and extending his hand. "You must all come see us before you go. We're seated over in the far corner."

As the producer/director walked away into the crowded second-floor dining room, Rodney asked, "Is that Helena, as in Helena Baxter the actress?"

"The one and only, yes," admitted Bettie. "Rex is her husband, director, and co-producer. He's British."

Vic checked the time on his wristwatch. "Let's finish our drinks. Then, we'll nonchalantly visit Helena Baxter's table. She's going to be leaving soon for half-hour call at the theatre."

Rodney's face held a quizzical expression, so Vic explained, "Every actor on Broadway is required to be in attendance at the theatre at least one half-hour before performance time, or earlier."

Bettie asked Julio where Helena Baxter was sitting, and the server pointed the way.

Once at the unobtrusive table in the corner, Rodney Clements was introduced to the group before Helena Baxter extended her hand to Bettie and Vic.

"Bravo, you two. Rex just told me the exciting news about your presentation this morning. I'm sorry I wasn't there to witness it for myself. It sounded just delightful and so creative. Imagine hiring a psychic! I've heard some of my friends talk about Mizz Mitzi and her extraordinary abilities. She makes for wonderful cocktail party chatter."

"Yes, indeed, congratulations, so well deserved," added a smiling Simone Caldwell, who did look astonishingly like Helena Baxter. Admittedly, the differences between the two women became more apparent when they were seated side by side.

After conversing for a few minutes, the Broadway star began pulling herself together to walk over to the theatre. "My dears, you three must stop by our apartment for a cocktail after the show this evening. We're having some folks over to celebrate getting through our first preview last night without any major calamities."

Rex quickly joined in, "Absolutely. You must come! We're at The Dakota, 72nd Street and Central Park West, Number 73. They'll be plenty to eat and drink, plus some surprises."

"And now, we must fly." Helena Baxter announced, theatrically sweeping out of the restaurant to wild applause from the star-struck Sardi's customers, who were thrilled to see a genuine Broadway actress up close.

"Let's go back to Thompson & Co," suggested Bettie to her co-worker, "We can give Rodney a tour of our humble offices."

Vic made his way briskly over to the elevator ahead of the others since it generally took a few minutes for the elderly operator to maneuver the manual contraption upward after pressing the brass call button.

All was eerily quiet as Bettie, Rodney, and Vic stepped out of the elevator into the seventh- floor lobby—a drastic change of atmosphere from the bustling restaurant just a few floors below. It was almost 7:30, so the offices were empty, with most employees heading home, or on their way to the theatre. Bettie led the way, indicating points of interest to Rodney, starting with her private office. That was followed by the other account executive stations, which led to the conference room, and then to the artists' bullpen.

They spent some time in the production department since Rodney seemed fascinated by the process of paste ups and mechanicals. These boards were a photo-ready assembly of all the elements of a show ad that were then submitted to the various publications for printing. This process needed skilled artists who had a good eye and a steady hand. The tools employed were a blue pencil, an Exacto knife, a T-square, and rubber cement glue—the fumes of which would provide the staff with a pleasant high for most of the day. Tobin's and Vic's offices were next on the tour, ending up at the art archives, clearly the pièce de résistance of any Thompson & Co junket.

"Golly, but this is impressive. It's literally a visual catalogue of hundreds of Broadway shows from the past forty years." Rodney whispered, demonstrating due reverence for the poster comps, as he became quietly overwhelmed by the amount of artwork stored in the room.

"It's very much the history of what might have been," Vic noted. "Keep in mind, all of this creativity has never seen the light of day."

One of the posters in particular, propped up on the railing, caught Rodney's eye.

"What show was this done for?"

Vic stepped back to allow extra room for the three of them to admire the artwork inside the cramped archives space. "There are no identifying markings on it, but I'm guessing it was created for *Fiddler on the Roof*. Harold Prince, the producer and director, often requested the services of Tom Morrow, one of his favorite illustrators. The poster that Morrow ultimately conceived for the final *Fiddler* art has become quite famous. This painting was among a group of several throw-away concepts."

"Such a shame. He certainly did Marc Chagall proud," commented Rodney, awestruck. "It's breathtaking, especially the color palette."

The policeman was unaware of how his instant identification of the artist in question was highly impressive to both Bettie and Vic.

"Over the years, we've adapted quite an array of famous art styles for our campaigns. I can show you faux Picassos, faux van Goghs, faux Magrittes, faux Dalis, and faux Monets," Vic continued, "The list goes on and on. Sometimes tapping into a certain classic art style is the key to creating a memorable show poster. People might be fond of a particular artist's work and are inclined to remember it, which could lead to their finding out more about the production, and hopefully buying tickets. At least, that's one theory of theatrical advertising." Vic laughed, "There are about a million others."

Bettie clutched Rodney's arm and said, "I have a terrific idea. Let's go back down to Sardi's and have a leisurely dinner. By the time we're finished, we can hop a taxi uptown to Helena Baxter's place for cocktails among the glamorous Broadway elite."

"I'm afraid I must kindly beg off. I have a...um...date later. But nothing's going to top meeting Helena Baxter tonight. My mom's positively going to freak out when I tell her about it. The other guys in my unit will be green with envy."

Before exiting the art archives, Rodney Clements turned to steal one last glance at the rejected poster art propped up on the railing under the museum-style lighting.

"Astonishing," he sighed.

Scene Eight

Stepping out of the Checker cab on the corner of West 72nd Street, Vic looked up to marvel at the gothic facade of The Dakota apartment building while offering a gentlemanly hand to Bettie in exiting the spacious taxi.

"They filmed the exteriors of *Rosemary's Baby* here a few years ago." Bettie remarked to her fellow film fan. "Mia Farrow. Ruth Gordon. Perfection."

As if the uniformed gatekeeper stepping out from his polished sentry booth to greet them wasn't intimidating enough, Helena Baxter's domicile featured classic European charm, a private vestibule, five wood-burning fireplaces, and a grand library that retained original 19th century architectural details. They entered into a foyer floored with highly waxed tiles and mellow indirect lighting. The huge living room, leading to a panoramic view overlooking the treetops of Central Park, tipped its elegant opulence over the edge.

"Welcome, my dears, and make yourselves at home. Please have Caprice fix you a drink at once," said Helena, ever the gracious hostess. "The performance went very smoothly tonight. We extend our humble thanks to the theatre gods."

Vic noted from past experience that it didn't take very long for theatre folk to get the party started. The expansive living room was already alive with thick cigarette smoke, the sounds of clinking glasses, raucous cocktail chatter, and a group of attractive guests fresh from their evening shows. The cast of *Don't Hang Up* was small in terms of Broadway, consisting of only five actors including Helena Baxter. Vic spotted Simone Caldwell across the room talking to an animated Ava Chasten, who'd obviously recovered from her afternoon headache. He also caught a glimpse of Terry Hagen snapping candid photographs of the partygoers. Vic wondered if she was still using his Canon F-1. His boss, Tobin Klein, was even in attendance. Tobin was notorious for quick hellos and even quicker getaways at gatherings like this one.

"I thought Olga was going to join you tonight?" Vic had yet to meet his boss' wife.

"She has an art class that she doesn't want to miss," Tobin said, "She's also not too keen on taking the trip in from Brewster on Metro North."

The party was filled with assorted theatrical types. Some dancers from the recent revival of *Gypsy* were in attendance. There were even a few bold-faced names as well as several by-lined entertainment columnists milling about. Over in the corner, Arne was in a serious-looking huddle, sharing a joint with Rex.

When the producer/director looked up and saw Vic, he excused himself, scurried over extending his hand, a waft of cannabis smoke in his wake, "So glad you could join us. The show went awfully well tonight. Another two weeks of previews and we should be in great condition to face the dreaded New York critics."

The director guided them over to the beverage setup. "This is our housekeeper, Caprice Fournier. She's acting as bartender tonight. What's your pleasure?"

Mademoiselle Fournier was your stereotypical idea of a French maid, minus the frilly white apron and stiletto heels. She was a forty-something ash-blonde, classically beautiful, and spoke with a perfect Parisienne accent, instantly bringing to Vic's mind images of 1) buttery croissants, 2) the Louvre museum, and 3) Catherine Deneuve movies. He also wondered if she was indeed the same housekeeper who'd lowered the boom on the unsuspecting Norwegian tourist fifteen years ago when she failed to stop a ten-pound dumbbell from its fatal fall out of the seventh-floor window.

Bettie had been chatting with Tobin. She noticed that a girlfriend of one of the young dancers from the supporting chorus of *Gypsy* had latched onto Arne Engels.

"Your job title sounds exciting for sure, but I haven't a clue as to what a general manager does," the young woman said with feigned interest, "Honestly, I get easily confused with a lot of theatrical terms—for instance, the function of the producer, as opposed to the director, as opposed to the stage manager?"

Arne flashed a devastatingly charming smile, "Basically, the general manager is the first person hired on any production. It's my responsibility to prepare and oversee the show's budget and timeline. This includes getting involved in scheduling every aspect of the staging process from hiring and casting to construction and rehearsal. I'd much rather hear about you."

Perry Chan, the young scenic designer, was over in the corner of the living room, taking in the extraordinary view. Dressed conservatively in blue slacks and a white shirt, he was alternating his attention between the sprawling Manhattan vista and the large goldfish bowl that housed two overfed aquatic residents. Vic excused himself and left Bettie and Tobin to their own capable devices.

The art director insinuated himself with, "Hey, Perry, I'm sure you've been hearing this a lot, but your scenery for the show is pure genius," They clinked cocktail glasses.

"Hello, Vic, it's been a while since I've seen you. I thought you'd call after our last dinner. Thank you so much for the kind words," said the young designer. "Is your agency handling the show? They never keep me up on the business end of things. The advertising's been just great."

"You know how crazy it gets, Perry. It's not as if you haven't been distracted as well. Working on the show must keep you very busy indeed."

"I'd always make time for you. I think you're well aware of that."

Vic opened his mouth to respond when he was literally saved by the bell as Hollywood producer Earl Quick and his far-from-blushing bride, Celeste Farris, made a blustery show-biz entrance.

Perry and Vic were close enough to hear their gracious hostess mutter, "Ugh, her! Doesn't that tramp ever stay home?" as Helena Baxter, with a concerted effort, took a deep breath before making her way over to the front door, arms extended in warm reception.

Watching Celeste Farris and Helena Baxter air-kiss provided the crowd with no end of gossipy excitement. The ongoing feud between the two Broadway superstars continued to be fodder for the supermarket tabloids. The actresses would sooner knife each other rather than embrace. Given that Helena Baxter's hubby Rex had now partnered with her ex-lover, Earl Quick, on his premiere producing venture—patiently putting up with Celeste Farris would become a necessary evil for her.

Vic became aware of shutterbug Terry snapping away, recording the momentous event.

As it turned out, the newlywed Mr. and Mrs. Quick had entered the apartment with Cal Lockheed in tow, whom they'd just cast in their upcoming revival. He was arm-in-arm with a ravishing woman whose slender figure conjured up the créme de la créme of Richard Avedon's celebrated haute couture mannequins.

"That's Celeste Farris' secretary," whispered Perry, "She uses a really funny stage name, but I can't remember it right now. Venus or Aphrodite, something like that."

Cal abruptly broke away from his group when he caught sight of Vic talking to Perry Chan across the room and headed over toward them.

"Well, darlings, I won the part. I'm going to play Dr. Bradman in *Blithe Spirit*. Believe me, I am over-the-moon thrilled. It ought to be outrageous fun working with Celeste again. That woman is a bundle of laughs," squealed the actor with delight as he glanced over at a vivacious Celeste Farris and her secretary talking to Helena Baxter, who was playing the tolerant hostess. "Given the opportunity to witness those two legendary ladies going at it hammer-and-tongs on occasion should provide ample entertainment during the rehearsal period."

Vic said, "I'm guessing that Helena Baxter will keep her distance and will do everything possible to avoid any confrontations. Besides, she'll be too busy with her own show to interfere with Rex's next project."

"That's if her play runs that long." Cal said, cattily, quickly adding, "Sorry, Perry."

"Oh, Cal, you're such a flaming bitch. Don't ever change," said the good-looking scenic designer, adding a wink.

"You should ask our hostess to do her caustic impression of housekeeper and chef extraordinaire Mademoiselle Fournier for you," Cal whispered, "Aside from possessing fine acting chops, Helena Baxter is an amazing mimic. It's one hilarious routine. She also does an extraordinary imitation of Celeste Farris. Maybe you'll be lucky enough to catch it sometime when she's had one too many cocktails."

The three men surveyed the noisy, smoke-filled living room. They were speculating on the identity of a tall, odd-looking character with wispy dark hair combed (to use the term loosely) in many directions. The gentleman was nattily dressed in a black suit and sported a pair of eyeglasses that sat crookedly on his face. None of them had ever seen him before.

Perry Chan, under his breath, declared, "Who the hell is that? He's kind of cute in a mad-scientist-from-a-*Frankenstein*-movie kind of way," then suggested, "Most likely somebody's plus-one. Let's take bets on how long he'll remain standing since he's downing those champagne cocktails faster than poor Caprice can pour them."

"I spy with my little eye that new publicist, Mark Rhodes, has just shown up," Cal observed, lighting his third cigarette since his arrival. "That boy is indeed quite a dish."

"The jury's still out on him. Mark certainly plays it close to the vest," said Vic.

Cal took a long drag on his Lucky Strike, and upon release, inquired, "What's Arnie Engels' story, darling? I hear he's popular with the ladies, but he's certainly hunky enough for one to consider that perhaps that nice Jewish boy might be convinced to play for our team occasionally—especially after a few stiff drinks."

"Poor hunk has severe allergies." snorted Perry, "If the pollen count's high enough, do you think he could possibly be had for the price of a Contac capsule?"

"You two biddies ask an awful lot of silly questions. Contrary to popular belief, I do not work in The Dakota information booth. Go find the answers out for yourselves. It's a party. I don't know about you, but I intend to mingle," Vic said, as he abruptly turned and made his way toward the center of the room, which was a beehive of activity.

It was then that Simone Caldwell sat down at the Steinway baby grand piano and began playing some familiar standard numbers, obviously yet another task she performed at her employer's request. The understudy/secretary was very adept at Gershwin and Cole Porter medleys and, of course, show tunes.

Helena Baxter approached the piano and posed, looking rapturously at the keyboard over Simone's shoulder as Terry Hagen took numerous snapshots. Rex joined her, wrapping his arms around his wife's waist, as some of the *Don't Hang Up* cast members entered the frame and began singing a song from *Funny Girl*. It was an inevitable Broadway cocktail party occurrence. Seemingly oblivious to all that, Earl Quick was having a lively conversation with Bettie during the spontaneous musical interlude.

In the midst of all of the show-biz hubbub, Tobin Klein surreptitiously took his leave. Moments later, from across the room, Vic noticed Celeste Farris' secretary exiting the apartment arm-in-arm with one of the more muscular chorus dancers from *Gypsy*.

"It's not helping my goddamn migraine, kids, but at least it's a good photo op," griped Ava, then shouting across to Terry, "I'll want some pictures of Cal Lockheed with Celeste Farris as well for when I announce his casting in *Blithe Spirit*."

"Please, give it a rest, Ava," said Helena Baxter, clapping her hands. "Attention, everyone, I have an announcement to make."

She waited until the guests had stopped their buzzing and settled into a tolerable hum.

"As some of you may know, our dear Caprice Fournier is an extraordinary chef and baker. She has graced our table, not to mention a number of these cocktail parties, with some of her delectable creations over the years. After much discussion, I have finally convinced Caprice to collaborate with me on a cookbook of her specialties. We just sealed the deal today with Simon & Schuster for a release next year." Helena Baxter gestured toward the strapping, young mad scientist with the bizarre coif, crooked eyeglasses, and the black suit.

"May I introduce Oskar Lindqvist, from that distinguished publishing house, who will be acting as our editor. Oskar, we're utterly thrilled. Please say a few words if you will?"

The editor tossed his head to one side in an effort to work some stray strands of hair out of his eyes while he held firmly onto his drink in one hand, a smoldering cigarette in the other. Although addressing the room full of guests, he seemed to focus his gaze on the carpeting, avoiding eye contact with anyone as he spoke.

"Tank you, tank you, Helena Baxter." Lindqvist said with an aggressively thick accent, "At Simon & Schuster, we believe dat an editor's relationship to a book should be an invisible one. I have had the honor of vorking with many celebrated authors in the past und look forward to my collaboration wit Helena Baxter und Caprice Fournier on their fabulush project."

The room broke into thunderous applause after which, Helena continued, "The first section of the cookbook, more of a lifestyle book really, will focus on canapés. To give some of the recipes a trial run, Caprice has made a wide variety of her favorites for you to taste this evening. My dears, you are all in for the treat of your lives."

The doors to the immense kitchen swung open to reveal Caprice, Simone, Rex, and Arne laden with large trays of exotic-looking appetizers, which they then deposited on the various tables strategically spaced around the living room. Some of the guests rushed over to acquaint themselves with the unusual Oskar Lindqvist, who was being photographed by Terry. The rest of the glamorous mob made a mad dash toward the canapé trays.

"Dangle food in front of theatre folk and they instantly mutate into a plague of locusts," observed Cal Lockheed as he reached for one of the fancy-looking hors d'oeuvres. "What did the Mademoiselle call this concoction, '*White Monkey Spread*,' I think she said? I hope it's not made with real simian meat, darling. One can never be too sure when encountering exotic gourmet dishes from the continent."

"Face it, Cal, the closest your palette's ever been to Parisienne haute cuisine was scarfing down an order of french fries at the Howard Johnson's on 46th and Broadway," said Perry Chan, reaching for a ham and banana hollandaise canapé that the chef had named, '*Around the World*.'

Terry now had her sights focused on Helena Baxter and Celeste Farris posing on either side of Caprice, who was gingerly balancing a small tray of her fancy delicacies on her arms, as if serving. The two legendary stage actresses were adept at changing their facial expressions with each and every snap of the camera. Mademoiselle Fournier maintained a perpetually frozen grimace throughout the entire process. Ava motioned to Oskar Lindqvist, who then stepped in and joined the ladies, making it a foursome.

At a safe distance, Cal commented, "Now that's a gaggle worthy of an Edward Gorey drawing," as he slid another *White Monkey* down his throat. "These canapés are really rather tasty after the initial shock wears off, darling."

Vic excused himself from the racy Broadway gossip session his circle was enjoying, to refresh his cocktail at the designated bar area. The art director was trekking across the immense living room, subconsciously eavesdropping on the various clusters of conversations he was catching along the way. Senso overheard fragmented phrases overlapping one another, unaware of who was saying what.

"…she actually crossed the stage in front of him during the scene…"

"…is having a hot and heavy affair with the producer's famous wife…"

"…when the jerk suddenly slapped me, I have to admit, I liked it…"

"…so, I moved closer to see if it was an original Warhol silk screen…"

"…it seemed to take forever for that old queen to die during Act One…"

Vic finally reached Caprice, fresh from her impromptu photo session, now back to her original station as bartender.

"Congratulations on the book. Simon & Schuster is a big deal," he said.

"I owe it all to Helena Baxter. It's her star name everybody's interested in."

Vic saluted Caprice with his freshly stirred cocktail, "Brava to you—don't sell yourself short. The canapés are delicious, creative, and highly unusual. They are sure to get noticed."

Positioned near an immense gothic fireplace, Bettie was sitting with Mark Rhodes, having a cigarette. This was the first time they'd ever managed to chat together without being part of a group. As expected, their conversation began with amusing exchanges, mostly involving work. Then, Mark abruptly asked, "Are you seeing anybody? I know at least ten guys who have their eyes set on you."

"Wanna laugh? I could say the same thing to you, too." Bettie chortled.

The publicist blushed, "I'm not sure I'll ever get accustomed to that."

"But, to answer your question, no, I'm not seeing anybody," she said. "I certainly don't have to explain to you that our workdays never seem to end. It's extremely difficult to meet anyone, especially if they have a somewhat normal schedule. Since I've started at Thompson & Co, I've broken more dates than I care to think about. What about you?"

"Honestly, I've even stopped trying." Mark admitted, brushing a stray ash from his tie. "Having Ava as a boss is a 24/7 job. She's been known to phone me at 3am as calmly as if it were the middle of the afternoon. I don't think the woman ever gets any sleep. She's nuts—but undeniably successful. I plan on learning an awful lot from her if I can put up with all the theatrical insanity of her office routines."

"Has she ever flirted with you?" Bettie asked.

"Ava flirts with every man she meets in her inimitable headachy, angst-ridden way. I guess some guys find all that moaning and kvetching attractive. I think she just comes across as being needy and extremely high maintenance." Mark put out his cigarette in a nearby ashtray and instantly lit another. "When you and I first met, I thought perhaps you and Vic Senso were a couple."

Bettie nodded, "Lots of people have gotten that impression. That's because we spend so much time together. Vic and I make for a terrific team at work, but we're just really good chums."

It was then that Bettie heard a loud crash followed by sounds of shattering glass. She and Mark abruptly turned their attention to the other guests gathered in the vast living room.

Bettie would later describe it as witnessing a film sequence in slow motion. She first noticed Arne Engels clutching his stomach, nearly capsizing the goldfish bowl, and dropping to his knees. Two of the *Gypsy* cast members were holding onto the nearest furniture to keep from toppling over, writhing in pain. They appeared dizzy and disoriented. Helena Baxter had her arms around Cal Lockheed, who could scarcely walk, endeavoring to lead the stricken actor in the direction of one of her four bathrooms. Vic ran over to provide a hand. Oskar Lindqvist, from Simon & Schuster publishers, was motioning to anyone nearby for assistance. Rex and Caprice clutched the ashen-faced editor's arms to lend physical support. They also began maneuvering him toward another of the apartment's bathrooms. The place erupted in utter chaos with panic-stricken partygoers screaming, aimlessly running amok, bumping into one another and, in the process, knocking over expensive bric-a-brac, antique *Louis Quatorze* chairs, and trays of assorted fancy canapés.

Scene Nine

Hours later, an exhausted Helena Baxter surveyed the wreckage of her cocktail party. The guests had been requested to stay put and not touch anything for the time being—until the EMT workers and the police finished with their assessment of exactly what had happened. The officers were dutifully collecting samples of the canapés and the cocktails. Cal Lockheed, Oskar Lindqvist of Simon & Schuster, Arne Engels, and two female chorus dancers from *Gypsy* had been rushed to a nearby hospital.

Caprice Fournier, in a highly agitated state of nervous collapse, had been given a sedative and ordered sent to bed. Ava volunteered to sit with her, mainly to remove herself from the annoyingly jittery crowd.

"I hope and pray that they're going to be alright," said Rex anxiously, turning to his wife, "My dear, I was just informed that a police detective is on his way up to talk with us. I think that's my cue to flush our stash down the toilet."

Helena Baxter nodded numbly, "Yes, of course, I understand."

The actress gestured to her equally shaken secretary. "Can you please get me a glass of ice water, Simone? And maybe make some coffee for everyone?"

Simone walked haltingly toward the kitchen as if in a stupor.

"How are Adam and Eve? Did the goldfish bowl topple over?" Helena Baxter asked.

As he headed away to destroy any evidence of marijuana on the premises, Rex assured his wife, "No, they're fine, dear. Swimming their little tails off."

Watching the proceedings from their position by the fireplace, Bettie and Vic performed a good old-fashioned double-take when the anxiously-awaited police detective finally arrived on the scene from the neighborhood precinct.

"Oh, my god, look, it's Copcake," said Vic, recognizing Rodney Clements. "I thought he told us he had a date tonight."

Bettie was aware that the detective's first priority would be to question Helena Baxter and her husband Rex about the party. She tried heading Clements off as he walked across the vestibule to check in with a few of his uniformed men.

The detective looked up when he realized Bettie was hovering nearby, waiting to speak with him. "Yes, miss?"

"It's me, Rodney. Bettie Balboa," she began awkwardly.

The policeman held up his hand, abruptly signaling for her to stop, "Um, miss, I'm afraid you must be acquainted with my brother. My name is Renny Clements," the detective quickly explained, "Rodney and I are identical twins. People often confuse us for each other. However, this isn't the time or place for chit-chat. Now, can you please sit back down and wait for one of our men to question you? I'd greatly appreciate it. That's all, thank you, miss. Step that way."

Bettie rejoined her intimate, huddled group, which included Mark, Perry Chan, and Vic. "Rodney failed to mention that he has an identical twin."

"This Clements brother means business," whispered Senso. "Those twin Copcakes may look alike, but the similarity apparently ends there."

"Who could ever have imagined there'd be two of them?" Perry Chan observed,

"One's heavenly enough."

Terry Hagen, seated nearby, leaned in, and said, "I met the twin brothers at a party a few weeks ago. I have Renny and Rodney lined up for a studio session sometime soon. I arranged it with them a while ago. They are painfully gorgeous, right? I'm hoping to pitch it as a pictorial piece for *Playbill*: *Hot Cops on the Broadway Beat*." Suddenly feeling guilty over having initiated such a frivolous conversation under the unusual circumstances, the photographer lowered her voice and added, "Has there been any word at all from the hospital on the status of the others?"

"I suspect that's why Detective Clements is here," offered Vic.

Celeste Farris and Earl Quick were sitting alongside Terry, watching the official proceedings. The detective had finished speaking with Helena Baxter and her husband Rex. Renny Clements was now clearly prepared to make a formal announcement to the rest of the anxious people in the room.

"May I have your attention, please?" Detective Clements began authoritatively, "I realize you must all be extremely tired and upset over what's happened here tonight. I ask that you bear with us for a while longer. It appears there were incidents of random food poisoning at your party this evening. Erring on the side of caution, I'll be questioning you about events leading up to tonight's unfortunate occurrence. At this juncture, we are trying to ascertain what was at fault—whether it was the food or the drinks, an accident, a prank gone overboard, or something more serious. Several rather stricken folks were removed by ambulance."

A synchronized buzz of comments was audible in the room.

Renny Clements continued, "Before we let you go back to your homes, there are just a few questions we'd like to ask. Some of the officers and I will be circulating around the room. Please be patient, and one of us will get to you in a timely fashion. After which, you will be released. Miss Baxter has kindly brewed some fresh pots of coffee." Following that, Detective Clements took a pocket notebook and a well-bitten pencil nub out of his pocket, performed a quick survey of the room, and called out, "Terry Hagen, can I start with you, please?"

The photographer nodded and joined the detective at his temporary station in the corner near the kitchen door, "Nice to see you again, Renny. How can I help?"

"You were covering the party tonight. Did you notice anything strange or out of the ordinary going on? Anyone tampering with food or beverages?" he began.

Terry shook her head, "No, it was just like all the other theatrical cocktail parties I've covered over the years. Oh, there was the special announcement that Helena Baxter and her housekeeper had signed a cookbook deal with a major publisher. They brought out trays of Mademoiselle Fournier's hors d'oeuvres for us to sample, then folks were singing while gathered around the baby grand Steinway. There was drinking and lots of smoking going on, of course. Cigarette smoking, that is."

A flash of a smile crossed Renny's face. It was gone as quickly as it had come. "About the special canapés, did you have any of them?"

"Yes, a few. Something called a *White Monkey*, I believe, and another appetizer made with gelatin and baloney." Terry then had an epiphany, suddenly blurting out, "Was there something wrong with the canapés? I tried several during the evening. They tasted just fine."

"Did you go into the kitchen at any point tonight?" the detective asked.

The shutterbug shook her head indicating a negative response.

"Well, I'm glad you're feeling alright. You can go on home now if you're up to it." Renny told her, "I promise that Rodney and I will be in touch to set up our photography session soon."

Celeste Farris stood up from her seat and captured the detective's attention just as Terry moved off to begin collecting her camera equipment. The detective waved her over, having instantly recognized the Broadway stage star and movie queen.

"It's an honor to meet you, Miss Farris," he said matter-of-factly, "Can I ask how you're feeling?"

"I'm happy to report that I've survived yet another of Helena Baxter's endless cocktail parties." Celeste Farris clearly wasn't in a particularly gracious mood at the moment, "Although this one does appear to have had certain casualties."

"Did you taste any of Mademoiselle Fournier's appetizers?"

"Yes, one or two. I cannot remember which ones they were. Apparently, they each had quaint little names. She was also in charge of mixing the cocktails."

Renny studied the famous actress with his piercing blue eyes, "Did you go into the kitchen at any point during the party, Miss Farris?"

"Certainly not. I rarely venture into my own kitchen."

"Can you approximate how much time lapsed from when the trays were brought out to when you first noticed guests falling ill?"

"I cannot say for certain, perhaps thirty minutes?" Celeste guessed.

"Did you observe anyone acting strangely tonight? asked Renny. "Were you aware of unusual behavior from any of the other guests?"

Celeste Farris gave it a moment's thought. "No," she ultimately declared.

"Thanks for your time. That'll be all for now. After I exchange a few words with your husband, you'll both be free to leave."

Dashing producer Earl Quick appeared wan and haggard despite his deep Hollywood tan. He had been mindlessly staring into the goldfish bowl.

"Were you in the kitchen at any point tonight?" the detective asked, admiring the older man's incredible head of wavy silver hair.

"Um, no…I mean, yes," answered the distinguished gentleman anticipating the next questions, "but I did partake of some of Mademoiselle Fournier's canapés. They tasted a bit unusual, but certainly not poisonous. She had also been manning the bar, but my cocktails were just fine. It had been a perfectly lovely party up until, well, you know."

Renny released the illustrious Mr. and Mrs. Quick, warning, "I may have further questions for you both tomorrow."

Detective Clements motioned Bettie Balboa to approach next. "Miss, did you notice anything unusual here this evening before folks started getting sick?"

"No, not at all."

"Did you taste any of the canapés?"

She looked around before leaning in and whispered, "Please don't tell Helena Baxter or Mademoiselle Fournier, but no, I didn't. Honestly, they looked disgusting. But, in all fairness, I was already stuffed from having had dinner at Sardi's." Bettie confessed.

The detective cracked a slight smile, "Were you in the kitchen at any time tonight?"

"Yes. I did drop in there," Bettie said, "more out of curiosity than anything. I wanted to see what a kitchen in The Dakota looked like. I talked with Simone Caldwell for a few minutes. I believe Terry took a few candid pictures of us then, too."

Renny Clements scrawled something in his pocket notepad using the worn pencil nub. One of his men approached and discreetly passed him a folded message. He looked at it, and then, scanned the room.

"Everyone, please leave your names and addresses with an officer," he announced. "We will be contacting you in the next few days for further questioning. It's quite late, and I realize tomorrow's a work day, so go home—get some much needed rest. We've appreciated your cooperation tonight under these extremely unpleasant circumstances."

"Dammit. I was hoping to be interrogated by Detective Dreamy." Perry Chan said, "I definitely wanted a closer look."

"Something tells me we'll all have that chance in due course— whether we want it or not." Vic extended his hand out to Bettie, "Shall we finally vamoose? It's nearly 2am, my lovely."

"I'd like to go to the hospital to check on Arnie, if that's okay," said Bettie. Averting her attention toward Renny's impending departure, "Detective Clements, would we be able to visit our friend Mr. Engels tonight for just a few minutes?"

"I'm on my way to the hospital now," the detective said, "Since you're acquainted with Rodney, and plain old food poisoning seems to be our culprit, I'd be happy to give you and Mr. Senso a lift. That is, if you don't mind riding in a beat up Chevy Impala?"

Before exiting, the detective said goodnight to Helena Baxter and Rex Merchant. "I've gotten clearance from the doctor to question his patients at the hospital. With your permission, I'll be returning here tomorrow morning to talk with Mademoiselle Fournier and Ms. Caldwell. If possible, please make yourselves available at that time as well."

"Yes, of course, detective," said Rex. "I'm sure there'll be no problem when you flash your credentials downstairs tomorrow, but we'll leave your name at the sentry booth in any case."

Ava emerged from Caprice's bedroom looking exhausted.

"How is she doing?" Helena Baxter asked, "Finally asleep?"

"Yes, thank God!" Ava dramatically took in a deep breath, "As she was nodding off, Caprice was babbling in English *and* French, no less, about her favorite Wusthof chef's knife having gone missing during the party. You'd think the woman would be more concerned about almost obliterating a good portion of the Broadway community tonight with her idiotic *White Monkey* canapés. But, apparently, that ten-inch piece of cutlery seemed more important. *'Où est mon couteau de chef Wusthof de dix pouces?'* she kept repeating. I remembered enough French from high school to decipher that phrase."

"Those gourmet knives cost a fortune, but I cannot imagine anybody walking off with one." Helena Baxter scoffed. "I'm sure it'll turn up eventually. The kitchen's been left in such chaos. The catering staff will probably find it somewhere under the rubble while cleaning up tomorrow."

Ava asked, "How would somebody sneak a razor-sharp, ten-inch chef's knife out of here anyway?"

Helena Baxter and Rex exchanged amused glances, and then looked back over at the publicist, who was gathering her things together, piling them into her massive Gucci tote bag which rarely left her side.

"Damned if I know, my dear," said Helena Baxter, raising her eyebrow in a theatrical expression of mock suspicion.

The battered hostess profusely thanked Ava for sitting with the heavily sedated Caprice. After the frazzled publicist exited the apartment, Helena Baxter and Rex surveyed the living room.

Overturned chairs, spilt drinks, broken Lalique ashtrays, and trod-upon canapés littered the expensive Persian carpets.

"Oh, Rex, I now understand what people mean when they describe something as a complete shambles," sighed Helena Baxter wryly, balancing Adam and Eve in their goldfish bowl on her lap. "My dear, I strongly suspect the wise thing to do now is move."

Scene Ten

"Ordinarily, a detective wouldn't have been called in tonight. Along with the EMT, a police presence would've been sufficient, but since there were high profile Broadway celebrities involved, our public relations people thought it judicious." Renny felt obliged to make conversation with the two passengers in his car.

"Because of the random nature of the poisoning, it's highly suspect as well. That's why we proceeded with the bagging of specimen samples and the questioning of the guests." the detective explained during their short drive to the hospital. "How do you two know my brother?"

"We work in the Sardi building," Vic told him from the back seat, "and run into Rodney occasionally when he and Fiona are making their Times Square rounds."

"It seems everybody knows everybody in the theatre world." Renny observed. "Rodney and I grew up in a small town and often comment on how the Broadway district has the feel of an isolated hamlet. I was mighty surprised to find that even I knew someone at the scene tonight. I'd met Terry Hagen, the photographer, just recently at a mutual friend's party. She's going to be taking our picture for *Playbill.*"

Bettie smiled, "The Theatre's an extremely tight-knit community. The playing field's pretty much confined to within a twelve-block radius. At times, I suppose it does have the feel of being a tiny village unto itself."

The hospital's intensive care unit seemed relatively quiet. Having accompanied the detective there had allowed Bettie and

Vic easy access to the area in which Arne was being held for observation. Detective Clements went off to find a phone booth while they visited.

"Helena Baxter really knows how to throw a party," said Arne, flatly.

Bettie, with tears welling in her eyes, hugged her colleague. "Oh, my god, I am so sorry this happened. How are you feeling now?"

"I felt like shit for about an hour. Now, all of the really horrible symptoms seem to have abated. What are you apologizing for? Do you know what caused it? The alcohol was certainly flowing but the only real food in sight were those…um…unusual canapés."

"We're waiting on official word from our detective. I think some of the other guests were brought here by ambulance." Vic slightly parted the dividing curtain surrounding the sectioned area and peeked out. "Uh-oh, everyone, brace yourselves. Renny Clements is heading back this way in a big hurry and he doesn't look too happy."

When the detective reached them, he pulled open the drape panel in one swift, theatrical gesture. "I just received word that traces of arsenic were found in some of the appetizers. And something worse—Oskar Lindqvist from Simon & Schuster has just died from arsenic poisoning."

The stunned expressions he detected on their exhausted faces lead him to adopt a calmer tone. After pulling closed the privacy curtain once again, "Naturally, this now puts tonight's event in an extremely different light. It appears that what we'd believed was a case of accidental food poisoning has actually been a deliberate attempt to cause serious harm. This has suddenly turned into a homicide investigation."

He seemed surprised by the news himself. "Do you have any idea who would've wanted to poison the party guests tonight, specifically Oskar Lindqvist?"

"I don't think any of us had ever seen or heard of him before tonight," Bettie said.

Vic observed, "Mr. Lindqvist had been introduced to our crowd for the first time this evening. The only people who were acquainted with him already were Helena Baxter, Caprice Fournier, and I'm assuming, Rex Merchant. Who'd want to kill a random stranger? Several of us sampled an assortment of the canapés. It appears only certain of the guests fell ill. Do you suppose that those folks were specifically targeted? Although, I don't understand why."

"Mr. Engels, do you recall which of canapés you'd tasted?" Renny asked, his pencil nub and notebook at the ready.

"I can't say that I remember what they were called, detective. I'm not even sure I could describe what they looked like. They were… just…canapés."

"Mr. Senso, you mentioned that you tasted a few of them as well?" Vic shrugged. "Yes, a few. I think one was named a *White Monkey*. But I didn't feel sick at all. The whole thing's so odd because the entire crowd was definitely eating from the same trays."

"Wouldn't somebody have seen the arsenic being added to the food? The living room was crowded and there were all sorts of people coming in and out of the kitchen, myself included." Bettie admitted, with a guilty tone in her voice.

"There were four separate trays scattered around the room. They were each filled with the assorted appetizers," said Renny.

"I have to admit, I made a point of tasting one or two from each of the selections," confessed Vic.

"We had just had a substantial Sardi's dinner, man! Where in the world did you put all that food?" Bettie smirked.

"It was my first Helena Baxter party. I was being a good guest," remarked the art director, sheepishly. "Have you spoken to Mademoiselle Fournier? She made the damn things."

"Unfortunately, the lady was in no condition to be questioned. She was given a sedative and sent to bed." Renny told them. "Mademoiselle Fournier is top of my list for questioning first thing tomorrow morning—especially in light of Mr. Lindqvist's death."

Unexpectedly, a muffled conversation was heard from behind the privacy curtain before it was abruptly pulled opened again.

"I thought I recognized some familiar voices," shrieked Ava, "What in the holy hell did Caprice put in her wretched canapés? Did I hear you correctly? That bizarre Simon & Schuster creature was murdered?"

"Excuse me, Ms. Chasten," the detective asked, "How did you get in here?"

"The hospital? Honestly, Detective Clements, I'm a Broadway press agent. I can gain access anywhere I damn well please. I've crashed parties at Gracie Mansion that had hired armed security. Bulldozing my way passed the intensive care desk after visiting hours was child's play. Besides, I came to check on Arnie."

"Hey, Ava, I'm happy to see you," said the stricken general manager. "I thought I was a goner a few hours ago. I'm feeling much better now, too. What an utter embarrassment this is for Helena Baxter, not to mention for shy little Caprice, the modern day Lucrezia Borgia of the Upper West Side. Poisoning her own cookbook editor with those godawful canapés. It's hysterical, really. Their little shindig tonight could singlehandedly have exterminated a large chunk of the theatre community. Just wait until the gossip columns get wind of this juicy story."

"I bet it'll be great publicity for the *Don't Hang Up* box office." Ava offered as an upside. She instinctively did a quick scan of the room for a telephone to no avail.

Detective Clements sighed and looked around the cramped quarters. "I'm going to check on the status of the other folks admitted this evening. Please, no one leave here or talk to anyone else for the time being."

The four exhausted party guests stared at each other.

"One saving grace is that Terry Hagen isn't lurking." Ava commented while checking out her reflection in a small dusty wall mirror, "The last thing we'd need for posterity is photographic evidence of how bad we all look after tonight's ghastly events. Well, not you, Bettie. You always look gorgeous, dammit."

"What do you think could have happened? It had to have been accidental, right?" Bettie asked, seeking assurance from the group.

"All of it seems so haphazard. Only some of us were affected. I suppose we could've been targeted. But, why?" asked Arne.

Vic thought a moment before speaking, "I guess we'll have to wait to hear what Mademoiselle Fournier has to say about it. I can't imagine she'd announce a new cookbook and then proceed to poison the guests—killing her publisher yet!"

"What the hell is in a *White Monkey* anyway?" spat Ava.

"Helena Baxter and little Caprice are going to be devastated," muttered Arne.

While the others continued talking, Vic pulled Bettie over to the corner of the draped enclosure, "I never did tell you the story I'd remembered about Helena Baxter and a ridiculous homicide she was accused of committing years ago."

Bettie was duly stunned, "How could you have forgotten to tell me gossip as sensational as that? And just why has everything we've done this week involved murder?" she hissed, eagerly adding, "Do you really believe our celebrity hostess could be a bit of a psycho?"

Vic said, "I think that's wildly improbable. However, Cal Lockheed reminded me the other night of Miss Baxter's previous association with crime. It seemed that some tourist died because she accidentally bashed him with a dumbbell tossed from her bedroom window. It was a major scandal in 1960. Apparently, the media coverage at the time was relentless."

"Not for anything, but Mizz Mitzi did predict murderous intent." Bettie quietly reminded him.

Vic nodded in agreement, "Yes, I'm well aware of that. Keep in mind that our psychic was also utterly specific in announcing that the malevolent vibes were emanating from someone at the table. Helena Baxter did not attend our presentation."

Bettie chewed her bottom lip before saying, "Of course, all of that is predicated on the assumption that Mizz Mitzi is a bona fide clairvoyant and not a flat-out fraud." She moved in closer to Vic and whispered in his ear, "We should continue this discussion later. I see the other inmates are attempting to eavesdrop."

Looking up, Vic was confronted by two weary faces intensely staring in their direction.

"What?"

"Anything you two want to share with the rest of the class, kids?" admonished Ava. "Don't you know it's rude to tell secrets? That is, unless you're telling them to me."

Detective Clements chose that moment to reenter the space. All attention instantly averted to him.

"The other patients are on the mend and should be released in the morning—as will you," Renny informed Arne, "barring any unforeseen relapses."

Bettie spoke up, "Are we allowed to ask you, detective, did you learn anything more from them? Cal Lockheed is a famous actor, and a rather observant man. He might've noticed suspicious details that we may have missed."

"Mr. Lockheed's still under sedation. I'll have to question him tomorrow. He was seriously affected by the poisoning as was poor Mr. Lindqvist, who succumbed. The two chorus dancers have bounced back nicely. However, they both pretty much hadn't a clue as to what happened. I'm afraid the ladies weren't much help."

Renny Clements took a deep breath before continuing, "I phoned Terry, the photographer, earlier tonight and asked that she develop the pictures from the party as quickly as possible. They could prove to be helpful. I strongly advise the rest of you to leave now, go home, and get some sleep." Even the detective's brilliant blue eyes were turning bloodshot from the late-night activities. "I know that's exactly what I'm going to do."

Hailing a taxi on the Upper West Side was much easier to do in the early hours of the morning. Bettie and Vic shared a cab heading downtown. Speculation continued.

"Caprice, Arnie, Rex, and Simone were assembling the trays. Since the gathering was so thoroughly informal, curiosity-seekers visited while the appetizers were being prepared. I noticed guests popping in and out of those doors a few times, myself included," Bettie said, droopy-eyed, "That means one thing for sure—any one of us at Helena Baxter's apartment tonight could have somehow poisoned the canapés while traipsing around that enormous kitchen. But why would any one of us want to deliberately murder Oskar Lindqvist, a complete stranger? It doesn't make sense."

Vic rubbed his aching temples and sighed, "But, Bettie, it also means the culprit might easily have been observed by any one the guests in the act of doing it. The poisoner was certainly taking a ballsy chance of being caught red-handed."

"Um, I just had another thought," mused Bettie dreamily.

They were drifting off to sleep in cadence with the bumpy motion of the taxi as it maneuvered the city's potholes, their heads bobbing against the plush checker cab upholstery.

Vic scrunched his thick eyebrows together, "Huh?"

Bettie slurred, "What if somebody did catch the poisoner in the act this evening, but for some reason, purposely hasn't told Detective Clements anything about it?"

Scene Eleven

Thursday - March 6, 1975
One day before the murder at the Hayes Theatre

The next day, Vic Senso was sitting at his Thompson & Co. drawing table by 10am. The morning papers hadn't yet printed a word about the death of Oskar Lindqvist at The Dakota the night before. The poisonings may have occurred too late in the evening for any coverage in the early editions, but Vic was certain that all of that was about to change when the afternoon editions hit the streets.

Vic's itinerary for the day included a meeting with Rex Merchant and Helena Baxter at their Dakota apartment to present and discuss quote ad layouts for *Don't Hang Up*, The stage thriller would be opening for critical review shortly. The appointment had been set up weeks ago, but given the circumstances involving last night, Vic was hesitant to simply show up as scheduled. The art director picked up the phone and dialed Merchant's number, unsure of how to begin a conversation with a client who'd just taken part in poisoning a room full of his wife's party guests the evening before.

Vic thought he could start with, 1) "Hi, I'm still alive." 2) "Do all of your parties end up at the hospital?" or 3) "May I have the recipe for *White Monkey*?"

He opted for, "Good morning, Rex. I hope everyone's feeling better today."

Don't Hang Up was being presented under the auspices of Fragment Productions. At least, that was how the official billing credit appeared on the *Playbill* title page. Fragment Productions was actually Helena Baxter, using a company name the television studio provided. It was a generous perk the network awarded the actress to keep their bankable star happy. It allowed her the liberty to mount and finance stage plays of her choosing—between the filming of her contractual appearances, which always made the studio millions of dollars.

Vic was first introduced to Rex last year at the Thompson & Co art presentation for the play. Since Merchant was acting as director of *Don't Hang Up*, he was opinionated during their initial meeting, but it was clear that his wife was calling the shots. Fortunately, he was a pleasant enough character, if perhaps a bit jittery at times about decision-making. He clearly relied on smoking vast quantities of weed to soothe his nerves. All told, Rex had proven to be intelligent, polite, and articulate. Working with him had, so far, been smooth sailing.

"Needless to say, we're a bit shaken up here. I cannot believe that poor Oskar Lindqvist is dead. But, that's no reason why we shouldn't forge ahead and keep to our advertising schedule. Helena's getting dressed as we speak, and even Caprice is up and about. I'll ask Simone to pitch in and make some coffee for our meeting this morning. We'll see you here at 11am as originally planned."

As luck would have it, the taxi that Vic snared in the midst of Times Square traffic sped uptown from his office and pulled in curbside just behind Renny Clements' Chevy Impala as the detective was checking in at The Dakota sentry booth.

"I believe we're heading to the same apartment," said Vic to both detective and sentry.

"Yes, your names are on the Mr. Merchant's list for this morning. Number 73. Go that way, please."

Vic was thrilled that The Dakota featured manual elevators and was impressed at how much quicker this lift ascended as compared to the relatively pokey ride offered at the Sardi building.

"Feeling better this morning?" asked Renny.

"Better certainly than Oskar Lindqvist, that's for sure." Vic blushed, "Sorry, that was in bad taste. Honestly, detective, I'm feeling…um…fresher, at least. The more I thought about it, the creepier the entire evening became. I was certainly one of the lucky ones to have escaped being poisoned."

The elevator operator discreetly looked askance at his passengers.

Renny expended an involuntary chuckle, "Yes, indeed you were fortunate," while seemingly checking out the highly polished ornate wood paneling.

Vic took a moment to admire the detective's handsome profile in utter awe of its classic perfection.

The operator pulled open the brass inner gate followed by his wrenching on the outer sliding door. The two passengers exited and instinctively knew in which direction to walk based on the previous evening. Simone greeted them in the private vestibule of Number 73 that led to a massive foyer, and eventually, the living room.

Helena Baxter and her husband were seated on the center sofa while Caprice had settled into an oversized antique chair accentuating her already delicate, waxen appearance. Simone draped herself on the edge of the Steinway piano bench.

"Before we get started, please accept my apologies for last night's debacle," said Helena Baxter, seemingly to both Vic and the detective, "Words escape me."

Both men remained silent, until Vic motioned with one hand, as if to clear the air of smoke, and said, "No apologies necessary. It's not as if you purposely poisoned the guests yourself, right?" He laughed nervously.

"Am I going to be placed under arrest, Detective Clements?" the actress asked.

"That's not why I'm here this morning." Renny quickly interjected before Vic Senso dug himself into an awkward conversational hole. "I realize you have business to attend to, so I'll keep this as brief as I possibly can. Of course, you're not under arrest. I do, however, have several questions. Are you aware of who might've wanted to kill Oskar Lindqvist?"

"Not in the least. We'd only just met the man. Ava called early this morning to tell us about the arsenic," interrupted Rex, "Do you have any idea how the poison got into some of the canapés?"

"Let me begin by asking Mademoiselle Fournier if she noticed any strange activities around the preparation of the food yesterday? Any delivery people or party guests hanging around where they shouldn't have been?"

Caprice answered in a hushed, nervous tone, "All of the ingredients arrived earlier in the day and none of the delivery men ever made it past the service entrance door. The party itself was quite informal. Several of the guests visited the kitchen at different points. They really seemed more interested in the size and decor of our vast scullery than in what was going on food-wise. I prepared the canapés with Simone's help. At the appropriate time, we asked the few lingering guests to please clear out of the kitchen. That's when Mr. Merchant and Arnie Engels were at hand to carry the trays into the living room. It was immediately after Miss Baxter finished making the announcement about our book."

Pencil nub and pocket notebook poised for action, Renny asked, "Can you recall who came into the kitchen during your preparation of the canapés?"

Caprice hesitated a moment in thought. "Honestly, I was extremely focused on my task. I was getting down to the wire in arranging the trays. I have a vague memory of Ava and the photographer getting in the way. That beautiful woman from the ad agency was looking around at one point, as was Oskar Lindqvist, our editor…our late editor."

"I'd been playing the piano for about a half-hour. After I stopped," Simone abruptly chimed in, "I rushed into the kitchen to help Caprice. I first had to ask Cal Lockheed and Earl Quick several times to exit into the living room to catch Miss Baxter's impending announcement. Rex and Arnie were about ready to carry the trays out."

Renny Clements looked around at the intimate group, "Did any of you notice stray guests milling about nearby, actually handling the trays or the appetizers?"

"I'm confident I'd have noticed anyone tampering with the canapés," said Caprice authoritatively. "No one touched them."

Helena Baxter, who'd yet to speak on the subject, suddenly interjected, "But someone had to have, my dear, unless you yourself poisoned them. Think."

Tears began to well up in Caprice's lovely eyes.

It was then that The Dakota house phone rang. Simone ambled over to answer it. She looked toward Helena Baxter, "Arnie Engels and Ava Chasten are downstairs."

The normally composed Broadway star suddenly turned pale, "The afternoon editions must've hit the newsstands. Tell them to come up."

Moments later, in typical Ava fashion, the press agent burst into the apartment handing out the publications that had just been released, "I picked Arnie up from the hospital after his discharge just in time for him to help me here with these. Batten down the hatches, kids, because things are about to get ugly."

The headlines across the board were devastating.

Helena Baxter did not physically touch any of the newspapers herself, as if closer contact would have made matters worse, but she listened in utter dismay to the fragmented excerpts her household was reading aloud from the various daily journals.

"...Broadway actress once again ensnared in sudden death scandal..."

"...Helena Baxter's arsenic poison party at The Dakota kills book editor..."

"...Suspicion haunts Broadway and television star in repeat performance..."

"...Accused of a tourist killing years ago, star Helena Baxter strikes again..."

"...Police interrogate the lady *always* in question: actress Helena Baxter..."

Rex put his arm around his wife's shoulders. She was visibly shaken to the core. The telephone, which accommodated multiple extensions, started ringing off the hook. Ava began to field the calls.

"It's so humiliating for you, Helena. I'm speechless," muttered Arne.

Angrily hanging up the phone after one heated conversation in particular, Ava announced, "Well, as expected, the Simon & Schuster deal is definitely off the table. I suppose having their editor drop down dead from eating one of those ridiculous canapés has put the kibosh on the cookbook project."

Caprice, drenched in tears, rushed from the room toward her quarters.

Helena Baxter and Rex watched her run off, but neither one of them was in any condition to follow her and offer emotional support. Simone decided to lend her crony a shoulder to cry on and followed the housekeeper to her bedroom.

Meanwhile, Renny cornered Arne and Ava.

"I didn't really have an opportunity to get your take on events. Tell me what you both recall about last night, most specifically when you were in the kitchen."

"Let's see," started Arne, "there were some guests looking around while Caprice and Simone were getting stuff ready. I remember seeing Bettie, Ava, oh yes, and Terry, the photographer. Oskar Lindqvist, too. I'm not sure, but I believe, at one point, Earl Quick and Cal Lockheed were checking things out. Rex and I were chatting off in the corner, biding our time until Caprice would give us the high sign to carry the trays into the living room following Helena's announcement. And no, I don't recall folks actually getting near enough at any time to administer arsenic to the canapés."

Ava jumped in and responded with machine gun rapidity, "I took Terry in there to shoot some pictures of Caprice and the appetizers. I even managed to snatch one without anybody noticing." Ava grimaced, "I thought it tasted like poison, I can tell you that much. I saw silver fox, Earl Quick. Cal was in there, too. I think he has a crush on Arnie. He was lingering, but was certainly not interested in anything Caprice and Simone were doing."

"Excuse me," the detective asked abruptly, "but you actually took an appetizer off one of the trays?"

SCENERY OF THE CRIME • 91

"Yes, that's what I just told you. I ate it rather quickly. I remember that it was called a *White Monkey*. I thought it smelled like one, too."

"No one caught you in the act of doing that? Not Mademoiselle Fournier nor Simone Caldwell?"

"That's correct," said Ava proudly, "and I even lived to tell about it."

Her statement clearly rendered Renny Clements wide-eyed and speechless for a moment. "Remarkable," he thought to himself, shaking his head in disbelief.

Vic was beginning to feel mighty uncomfortable witnessing the proceedings. He had arrived innocently enough to present advertising layouts, not expecting to attend a police interrogation, however entertaining it may be watching the magnificent Renny Clements in action.

He found it endearing to observe the handsome detective jotting down selected facts in his battered notebook with a pencil nub. Renny was using the palm of his left hand as a flat surface upon which to rest his well-worn spiral pad while he scribbled. Vic was utterly captivated.

"I've questioned pretty much everyone about last night," mused Renny, "and find it bewildering that, considering all the foot traffic walking through the kitchen, no one noticed Ms. Chasten steal and eat one of the canapés."

"It could be something that a person wouldn't register as having seen. After all, we see people nibbling tidbits in the kitchen all the time. It's a non-event. Why would anyone take note of it?" asked Helena Baxter, "Grant it, touching the trays was clearly verboten at the party, but quite honestly, I wouldn't even have been surprised if I'd caught Ava going through my lingerie drawer. For her, it's normal behavior."

The publicist smirked and nodded in complete agreement, inadvertently rearranging the massive red curls piled on the top of her head.

The detective remarked, "I suppose it speaks volumes as to why no one in your crowd remembers witnessing any food tampering."

Helena Baxter further explained, "One more thing to keep in mind, my dears, is that you're dealing here with actors and theatrical types who are much too self-absorbed to notice anything unless it directly affects them or pertains to them. Believe me, I include myself in that category. I am typically oblivious to my surroundings unless I'm on stage or making a personal appearance." She gazed at her husband and squeezed his hand, "I have Rex by my side to take care of those details for me, thank goodness, don't I, my darling?"

Rex presented his wife with a beaming smile, "Yes, love."

Renny Clements stood and addressed the lady of the house, "Miss Baxter, can I use your telephone, please? I'll be leaving after I make a quick call."

"Over here, detective," Ava signaled to him and pointed at a vintage gold Victorian rotary instrument that reflected the rest of the designer decor around them.

"If you'd prefer," said Vic, turning his attention to both Helena Baxter and producer Rex sitting close together on the sofa, "I can come back another time to show you these ad layouts."

"Not at all, my dear," Helena Baxter was once more in grande celebrity mode, "Let's get it over and done with. We have so much more to accomplish before opening night." She hesitated and, with a hint of a wince in her facial expression, continued, "That is, if we still have a show to do after these monstrous newspaper stories hit the streets."

As if on cue, Arne emerged from the kitchen, having commandeered the wall phone stationed near the pantry, "One good thing might come from all this yet. I just talked to the box office treasurer. Our *Don't Hang Up* ticket sales are going through the roof. We're selling seats like mad!" He sniffled and sneezed into a handkerchief.

Ava smiled, "No doubt about it. If you can survive the nasty storm ahead, it's a proven fact that bad publicity is always great for business. And, kids, this is really, really bad."

Scene Twelve

The next morning, Bettie took a taxi from her apartment directly to the hospital. Acting on impulse, she decided to look in on Cal Lockheed who was still being held for observation.

"How are you feeling this morning?" Bettie asked as she took a seat on one of the molded plastic chairs

"Well, darling, I'm still shaken, but breathing. What the hell happened?"

Bettie recounted the evening's events following the EMT activity and the arrival of the police. She told Cal that it had been determined that arsenic had somehow been introduced into some of the appetizers, and that the cookbook editor from Simon & Schuster had died as a result.

"Nerdy Oskar Lindqvist? How perfectly ironic is that?" Cal asked rhetorically.

As timing would have it, Renny Clements arrived at the hospital to question the stage performer after winding up his visit with Helena Baxter at The Dakota. Bettie was quietly conversing with Cal when Renny walked in. He was pleased to find the actor in good health and lively spirits. After a quick nod in Bettie's direction, the detective turned his attention to the man in the bed.

"Mr. Lockheed, I'm very happy to see you looking better today. I'm Detective Renny Clements. Please allow me to ask you a few questions about the party last evening."

"Oh my good gracious, darling, you're identical twins!" Cal hooted, "I know your brother Rodney and his horse, Fiona."

Lockheed was mindful that Renny was not there to socialize. "Of course, detective, I appreciate your concern. How can I help you?"

"It seems you were taking a tour of the kitchen just before Helena Baxter's announcement about her book. Did you happen to notice anyone tampering with or getting close to the canapé trays who shouldn't have? Perhaps you noticed something that may not have necessarily registered as important or noteworthy at the time. You know, someone acting oddly, or seemingly out-of-place, considering the surroundings?"

Cal Lockheed stared straight ahead, brows knitted in concentration, "Um, I don't think so. There were several others in the kitchen at that time. Caprice and Simone, of course, were in the midst of administering finishing artistic touches. I was circling with the dazzling Earl Quick. Rex and Arnie were off in the corner, well away from the marble counter. Ava and Terry were moving all over the place, taking lots of photos at different camera angles. Oskar Lindqvist was nosing around as well. Bettie, I believe you were there, too."

The account executive nodded in agreement, "Yes, I'd already mentioned to the detective that I was part of the kitchen entourage."

"Do you have any idea of who might've wanted to kill Oskar Lindqvist?" Renny asked the ashen actor.

"I don't believe any of us had ever set eyes on the creature before last night," said the actor. As he spoke, Cal took note of how ravishingly lovely Bettie managed to look, even under the crappy fluorescent lighting, while he disclosed, "I suspect you must already know, detective, that Helena Baxter was involved in a murder once before?" Lockheed arched his right eyebrow for emphasis.

Renny was taken aback, "Excuse me, no, I didn't know that. When was this?"

Ever the performer, Cal Lockheed knew when he'd captured an audience's undivided attention. He spoke languidly and clearly as if reciting a dramatic passage from Shakespeare, "It was probably about fifteen years ago. It's practically become a show business urban legend, and it's guaranteed to get a big laugh at Broadway cocktail parties whenever its told." The actor launched into the story.

"Let me stop you right there for a moment. You seem remarkably clear on the details so far, Mr. Lockheed. Is this murder common knowledge in the theatre world?" Renny asked.

"Well, it was front page headline news for many, many weeks at the time. However, I'm sure most people have forgotten by now. The specifics are fresh in my mind because Vic Senso and I were laughing about it the other night at the first preview of Helena Baxter's new show at the Hayes. It jogged my memory of the various publicity stories and rumors circulating about it. I'm just getting to the funny part about the fatal dumbbell. Shall I venture to continue?"

Renny Clements urged, "Yes, please go on."

Propped up in his hospital bed, Lockheed finished the story.

"The whole incident was eventually written off as an unfortunate accident, not a homicide at all. The event has become somewhat of a joke over the years, I'm afraid."

"Poor Helena Baxter." Bettie sounded genuinely distraught, "The press will surely make mincemeat out of her again after this."

"Mr. Lockheed, thank you for that interesting bit of information," said Renny, "I'll be certain to follow up and look into it further."

They were about to exit but were brought to an abrupt halt.

"Stop! Wait a minute!" Cal Lockheed declared with a theatrical gesture, "There was one other thing I suddenly remember about activity surrounding the canapés. It was funny. Simone was politely pushing us out of the kitchen as Rex and Arnie were moving into position to gather up the trays. That's when I saw her do it."

Renny Clements leaned forward, pencil nub in hand, "Go on, Mr. Lockheed, you saw who do what?"

"Ava Chasten. She popped one of the appetizers into her mouth. I don't think she was aware that anybody watched her swipe it. The kitchen at that point was chaotic to say the least. It was certainly amusing, but I doubt it'll help you figure out how the arsenic was administered to all those exotic delicacies."

Renny once again asked the actor if there were any other details he could recollect about Helena Baxter's party.

"I think I've told you all I know about the last-minute activity in the kitchen. The rest of the evening was extremely pleasant—a typical theatrical cocktail party with attractive people smoking like mad and getting drunk—similar to hundreds of others I've attended over the years. You might ask Terry to show you her photographs when they're developed. She was furiously snapping away throughout the night."

"She must've taken hundreds of pictures," Bettie said. "Terry always does."

Renny slipped the pencil nub and worn-out notepad into his pocket, "I plan on visiting Ms. Hagen's studio very soon. I'm told the doctor will be releasing you in an hour or so. Will anyone be picking you up?"

"I'll make a few calls. I shouldn't have too much of a problem finding someone to escort me home. I live in a duplex apartment down on Varick Street near the entrance to the Holland Tunnel. Most of my friends are stage performers and don't work daytimes unless it's a Wednesday, Saturday, or Sunday matinee. Today's Thursday, correct?"

"Indeed, it is, Mr. Lockheed," the detective assured him. "If you happen to remember anything you might deem important or helpful, please give me a call anytime."

Cal stared into Renny Clement's intense blue eyes. "You can count on that. I hope you get to the bottom of things soon."

The detective and Bettie were gone for a full five minutes before Cal hopped out of his bed. He grabbed some loose change from the pocket of his pants which were neatly folded on a nearby table. He also nabbed his crushed pack of Lucky Strike and a cigarette lighter. Still dressed in his flimsy paper hospital gown, he confronted the first nurse's aide he could find. "Can you tell me where I can locate a phone booth, darling?"

The petite blonde candy-striper pointed the way and watched as Lockheed quickly sashayed down the corridor with the back of his gown coming untied. Cal found the pay phone and took a seat. He nervously lit up a cigarette and proceeded to rifle through the mammoth Manhattan directory which was judiciously secured in the booth by a chain. He dropped a dime into the coin slot and rapidly dialed a number. The phone at the other end of the line rang twice before the call was picked up.

"I think we need to talk," the actor whispered into the receiver, "That detective just questioned me at the hospital. You might be surprised to learn that I saw what you did at Helena Baxter's soiree last night." Cal was unconsciously twisting the phone cord around his index finger, "Naughty, naughty. Don't worry, I wouldn't dream of telling a living soul. I ask you, darling, whatever were you thinking? You might've killed *me!*"

Scene Thirteen

Terry Hagen's studio was located at 43rd Street and Tenth Avenue on the ground floor level. It was a spacious, yet comfortable workspace, organized and neat, with floor-to-ceiling picture windows facing north, running the length of the loft-sized room. The celebrated theatre photographer often preferred taking advantage of the abundance of natural light for her studio sessions, but had astutely installed blackout shades at some expense, anticipating several set-ups where the lighting would need to be controlled. In some cases involving major stars, there was the considerable issue of privacy.

Vic walked through the heavy industrial door, which was painted bright blue, "You can feel a rush of creative vibes the minute you step into this foyer. Just being here immediately makes me feel like more of an art director."

Terry blushed, "That's so sweet of you to say."

The ferocious yapping of a small dog suddenly filled the air. It took a moment for Vic to find the source of the racket and to lay eyes upon one of the ugliest and fattest chihuahuas he'd ever seen—and it was lumbering in his direction, teeth bared.

"Meet Tu-tu. I've had him since childhood," explained Terry.

Before Vic even had a chance to comment, Tu-tu dug its fangs into his pants leg, growling and snarling like the Hound of the Baskervilles. Terry seemed oblivious to the animal attack happening right under her nose.

"Um…is Tu-tu trained to kill visitors?" Vic joked facetiously, attempting to detach his pants from the dog's toothy grip.

"Oh, he just gets excited when we have company. My tiny Chihuahua thinks he's a guard dog. He just doesn't realize that he's only nine-inches tall."

"Um…and about a hundred years old, I'm guessing?"

Terry laughed, "Counting in canine years, Tu-tu's older than that."

"Really? Whatever do you feed him?" Vic had finally gotten loose, moved over to the other side of the studio, and casually leaned up against a nearby worktable.

"I know it sounds rather strange, but Tu-tu has managed to exist on a steady diet of rare hamburger meat and Chapstick."

"Did you say Chapstick?"

Terry nodded, "Not often—only as a treat. When I was a child, I used to apply it to his mouth when we played pretend dress-up and lipstick. He grew to like it. Tu-tu could ferret out a tube of the stuff wherever I hid it in my room—like those talented pigs sniffing for truffles."

"Doesn't eating Chapstick make him sick…um…or delirious?" Vic thought he'd clearly discovered why the dog appeared to be a total psycho.

"He's accustomed to it now. At first, he'd suffer from an occasional loose stool, but soon got over that. The vet said it was fine as long as he didn't eat the packaging. Tu-tu's gotten so good at extracting the lip balm from the holder, he can adeptly perform a removal operation in no time flat." Terry beamed proudly.

Vic smirked, "Personally, I've cut my Chapstick habit down to a tube a week." He watched as Tu-tu ploddingly dragged himself along the far wall of the studio back to his dog bed where he threw himself into the worn cushion with a huff and began snoring like a champion thoroughbred.

"Have you recovered from last night? Terry asked, "I think most of us went home with jangled nerves. What do you think could have happened? I was preoccupied taking pictures, trying to get Ava off my back throughout the entire event, and can honestly say that I didn't notice anything wrong until the guests started dropping like flies." Terry sounded genuinely mystified.

"Helena Baxter could easily have wiped out half the population of the Broadway theatre community last night. I mainly hung out with Perry and Cal. Even managed a short conversation with Caprice Fournier, who seemed cool as a cucumber. I doubt that she's responsible for the poisonings." Vic said emphatically, "It had to have been accidental. Detective Clements refers to it as a murder."

"Well, she did make the canapés. Come to think of it, she was pitching in as bartender to boot. One might suspect that Helena Baxter is a demanding employer. Arsenic could just as easily have been mixed into the cocktails." Terry motioned Vic to follow her over to one of the long worktables. On the cluttered surface, she had fanned out a variety of printed contact sheets from their photo briefing at the Hayes Theatre. Her favorite frames were circled in red grease pencil.

Vic noticed his Canon F-1 brazenly on display at the end of the counter but decided not to make a big deal about it. At least he knew the camera was still intact.

"What do you think about Johanna Jay's retouching abilities?" Vic inquired, as he caught sight of an exceptionally closeup shot of Helena Baxter.

Terry shrugged, "She's by far the best of the lot. I dabble doing my own discreet touch-ups, but only to a point. Actors and actresses are very picky when it comes to their public personas. I much prefer leaving that end of things in your capable hands. Why do you ask?"

"I plan on hiring Johanna to airbrush the photos for *Don't Hang Up*. From what Tobin has told me, Helena Baxter can sometimes be a bit of a barracuda about the approval process."

Terry widened her lovely blue eyes, "I'm not surprised. Theatre actresses of a certain…um…maturity can keep the illusion of youth alive a lot longer than movie stars. The ladies of the Broadway stage needn't concern themselves with extreme camera closeups. They can still safely maintain an aura of ageless glamour from row E in the orchestra, safely forty feet away. But rest assured, the front-of-house and publicity photographs are a totally different ball of wax. They had better look flawless."

Vic nodded in agreement, "I'm working on another show right now where the leading lady's as mean as a snake about her pictures. We're actually going to have to schedule another studio session, which will be quite costly. I told the hapless photographer that on this go-round, he should seriously consider shooting this actress 1) through vaseline, 2) through gauze, or 3) through an Indian blanket."

"As terrible as it is to admit, I'm gratified to hear that other artists have similar trials and tribulations with unreasonably demanding clients. On the other hand, I love juicy theatre gossip. Who's the actress?" Terry asked with exaggerated enthusiasm.

Vic dramatically leaned in and whispered the name in her ear. He caught a slight whiff of a sweet, seductive perfume as he did so.

"Oh, yes, I've heard that she can be a total witch," Terry squealed gleefully, "I'd love the extra income, but I'm certainly glad the producers decided not to use my services on that show."

The photographer and the art director became immersed in conversation about the *Don't Hang Up* advertising layouts. A quarter of an hour later, the jarring sound of the door buzzer distracted them.

When Ava Chasten hesitantly walked into the studio, Tu-tu once again sprang into action. The chihuahua went from a deep sleep into a lively (for him) sprint in seconds flat. The publicist had come prepared. She pulled a small paper sack, just purchased from the neighborhood drug store, out of her enormous Gucci tote.

"Yoo hoo! I have something for Nosferatu-tu." Ava said playfully, rattling the contents of the bag. "Come and get it."

Terry called out, "I'm in here, Ava, with Vic Senso."

"This isn't my first time under attack," Ava said as she emptied the contents onto the cement floor. Four tubes of Chapstick, in a variety of flavors, spilled out around her feet as Tu-tu abruptly ceased his yapping to revel in the sudden overabundance of greasy treats.

Ava looked triumphantly at Terry and Vic, "That little rat has bitten into too many of my Capezios over the years. I decided to arrive armed this time."

"Tu-tu will love you forever," smiled the gracious photographer. The growling chihuahua circled Ava's legs as he systematically collected the rolling tubes in record time. "Good...um...boy, Nosferatu-tu."

"I've asked you again and again not to call him by that awful name. It disturbs me," scolded Terry with a sense of humor.

"Oh, please!" Ava ranted, turning her attention toward Vic, "Have you met this...um...thing?" she asked the ad man, pointing at Tu-tu, who did appear quite insane, "I firmly believe that he's just got to be a vampire dog. That chihuahua's about a hundred and fifty years old in canine years."

"Yeah, I meant to ask you about that, Terry. Admittedly, you've had Tu-tu since childhood. How's that remotely possible? You're around my age, right? Twenty-nine?" Vic scratched his head for effect, "That would make Tu-tu at least twenty-five years old. I've never heard of a small dog living that long."

"Nosferatu-tu." Ava repeated emphatically, "I'm telling you all, he's one of the undead. Just watch him lumbering around the studio here. He avoids all sunny areas and drags himself along the walls on the shady side of the loft. From what Terry tells me, he'll only eat rare ground beef. He's got huge fangs, for God's sake. I doubt that he even casts a shadow. I'll bet he growls at garlic, too. What further proof do you need?"

Vic said in an embarrassed tone, "For years, my mother had me believing that our beloved pet parakeet lived an extraordinarily long life until mom confessed that she kept replacing deceased Twinkies with new birds that looked identical."

Terry grimaced and seriously considered the possibility. "I hope that's not the case here. I think I'd have noticed the difference."

As Ava and Vic exchanged ironically wide-eyed glances, the buzzer sounded again.

The blue metal door opened admitting Detective Renny Clements into the studio. "Hello? Ms. Hagen? Terry?" he called out tentatively.

Tu-tu sprang into action and began snarling, barking, and growling as he hobbled toward a fresh victim.

"Is that Renny Clements? What a pleasant surprise. Come in, please," said Terry, "It's like a mini reunion at my studio today. Ava Chasten and Vic Senso are visiting as well."

They were all stunned when Tu-tu came to a grinding halt and ceased his vicious vocals. The chihuahua sat down complacently at the detective's feet.

"By any chance, do you carry Chapstick in your pockets?" Terry inquired.

"Or a crucifix?" Ava suggested.

Renny burst into involuntary laughter, "I do believe that's the first time anyone's ever asked me that question. The answer's no, by the way, on both counts." The handsome detective casually squatted down and scratched behind Tu-tu's ears. Vic could swear he heard the chihuahua purring.

Ava folded her arms defiantly, "I stopped by to pick up those new headshots. I've a meeting with Geraldine Page at the Music Box in ten minutes. Why are you here, Vic?"

The art director looked in Renny's direction, "We're discussing new ad layouts for *Don't Hang Up*. Opening's a week from today."

The two men smiled cordially and firmly shook hands.

"Nice to see you again," Vic assured the detective.

Terry slipped the envelope containing the printed pictures, labeled *Absurd Person Singular,* into the publicist's cavernous Gucci tote bag.

"Excuse me. Must dash out now," said Ava hurriedly, "Sorry I can't stay to chat."

He waited until he heard the heavy blue door slam shut before Renny turned his full attention to Terry Hagen.

"I wonder if I could see some of the photos you shot at Helena Baxter's party. Particularly those taken in the kitchen. By the way,

I looked back at my notes. Why did you tell me you hadn't been in the kitchen when I first questioned you?"

Terry blushed, "I was so terribly nervous. Now I feel like a total idiot about it. I don't know why I denied being in there. I obviously have plenty of photographic evidence to the contrary."

"It happens to a lot of people when suddenly confronted by the a policeman under unpleasant circumstances." Abruptly changing the subject, "How long have you been in this space?" Clements asked, scanning the studio.

She hesitated a minute, "About six years already. Crazy, how time flies." Terry sighed, "I can only afford the rent here because most people in their right minds wouldn't live or work this far over on the westside—where your neighbors are sure to be prostitutes, addicts, and actors," she jovially explained to the detective. "I hope you don't mind, but Vic Senso from the advertising agency was here to show me some layouts. We have a photo session on Friday at the Hayes Theatre for post-opening quote ads. Deadlines, you understand."

"Not a problem in the least," Renny assured her while smiling over at Vic.

The detective was making his way around the studio admiring the various black and white prints that Terry had pinned up on random walls to great artistic effect.

Tu-tu had quietly shuffled back over to his bed, once again positioning himself comfortably on the cushion that was nestled in the studio's darkest corner. The chihuahua was soon fast asleep sprawled atop his fresh treasure trove of Chapstick, courtesy of Ava Chasten.

Terry was clearly searching for something as she spoke over her shoulder.

"After the horrible incident at Helena Baxter's apartment, I just couldn't get to sleep. So, rather than tossing and turning all night, I processed the film from the party and made some prints I thought might interest you. I had a sneaking suspicion that you'd eventually ask to see what I'd shot." She pulled a flat box from a small stack on her desk and said, "I hope you and Rodney haven't forgotten your promise to pose for me sometime soon. I think *Playbill* would be most interested."

"Are you kidding? Rodney won't let me forget it." Renny laughed.

As Terry sorted through the pile of photo prints, the detective noticed a headshot of an attractive blonde pinned on the wall over her desk. He moved in for a closer look and was struck by a remarkable facial resemblance.

"I recognize most of your celebrity pictures, but I've never heard of this actress. She looks very much like you." Renny said, pointing to an older-looking faded print. "Dagmar Vanderhagen," read the detective aloud from the twelve-point type labeled under the headshot.

Terry smiled fondly, "That's my mother. She tried her hand at acting for a brief time while I was away at boarding school. Beautiful, isn't she?"

"The resemblance is practically unsettling." Vic commented, squinting at the print.

"Vanderhagen? You shortened your last name?" asked the detective.

"Vanderhagen is such a mouthful. I thought Hagen looked much better on my business cards. Lots of people in show business abbreviate their names in one way or another," Terry explained.

Renny sorted through the collection of prints from The Dakota gathering. Vic quietly moved into an advantageous position and began checking out the candids from over the detective's shoulder.

"I'll be damned. I don't see anything wrong going on in any of these shots. Am I missing something?" asked the detective, "Although, I have noticed that you failed to snap Ava Chasten sneaking a canapé off one of the trays. That's not meant to be a criticism. It just makes me realize your camera cannot catch everything."

Terry agreed, "Believe me, I've studied the entire lot of those prints twice, three times. I do not see one single thing that appears remotely suspicious. Certainly not a murder."

Vic added his two cents, "It's just another glamorous Broadway party to me. I must say, Terry, you do manage to capture everyone looking their best."

The trio stood silently shuffling the photos around, taking careful inspection at some of the kitchen candids, but to no avail. The only sound in the studio was Tu-tu's obnoxious snoring.

"What aren't we seeing?" Renny pondered aloud.

ACT TWO
Scene ONE

Vic had been hunched over his drawing table for about an hour when Bettie took a break from her busy morning, appeared at his door, and plopped down in his office guest chair for a chat. Tobin happened to be walking by and visited as well. Bettie and Vic eagerly recounted numerous unsavory details for their boss regarding what'd he'd missed by darting out of The Dakota before the real dramatics began.

"I bet Olga was upset," said Vic, "She could've been part of all the excitement last night. A homicide at a party had to be more thrilling than her art class in Brewster."

"My wife would be perfectly happy to never set foot in Manhattan again. I try to coerce her into coming to several Broadway openings, but Olga prefers the quiet life in Westchester to the excitement of the theatre, I'm afraid."

"Regardless, I'd love to meet her sometime." Bettie said.

"What a helluva mess," Tobin declared. "Do you think *Don't Hang Up* will be forced to close in previews?"

Vic said, "Not on your life. Arnie announced that they are selling out at the box office. Everyone wants to see Helena Baxter in the flesh. It's somewhat of a circus mentality, you know, everybody's intrigued in various degrees by a side show."

"That certainly works in our favor however much I'd hate to appear mercenary at a time like this. By the way, did Merchant and Helena Baxter approve your quote ad layouts?" asked Tobin.

"They were thrilled with them. Helena Baxter especially liked the concept of using photographs rather than the poster artwork in the newspaper spreads. That's to be expected, naturally, since her image will be sure to appear in all of them."

Bettie inquired, "There's no doubt about it now—Helena Baxter is our box office draw. Do you think we're still on track to shoot our visuals tomorrow as scheduled? Fortunately, the photographer, the supporting cast, and our leading lady remained unharmed, thanks to the theatre gods. I'm grateful that we're all still breathing. Arnie rode up in the elevator with me, so I know he's ready for business-as-usual. I'll check in with Terry to see if she's still on board."

"By all means double-check, but I just came from her studio and she seems well prepared. My God, that chihuahua of hers is terrifying. You haven't lived until you've witnessed Broadway's scariest canine munching on a Chapstick. It's a sight to behold." Vic shuddered.

"On another front, I want to show Tobin the poster comp I unearthed yesterday. I suspect it's a Tom Morrow painting from 1964 and was rejected for *Fiddler on the Roof*." Vic motioned for his boss to follow him. "It should just take about fifteen minutes. It'll probably look familiar to you, Tobin. I'm sure you were responsible for having it done in the first place. Both Bettie and I think that, with slight revisions, it could work as a possibility for the basis of our *Blithe Spirit* ad campaign."

Bettie returned to her desk as Vic and Tobin walked through the production department to the art archives room.

Vic switched on the directional canisters positioned above the poster railing, "What do you think? It certainly shows potential."

"Chalk it up to the new lighting, but the colors look extraordinary. It's stunning. Oh, yes, I agree, with some revisions in the concept, we could definitely present it as an artwork option to the *Blithe Spirit* group. Correct me if I'm mistaken, but I thought they were very much smitten by one of the pieces you presented at the meeting yesterday, am I right? They were fairly enthusiastic about it, actually."

"They seemed much more excited over your sleight-of-hand trick."

Tobin boasted, proudly, "The art of misdirection, Vic. It'll get them every time. That group was so enthralled feasting their eyes on the presence of our remarkable Mizz Mitzi, they were totally unaware of my manipulating the wire that slammed the door shut."

Both men were amused over their recollection of the event.

"In terms of the *Blithe Spirit* artwork, I always feel more comfortable having a backup Plan B just in case." Vic explained to the creative director, "We can bide our time to see how it plays out. With all this craziness over Helena Baxter's arsenic party, I'm sure Rex has bigger issues on his plate right now that will take precedent."

Tobin stepped back for a better look at the painting, "Well, it's a terrific option. I honestly can't say I remember this Morrow piece, but it was over ten years ago, and we've created ad campaigns for hundreds of shows in between."

He made his way around the space, checking out each of the aisles, which now employed the new modular system, vertical and horizontal racks, cabinets, and flat files. "The archives are getting awfully cramped. We might have to eventually think of an alternative storage area for all of this artwork."

"It'd be awful to have to move the archives off site. It's a great convenience having all this reference here at our immediate disposal," said Vic.

"I develop a headache just thinking about having to safely transport it all," Tobin Klein admitted to the art director. "I suppose now that we've installed this state-of-the-art modular system at some expense, we've bought ourselves a few years before we need to seriously consider it, thank goodness."

Bettie knocked on the door and joined them. "We're all set for shooting set-ups at the theatre tomorrow afternoon. I guess the sound of the cash register bell ringing repeatedly in the box office has calmed everyone's jangled nerves."

"Helena Baxter is one brave lady." Vic said in admiration.

Often likened to nails on a chalkboard, receptionist Marsha's dulcet tones hit the office intercom system airwaves, "Phone call for Tobin Klein. It's your dentist." Tobin rolled his eyes and excused himself to pick up the nearest extension located in the production department.

"I thought we should go to the show again tonight, Vic, to lend moral support." Bettie said, "So I asked Arnie to set up tickets for us. You'll be thrilled to know I called Rodney Clements and asked if he could get the night off at short notice. And what do you know? Copcake's going to be my plus-one."

Vic beamed, "Look at you. Women's Liberation at work! Good going."

"Arnie told me that because it's now the hottest ticket in town, he couldn't manage pairs together in the orchestra tonight. You and your date will be sitting in a different row," Bettie coyly announced.

"No problem. I'll call and ask the charming Mr. Engels if he can at least wrangle aisle seats for me as a consolation prize. My legs would thank him profusely. The bigger issue is whom to ask to be my date. I'll have to give it some serious thought," mused Vic, playfully drumming his fingers against his chin in contemplation. "It's a quandary. So many to choose from." Vic said facetiously, "Anyway, I have enough work to keep me busy until I decide."

"What's on your plate for this afternoon?" Bettie asked.

"Arthur Cantor asked to see some fresh print ideas for *In Praise of Love*. The show's been running at the Morosco since the end of last year and Terence Rattigan's now complaining to the producer that the ads are looking stale."

Bettie commented based on experience, "You and I both know that usually translates as the box office is sluggish or the playwright's agent wants his client's billing credit to be more prominent in print."

"Either way, I'll have to deal with it," sighed Vic, "Next up, there's The Theatre Guild asking for a new look for *Absurd Person Singular* at The Music Box. I agree they could use a change, but it's almost impossible to get six actors to agree on anything that needs unanimous approval. It'll most likely become an exercise in futility, but they're prestigious producers. I suppose an effort must be made to appease them in any case. What about you?"

"I have a long list of client phone calls to return. Marsha left a stack of messages on my desk this morning. As it stands, half the day tomorrow will be spent at the photo shoot, so I've got to buckle down while I can. Catch you later." The account executive waved her goodbye as she briskly walked in the direction of her office.

Vito Lanzetta showed up at Thompson & Co like clockwork at 5:20pm. He killed some time reading Daily Variety, stacks of which were available at the reception area. He leafed through the pages while waiting for Marsha to end her workday.

Bettie was questioning Marsha about some of the telephone messages she had received earlier.

"This message shows a distinguished gentleman with a mustache." Bettie pointed out. "He looks familiar. Oh, It's Earl Quick."

"Yes, that dashing older man from your presentation yesterday, the one with the tan…from Hollywood." Marsha assured the account executive. "He's married to that movie star."

Bettie widened her eyes, "It captures him perfectly."

"Yes, that's the one. I couldn't remember his name."

"What did he want?" Bettie asked.

Marsha turned down her mouth, shrugged slightly, and replied, "I guess he'll tell you himself when you return his call."

Bettie, somewhat in disbelief, glanced over at Vito Lanzetta, whose thick, muscular frame filled much of the sofa. He appeared engrossed in his magazine, but Vito looked up for a brief moment and caught the account executive's eye, having just overheard the exchange between Bettie and his ravishing lady love. A shadow of a smile crossed Vito Lanzetta's swarthy features.

"Who is this next message from? It just looks like a giant pill."

"Oh, mah gawd, that's the crazy redheaded publicity lady from upstairs," laughed Marsha, "You know, she always has a headache and scrounges around searching for Execdrin or aspirin all the time."

Bettie smiled involuntarily, "And what did she want? Wait, don't bother to answer. She'll tell me herself when I return her call, right?"

Marsha nodded.

A loud whir and clang announced the arrival of the elevator. The door was pulled open to reveal a breathless Rodney Clements, still decked out in his Mounted Police Unit uniform.

"Hey, Bettie, I don't have much time to chat. Fiona's tethered to the fire hydrant in front of your building with Guy Anderson babysitting her. Quick question for you—can I borrow the painting that Vic showed me last night in your art archives? You know, the faux Chagall? I'd like to show it to a colleague of mine at the precinct. I'd return it right away."

Since there was limited room in the reception area, Vito Lanzetta, in a gentlemanly gesture, immediately rose from the sofa and walked over to perch on the corner of Marsha's desk.

Bettie took his place on the couch and gestured for the officer to join her. "Catch your breath. We can talk here. What's so urgent?"

"I was thinking about that painting all last night," he said.

As he spoke, Rodney briefly glanced over at Lanzetta, who was peering in his direction. Vito turned away when he realized the policeman'd caught him staring.

Bettie frowned. "I'm afraid our creative director, Tobin Klein, wouldn't allow it. He's Vic's boss, and very strict about the art archives rules. That's rule number one. Nothing is ever to leave that room. Ever."

As if prepared for that response, Rodney shrugged, "It was worth a shot. Would it be alright if I brought my Polaroid camera down here to take a picture of the painting?"

"I'll check with Vic, but I'm sure that'd be no problem at all."

Rodney stood up. "Wonderful. I cannot thank you enough. That'd be great. We can arrange a time over dinner tonight. Now, I've got to sprint back to my unit, shower, and change for dinner and the theatre. I'm really excited about seeing the play with you."

"With today's vicious media coverage about the poisoning, Helena Baxter's going to need some friendly moral support in the audience tonight," she told Rodney as he rang for the elevator.

The officer nodded a goodbye to Marsha and Vito across the reception room as the doors closed.

After returning to her desk, the advertising account executive could detect the faint scent of Paco Rabanne cologne on her own clothing.

Bettie wondered, did Vito Lanzetta bathe in the stuff?

Scene TWO

Vic phoned Arne and asked the general manager if he could change his tickets.

"Have mercy on me. I really need the leg room," he begged.

Arne sneezed as he took a peripheral glance at the diagram at hand, "The aisle locations in the orchestra are already spoken for. I can easily offer you all the comfort you could possibly need if you're willing to occupy our box seats. You do realize, they afford only a partial view of the stage. But you'd have ample space to stretch, and privacy to boot. We never list the boxes on the chart for sale anyway. Too problematic."

"That sounds ideal, Arnie. I really appreciate the switch. Thanks."

Vic's next call was to Perry Chan, who was paged backstage at the Hayes Theatre. The scenic designer was breathless when he picked up the phone.

After briefly discussing the repercussions of Helena Baxter's disastrous cocktail party the night before, Vic ventured further with, "Perry, I don't know if you were planning on sticking around at the theatre, but I've arranged box seats for the performance tonight as a demonstration of moral support for our star. I thought maybe we could sit together and you could perhaps suggest elements of interest for Terry Hagen to use as backdrops at tomorrow's shoot."

The designer heaved a thought-provoking sigh, "Are you asking me on a date or to help you with work?" Perry inquired, facetiously.

"A bit of both, actually. If I took you to dinner first, would it count as a date?"

"It would be a step in the right direction," laughed the set designer, "You might even get lucky if you play your cards right."

"Could you meet me at Sardi's at 6:30?"

"I'm bolting out of the stage door already," said Perry, hanging up.

Vic passed Bettie's office on his leisurely stroll to ring for the elevator. She was in the process of gathering her things.

"I'm meeting Rodney downstairs at the second-floor restaurant for a quick bite before the show." Bettie casually checked her hair, eyeliner, and lipstick in the office mirror as she spoke. As usual, she looked perfect. "What did you decide to do?"

"I asked Perry to join me. We're having dinner at Sardi's as well. Come on, we can elevate together," joked Vic.

Bettie grabbed her Fendi shoulder bag, "I'm not sure it's correct to use the term 'elevate' when you actually plan on going down."

"Ha! Plan on going down?" Vic laughed, "Bettie, you're slipping—you've left too easy an opening for me. After all, I am on my way to hook up with Perry."

"You're a pig." Bettie punched Vic's arm just as the elevator doors opened.

The operator greeted them with a wide smile. "Good evening, folks. Where to?"

"Oh, we're going down! All the way down to the second floor, if you please, sir," Vic commanded, playfully, "And make it snappy. We have some hot dates waiting for us at Sardi's."

"Hop in," joked the operator, "I'll set the control dial for accelerated speed. Hold on to your hats!"

The elevator started moving slowly with a sudden jolt, producing odd scraping sounds, rattles, and several clangs before reaching its destination a few floors below.

Bettie had arranged, with the assistance of her waiter friend Julio, for a quiet table in the far corner. She spotted Officer Copcake Clements almost immediately and walked across the crowded restaurant to join him.

Perry was just arriving, via the first-floor stairway, as Vic was scanning the room in search of him.

While a busboy poured ice water in their glasses, Perry couldn't contain his obvious excitement, "I hear that the town's buzzing over the poisoning last night. The papers are all over the story today with the most horrendous headlines. Some of them are actually hilariously funny to read—if you find humor in that sort of thing," Perry quickly added. "Helena Baxter must be so humiliated being hauled over the coals like this for a second time. What did that remarkable looking detective have to say about it at the hospital?"

"He asked us a lot of questions about what we'd witnessed. He was especially interested in all of the activity going on in the kitchen just before the trays were carried out. By the way, did you know our detective's twin brother, Rodney Clements, is Bettie's date for the theatre tonight?" Vic tilted his head in the direction of her table situated across the noisy room.

"Good for her," cheered Perry, "It's a miracle of nature that there are actually two of those hunks existing in this world. Both are magnificent matching specimens. Let's keep our fingers crossed that Rodney's been gossiping with his sibling about the murder at The Dakota, and perhaps our beautiful Mata Hari will get some information out of him."

Vic winked with a sly smile on his face, "I'm counting on it."

"This is my first dinner at Sardi's restaurant," confessed Rodney shyly, looking around at the caricatures of legendary Broadway actors and actresses lining the walls. "It's a little intimidating." They were sitting under framed drawings of Elizabeth Ashley and Zero Mostel.

"You'll get used to it after a few meals," Bettie assured him, "I hope you realize that you're a bit of a local celebrity yourself. Well, you and Fiona, of course. Everyone in the business recognizes you—with or without your horse. You're the unofficial toast of the Broadway."

"It must be a lot fun to be really famous," mused the policeman, "I get to sample a slight taste of stardom when I make my rounds in Times Square. Talking to tourists who ask a million personal questions, signing autographs, having my picture taken. Hey, maybe when Terry Hagen photographs my brother and me for *Playbill*, we'll hit the major leagues."

"The combination of your good looks, and the fact that you're working in this high-profile neighborhood filled with hungry agents looking for prospective clients, I'd predict the chances are promising," said Bettie, "If that's what you really want. You'd pretty much be forced to live under a microscope once you've become a household name. It comes with the territory. Take Helena Baxter, for example, and what agony she must be going through today. Under suspicion of murder…again."

Rodney's tone turned serious, "My brother told me about the party at her home last night. Some of the newspapers are treating it like a bad joke. Imagine inviting guests to try out some recipes for a new cookbook, and then proceeding to poison everybody—actually killing the publisher's editor."

"I was there at The Dakota last night. I met your brother Renny, you know."

"Oh, right," admitted Rodney, "He mentioned that you were with Vic Senso. Mind if I ask, are you two an item?"

Bettie laughed a bit too heartily, "Heavens, no! We're just great friends and we often work together as a team at the ad agency."

"That's good to hear," said Rodney, blushing as he abruptly changed the subject, "What do you think was going on at The Dakota last night? Who do you suppose was originally intended to be the main target?"

"I honestly don't have a clue," Bettie took a sip of her ice water, "I never really gave it a thought, but I would venture to guess that Helena Baxter herself was the target. It was her apartment and the poisoner could only be assured of her presence there at the gathering. If one looks at it in a certain way, there were only four people who were guaranteed to be in attendance: Helena Baxter, her husband Rex, Simone the secretary, and Caprice the housekeeper. They all live and work there. If you're at all familiar with theatre people, you'd know the other guests were optional and could not have been relied upon to show up. As it was, Vic and I were last-minute invitees. It's lucky you had other plans, or you may have ended up being one of the poison victims. That's what makes it all seem so incredibly random. I don't know what to make of the whole puzzling mess."

Rodney snapped a breadstick in half, "The media paints Helena Baxter as a highly-strung personality who'd been involved in a murder once before. Apparently, she accidentally clobbered a Swedish man with an exercise dumbbell some years ago."

"In actuality, she wasn't even in New York when that tourist was killed," said Bettie, "I just recently heard the whole story. It was a proven fact that Helena Baxter was out-of-town doing a play in summer stock. It was a terrible accident, not a murder at all."

"My brother Renny's a great detective. I'm sure he'll get to the bottom of it." Rodney looked longingly into the breadbasket. "I love carbs," he said, helping himself to a salted roll.

Vic and Perry had just finished giving their dinner order to the plump waiter in attendance.

"Did our handsome detective ever get around to questioning you last night?" Vic asked the scenic designer.

"I felt totally ignored. So did Mark Rhodes. We kept waiting to attract Renny Clements' attention." Perry complained, "One of the other cops took our statements. No matter. I didn't really witness anything of importance that I know of—unless you consider gazing into a goldfish bowl worth mentioning. Come to think of it, those little devils did appear to be rather suspicious looking. They kept staring back at me."

"Those goldfish were lucky to have escaped becoming an ingredient in the canapés. God knows what Mademoiselle Fournier mixed into some of those concoctions. Poisoning her editor certainly put the kibosh on her cookbook deal with Simon and Schuster. The poor thing had to be heavily sedated last night, she was so utterly distraught." Vic looked fixedly at the warm breadbasket but refrained from taking anything.

"It'll be fascinating to watch the performance this evening aware of the awful stress our leading lady must be experiencing. I'm sure the box office is jubilant over all the sudden clamoring for tickets, but in all fairness, Helena Baxter's the only one who has to walk out on that stage tonight in front of hundreds of people who suspect her of committing cold-blooded murder."

"As they say in Variety, 'That's show biz,'" quoted Vic, adding a forced grimace.

Scene Three

There are some theatrical events which generate such palpable excitement in the audience, you can sense the crackle of electricity in the air while waiting for the curtain to rise. The Thursday evening presentation of *Don't Hang Up*, starring Helena Baxter, ranks among them. The waves of love and support that washed over the footlights onto the stage must've galvanized the legendary actress to give one of the best performances of her lengthy and successful career. The crowd went wild as Helena Baxter made her first entrance onto the boards, sustaining thunderous applause for a full ten minutes. It was a personal triumph for the celebrated stage star who had been skewered and humiliated by the news media, not only in the recent past, but earlier that same day.

After the curtain came down, Vic and Perry made a mad dash backstage. They wanted to be among the first to congratulate the diva on her bravery and talent. Helena Baxter's dressing room was already filled with well-wishers. Publicist Ava Chasten was front and center, attempting to wrangle the mob into some semblance of organization in order to clear a path for the press, who were anxiously armed with cameras. Terry Hagen was among them. Mark seemed overwhelmed, assigned by his boss with maintaining crowd control.

Vic noticed Bettie and a star-struck Rodney Clements shoved into a corner across the room amidst all the bedlam. Simone was attempting to make her way towards her employer. However, the noisy crowd parted like Cecil B. DeMille's Red Sea in *The*

Ten Commandments when Celeste Farris entered the dressing room. She was escorted by Earl Quick, her distinguished silver fox of a husband. Actor Cal Lockheed was also in tow. Sulky general manager Arne Engels followed not too far behind.

Arms outstretched, Celeste Farris dramatically sauntered across the room and embraced Helena Baxter, "*Ma chére amie,* however do you do this play every night?"

The actress was too shaken by the evening's events to utter any response as the sound of wildly clicking cameras filled the room. In the past few hours, her emotions had been put through the proverbial wringer.

Helena Baxter had vomited into a bucket moments before she walked out onto the stage this evening, not knowing what to expect from the eight-hundred-or-so people sitting in the sold-out audience. Boos and hisses? Total silence? Crickets? A deafening ten-minute ovation quickly followed, which bought her some time to erase her fears and hesitations, before proceeding to give a performance.

Now—here she was—being air-kissed by a hideous Medusa while the enthusiastic media shutterbugs crammed into her dressing room and shouted in her direction. She loosed herself from Celeste Farris' clutches as delicately as possible while being confronted by a barrage of ridiculous questions posed by the members of the press.

"How did it feel to be on stage this evening, Miss Baxter?"

"Do you know who poisoned Oskar Linqvist last night, Miss Baxter?"

"Miss Baxter, how brisk were ticket sales at the box office today?"

"Are you and the Baxter household being questioned by the police...again?"

"Will *Don't Hang Up* open on Broadway as scheduled, Miss Baxter?"

Ava raised her arms and used her forceful tone of voice to put a stop to it, "Ladies and gentlemen, Miss Baxter will not be answering questions or granting interviews at this time. She is, however, delighted to pose for your cameras as long as you remain respectful and keep your distance."

Thirty minutes later, most of the masses had dispersed. Bettie accompanied her bashful date Rodney over to meet the stage star.

"My goodness gracious, I didn't expect to see you here tonight, detective," said Helena Baxter, "I thought you'd have seen more than enough of this theatre crowd for one day."

Bettie explained, "This is Renny Clements' twin brother, Rodney. He's a big fan."

Last night, when first introduced to the detective, the actress had been terribly distracted by the fact that her guests were dropping like flies. Now, in the safe and cozy atmosphere of her dressing room, Helena Baxter felt a girlish flutter, in reaction to the policeman's extraordinary good looks, when Rodney took her hand.

"Oh, you're identical," the stage star purred, "Charming, simply charming."

Snapping out of his cannabis haze, Rex Merchant was amused at his famous wife's realization that there were two Clements siblings. He shook Rodney's hand vigorously, "Your brother has been just wonderful to us. It's a pleasure to meet you."

"I felt sure that the audience was going to boo her right off the stage after all the bad publicity earlier today," said Arne, as a whispered aside to Celeste Farris.

"Wouldn't that have been ducky? Oh, well, if wishes were fishes…" mused the glamorous Mrs. Quick, who was shimmering in a sea-green ensemble, just slightly overdressed for the occasion.

Arne noted that he found this to be one of Celeste Farris' most endearing qualities. She was always outfitted as if she were being presented to the Court of St. James. She invariably endeavored to live up to her public's image of 'legendary star of stage and screen.' It was an ingrained holdover from her Old Hollywood studio-system training.

Terry, who was the only photographer granted permission to stay behind, leisurely circulated around the dressing room snapping candid shots. The lovely blonde brushed past Vic and said, "I promise to return your Canon tomorrow. I'm thinking I need to buy one just like it right away."

"Okay, folks, there's been enough excitement for one day." shouted Ava, "How about we allow Miss Baxter to call it a night? We do have a photo session planned for tomorrow afternoon on stage and she needs her rest. I'll be seeing some of you there."

The room cleared out after a few minutes.

Rodney was thrilled, "Wait until I tell Renny about this!" he exclaimed.

Mark was occupied with listening to his boss's long list of assignments to be carried out the next morning, but watched as Bettie and Rodney exited the dressing room together. Mark thought, if he was planning on asking the advertising account executive out on a date, he shouldn't wait too much longer. It was apparent that Officer Clements would be massive competition for Bettie's attention.

Celeste Farris and her entourage, which consisted of husband Earl Quick and actor Cal Lockheed, announced that they were heading over to Sardi's for a light after-theatre supper.

"Save me a seat," Arne called out to them, "I'll catch up with you shortly."

Simone, who appeared to be utterly exhausted, was collecting Helena Baxter's things. "I'll take these to the car and wait for you there," she said, quietly.

"I'll go along with Simone," said Rex, "Take your time changing, love."

Helena Baxter was finally alone in her dressing room. She placed her wig on the nearby stand and decided she'd remove her makeup at home. Suddenly sapped of all energy, she looked at her reflection in the mirror and began sobbing.

How much longer could she endure this? She had truly pulled a rabbit out of her hat on stage tonight. The audience could just as easily have torn her to pieces rather than applaud. She'd barely survived the atrocious publicity the first time around, fifteen years ago. It was clear to her that she was being targeted. The actress was also actively concerned over Caprice Fournier's state-of-mind. The woman was fragile on the best of days. These poisonings, and Oskar Lindqvist's death, were likely to push her housekeeper completely over the edge.

How in the world did it happen, anyway? There had been so much foot traffic in the kitchen before the trays had been carried out. Anyone of her guests could be responsible. Who would want to sabotage her book deal, not to mention her entire career? Who could possibly hate her so much—and for what reason?

Celeste Farris was the obvious frontrunner. Their rivalry and bitter feuds were now legendary in the tabloid press. Not only had the blonde witch stolen her Hollywood fiancé, but she was now constantly hanging around the theatre and backstage in her guise as Mrs. Producer. Helena Baxter honestly felt that Celeste Farris reveled in her rival's suffering. The vindictive actress probably wouldn't choose to put Helena out of her present misery by killing her.

Last night, she had arrived at the conclusion that the culprit was to be found among her intimate circle of friends, and the realization made her terribly uneasy. Obviously, there has to be a motive behind why the poisoner has taken such desperate measures. Helena Baxter was terrified about what might happen next.

It was torture waiting for the other shoe to drop.

Vic and Perry braved the evening drizzle as they walked to the Times Square train station. Although Vic was a major proponent of hailing a taxi, the advertising art director was aware of Chan's monetary limitations—always on a budget, as frugal as they come. Since Perry had invited him downtown to his apartment on Barrow Street for a nightcap, Vic conceded to waiting for the E train. He was ever hopeful that the New York City Transit Authority was serious about eventually sprucing up the system, using as a first step the unveiling of Massimo Vignelli's redesign of the subway map months before. At least on paper, the new look promised a clean, safe, and enjoyable environment.

As it stood at eleven o'clock that evening, the station was dank, dirty, and jam packed with hookers, pimps, addicts, and former mental patients the state had turned out into the streets—all of whom had jumped the turnstiles to avoid the nasty weather for a while. The train that ultimately arrived to transport them to the West Village was a confusion of graffiti. It held all the charm and sophistication of a garbage can. Vic silently swore to himself that he'd only ever take cabs after tonight, regardless of Perry's stringent personal principles.

"I'm afraid to sit down, I might catch crabs, or lice, or something." Vic carped.

"Don't be such a princess. Take a seat. I want to dish about what happened tonight." Perry Chan pretended to wipe the questionable surface with his sleeve.

Vic took the bait, "Helena Baxter certainly dodged a major bullet. She was fearless and it paid off for her big time. The theatre audience couldn't have been more supportive. I don't know how she was able to do it. The lady definitely has bigger balls than I do. Mark told me she threw up in a bucket just before making her entrance on stage this evening. Yet, seconds later, she appeared before a full house looking confident and radiant. That's the mark of a truly great actress."

"Let's hope she can get through the preview period without having a complete nervous breakdown." Perry said, "We still have several days to go before opening night. That amounts to an awful lot of pre-curtain vomiting."

Vic moved in closer to Perry and whispered over the roars and screeches of the speeding train and its timeworn wheels, "What did you think of Celeste Farris? Her insincerity knows no bounds. It's so obvious that she dislikes Helena Baxter intensely. I hope Terry caught their embrace on film. It was something that defies description. In this instance, a picture *would* actually be worth a thousand words."

"Those two are like oil and water. I cannot believe Helena Baxter is allowing Rex to co-produce and direct *Blithe Spirit* with Celeste Farris' husband—starring Celeste, no less! Maybe the four of them relish all the drama and turbulence," deduced Perry, as he kept a watchful Manhattan eye peeled for any suspicious-looking characters who might be populating their graffiti-coated subway car.

"At The Dakota party last night, I overheard some folks gossiping about a hot-and- heavy love affair involving a producer's actress-wife. Do you think it's possible that British pot head Rex is screwing around with Celeste Farris?" asked Vic.

"From what I know of Celeste's reputation, it'd be difficult to believe that she's *not* sneaking around with someone behind her husband's back."

"She and Earl Quick were just married a few weeks ago."

"So, what?" Perry smirked, "Grow up, it's 1975."

"It never crossed my mind until now, but maybe Rex and Celeste Farris were trying to bump off Helena Baxter last night by poisoning her canapés."

"Well, if that was the plan, they missed the mark by a mile. Not to mention the fact that they could have wiped out almost half the population of Broadway in the attempt. I'm sure there must be a thousand better ways to murder your wife than to do it in public surrounded by friends, co-workers, and with a photographer in attendance," said Perry.

"I suppose you're right. Maybe I'm looking at this picture backwards. That love affair rumor going around might involve a totally different couple," murmured Vic, "After all, Helena Baxter can also be described as a producer's actress-wife."

Scene Four

The next morning, Bettie had barely reached her office door when the phone on her desk began ringing. It was Rodney.

"Is it convenient for me to visit the art archives this morning around 11?"

"Yes, that'd be perfect. See you soon."

Bettie was leafing through some of the previous day's messages Marsha had left on her desk. The account executive often thought of the small pink sheets of notepaper as secret cryptograms that she was determined to decipher. A cleverly detailed sketch of a camera could translate as a directive to return Terry Hagen's call. The nicely rendered drawing of a woman holding a baby could possibly serve as a reminder that Bettie should phone her mother. As maddening as it was, flipping through the messages made a bit of a game out of what would ordinarily be considered a mundane task.

Bettie walked over to Vic's office to tell him about Rodney's impending visit.

"Hey, aren't those the same clothes you were wearing yesterday?" Bettie asked him, fully aware that indeed they were.

Vic smiled, "Your powers of observation astound me, Miss Marple."

To fill the awkward silence that followed, she switched gears, "Wasn't the audience reaction just incredible last night?" Bettie remarked. "Rodney was beside himself with excitement over meeting Helena Baxter and Celeste Farris."

"You scored major points there. Officer Copcake certainly seemed to be having a terrific time," observed Vic, "By the way, I think Mark was a bit thrown off by seeing the two of you together."

Bettie feigned innocence, "Oh, really? Do tell."

Vic sighed knowingly and abruptly changed topics, "Have you been privy to any recent rumors about Celeste Farris being involved in a torrid love affair?"

"Well, our very own Guy Andersen, the Hedda Hopper of lobby attendants, fed me a blind item about the famous wife of a Broadway producer who's possibly been fooling around, if that's what you're referring to? Why, what've you been hearing?"

"At The Dakota party, I overheard someone speculate that a producer's illustrious actress-wife was having a steamy affair. I'm guessing that it can be none other than Celeste Farris."

"If Helena Baxter weren't having so many other major distractions in her life right now—like previewing in a new Broadway play, writing a cookbook, and casually poisoning her party guests—she could fit that description, too. You're probably correct, though. It's much more likely that Celeste Farris is screwing around," said Bettie, "I cannot imagine someone as sweet and courtly as Helena Baxter actually cheating on her husband."

"I tend to be in agreement with you on that," Vic nodded as emphasis.

Bettie looked around anxiously, "Rodney's on his way here to shoot a Polaroid of the faux Chagall in the art archives."

"I'm guessing Officer Copcake wants to show off the Morrow painting to another art lover at the precinct," said Vic.

Punctually, at eleven o'clock, the elevator doors were pulled open. Rodney Clements stepped out into the Thompson & Co reception room.

Bettie, Rodney, and Vic made their way through the bustling advertising offices toward the art archives.

As they breezed through the various departments, Rodney peered around the vibrant agency at work with intense enthusiasm, seemingly committing every detail to memory. He'd previously seen the offices after working hours.

Vic walked a few steps quickly ahead. He used his body to prop open the door to the art archives as he reached into the darkened room and switched on the overhead lighting canisters. He guided them inside with a broad smile. Vic heard Bettie gasp as he turned his attention to the display railing.

The faux Chagall painting was nowhere to be seen.

Muttering to himself, Vic performed a quick search around the storage space, but it was quite evident that the poster comp was gone. He was rendered speechless.

Bettie broke the uncomfortable silence, but sounded distraught, "What could've happened? It was here yesterday."

Rodney was perfectly cool and composed, "Is there somewhere less populated that we can talk, the three of us?" he asked.

They chose the conference room. It was windowless and provided total privacy.

Bettie offered Copcake a seat at the head of the conference room table. The two of them quickly claimed chairs in close proximity.

Rodney softly cleared his throat before speaking, "Please allow me to preface this discussion. I don't pretend to be officially affiliated with anything I'm about to tell you. There's a small division at our precinct—so small that only one detective works it—name of Volpe. He's dedicated to recovering lost or stolen artwork treasures, as well as the illicit traffic of cultural goods. With my intense interest in Fine Art, I sometimes hang out with the man in charge. I'd like to thank you, Bettie, and Vic, for allowing me access to view what I described to him as a faux Chagall painting.

"When you so kindly gave me a tour of your art archives, I was struck by that particular painting. I have a great memory for detail and recalled a photo Detective Volpe had shown me a while ago of a lost Marc Chagall canvas. It was among several masterpieces that had been stolen in an audacious robbery from the Neils van de Velde Museet in Oslo, in 1957. It has never been recovered."

Rodney slipped a photograph out of his uniform pocket and slid it across the table surface. Both Bettie and Vic recognized the painting in the picture as their faux Chagall from the art archives.

"This print was made from a transparency from the van de Velde Museet's files. The artist's signature on your painting was in approximately the same location toward the bottom of the canvas." Rodney said.

"I don't understand. How is this possible?" Vic was dumbfounded, "Maybe our theatre poster artist had seen the original on a vacation trip abroad and recreated it later on from memory. I scarcely think that the actual original painting could have ended up here at Thompson & Co."

Rodney interjected, "Look closely at the base of the canvas, Vic. Where the artist had signed it."

"Yes, it clearly reads Marc Chagall," observed Bettie, moving closer to the image.

Vic said, "Our canvas was distressed in that area. All we could see was the 'M.'"

"Yes, I noticed that as well." Officer Clements remarked, "I believe the painting was damaged during the robbery or possibly sometime afterward in the transporting of the canvas from location to location."

"I only recently discovered the painting in our archives," said Vic, "Both my boss and I are certain we've never seen it before. It was grouped in a vertical file towards the back shelves in that crowded room. It may have been sitting there for years, for all we know. But, where in the world could it have come from? Who'd have hidden it in there in the first place?"

Rodney placed his hands on the table, "Quite honestly, I'm not surprised it has disappeared again. Someone connected to the theft itself, or to an underground network that is instrumental in moving it from place-to-place, country-to-country, must have realized that you'd uncovered it, Vic. It only serves to assure me that what was stolen from your archives is indeed the original Chagall masterpiece."

Bettie asked timidly, "So what do you suggest we do now?"

"I strongly urge you to do nothing," Copcake was quite emphatic, "Volpe will take it from here. It entails making phone calls to several of his contacts. You've established a fresh trail, and that alone is an instrumental new piece to this puzzle."

"Don't you find it a bit strange that a painting stolen almost twenty years ago in Oslo possibly ended up here at a theatrical ad agency in Manhattan?" asked Vic, scratching his head for maximum effect.

"Ever since the unbelievable theft of da Vinci's *Mona Lisa* from The Louvre Museum, I can pretty much believe anything bizarre as far as the world of priceless art is concerned. You know, Leonardo's masterpiece was missing for two years—hidden in a janitor's closet—before the thief himself wrote a confession and returned it safely to an art dealer in Florence." Rodney Clements moved his chair back and rose to his feet.

"I'm sorry things didn't work out today," apologized Bettie.

"Well, it definitely is disappointing, but the Chagall cannot be too far away right now. I'm confident that Volpe and his Art Theft Detail liaisons will track down its whereabouts soon. I'm in your debt for providing us with such a substantial lead."

They solemnly escorted Rodney to the elevator. No sooner had the clanging of the noisy lift announced its descent before Bettie grabbed Vic's hand, "Come with me. Right now!"

They raced all the way back to the art archives room. Bettie opened the door and shoved Vic inside, "Well?" she asked impatiently, closing them in.

"Huh? What are you going on about?" Vic was clearly bewildered.

Bettie widened her eyes in disbelief, "Oh, come on, Vic. Can't you smell it?"

"I honestly don't know what you're talking about. Smell what?"

"Paco Rabanne," she said.

Scene FIVE

Friday - March 7, 1975
The day of the murder at the Hayes Theatre

"It's nuts. First, we hire a clairvoyant who announces that there's possibly a killer in our conference room. Then we experience mass poisonings and a homicide at a cocktail party. Now we're involved with what appears to be an international art theft at our offices," said Vic, "What's next? I feel like we've been dropped into the middle of a television Movie of the Week melodrama. How do we begin trying to figure out what in heaven and hell is going on around here lately?" The art director was nervously organizing the markers and pencils on his drawing table as he spoke.

Bettie reminded him, "Vic, let's keep our heads on straight, okay? We have a job to do right now. We're due at the Helen Hayes in about fifteen minutes. If we're there early, we can connect with Terry before starting the photo set-ups. I think we need to focus on the task at hand. Try to forget about the stolen painting right now, and let's get this shoot under our belts."

"I'm all for that, too. Hopefully, the rest of the day will go smoothly," Vic crossed his fingers, reinforcing his wish.

"I suppose it actually couldn't get any worse," said Bettie.

Vic winced, "Please, don't say things like that! Are you trying to give us *Malocchio*? We're having a crazy enough time without throwing bad luck into the mix."

"Oh, don't be so superstitious," she laughed, "We call it, *Mal*

De Ojo in Cuba. My mother gifted me with this onyx stone for protection," Bettie pointed to the black gem at the end of a delicate chain hanging around her neck. "So, that puts me in the clear."

"I'm about as safe as you are, then," said Vic as he pulled a horn-shaped *cornicello* charm from his pants pocket. "My mom insists I always carry it with me to avoid the dreaded *Evil Eye*. I guess it's been working for me overtime lately."

Bettie laughed, "Just goes to prove that Cuban and Italian mothers are a lot alike."

"However, yours supplies more tasteful jewelry," said Vic.

Tobin stepped into Vic's office, "Are you about ready to go to the Hayes? I thought I'd tag along with you both just to schmooze for a bit. I have another meeting back here in an hour, so it'll be the ideal excuse for me to dart out of there once Terry starts taking pictures."

"I find it hilarious, Tobin, how you are always prepared to leave somewhere before you actually even get there," Bettie said, "Let's go."

Klein laughed, "I guess my wife's trick of avoidance behavior is beginning to rub off on me. Olga's worse than I am."

On their brief walk over to the theatre, they updated Tobin on the surprising news regarding the stolen Chagall, being sure to add Copcake's strict directive to do nothing until he contacted them.

"You realize, after all this hubbub, it simply might turn out be just a rejected poster comp for *Fiddler done* by one of our staff artists years ago." Tobin said.

When they reached the Helen Hayes Theatre on 46th Street, there were a few stagehands leisurely smoking outside the entrance. One of the friendlier union guys instructed them to enter through the front of the house since the doors were unlocked.

"Simone Caldwell just arrived a few minutes ago," one of the crew mentioned.

Vic adored the facade of this Broadway theatre in particular. It was predominately made of terra cotta, and featured a filigree pattern on its walls, consisting of amber and ivory, with areas of blue glass tiles at the intersection of the lattice.

Once inside the front doors, they noticed that the spacious lobby was occupied by members of the press. The journalists and their staff photographers were impatiently hanging around. Ava had invited some key reporters to cover the photo shoot as a behind-the-scenes gossip item—good publicity for the new play during its preview period.

Tobin said, "I'm going to run downstairs to the restroom. I'll catch up with you."

Vic and Bettie took a look at the 40"x 60" easel, commonly designated as an advertising 'A-frame', which was propped near the box office windows. It read: Limited Engagement! / Box Office Now Open! / Preview Performances at Poppular Prices! / Helena Baxter starring in *Don't Hang Up.*

"Unbelievable! There's a typo on the board. Dammit, didn't anybody proof-read that sign before it left the display house?" Bettie was livid, "I'll call Jerry at King's to have it corrected as soon as we get back to the office. In the meantime, let's ask the box office to move it out of sight for the time being."

It took five minutes to deal with the issue. Once that problem was resolved, Vic and Bettie opened the inner lobby door and entered. Before their vision could adapt to the semi-darkness of the vast orchestra seating area, an ungodly scream, followed by a deafening crash of cymbals, boom of drums, and scrapping of metal—later likened to the sound of garbage cans being tossed downstairs—assaulted their ears.

"What the hell could be going on in there?" Vic voiced over the cacophony.

Just as suddenly, it all fell completely silent.

Bettie and Vic ceased moving and peered down the aisle toward the stage, their eyes gradually adjusting the dim light. There was no one to be seen.

"They must all be on a lunch break. It's a union rule, no matter what," whispered Bettie, now holding on to Vic's arm.

All was still.

They could see that the scenery was fully lit, set-up, and ready to be photographed. Vic's attention was drawn to Perry Chan's brilliant wall of headshots. The sea of framed smiling faces stared back at him. A chill ran up his spine as he detected movement from behind the wall on the set facing the head shots. Maybe it was a reflection off the glass.

Tobin abruptly burst through the lobby door behind them, "What the hell caused that racket? I thought I heard a scream."

The three of them stepped slowly down the aisle, checking over their shoulders along the way for any signs of movement.

Bettie later recalled that's when she first became aware of the sounds of people running, some of them shouting, as she, Vic, and Tobin reached the stage. They used the rehearsal steps on their right to climb onto the performance area. She stood frozen with apprehension when she realized that the trap door on the floor of the set was open, exposing a dark, gaping abyss. It wasn't immediately apparent due to the stage lighting scheme.

She saw Rex Merchant, Ava, and Mark run onto the stage from various backstage locations. Perry and two of the carpenter crew appeared next. Lester, the stage doorman, meekly peered around the curtain. Close behind were wheezing Arnie and a breathless Terry. Oddly enough, Bettie observed Celeste Farris, Earl Quick, and Cal Lockheed—of all people—now congesting the scenery. What were they doing here?

Vic hesitantly approached the trap door. It took a few seconds for his eyes to adjust to the relative darkness below as he stared into it. The others reached it just seconds after the art director.

"Look at all the blood…" Arne Engels was stunned.

"What else can you see down there?" Perry had his hand up, half-covering his eyes.

"I think someone's fallen in. It's so dark, it's difficult to tell…" this, from director Rex Merchant.

"It's a woman. She's not moving at all…" Ava squinted into the shadows.

"Oh, good Lord, it's Helena Baxter..." said Vic, "...and I think she's dead."

In an effort to garner as much publicity as possible for the new play, Ava Chasten had previously invited several of the journalists, who typically covered local theatre happenings and gossip, to this particular *Don't Hang Up* photo shoot.

The reporters instantly bolted out of the Helen Hayes heading toward the nearest phone booths in order to report the unanticipated scoop to their various newsrooms. They'd clearly heard Vic Senso's horrified pronouncement ring out from the stage of the empty theatre. What began as a routine publicity photo shoot for a new Broadway show had unexpectedly turned into a more momentous narrative. As a result, the media was quick to circulate the news of Broadway legend Helena Baxter's grisly demise.

WINS Radio used the shocking item as the lead-in to its *"Newswatch never stops"* broadcasting, which supported their tagline, *"You give us 22 minutes, we'll give you the world."* It referenced the station's format clock which would return to their top stories every twenty minutes. The account of Helena Baxter's death was repeated ad nauseam for hours.

Broadway Star Has Fatal Stage Accident was a "Special Bulletin" headline splashed across several local New York City television stations, interrupting regularly scheduled daytime programming.

The New York Post, naturally, created the most vivid headline for their Late Edition with: *Helena-Over-Heels—Trapdoor Topples Towering Talent*.

The news of Helena Baxter's death spread like wildfire throughout the media.

Scene Six

Due to a trick of lighting, it was the second time in the past week that Vic Senso had mistakenly identified understudy Simone Caldwell for her boss, Helena Baxter.

The members of the press had overheard the art director utter his bleak observation aloud from the stage of the Helen Hayes.

However, it wasn't long after the journalists had vacated the theatre to report the deadly disaster to their various news sources that Helena Baxter herself appeared from the wings—alive, and fully intact. By that time, however, it was impossible to stop the erroneous report of the star's death from seeping into every entertainment-oriented network of mass communication.

"Is everything alright?" the actress asked, "What was that horrible commotion? It sounded like all hell breaking loose."

This swiftly triggered everyone into action. The group standing around the open trap door on stage realized at once that the woman who'd fallen must've been Simone Caldwell. Several of them ran down the stairs to the trap room to lend a hand in the event that Simone was still breathing. Although, the consensus, among those on stage looking into the darkened void, determined from the amount of blood spilled, there would be little they could do until the EMT arrived. Vic could already hear the ambulance sirens approaching the theatre as he and some of the others were dashing toward the space beneath the performance area.

The trap room was a large open chamber under the stage of the Helen Hayes Theatre used for scenic effects. Included among its many functions, it allowed the stage floor to be leveled, extra electrical equipment to be attached, and most importantly, it was essential for the placement of the trap doors leading onto the stage. The room was unfinished and doubled as a storage area. Vic speculated that the combination of Simone's fall from a great height onto the massive stockpile of items below was what ultimately killed her. Although, truth be told, he could barely bring himself to look at the mangled, bloody body that confronted the group when they reached the trap room.

Fortunately, the EMT workers, as well as a legion of stern officers from the police department, arrived moments later and sharply ordered them to go back upstairs.

"Oh, my dears. Oh, my dears," Helena Baxter kept repeating.

Rex wrapped his arm around his distraught wife's shoulder as he gently accompanied her back to her dressing room. Almost everyone else was in too much of a state of shock to move. Ava looked as pale as a ghost.

"They don't make aspirins colossal enough for something like this," she lamented.

One of the older policemen employed a booming voice and announced, "Folks, I urge you to move away from the trap door and exit the stage area. Use the rehearsal stairs on your right in an orderly fashion."

"That's actually referred to as stage left, sergeant," Ava corrected the man sternly, "You've been working in the theatre district for years, you'd think you'd have learned the lingo by now."

"Lady, you must be confusing me with Laurence Olivier. Get moving," the officer snapped gruffly, and continued addressing the rest of the group, "Take seats in the front rows until it's your turn to be questioned. Please be prepared to wait for some time, and don't hesitate to alert any of the other policemen if you're feeling unwell, require a glass of water, or the restroom."

The sergeant allowed clearance for Lester Potts to resume his vigil at the stage door. The members of the carpenter crew were led backstage to an isolated area for questioning by a senior officer.

Everyone else had comfortably settled into the first few rows of the orchestra.

Vic quickly secured aisle seat B101 to accommodate his long legs. Bettie and Tobin sat to his left. Mark broke away from Ava, who was nervously pacing the theatre floor, and grabbed the seat directly behind Bettie. Perry Chan and Terry Hagen left an empty gap between them in row A, but were engaged in a hushed conversation, nonetheless. Arne, Celeste Farris, Earl Quick, and Cal Lockheed occupied locations on the opposite side of row B. The chattering of the assembled witnesses abruptly ceased when Detective Clements made his entrance onto the boards and stepped into the center stage spotlight.

His demeanor was quite solemn, comparable to a brooding Shakespearean prince, as Renny began addressing the rapt audience, "It appears most of us need no introductions. After the unsettling events of the last few days, we are again confronted by a second fatal tragedy. Simone Caldwell, Helena Baxter's long-time understudy and secretary, was pronounced dead by the medical examiner who was quick to arrive on the scene. We know that an incident occurred less than thirty minutes ago in which she fell through the stage trap door to the room down below. There are a few questions that immediately must be asked. Who left the trap door open and unguarded? Why was Ms. Caldwell on stage alone? Despite the fact that the space directly beneath is typically reserved for storage—who is responsible for piling folding chairs, drums, cymbals, and empty trash cans in a dangerous heap under the trap door opening?

"According to the M.E., although the fall from the stage measures nearly a thirty-foot drop, the fact that Ms. Caldwell landed onto sharp-edged surfaces is what most likely led to her death. The razored rim of one of the drum cymbals sliced an artery in her neck. There is sufficient cause to consider this more than a dubious accident. This event is being treated as a premeditated homicide. The entire theatre is now an official crime scene, and unfortunately, you are all considered suspects.

"Each of you were in the house at the time of the incident. Based on the lethal poisoning at The Dakota on Wednesday evening and the fatality today, I believe that someone is targeting Helena Baxter. We've all recognized that Ms. Caldwell and Helena Baxter shared certain physical qualities that often led to confusion and, in certain lighting, to misidentification. I think that this accident was meant for Helena Baxter. That Ms. Caldwell was mistaken for her employer—with tragic results.

"Mr. Perry Chan. Are you here? We didn't meet the other night at The Dakota gathering. I understand that you designed the scenery?" Renny asked.

"Yes, ye...yes, sir," stuttered Perry nervously.

"What was the purpose of this trap door? It's certainly not meant to be kept open during the performance?"

Chan stood up automatically when responding, due to years of strict Catholic school training by the sternest of Franciscan nuns, "No, detective. The trap mechanism is set to open only when the scenery has moved forward on the track. It's a special effect device used to make it appear that someone has been hiding in the armoire— designed as a scare tactic to shock the audience at the dramatic climax of the play. It should only be in use when the armoire is moved into place. At the proper moment, it elevates the actor from the trap room below up to the stage as if he's been hiding in the cupboard throughout the entire scene."

"Who works the mechanism?" asked Renny.

"One of the backstage crewmen, but truth be told, anyone who's been in the theatre during rehearsals has seen how it is handled. It's done manually, no special training really required. A child could maneuver the controls," Perry explained.

Even at a distance from the stage, Perry found Renny Clements' icy blue-eyed gaze highly intimidating.

"Where were you when you heard all the noise?" the detective asked.

Perry hesitated before answering, "I was in a little room upstairs designated for use as my office. I was checking out some last-minute measurements for a section of the scenery that was proving to be problematic."

"Was anyone with you to corroborate your whereabouts?"

"No, I was alone," the set designer responded uncomfortably. "I heard a horrible scream followed by a hell of a lot of crashing and banging. So, I came running."

Renny pulled out his worn notebook and pencil nub, "You could hear all of that from upstairs on the second floor with the door closed?"

"I had the door propped open," Perry informed him meekly, "It can begin to get hot in that small room very quickly."

Chan answered further questions in an equally jittery manner before Renny moved on to Terry, who also appeared noticeably ill-at-ease.

"Are you alright, Terry? Is something bothering you?"

"I might as well fess up now, detective. I ran to the trap room with the others as soon as we realized someone had fallen down there. I had my camera with me, of course, and shot some photos of the scene—and of poor Simone in that awful condition. I know I shouldn't have snapped the pictures since it was all so grizzly and horrible, but I suppose the guerilla-journalist side of me took over for a few intense moments." Terry confessed.

Renny frowned a bit, "You realize, of course, I'm going to have to confiscate that film, Terry."

The lovely photographer crossed her legs as she responded, "Well, that'll turn out to present just a slight bit of a problem. I cannot seem to find the camera. I set it down during all the commotion. I've looked absolutely everywhere. It's nowhere to be found."

"During all of this pandemonium, someone stole your camera?" Renny asked incredulously.

Terry shifted in her seat. She looked remorsefully over at Vic, who was snugly slouched in the row behind her, as she answered, "Well, it was not actually my camera. It belongs to Vic Senso. It was his Canon F-1. I intended to use it for our session today, and then return it to him."

"That figures," Vic muttered under his breath. Straightening out his posture in seat B101, he quickly added, "I certainly haven't seen it, detective."

Bettie stifled a slight guffaw.

Renny continued directing questions at Terry. "Where were you when you first heard the scream followed by all the noise?"

"I had just darted into one of the empty dressing rooms on the second floor to load my camera. That is, Vic's camera. The Canon. I needed an isolated spot that could provide absolute darkness. I was only in there for a minute or two," said Terry.

"Did anyone see you?"

"Not that I know of, I'm sorry to say." Terry seemed genuinely forlorn, "But, as it happens, I can corroborate Perry's story. As I was searching around for an empty room, I caught sight of him through the open door. He was using the space as an office."

"Perry, did you see Ms. Hagen outside your door sometime before the commotion began?" asked the detective.

The scenery designer shrugged, "Wish I could say I did, but I didn't. I was focused on the task at hand, you know, calculating some geometry." He twisted his lips into a frown aimed at the photographer, "Sorry, Terry."

Detective Clements then turned his attention to row B stage right, where Celeste Farris, her husband Earl Quick, actor Cal Lockheed, and general manager Arne Engels were sitting in succession. Renny seemed about ready to launch into their interrogations. Instead, he abruptly asked of no one in particular, "Is it possible for someone to get me a chair?"

One of the young officers instantly ran on stage and provided a battered metal stool. The detective removed his suit jacket, threw it to the floor, and took a seat. The suspects located in the front rows of the orchestra were now presented with the provocative tableau of Renny Clements sitting beneath the flattering stage spotlight. Unbeknownst to him, the detective's muscular frame and angular facial features were being given the full star treatment. It did not go unnoticed by the intimate audience.

"Miss Farris, can you tell me where you were, please?"

Celeste employed her renowned talent for projection to relay her response. Her voice filled the Helen Hayes up to the rafters of the rear balcony section without the use of electronic amplification.

"It was just coincidence that Earl and I were in this theatre at all today. We had an appointment with Arnie to tour the facilities since it seems likely that our production of *Blithe Spirit* will be housed here next season following the run of *Don't Hang Up*. Although I've played the Hayes many times in the past, it's always important to check out any improvements and updates that have been made—or need to be addressed. Our dear friend and cast member, Cal Lockheed, tagged along. We four were planning on enjoying a luncheon at Sardi's after our excursion today."

The celebrated blonde actress, who'd been sitting on the aisle in row B, now stood to dramatize the rest of her response, "When we heard that blood-curdling scream, my husband and I were in the midst of a conversation with our publicity person, Mark Rhodes. You know, he works with Ava Chasten. He was asking about my preferences in terms of backstage press protocol. We were standing not too far from the stage door exit. I'm certain of that because I recall noticing Lester Potts nearby, standing at his post. Needless to say, we were all startled out of our wits. We quickly determined that all the fracas was coming from the onstage area nearby. I remember feeling a terrible sense of dread as we began running in that direction. Oh, it was simply terrible, terrible." Celeste Farris, having played her scene, gracefully resumed her seat in B113.

With the theatre lighting serving to make his silver hair appear even more remarkable, Earl Quick spoke next, "My story is much the same, detective. I was with my wife the entire time. The incident occurred during the required union lunch break, so things were fairly quiet. People were off on their own and scattered in all directions, as opposed to the typical hustle and bustle that accompanies a full rehearsal on stage. I didn't notice anything suspicious or unusual for the duration of our backstage tour, that is, not until we heard that godawful scream followed by complete bedlam."

Renny turned his attention to Cal Lockheed. Clements had last interviewed him when the elegant actor was propped up in a hospital bed, still in a highly weakened state from arsenic poisoning. Cal appeared fully recovered.

"Mr. Lockheed, I'm glad to see you out and about. Can you share your whereabouts during the time in question, please?"

"Thank you, detective darling, that's sweet of you to say." Lockheed launched into his story, "Arnie was conducting a tour of the house for Celeste, Earl, and myself. Just before all the furor began, I stopped to chat with Ava. Across the stage, Mr. Engels motioned for me to join him. Celeste and Earl moved off to speak with Mark. I bid Ava adieu and caught up with Arnie. He was pointing out where he thought my dressing room might be positioned for *Blithe Spirit*. We were discussing the advantages and disadvantages of having a dressing room on the stage level when we heard the scream followed by all the terrible pandemonium." Cal shuddered a bit.

"I can pretty much corroborate that chain of events, detective," said Arne, his nasal passages filling up with backstage dust, "There were a few folks milling about. I could see them peripherally, as well as in the background, over Cal's shoulder while we spoke. I honestly couldn't tell you who they were. I was more aware that people were walking around rather than who the specific people were. Does that make sense?"

"Yes, I understand," Renny Clements nodded as he scribbled in his notebook.

Ava abruptly decided that it was her turn to be heard, "I was using the wall phone in the backstage area when all hell broke loose," said the publicist, who had finally chosen to settle in a row D aisle seat, "but I could see Arnie and Cal through the scenery on the opposite side of the stage having their conversation. As usual, Cal was doing all of the talking, but Arnie's always been a good listener. Besides, you always know when he's in the vicinity by the sound of his incessant sneezing. They were hardly being discreet about smoking backstage, a constant cloud surrounding their heads. The main set and trap door were blocked from our view by an immense backdrop. It created a narrow walkway to enable actors and crew to walk across the stage without being seen by the audience."

Renny turned his attention to Lockheed and Arne, "Can you gentlemen confirm that Ms. Chasten was, at that time, on the phone and within your sights?"

"Absolutely, yes," they both agreed, with Cal adding, "I could clearly see her from where I stood, detective. Granted, she was across the stage standing behind the backdrop as were we. Once or twice, depending on the angle, I'd lose sight of her as she paced while talking, but I could still hear her side of the conversation. It was too bad the party at the other end of the phone line couldn't witness all of Ava's outlandish hand and finger gestures. But, whoever it was, was certainly getting an earful. I've never heard so many four-letter words used in a sentence. They were, um, quite vivid."

"I was talking to my mother," Ava explained.

After a moment of stunned silence, Bettie spoke next. "I don't believe you've met our boss, Tobin Klein, from Thompson & Co. He's Vice President and Creative Director," she said by way of introduction to the detective.

"Mr. Klein, your whereabouts at the time, please?"

"I had just arrived at the theatre with Bettie and Vic. One of the stagehands directed us to enter through the front lobby doors. I decided to use the restroom before the photo shoot began and made my way downstairs. I couldn't have been gone more than five minutes. I caught up with the two of them just as I heard the scream followed by the horrendous noise," said Tobin.

Renny shifted his position on the stool as he asked, "Did you happen to see anyone down on the lower lobby level?"

"On the contrary, it was rather deserted, actually. The restroom was empty as well," said Tobin, "I didn't see anybody until I walked back upstairs to join Bettie and Vic."

Detective Clements turned his attention to the next witness in line, Bettie Balboa. Renny's brother seemed quite smitten with the beautiful advertising executive. Rodney was gabbing on and on last night about how exciting it was to see the play and then to be escorted backstage. Meeting Helena Baxter in the star's own dressing room was the Oklahoma boy's dream come true—a close encounter with a real Broadway celebrity—all thanks to Bettie.

"Vic and I stopped to talk to the folks manning the box office about the A-frame standing in the lobby," she began, "That discussion probably lasted about five minutes, I'd guess. We then passed through the lobby doors to the back of the orchestra section. My eyes were still adjusting from the brightness of the sunny day outside to the dimness of the theatre when we heard the scream. It was followed almost at once by that ear-piercing commotion of crashing metal. We couldn't imagine what had caused it. Vic and I were walking toward the stage when Tobin caught up with us."

Renny asked, "Did you see anyone else in the theatre?"

"Not at that point, no. That was partially what made it so eerie," Bettie answered, "We ran up the rehearsal steps to the stage and realized that the trap door was open. Everyone came running out from everywhere at that point to locate the source of the noise."

"Mr. Senso, what's your take on the sequence of events?" the detective requested.

Vic stood before speaking, "Bettie has pretty much summed up our movements accurately. We were together the entire time. I do have something to add, however, if I may be allowed to ask a question."

"Of course," said Renny with a slight smile.

Vic continued, "As we made our way down the aisle toward the stage area, I thought I saw some movement near the scenery. As I was running up the rehearsal stairs, it definitely caught my attention. Now that I've been sitting here a while, I've been focusing on the wall of framed head shots. I wanted to ask Perry if any of the pictures have recently been switched around? I do believe something has changed or perhaps been removed. I just know that when I glanced at the headshots while we ran up the steps, the pictures were different than they are now."

Detective Clements looked over his shoulder at the wall of

headshots, "Do you think someone has rearranged the pictures? Substituted one photo for another?"

"I honestly couldn't tell you. I just know that they are different now," said Vic.

Chan stood up, "Nothing's been replaced on that wall. The headshots are hung exactly in their original positions. Maybe it was a trick of light in all the excitement—some movement on stage reflecting off the glass of the frames."

Vic walked nearer to the apron of the stage, "Detective, I make my living closely studying and memorizing visual imagery. I can swear something has been altered on that wall from the time when I ran up with Bettie and Tobin to check out the trap door till now."

"I'm not doubting your impressions at all, Vic, but I can assure you that all of the framed headshots are in their original configurations," declared Perry most emphatically, clearly on the verge of losing his composure.

"Did any of you share a similar perception?" Renny scanned the mystified faces of the assembled group. "Can someone offer a possible explanation?"

Bettie meekly admitted, "I'm afraid I was too preoccupied with reaching the trap door. I wasn't looking around at anything else."

"I will double-check my grid design for the headshots," Perry offered through clenched teeth, "but I'm certain nothing has been rearranged or removed."

Vic looked askance at the scenic designer and shrugged his shoulders.

Publicist Mark Rhodes, seated behind Bettie whispering droll comments in her ear throughout the proceedings, was next up.

"I was standing near the stage door exit talking with Celeste Farris and Mr. Quick. There was some activity around us, but I couldn't tell you exactly who was coming and going. I believe Lester, the doorman, had us in his sights the entire time—until we all heard the scream."

Renny Clements slid off the battered metal stool and grabbed his suit jacket from the floor, "I thank you all for your patience and your assistance. Please contact me if you think of anything noteworthy to add to your statements. I may be in touch soon for further questioning. You're free to leave the theatre."

The detective made his way downstage for a closer view at the wall of framed headshots. He was promptly aware that someone had joined him. They were now standing shoulder to shoulder. Without turning his head, Renny's gaze shifted sideways at Vic, who was leaning forward, intently studying the black and white images of the smiling actors' and actresses' faces.

Vic glanced over at the painfully handsome detective, "I'm not imagining it," the art director whispered, "Honestly, I'm not prone to hallucinations."

"No one claims you are," said Clements with a laugh, "Allow your thought-process a bit of time to gestate. When you decipher what you believe you saw, you can call me anytime of the day or night."

Vic mumbled aloud as he reflected, "I don't care what Perry Chan claims. How do you suppose someone could have switched one of these pictures without any of us noticing? And why would they?"

Scene Seven

Detective Clements walked downstairs to the trap room, now designated as the primary crime scene. The place was teeming with police officers, fingerprint and evidence technicians, forensic investigators, and homicide squad analysts. The judicial photographer was still at work snapping pictures of the deceased, including the areas near and around her lifeless body.

"You'll pardon the really terrible pun, but this entire scene looks staged," said Renny to his friend, Dr. Patrick Wheeler, the medical examiner.

Patrick was a big man. Big build, big smile, big heart, big talent. His trusty big black bag accompanied him almost everywhere. He moved around the room very quietly, exuding a genuine impression of expert calm.

"Well, I can tell you that the scene was deliberately constructed," the genial Dr. Wheeler reassured Renny, "The steel folding chairs, empty metal trash cans, random pieces from old drum sets, cymbals, anything it seems, that could create a great deal of commotion, was thrown into a huge pile underneath the trap door. I believe the forces of gravity took over when the victim dropped through into the haphazard position we now see here. The cymbals must've sliced into her neck as she fell into them. It actually seems as though she's purposely sitting in that huge broken drum."

"This room's normally used for random storage. Most of these items may have been here already. All the killer had to do was pile them under the trap door. I agree that it has the look of a bad burlesque sketch gone haywire," Renny observed, "Ms. Caldwell's crash through the drum skins resembles a broken, bloody doll thrown into the percussion section of a derelict orchestra."

Dr. Patrick Wheeler smiled, "Sounds as if these creative theatre types are rubbing off on you, Clements. That was most descriptive."

"I think the fact that it looks almost comical renders it even more horrific," the detective observed, "This crime scene makes me want to cry—and laugh."

"It's is an extremely malicious murder, more than most, I'd venture to guess. Our killer wanted the victim to look ridiculous—and has succeeded," amiable Dr. Wheeler pronounced. "At least the forensic photos will always be kept confidential."

Renny clicked his tongue. "I have a sickening feeling it's possible that several shots of this grizzly scene will somehow leak to the press."

"Why's that?" asked Dr. Wheeler.

"I suspect that the intended victim here was Helena Baxter. She's a famous Broadway star—and anything she does makes it into the news. Someone obviously has targeted her. There was a mass poisoning at her book announcement party two nights ago resulting in a homicide. I suppose, since that attempt failed to do her in, it's led to this tragedy," said Renny disgustedly.

"Simone Caldwell has often been mistaken for Miss Baxter, especially given certain lighting. I believe our killer thought it was Helena Baxter who'd been murdered. One of the first witnesses was theatre photographer, Terry Hagen. She was carrying her camera with her when she and some other folks discovered Ms. Caldwell's body. She took several pictures of the crime scene. Terry admitted to me not thirty minutes ago that her camera's since gone missing," the detective felt an ache in the pit of his stomach, "That camera being stolen does not bode well. There's only one noxious reason I can think of for it to have disappeared."

Dr. Wheeler said, "I hope you're wrong about that," as he continued with his work.

A young officer approached, "Detective Clements, there's a

man here who says he's a witness and has something important to give to you. I can't get rid of him."

Renny turned and peered across the dark storage chamber. He realized that it was Vic Senso who was anxiously waiting in the shadowed corner.

"Taking lessons from Ava Chasten, are you? How long have you been standing there?" the amused detective inquired.

Vic's lips curled into something resembling a nervous smile, "Funny thing. I pretty much followed you down here. I told Bettie and Tobin that I'd meet them later at the office. It's fascinating to witness an actual police procedural in person. Um, you weren't gone from the stage but a minute when I noticed this little item among the props on the set." Senso held out his Canon F-1 camera. "I figured it would be okay for me to handle it since my fingerprints would be all over the damned thing anyway."

"Did you check for the film?" Renny asked.

Vic said, "I thought I'd wait for you to do that. It'd be considered evidence, right?"

Procuring a pair of crumpled disposable vinyl gloves from the pocket of his suit, Renny suggested, "Let's find a dark room."

Briefly daydreaming about how much he'd enjoy hearing those words coming from the detective's mouth under different circumstances, Vic quickly snapped back to reality.

"After you'd walked away onstage, I glanced over at the desk that's positioned in front of the headshot wall," Vic quickly explained, "and there it was—my lost Canon—nestled among the typewriter, pencils, stapler, tape dispenser, tissue box, and other scenic props."

Renny found a small, dark washroom. Vic waited outside the door. It didn't take but a moment for the disappointed detective to emerge. "Well, it's empty. Someone's stolen the film," he announced. "This is bad. Very bad."

Vic was at a loss for words.

Clements handed the camera off to a passing policeman with the directive, "Bag this as evidence, officer."

As he began walking toward the trap room exit, Renny said, "I'm on my way upstairs to her dressing room to speak with Helena Baxter and Mr. Merchant. Vic, I'd appreciate it if you'd come along with me. I've heard you're somewhat of an expert on the scandal involving Miss Baxter about fifteen years ago. I learned about it just recently from Mr. Lockheed while at the hospital, although he seemed a bit sketchy on the details," said Renny.

Vic said, "I'd hardly call myself an expert. I do admit to being a true-crime enthusiast. Even as a kid, I was fascinated by jewel heists, kidnappings, and especially murder cases. On Sundays, the only section of the Daily News I was interested in reading, after tearing through the *Dick Tracy* and *Prince Valiant* comics, of course, was the week's special feature *Justice Story*. I couldn't resist soaking up articles with lurid titles like: *The California Chop-Chop Murder*, *The Killer Cowgirl*, and *My Headless Valentine*." Vic paused a moment and took a breath, "Am I scaring you, detective? Or worse, am I incriminating myself?"

"It sounds like a healthy teenage morbidity to me," Renny laughed, "Go on."

Vic continued confidently, "There are some sensational stories that stuck with me. The hoopla surrounding the Helena Baxter scandal is one of them. It involved everything I lived for—a glamorous Broadway star, mysterious circumstances at The Dakota, sudden death, and lots of bad publicity and outrageous speculation. I can vividly remember silly details—that the victim came from Norway...that Lauren Bacall was Helena Baxter's downstairs neighbor...that it was a ten-pound exercise dumbbell that fell from the seventh-floor window...I could go on."

The detective found it difficult to control his own enthusiasm, "I decided to visit the Public Library yesterday to see if I could dig up any other information on the case. Isn't it just about the most beautiful building in New York City?" mused Renny, "I spent most of my time in the microfiche reading room. They have millions of periodical back-files. It's incredibly impressive—almost intimidating. Surprisingly, the articles relating to the Helena Baxter case didn't contain a huge amount of detail about the accident itself. I venture to guess that you can remember more minutiae about the story than I learned doing all that research at the library."

"I have one question, Renny. Have you just unofficially appointed me as your 1) Dr. Watson, 2) Barney Fife, or 3) Ethel Mertz?" Vic inquired facetiously.

"Let's just refer to you as an 'expert' who's assisting me in this particular aspect of the investigation."

"Okay, that works for me, detective," declared Vic, smugly.

Renny said, "In a homicide, any information can prove vital. The more we learn about Helena Baxter, the more opportunity we have to deduce who might be targeting her—and for what reason."

"Not for anything, but it's Simone Caldwell who's been killed. How can you be certain Simone wasn't the intended victim to begin with?" Vic asked.

"She may very well have been—and I'm working that angle also. But, I strongly believe that between The Dakota incident resulting in Oskar Lindqvist's death, plus today's premeditated murder—it's all linked to Helena Baxter. Are you sure you feel comfortable helping me with this, Vic? I realize it's completely foreign territory for you."

The art director nodded his assent vigorously.

Renny knocked on the dressing room door and waited until he heard a voice call, "Come in," before entering.

Helena Baxter was seated at her dressing table holding a drink. A half-full bottle of Glenlivet scotch was close at hand. Her husband, Rex, was standing near a rack of costumes. He also had a glass of the malt whiskey clutched firmly in his grip.

"Greetings, detective," Helena Baxter said, "We've been waiting for you."

Clements motioned to Vic, "I believe you know Mr. Senso from Thompson & Co. I asked him to be here."

Both Helena Baxter and Rex were either too shell-shocked from the morning's events, too stoned, or too polite to ask why.

Instead, the actress nodded and motioned for the two tall men to take seats on her guest sofa.

"Rex and I have been listening to the report of my death on WINS Radio. Honestly, my obituary contains some of the best reviews I've ever received in my career. I sincerely hope the critics don't want to take it all back when they realize there's been a terrible case of mistaken identity." Helena Baxter sighed, cynically.

"Is Simone indeed dead, detective?" Rex asked meekly, hoping he'd waved away the lingering aroma of cannabis that had filled the dressing room earlier.

"Yes, I regret to tell you that Ms. Caldwell's been murdered. She fell through the trap door onto a pile of steel folding chairs, percussion instruments, and metal garbage cans that had been deliberately collected under the opening. Unfortunately, the sharp edge of a drum cymbal struck her neck." Renny explained gently in a subdued tone of voice.

"Bloody hell, why would anybody want to do this to Simone?" Helena Baxter moaned, angrily adopting one of her husband's preferred British expletives.

"That was one of the questions I was going to ask you," said the detective. "Did Ms. Caldwell have any enemies?"

"Ms. Caldwell kept pretty much to herself. She was an extremely private person. Truth be told, she lived a quiet, simple life with us at The Dakota. Our schedule is fairly regimented when my wife's doing a play," Rex explained, "We sleep in until about 10 o'clock, exercise, have a good breakfast, read the daily trade papers, get to the theatre, rehearse and/or grant interviews to the press, catch a brief nap in the dressing room, and then, it's all hands on deck for the 8 o'clock performance. If all went well of an evening, we'd go to a restaurant for a late night supper with friends. If things at the show were problematic, we'd go home, have a cocktail, and chill out instead."

"Did Simone have any romantic interests?" Renny asked.

"A few short-lived affairs over the years, but certainly nothing recently." Rex offered.

"I believe Ms. Caldwell was involved with you in the accidental death of a tourist some years ago. Can you tell me about that, please?"

Helena Baxter seemed prepared for that line of inquiry, "Most of the press hoopla surrounding that horrible scandal was, unfortunately, centered upon me. Although it was a regrettable series of events, the publicity relentlessly focused on the fact that I had placed two exercise dumbbells on my window ledge to support a screen I'd temporarily put in place of an air conditioner that had been sent out for repairs.

"As timing would have it, I was offered a part in a play in summer stock. I accepted and left Manhattan for a time to work in Westport, Connecticut. While I was gone, the air conditioner was fixed and ready to reinstall. My housekeeper, Caprice Fournier, wanted to clean the area first. She asked Simone to give her a hand. In moving the screen, one of the dumbbells was dislodged and fell from the seventh-floor window. It struck an unsuspecting tourist and killed him instantly. Although I was nowhere near the apartment, I was accused of what was erroneously reported as a homicide. It turned into a mass media feeding frenzy."

"I can well imagine," Renny sympathized, "How was it eventually resolved?"

"The widow was flown in from Norway with her child to identify the body. All that publicity made everything even worse. The media ran daily stories insinuating all sorts of ridiculous claims. Everything from my having an illicit love affair with this tourist whom I'd never met, to even more outlandish allegations of my having a relationship with his wife—compliments of the old French film, *Diabolique*—which had just been aired for the first time on network television in New York City. It's altogether too insane to even mention after so much time has passed."

"Do you recall the deceased man's name?" Renny asked.

"He had come to New York for some sort of convention. He was wearing an I.D. tag pinned to his shirt, which is why I remember it at all. Magnus. That was his name, Magnus."

"First name?"

"I have no idea what his first name was. I'm not sure I ever knew it," answered Helena Baxter, "But Mrs. Magnus was a force-of-nature. And a publicity hound. I never did find out what happened to their poor child. Such a horrible mother."

Renny asked, "The child, was it a boy or a girl?"

"As it happens, I don't know. I never saw the offspring. But, I believe it was a teenager, not a toddler," the actress said, taking a sip of her amber drink.

Clements stood to indicate imminent departure, with Vic following his lead. The detective asked, "I realize you and Mr. Merchant must have a million decisions to make about the show tonight. One last question, where were you today when you heard the scream?"

Rex seemed eager to respond, "I was just coming from a meeting with Celeste Farris and her husband. Arnie was giving them a tour of the theatre and the backstage area. We're co-producing a show here at the Hayes for next season and it's customary for the upcoming tenants to have a look around. Cal was with them. I'm afraid I was totally flying solo and on the way to join my wife in her dressing room when all hell broke loose."

"Did you see or notice anything suspicious beforehand?" the detective asked.

Rex shook his head, "No, not in the least."

Renny looked over at Helena Baxter, who was in mid-sip.

After a dramatic pause, the actress answered, "My alibi is equally as feeble, my dears. I was alone here in the dressing room doing my makeup for the photo session we were to have with Terry Hagen," Helena Baxter nodded toward Vic, "and the advertising agency. I seemed to have been the last to arrive on the scene. It took me a few minutes to throw on some clothing when I realized something horrible must have happened due to the sudden commotion."

"I trust you understand I will be contacting you again as the investigation progresses. Thank you for your cooperation." Clements opened the door and motioned for Vic to exit. Renny smiled and quickly followed him out.

Both the stage area and backstage corridors were still teeming with an active police presence. The Homicide Squad was being quite thorough.

"Do you have any plans for tomorrow?" the detective asked as he walked Vic toward the stage door exit.

Vic shrugged, "Saturday? Yes, my usual glamorous weekend routine—I sleep late and then clean my apartment. Why do you ask?"

"Would you mind joining me at the library in the morning? I have a feeling you'd be much more successful at this Helena Baxter research business than I've been. Certainly more familiar with which publications would be likely to have covered the scandal. I've never even heard of a *Justice Story.*" Renny confessed.

"I know this'll seem ghoulish, but it does sound like it'd be fun." Vic twisted his lip into a grin, "I do have one important question, however."

The detective arched his sublime eyebrows, and nervously blinked, "Which is…?"

"Where will you be taking me for breakfast?"

Scene Eight

When Vic arrived at his office fifteen minutes later, Bettie had already received panicked phone calls from the production's general manager and the press agent. The decision had been made by Helena Baxter to immediately drop out of the cast of *Don't Hang Up*. Following the aftermath of Simone's murder, the actress couldn't justify continuing with the play. She was suddenly incapable of controlling her nerves and was living in abject fear for her life. Helena Baxter didn't appear to be all that terrified when he and Renny spoke with her less than thirty minutes ago in the dressing room. Vic chalked up her elegant composure to good acting—and frequent sips from a tumbler of Glenlivet.

"The topper is that the show's not closing," Bettie announced, "Rex asked Celeste Farris to take over for his wife in the starring role. My guess is that ticket sales continue to be quite brisk, and that the producers want to avoid losing scads of money if at all possible. The plan is to cancel performances for the weekend and resume again on Tuesday the eleventh. They're not even pushing back opening night. It's still scheduled for Thursday the thirteenth. Apparently, Celeste Farris is a quick study. She was already familiar with the material. Rex had been giving them progress reports on the state of *Don't Hang Up* since he'd been spending a lot of time with her and her new husband discussing the show they're producing together next season. All three had partnered up a few weeks ago for *Blithe Spirit*."

"Excuse me, but isn't the stage at the Hayes considered a crime scene?" Vic asked.

Bettie was flipping pages on her desk calendar as she answered, "No, but getting anywhere near the trap room is strictly verboten, I expect. Maybe the producers have received special dispensation from The League, or from The Pope, or from Helen Hayes herself for all we know!"

"Unfortunately, it's back to the drawing board as far as the advertising is concerned," lamented Vic, "All of the approved newspaper layouts have just been rendered unusable. The window cards have to be reprinted with new star billing, the theatre marquee updated, as well as the *Playbill* title page reset, front-of-house displays redesigned—and that's just for starters. It's going to be a late night for me and the production department."

Marsha appeared holding a massive amount of phone messages for both Bettie and Vic. The receptionist had gotten some of Bettie's notes mixed up with Vic's. As a result, she spent several minutes awkwardly reorganizing the pink papers into two correct piles before distributing them. Marsha muttered, "Damn, there were a lot of calls," before scurrying away in the direction of her desk.

"I was going to ask her how Vito Lanzetta is doing—you know, nonchalantly, of course," Bettie said with a hint of mischief in her voice, "But, I didn't have the heart. Marsha looked like a frightened deer caught in the headlights. There's always the possibility that she would start crying, or worse, pass out cold in the middle of the office."

"Good thinking. We have no time for that drama right now," said Vic facetiously, "Our sweet little receptionist does seem nervous as a tick. We should definitely put her behavior on our list of suspicious things to investigate—after we find out who's responsible for the recent art theft, the mass poisoning, and, oh yeah, the homicides."

The door to Vic's office unexpectedly burst open.

"Prepare yourselves for a real media shit storm!" frazzled publicist Ava announced, barging onto the scene, "It appears that somebody leaked the photos of Simone Caldwell's dead body to the press. Worse…to the sleazy tabloid press. I might've been able to talk sense into *The New York Times* or *The Daily News*, but this is the type of sensational, disgusting story that *The Post* and *The National Enquirer* live to print. It's like a tidal wave—it cannot be stopped. Migraine City, people!"

Mark and Arne quickly followed behind, practically falling into the art director's office. The two men had been trying to corral Ava from aimlessly running amok throughout the Sardi building. Normally a bundle of nervous energy, the fact that someone maliciously released the scene of the crime photos threw the red-haired publicist into hyper-drive.

"It's so humiliating. Terry's pictures of the trap room look like still frames from a live-action Road Runner cartoon. She captured Simone in an unintentionally comical pose—splayed out, sitting in a broken drum having crashed through its skin. The only things missing are animated birds circling her head, chirping sound effects, and exes crossing out her eyes," Engels reported excitedly as he blew his nose. "Even her tongue is grotesquely protruding from her mouth."

"The press even acknowledges that although the scene was horrific, it ultimately emerges as macabrely humorous the more you look at it," added Mark. "Simone would be devastated."

"I hate sounding crass, but a corpse cannot be embarrassed by bad publicity," rationalized Ava, "We do have to contend with Helena Baxter's reputation, however. The fact that the media will be dredging up that old dumbbell murder story yet again—that's what's totally humiliating. She'll never shake that stigma after all this brouhaha hits the newspapers."

Ever the meticulous planner and level-headed general manager, Arne attempted to generate some order from the desperate panic that was beginning to permeate the small office space.

"Look. Let's get our acts together. It's already been decided that Helena Baxter is out of the show and that Celeste Farris will be her replacement. Bettie, can you please rework our media plan? Show us what you think we need to spend in order to tout our new star really quickly. I realize all the production charges will have to include overtime, but so be it. Vic, can you arrange for Terry to take pictures of Celeste as soon as humanly possible? The photos could be used for both press and advertising until we can produce an alternative campaign. Get your art and production departments to hunker down. There's lots of collateral material to redesign very quickly—including the front-of-house, theatre marquees, and the program title page. Ava, make a last-ditch effort to talk sense into the media. There has to be an editor among them who has a conscience and some sensitivity. Mark, please update Celeste Farris' bio for *Playbill*, and keep Ava from coming apart at the seams. I'm heading over to the Hayes to see what's doing there. Merchant and Quick are attempting to actually get some work done on revamping *Don't Hang Up* in order to reopen for previews on Tuesday. Godspeed, y'all."

Everyone immediately vanished to their respective posts just as quickly as they'd appeared. Vic dialed his phone and was holding his breath until Terry picked up her studio extension on the third ring.

"Terry here," she said breathlessly, only the sound of Tu-tu the chihuahua to be heard growling in the background.

"Hello, it's Vic Senso," said the art director hurriedly, "Are you free to meet me at Celeste Farris' apartment right away? I need you to take some shots that can temporarily serve as an interim advertising campaign until we design a new one. Ava will be using the shots for publicity as well. I've already spoken to Miss Farris. She'll make herself available in an hour at her place at the St. Regis on 55th Street. Do I sound duly harried?"

The photographer picked up on the urgency of the situation, "Hold yourself together, honey. Help is on the way. I'm already out the door, Vic—with my own camera this time," she joked lamely, "See you shortly."

It was a tossup for Vic and Bettie whether they should hail a taxi or briskly walk over to 55th Street from their offices. Midtown traffic, especially of the crosstown variety, could be particularly brutal on a weekday afternoon. On Fridays, in Times Square, it was typically proven to be godawful. Decision made—they started the trek.

The larger newsstands along their route were already displaying the late edition headline stories. Many of the tabloids were falling over themselves to correct the fact that they'd initially reported the wrong murder victim.

"Helena Baxter: Back from the Dead" —*The New York Times*
"Slaughter on West 46th Street"—*The Daily News*
"Understudy Sent to Undertaker"—*Newsday*
"Helena Baxter's Still Knocking Them Dead"—*The Post*

Each glaring front page headline was accompanied by a 4-column wide, black, and white, screened reproduction of the macabre Simone Caldwell murder scene. As they made their way uptown, then over toward the east side, Bettie and Vic observed passersby snickering at the grotesque crime scene pictures on full view for those thousands of pedestrians indulging in daily Manhattan foot traffic.

Bettie said quietly, "I can now understand why Helena Baxter has decided to remove herself from public display. This story is about as seriously ugly as it gets."

They walked across the vast St. Regis lobby to the elevators and rode up to the penthouse floor. Vic immediately recognized the woman who came to the door as Celeste Farris' secretary, whom he had only seen from a distance at Helena Baxter's ill-fated cocktail party. Her features were exquisite and her complexion was luminous. She was crisply dressed, and stunning.

"Miss Farris is expecting us." Vic said by way of introduction, "This is Bettie Balboa and I'm Vic Senso from the Thompson & Co advertising agency. We have an appointment."

"Please come in." The slender older woman stood gracefully at attention in her stylish black suit, her voice lilting, calming, and smooth as fine silk, "I'm Venus Pluto, her secretary. Can I get you something to drink? Coffee, perhaps? Her Majesty is still getting dressed and into makeup. She's been holed up all morning in the bedroom, woodshedding."

Vic and Bettie laughed as they took their seats in the elegant living room. "We're waiting for our esteemed photographer, who will hopefully be joining us shortly," explained Bettie.

"This awful murder is simply tragic," the secretary whispered in a conspiratorial tone as she threw herself on the sofa next to Bettie, "I understand you were both at the theatre when it …uh… happened this morning. I've met poor Simone a number of times lately because of *Blithe Spirit* going into production this Fall. You suppose there's a maniac on the loose? Do you think Celeste's life will be in any danger?"

"Don't get your hopes up, Venus. I'm sure I'll be perfectly safe at the Hayes," said Celeste Farris gliding into the room and delivering a true star entrance. "It's your coffee that just might kill me."

Vic stood and clutched the actress's ice-cold hand, "We cannot thank you enough for agreeing to do this today. I realize how shaken up you must feel."

"We're actually feeling no pain at the moment," Celeste Farris admitted, "Truth be told, Venus and I are as numb as zombies. We've been guzzling martinis ever since I got back from the theatre,"

"Oh my stars, we're soused alright," the secretary readily agreed, abandoning her semblance of quiet efficiency, "Her Majesty needed something to calm her jangled nerves. I haven't seen her in such a hysterical state since her wig got carried off on a prop spear on her opening night performance of *Medea*."

Celeste Farris bristled, "Dear Venus. She has the memory of a bull elephant and the mouth of a…"

The rest of her sentence was abruptly cut off when the doorbell rang and the barbed secretary precariously rose to respond.

From the nearby living room, Vic and Bettie could hear Terry at the front door announce, "I'm here to shoot Miss Farris."

"Shooting's too good for her," snapped Venus, "but come in anyway, honey."

Celeste Farris summoned a gratuitous smile as she greeted the photographer.

"The buzz on the street is that your pictures of Simone are plastered all over the front pages of the tabloid newspapers. It's simply unforgivable and cruel. Who do you think stole your camera?"

Terry blanched, "As you heard me tell Detective Clements, I honestly have no idea. I don't even remember putting the Canon down anywhere. It's making me sick to my stomach. I've always dreamed of my work being printed on the front page of The New York Times, but certainly not under such horrible circumstances."

"Venus, call downstairs and ask the concierge to send up all of the afternoon papers he can get his manicured hands on," barked Celeste Farris a bit too gleefully, "I'd like to assess the damage for myself."

"Yes, Your Majesty," said Venus, bowing multiple times as she precariously backed out the room.

The actress sauntered over to the largest window, "I suggest we shoot this thing before my makeup gives out and we lose this flattering afternoon light."

Suddenly struck with another train of thought, Celeste Farris asked, "By the way, have any of you seen or heard from Cal Lockheed? I've tried calling his apartment numerous times to no avail. Even his phone answering service cannot seem to track him down. Either he's found a new romantic interest, which could happen on a dime, or he'd decided to take a job out-of-town without telling his nearest and dearest friends."

Vic and Terry shrugged, shook their heads in the negative, and began working on getting the most out of the natural mid-afternoon glow. It reflected most flatteringly on the Broadway star as it flooded into the beautifully appointed hotel suite.

"If you don't mind my saying so, your secretary is a hoot," remarked Vic.

"We've been close friends for eons. Venus Pluto is actually her real name. Can you believe it? Everyone thinks she created it as a stage name," snorted Celeste Farris. "Her mother is an astronomer and her father is an astrologer who legally changed his last name to Pluto. I kid you not. The poor thing didn't stand a chance of being given a normal handle. Venus and I met over twenty years ago when we were featured as a burlesque comedy team in a lousy Broadway-bound musical that closed out-of-town."

Suddenly, a sultry voice projected from across the room, "The minute that turkey shut down, I decided not to keep kicking my legs over my head for a living," said Venus, again joining the group, having finished her phone call to the St. Regis concierge desk, "Cal was part of that company as well. The three of us bonded. For some godforsaken reason, Her Majesty and I remained the best of friends, more like sisters. We wanted to continue working together. Her career skyrocketed, and I became more comfortable dealing with the day-to-day details that make her life run as smoothly as possible. Don't get me wrong, I think stardom is terrific—but, only from a distance. I'm lucky enough to enjoy a lot of the perks of Her Majesty's celebrity without having to live under a microscope. Cigarette?"

"No smoking allowed while we're shooting," Celeste reminded them.

Venus casually took a seat on a lushly cushioned chair as she spoke directly to Terry Hagen, "A hint of a silvery haze might enhance the shots, honey. It all comes down to smoke and mirrors."

Vic was unexpectedly struck by the secretary's offhand comment. But, for the moment, he couldn't quite figure out why.

Scene NINE

Renny asked Vic to meet him at The Automat on Third Avenue and 42nd Street.

It was a far cry from the glamorous breakfast the art director was anticipating. However, it did offer him a final peek at a quickly vanishing piece of contemporary Manhattan life he was sure to miss when it was gone. The eatery was an immaculately clean, vast rectangular space filled with highly lacquered tables. A jaded, Camel-smoking cashier converted Renny's small wad of one-dollar bills into brass tokens. The detective could then drop them into a coin slot that would dispense anything from a corned beef sandwich to a massive wedge of lemon meringue pie.

"The sky's the limit this morning," joked Renny, "What's your pleasure?"

Vic smiled, "I noticed a huge slice of coconut layer cake that'd satisfy me to no end. It's been years since I've eaten cake for breakfast. So decadent."

The detective deftly slipped some tokens into the appropriate slot and rotated the porcelain-centered, art deco chrome-plated knob. Seconds later, the compartment next to the slot revolved into place to present a generous slice of cake through a small glass door that opened and closed. It was served on a sturdy Horn and Hardart plate that weighed more than the cake itself.

After Vic reached in and removed the coconut indulgence, a behind-the-machine staff member quickly slipped another piece of cake into the vacated chamber. It was a nifty bit of theatrical stage trickery performed without fanfare countless times daily at The Automat on Third Avenue.

They filled their cups with piping hot coffee. A precise amount came gushing out of the dispenser at an exactly calibrated temperature.

"These chrome dolphin-head spouts spitting out our hot beverage were modeled after a fountain found in the ruins of Pompeii," said Vic, as he carefully balanced his tray so as not to spill any of the dark steamy brew.

"You must know an awful lot about art," said Renny.

"Enough to make a living," Vic assured him, "Plus, I took quite a few Art History classes at Pratt Institute."

"My brother Rodney is quite knowledgeable about Fine Art, too. But, I'm not forgetting your impressive expertise involving true crime, either."

"That was strictly extracurricular studying," Vic smirked, as they scouted around for an isolated table, "After all, it's why we're on this research mission at the library on a Saturday morning."

"Let's maintain that's one of the reasons," Renny said, taking a seat.

"Could the other reason possibly be that you're testing the waters in order to hit on me?" Vic asked boldly, hoping he was correct.

"I wouldn't phrase it like that—but when you put it that way—yes?" It was still posed as a question.

Vic heaved an exaggerated sigh of relief. "You beat me to the punch, detective. I had every intention of coming on to you at some point during today's expedition. I realize we're living in an era of Gay Liberation, but I still believe it pays to be cautious in terms of outing yourself. After all, we both have our careers to consider."

"Working in theatrical advertising must be a much more relaxed atmosphere." Renny said, "It's show business, for goodness sake."

Vic leaned in closer. "You know, when I first got the job, I expected the office to be a highly flamboyant environment. Turns out, the agency is much more stodgy and traditional in terms of its executives and employees. Everyone pretty much keeps their personal life close to the vest. I'm happy to follow suit, but I'm tenacious in not hiding the fact that I'm a gay man. There's simply no need to advertise it at the office."

"We just don't discuss the topic at the precinct at all," said the detective.

Vic joked, "There was every possibility of you slapping me in handcuffs today after breakfast. I was determined to confess my lewd ulterior motive for helping out with your investigation. I much prefer this happy turn of events."

"I'm glad that's all settled," the detective laughed.

Renny had chosen an almond horn for his decadent breakfast extravagance. He was about to take his first bite and closed his eyes in sweet anticipation.

"That's about a thousand calories right there," Vic laughed, interrupting the detective's private reverie, "Not that you have to worry about that, of course."

"Believe me, I'm not going to lose any sleep over it." Renny said seriously, "I put in enough hours at the precinct gym to ward off any guilt."

"What's our game plan this morning?" Vic asked.

"I'd like us to collect as much detailed info as we can regarding the dumbbell story involving Helena Baxter. I've already submitted a request for the official police records from 1960, but it takes forever to get them sent over from wherever the hell they're stored. Some place in New Jersey, Pennsylvania, or Timbuktu, most likely."

"Do you really think it could be connected to what's going on now?"

Renny sighed, "I have a gut feeling that it might be. Someone's clearly targeting Helena Baxter. I suspect it could be connected to the one really awful event in her past for which she wasn't even responsible. It's a good enough place to start anyway."

"I've heard a rumor that her husband Rex might be having an affair with Celeste Farris," offered Vic.

"I typically keep a sharp eye on spouses in a case like this. My team's already maintaining a close watch on Mr. Merchant." Renny licked the tip of his finger and proceeded to gather the almond horn crumbs on his plate. He then slowly slipped his finger into his mouth to savor the last morsels of the pastry.

Vic was about to comment on the wondrous fact that the detective managed to momentarily transform a simple Automat breakfast into a sensual experience, but quickly thought better of it.

Renny took a sip of his coffee and asked, "Have you been able to work out how the framed headshots could have been switched on the scenery wall?"

"Something keeps nagging at me about that. On one hand, I have to believe that Perry Chan knows what he's talking about, but I can also remember feeling certain that one of the pictures had been moved or changed. I know my nerves were jangled and in a state of shock, but I still think the answer's on the tip of my tongue, so to speak. It'll probably pop into my head and wake me up from a deep sleep at four o'clock in the morning sometime."

"You'll let me know the minute you figure it out, right?" the detective suggested emphatically.

"My very first phone call will be to you—day or night," Vic promised.

Renny and Vic left The Automat and walked west across 42nd Street toward the library located on Fifth Avenue. It was a sunny Manhattan morning which provided perfect lighting for the main branch's Beaux-Arts architecture and ornate detailing. The entrance was flanked by a stalwart pair of stone lions that serve as the library's icon. The building had been rightly declared a National Historic Landmark just ten years before. It was one of Vic Senso's favorite places.

"Did you know that these lions have names?" Vic quizzed the detective.

Renny shook his head as they mounted the front staircase, "Can't say that I do, no."

"The one on the right is called Fortitude. The other one is Patience. They were named during The Depression in the 1930s by then Mayor LaGuardia."

"You should write the answers for that game show, *Jeopardy*. That'd be a good one," Renny smiled, "Time to get to work. Let's split up and see what details we can dig up about the notorious dumbbell incident. I'm going to head back to the microfiche room."

"Shall we meet in about two hours to compare notes?"

"Sure. Where do you suggest?" Renny asked.

"There's a fountain sculpture of Lady Godiva directly behind the Patience lion on the south side of the main entrance," he looked at his watch, "Since it's such a beautiful day outside, let's connect there at 1:30," proposed Vic.

"You certainly know a lot about fountain statues," laughed the detective, waving as he bolted up the interior staircase two steps at a time, "Happy hunting."

The vast Rose Reading Room was quietly bustling with activity. Vic spent the bulk of his time there. He eventually grew restless and needed to stretch his legs. Senso then ventured over to the Periodicals Room located on the first floor. The art director jotted down some detailed notes from the various news articles and gossip columns he'd unearthed. There was certainly no shortage of print media coverage of the story in 1960.

Pictures of Helena Baxter from some of her past movies and Broadway triumphs usually accompanied the commentaries. Vic did manage to find one photo of a distraught Caprice Fournier and Simone Caldwell taken near the ill-fated window at The Dakota. He hit pay dirt when he discovered one blurry picture of the victim, Mr. Magnus, made even fuzzier by the muddy newspaper screen required to print photo reproductions for tabloid publication. Vic asked one of the library staff to make a few Xerox copies for him, but he kept his requests at a minimum for $1.00 a pop. Before he knew it, a glance at his Bulova told him it was time to meet up with Renny Clements.

The detective had arrived at the appointed spot and was perched on the rim of the ornate fountain's base. He and Vic compared notes under the shadow cast by a pedestaled stone urn. Vic chose to lean up against the massive base of the Grecian replica as he organized his roughly scrawled notes and Xerox copies. They wedged themselves in a tight space between Lady Godiva and the enormous Greek replica. It provided as much privacy as they could possibly hope to achieve in public on 42nd Street and Fifth Avenue.

Vic enthusiastically began, "As they say in all the television murder mysteries, *'What have you got for me, detective?'*" After a brief pause, he added, "That's my way of asking, Renny, would you mind going first?"

"Not at all," said Clements, as he comfortably launched into his presentation of the facts he'd just uncovered. "I wanted to start by researching Oskar Lindqvist, the victim of The Dakota poisoning. Interestingly enough, I couldn't find any background material on him until he became an editor at Simon & Schuster. His description on their staff roster is quite brief. He was raised and educated in Europe where young Oskar acquired a great love of books and fine cuisine. Mr. Lindqvist has never been married. He'd been employed at the publishing house since 1970 and has edited several prestigious celebrity-oriented cookbooks. As far as I could tell, he's never had any encounters with theatre-types or Broadway in any capacity. His collaboration with Helena Baxter and Caprice Fournier appears to have been his first introduction into the world of the legitimate stage."

"I found nothing whatsoever on Oskar Lindqvist aside from a photograph of him and some literary types from a 1973 issue of *Intervista Magazine*," contributed Vic. "It was taken at a book launching for Graham Greene's *The Honorary Consul* at The Plaza Hotel. You'll be happy to know Mr. Lindqvist was wearing what appeared to be the same godawful tie he wore at Helena Baxter's soiree the other evening."

"That's…um…creepy. So, let's move on to Mr. Magnus. Considering all of the materials I read through, only a few articles actually referred to him by name. He was wearing an identification tag from the conference he'd been attending at The Plaza Hotel—hey, there's a possible connection there, but it's doubtful—and had it pinned to his jacket. Under the words **ICOM welcomes** printed in red Helvetica type, he'd written, in his own hand with a felt-tip marker: **Magnus.** The poor fellow was here from Oslo as a member of the International Council of Museums convention. ICOM is a non-governmental organization that partners with entities such as the World Customs Organization in order to carry out its international public service missions. These include protecting world cultural heritage in the event of natural or man-made disasters. It was only the second day of a four-day session. On his extended break, he chose to walk up Central Park West to become familiar with this unique area of Manhattan. Mr. Magnus' personal tour ended abruptly when he was hit on the head by Helena Baxter's falling exercise dumbbell as he approached The Dakota. Little did he know his death would become somewhat of a laughingstock in the Broadway community."

"Count Carl Magnus is the name of one of the main characters in *A Little Night Music*. It's a Stephen Sondheim-Hugh Wheeler musical that recently ended a long run at the Majestic Theatre," said Vic embarrassingly, "I apologize for being a big Broadway nerd, but it was a great show, and the name Carl Magnus stuck in my mind."

Senso leafed through the Xerox papers in his hand, "I found a photo of our Mr. Magnus from *The Village Voice*. It's not a very clear reproduction, but it's enough to give us an idea of what he looked like."

Renny squinted his ice-blue eyes and studied the picture for a few seconds, "When I first glanced at it, I thought he looked familiar, but it's gone now," he grudgingly admitted, handing the paper back to Vic.

"I know you feel his background will be of help," Vic said, "But, I believe Mr. Magnus himself was just a victim of circumstance—being at the wrong place at the wrong time. His wife, however, sounded like a real piece of work."

"What did you find out about her?" asked the detective.

"By the time the Widow Magnus flew here from Norway, she had already employed a high-powered lawyer. I get the impression that the grieving Mrs. M. immediately saw dollar signs when informed of her husband's accidental death and the involvement of a famous Broadway actress. It appears that she dragged her poor teenage child along with her to the United States to wring all the sympathy possible out of the tragic situation."

"Was the teenager a girl or a boy?"

Vic shrugged, "The media handles the identity of juveniles prudently. I really couldn't find any reference to the child's sex in any of the coverage. Only the age: fourteen. That'd make the little Magnus offspring about my age—twenty-eight or twenty-nine."

"And mine," added Renny.

Vic laughed, "Not to mention half the people we know. Right off the top of my head, I can name Perry Chan, Terry Hagen, Arnie Engels, Ava Chasten, and Mark Rhodes, who are all in that approximate age range."

"You're leaving out Bettie Balboa and Helena Baxter's young husband, Rex Merchant. Let's not forget our first murder victim, Oskar Lindqvist, who was poisoned at the cocktail party," said Renny.

"That's quite a long list if you really believe the murder is connected to the old dumbbell case and little Magnus junior. I suppose it's an extremely likely revenge scenario considering Caprice was involved in the poisonings as well as Ms. Caldwell," the art director said as he leaned in closer to the detective and pulled a sheet of paper from the stack in his hand, handing it over to Renny, "But, this is by far the most interesting thing I learned today."

Clements scanned the printed copy through his thick double-row of black eyelashes, and looked up wide-eyed, "Somehow, Helena Baxter forgot to tell us that the charming Mrs. Magnus was hounding her for a while after all the bad publicity. Following her everywhere she went, it seems."

"Enough so as to lead Helena Baxter to request a restraining order," said Vic.

"It says here it was soon after that the lawyers came to an agreement on suitable compensation for widow and child," read the detective.

Vic was clearly at home in this true crime mode, "We should find out where Mrs. Magnus is now. Did she go back to Oslo? Did she stay in New York City to make Helena Baxter's life miserable? Can she somehow be involved in Simone's murder?"

Renny crossed his fingers, "That's what I'm hoping the official police files will tell us—if and when they ever get delivered to me at the station."

"I don't know about you, but after all of this investigative research, I'm starving." Vic said, "How about you?"

The detective grimaced, "I feel like we've just had breakfast."

"I ate a slice of cake, Renny. And you, scarfed down a measly piece of pastry," Vic quickly gathered up his papers in an exaggerated huff, "Come on, I'll treat you to a proper lunch at Sardi's. But, since it's Saturday, I'm warning you, we may have to fight off a battalion of ravenous blue-haired matinee ladies to get in the door."

Scene Ten

Bettie phoned Vic on Sunday morning to get the low-down on the 'Library Caper,' as she playfully called it. She'd first made herself comfortable by pouring piping hot coffee into her favorite porcelain hand-painted cup. Bettie then sat up and leaned back on the cushy down pillow fluffed and positioned between her and the ornate honey oak headboard of her queen-size bed.

"So, spill the beans. Was Detective Clements brilliant?"

"I felt just like Dr. Watson lending a hand to Sherlock Holmes," Vic beamed.

"Knowing you, I'm guessing it was probably more like an episode of *The Snoop Sisters*," chided Bettie laughingly, as she lit a cigarette, "What'd you find out?"

Vic filled her in on the information he and Renny had uncovered, including the restraining order that Helena Baxter requested because of the creepy Mrs. Magnus…confirmation that the hapless victim came from Oslo, to be exact…'We even found a blurry picture of him from *The Voice*!'…and that the tragic Norwegian visitor was in New York City as part of the International Council of Museums convention… oh, yeah, also at the time of the father's accidental death, Magnus, Jr. (sex yet to be determined) was fourteen years of age."

"The widow was following Helena Baxter around? Do you think that twisted Mrs. Magnus could possibly still be in Manhattan?" Bettie asked.

"Renny's hoping that that information will be included in the police files."

Bettie sounded smugly confident, "In case you think you're the only resident sleuth on the case, I've got a bit of investigative insight for you, following another trail. Our yappy lobby attendant, Guy Andersen, told me something terribly interesting along with his usual star-struck list of celebrity sightings and blind items. He whispered on the Q.T. that Helena Baxter has been a frequent visitor lately to the Sardi building—and it isn't for the cannelloni. Guy seriously believes she's making her way to one of the upper offices under the guise of catching a bite to eat at the second floor restaurant between gigs. I think she's having an affair. Andersen agrees—and he's got a keen nose for situations like this."

Vic baited, "Perhaps it's for some totally innocent reason. She may be shopping around for a new agent and doesn't want anyone to know."

"My women's intuition is telling me otherwise," Bettie took a deep puff on her Virginia Slims.

He could hear her triumphant inhaling of the slender cigarette and could imagine that exquisite face surrounded by the eventual release of hazy smoke.

"I suppose anything's possible." Vic laughed, "Especially this week when much crazier things have already happened."

"Maybe Helena Baxter was trying to poison her hubby at their own cocktail party and the plan somehow went awry? Oskar Lindqvist died instead." Bettie suggested.

Vic wasn't convinced, "So how do you explain Simone's murder?"

"Simone might've seen her boss administer the arsenic and was blackmailing her. You have to admit, that's a distinct possibility."

"Playing devil's advocate, I gave speculation to a couple of other possibilities I haven't shared with anyone," Vic told Bettie hesitantly, "1) That Helena Baxter herself, after years of unsavory publicity, finally snaps and takes revenge on the two women who are ultimately responsible for Mr. Magnus' death—Simone, by killing her, and Caprice, by hanging the specter of poisoner over her head now and forever. 2) That Rex's first attempt to kill his wife at the cocktail party had disastrous results, and afterward, in a second attempt, he mistakenly identifies Simone Caldwell as Helena Baxter in executing the trap door murder. Rex really can't account for his whereabouts in the theatre during the time leading up to the homicide. 3) That either the widow and/or offspring of Mr. Magnus from Oslo are at long last seeking revenge for his untimely death by flying dumbbell."

There was a brief lull in the conversation while each of them collected and processed those possibilities. Bettie finally broke the silence, going off on yet another tangent.

"Venus called a few moments before I phoned you. Celeste Farris has requested our attendance at the Helen Hayes for their first full run-through of *Don't Hang Up* this afternoon. The schedule is absolutely breakneck. Today, there's the first complete run-through. Tomorrow, the final dress rehearsal with an invited house, and Tuesday the show has its first performance—with the new leading lady—for a sold-out audience. Matinee and evening shows on Wednesday, then it's opening night on Thursday."

"The mind boggles!" Vic theatrically exclaimed adding, in a normal tone of voice, "Have you heard anything from Copcake about the Chagall?"

Bettie answered, "Not a peep."

"What time's the run-through today?"

"It's scheduled to start around five o'clock. Want to go together, or are you bringing a date?"

Vic hesitated for a moment, "I think I'll ask Detective Clements if he'd be interested in being there. How about you?"

"I'll be sitting with Mark," Bettie told him. "I spoke with Tobin earlier and he declined. It'd be a bit of a schlepp for him coming in from Westchester."

"What's doing with you and Mark anyway?" Vic asked.

"Nothing really. I enjoy his company and I think the feeling's mutual."

"You'd make beautiful babies."

"That's putting the cart well before the horse, Mrs. Levi." Bettie admonished.

Vic laughed, "Just a suggestion from the future godfather."

Bettie volleyed back with, "Any sparks between you and Detective Dreamy? Do you think he's straight?"

"I'm typically awful at figuring out the sexual inclinations of the guys that I'm attracted to. My tried-and-true test on borderline cases is to check out their shoes. So far, Renny has only worn classic loafers which, as we all know, are the asexual pump of choice. He's definitely playing it safe."

"It gives us something else exciting to investigate. Perhaps I'll interrogate Copcake one of these evenings," said Bettie.

"Don't you dare. I would like to crack the case myself. I've already started laying the groundwork. Besides, the unnaturally handsome Rodney Clements has only been seen wearing thigh high black leather boots. We all know what that usually means," Vic teased the advertising executive, "Marquis de Sade chic."

"He's a policeman who rides a horse. It's part of his uniform, dopey. What would you expect him to wear—clogs?" scoffed Bettie.

"What type of shoes did he have on when you took him to the theatre?"

Bettie shrugged on her end of the line, "Believe it or not, I didn't spend a minute checking out his footwear. Those dreamy blue eyes of his are hypnotic."

"Oh, well, there's always next time," suggested Vic.

"So, I'll see you at the Helen Hayes this afternoon?"

Vic brayed, "Wild horses couldn't keep me away! Celeste Farris taking over for Helena Baxter is a monumental chapter of theatre-history-in-the-making. My gay card would be immediately revoked if I dare miss it!"

There were about thirty people seated in the audience to witness the revamping of *Don't Hang Up*—all were close friends of the star and/or working on the production. Vic was sitting between Perry and Renny in row D alongside Bettie and publicist Mark Rhodes. Behind them were blatant canoodlers Ava Chasten and Arne Engels. Helena Baxter's director-husband Rex was prepared to take notes and chose to take up temporary residence in K107, the dead center of the orchestra. Co-producer Earl Quick darted over to the same section and ensconced himself one seat away from Rex. Thin and stately Venus took an aisle position in row B. Terry was in attendance as well, moving from section to section in order to consider the best angles. She would be shooting production stills during the final dress rehearsal scheduled for the next day, Monday.

Two recent additions to the list of *Don't Hang Up* employees were Celeste Farris' newly-hired bodyguards, John Elmo, and the equally imposing John Sylvester. They were stationed on either side of the proscenium for the performance. Both were built like football linebackers and were neatly packed into solid gray wool suits. John Elmo was black, had a perfectly coifed afro, and possessed smoldering good looks. John Sylvester was white, with a blond buzz-cut, and had an angular face that was born to be plastered on cereal boxes.

"They are the salt and pepper dispensers of personal security." Vic observed. "Where in the world did Celeste Farris find them—central casting?"

Ava, sitting directly behind Vic, momentarily released herself from Arne's attentions and leaned forward in her seat, "Aren't they divine? A movie star client of mine hired them last year. The two Johns always make for an interesting background in candid paparazzi shots."

"Speaking of shots. Vic, have you given up on your idea that the headshots were switched on the wall of my set?" asked Perry pointing up at his scenery, "I double-checked my sketches. Nothing's been tampered with there."

"Sorry to sound like a broken record, Perry, but I'm convinced something had been changed around or perhaps been removed. I know that when I glanced at the headshots while running up the rehearsal steps the day of the murder, my impression was that the pictures were different somehow than they are now," Vic remained adamant.

Renny chimed in, "As I've told you before, my advice is to relax about it. Whatever it is will come to you when you least expect it." The detective gave Vic a reassuring pat on the thigh.

Bettie caught the friendly gesture, attracted Vic's attention by comically pursing her lips and rapidly batting her eyelashes, "I totally agree with you, Renny," she purred.

Earl Quick rose from his seat and mounted the rehearsal stairs, taking center stage. The theatrical lighting gave his massive mane of wavy silver hair an unnatural shimmer. He waited for the mild buzz of conversation to die down.

"Thank you, friends, and family, for lending your support to one of Broadway's greatest stars in her incredibly courageous endeavor to keep *Don't Hang Up* on the boards. As you know, due to the tragic death of Simone Caldwell, Miss Helena Baxter has decided to drop out of the production. My incredible wife, Celeste Farris, has been woodshedding and working tirelessly with her director, Rex Merchant, in order to keep to our schedule of opening for critical review this coming Thursday evening. This afternoon will be her first full dress performance. Enjoy the show."

With that, Quick darted back down the stairs to his seat in row K as the small audience of thirty applauded wildly.

The play began. Celeste Farris, the stage professional, looked at ease, as if she'd been performing the role for weeks. The run-through was proceeding without a hitch—although Vic would hardly have been a good person to ask. The art director was fixated on the wall of headshots. His attention would sporadically revert to the progress of the performance, but truth be told, the puzzle of the possibly switched framed photos obsessed Vic enough to border on utter distraction.

To add to his recollection of the event, he was now vaguely aware that as they ran up the rehearsal steps, he detected movement from behind the scenery wall facing the headshots. Maybe it was a reflection off the glass, but Vic was now mindful of the impression that someone had been lurking there. Of course, the awful discovery of the open trap door and catching sight of Simone's dead body abruptly stole all of his attention. In the ensuing chaos, the art director focused his gaze elsewhere. He decided to take Renny's advice and put it out of his thoughts.

Now having seen *Don't Hang Up* a number of times, Vic watched as Celeste Farris gave the role of the jaded agent a slightly harder edge, proving most effective when pitted against her supporting cast of characters. Celeste Farris lent her portrayal a vivid strength that slowly begins to deteriorate when an unhinged actor-client in the play confronts the agent in her isolated office. It was difficult to believe that the actress hadn't been studying the role for weeks.

Perhaps Rex, the British wunderkind, aware of his wife's mounting fragility, suggested to his new co-producers that Helena Baxter could likely drop out of the production? Although the play itself had its weak points, the leading part was a plum vehicle for any actress worth her salt. Celeste Farris, if offered the role, wouldn't foolishly let an opportunity like that pass her by.

The jarring sound of surrounding applause snapped Vic out of his daydreaming. Act One had just ended. Even The Johns were wildly clapping.

Act Two proved to be in even better shape. The curtain came down on the afternoon run-through to an enthusiastic, albeit limited, audience. Director Rex Merchant wanted to change the blocking of the curtain call, so the invited audience was deprived of that bit of business.

Celeste Farris did step forward to thank everyone for their support. A slightly stoned and bloodshot Rex joined her center stage and clasped her hand.

"If you're up to it," the director announced to the intimate group, "Please join my wife and me around 8pm at The Dakota for some celebratory champagne and a toast to our new leading lady. We'll dispense with hors d'oeuvres—for obvious reasons."

A smattering of awkward laughter ensued before Rex continued.

"However, they'll be plenty of pretzels and chips served straight out of the box."

Arne Engels exited the theatre well before the rest of the crowd. He was heading uptown to lend a hand to Helena Baxter and Caprice before the onslaught of thirty-or-so thirsty guests. Silently tolerating Ava's annoying supervision, Terry was snapping a few publicity pictures of Celeste Farris and her director, Rex. Quick stepped in to join them for some shots of the happy threesome with stage scenery as background.

Ava hoped to quickly send the photographs over to Liz Smith, by messenger, to run in her column's early edition. Terry'd even hired an assistant to stand by. After shooting a complete role of film, she handed the Kodak canister off to her energetic apprentice for processing, printing, and delivery. Terry was not about to miss out on another Helena Baxter bash at The Dakota.

When Arne arrived at Helena Baxter's apartment, Caprice answered the door looking distressed. The housekeeper was muttering random phrases, not quite full sentences, with Arne catching various snippets, "...going to blame me forever...what can I tell them...*les saints me protégent*...Simone wanted to find out more..."

Arne took hold of her trembling shoulders gently, "Caprice, what's happened? You look terrible, are you alright? Where's Helena?"

It took the housekeeper a few moments to snap out of her dream state.

"She's still getting dressed," Caprice answered slowly, "I don't know how Rex can subject her to a situation like this. Inviting his wife's worst enemy here to celebrate taking over a role Miss Baxter's originated. It's mental cruelty, it's sadistic is what it is. Everyone thinks he's so *jovial* all the time. Rex Merchant is a narcissistic monster."

"That's enough, Caprice!" shouted Helena Baxter, emerging from the direction of her bedroom, "It's going to be a difficult enough evening to get through without your caterwauling."

Arne noted that the Broadway star looked none the worse for wear. In fact, Helena Baxter appeared ravishing in a deep green cocktail dress.

"I think it best if you retire to your bedroom, Caprice. I will tell you about the party tomorrow morning at breakfast. The stress of the last week is taking its toll on you," observed Helena Baxter, "Now that Arnie's here to pitch in, we can certainly handle the gathering tonight. It's simply uncorking bottles of a semi-decent champagne, arranging some Mister Salty pretzel sticks and Planter's potato chips served directly out of the box. Heaven help us for consenting to that repulsive suggestion from Ava Chasten, who probably hasn't thrown a party since 1968."

Helena Baxter accompanied Caprice across the vast living room and down the hallway to the housekeeper's bedroom. Arne watched them open the door and go in together. Helena Baxter lingered there for ten minutes before she emerged. The actress was dabbing her forehead with a lace hanky and smoothing out the front of her gown in preparation for the onslaught of guests.

The general manager gently placed his arm around her waist and guided her toward one of the plush sofas. Arne nuzzled his face in her hair and softly kissed her neck. Helena Baxter leaned into the cozy and affectionate gesture as she straightened his elegant silk tie.

He whispered, "Honestly, I can handle all this until Rex and Earl get here to help. Why don't you sit down and I'll fix you a drink," Arne suggested, "It's Glenlivet on the rocks, right?"

Helena Baxter gratefully took the general manager up on his offer.

"Oh, Arnie, I am totally exhausted. What the hell was Rex thinking?"

"I'm not sure thinking of any kind was involved at all, knowing your genius pot head husband." Engels said, as he stacked some vinyl albums on the Stereo system record player, "I'll just put on some easy-listening cocktail music. It always helps fill the void."

Helena Baxter leaned her head back on the plush *Louis Quatorze* sofa. She took a few sips of her drink and drifted off. In less than fifteen minutes, The Dakota sentry booth gatekeeper announced the arrival of the Helen Hayes Theatre contingent.

It wasn't long before everyone had shown up. The celebration was proceeding full throttle, with raucous laughter, theatre war stories told, and general Broadway chitchat filling the smoke-filled atmosphere.

Celeste Farris, arriving last, made a sufficiently grand entrance. Wearing a gold sequined cocktail dress, she swanned her way into the room to thunderous hoots and applause from the enthusiastic guests. John Elmo and John Sylvester stood staunchly behind her the entire evening, shadowing her every move.

"I approve of their muscles," joked Perry Chan, as an aside to Vic.

Helena Baxter was first to greet Celeste Farris at the door, "I'm told it went splendidly. How wonderful for you, my dear."

Terry was shooting candid shots around the room, still being hounded by Ava, "Call your assistant and find out if Liz Smith received those prints yet."

Unfortunately for him, Detective Renny Clements had to report back to work, and sadly begged off attending the event.

Surprisingly, Tobin showed up for a quick drink and to offer his heartfelt congratulations. As usual, the creative director offered apologies ahead of time for having to leave early due to a previously scheduled engagement. He and his equally elusive wife, Olga, were expected at a neighbor's birthday celebration.

Venus had quickly latched on to Vic and Perry with the explanation, "Honey, I always make it a point to talk to the handsomest men in the room at these affairs. The conversations may not be any more stimulating, but the gorgeous view is guaranteed to hold my attention."

Both Rex and Earl were playing it low key, amidst the crowd of theatrical revelers, and remained very much in the background quietly chatting on a remotely placed settee.

Arne, having donned a chef's bib apron for comic effect, was hunched over the Mister Salty pretzels and Planter's potato chips set-up, meticulously fussing with finishing touches.

As is typical with any cocktail party involving Broadway types, networking was in high gear. The guests moved about the spacious apartment willy nilly and sought out sundry conversations in which to take part.

A quick survey of the room during various times that evening found Ava Chasten trading gossip with Celeste Farris while The Johns eavesdropped with rapt attention…Rex and Tobin could be heard laughing unnecessarily loudly at several of Venus's off-color burlesque reminiscences as they passed around a joint…Mark was suavely chatting up Helena Baxter…Vic was in a serious huddle with Terry who'd stashed her camera on a table in the foyer and was enjoying a cocktail…and Bettie was getting an earful from Perry.

The celebratory sound of popping champagne corks could be heard periodically throughout the evening. The bubbly booms intermittently brought applause, cheers, and impromptu toasts from several of the Theatre Elite. The needle was abruptly lifted from the Stereo record player. Although Simone Caldwell was no longer there to sit at the piano, an endless line of talent was on display, as each able entertainer took a turn playing a show tune.

Later in the evening, Bettie was admiring the panoramic view of Central Park with Mark. She was getting the impression that he wanted to ask her out, but something was holding him back. They sat on a divan positioned near the window. Mark leaned forward and was tapping on the glass of the goldfish bowl. Bettie turned to take a cigarette out of her purse and caught sight of what she knew to be Caprice's bedroom door. It was slightly ajar. No one came out.

"I hear Mademoiselle Fournier has been a complete nervous wreck over everything that's been happening." Bettie lit her Virginia Slim as she continued, "More so even than Helena Baxter herself. Um…Mark, you shouldn't tap on the glass like that, you know."

Mark smiled and shrugged, "Why not? I just want to say hello to the little guys."

"Their names are Adam and Eve. Tapping on the glass is a big no-no. It scares and disorients the poor fish. It causes them to swim away from the noise and hide even more," said Bettie peering down into the crystal-clear water.

"I didn't realize I was sitting next to Jacques Cousteau." Mark snorted.

"My older sister and I had an aquarium when we were kids," explained Bettie.

Having abandoned his apron, Arne abruptly appeared and lifted the fishbowl from its place on the table, "Helena Baxter would not approve of you frightening her pets. Everyone's nerves are jangled enough around here already."

Bettie and Mark snickered. They noticed that Arne looked over in the direction of Caprice's bedroom as he spoke. He managed to utter, "Oh, damn!" as he shifted the angle of the bowl to maintain balance since it was an awkward object to carry, and its smooth surface quite slippery to hold on to.

Arne couldn't continue his juggling act for long. The bowl tipped over, capsizing itself so that the water sloshed all over him as it went crashing to the floor. Some of the liquid splashed onto Mark and Bettie as well.

"Oh, no—Adam and Eve!" screeched Helena Baxter from across the room.

Almost immediately, Rex burst out through the kitchen door clutching a roll of paper towels. He was followed by Earl Quick, who was gingerly balancing an exquisite replacement fishbowl filled with water as he crossed the room. Vic and Perry appeared next armed with a dustpan and broom.

"It's a frigging fish triage," squealed Ava.

Several of the guests successfully pitched in to rescue Adam and Eve. The golden couple were carefully scooped up from the floor and safely deposited in the fresh glass vessel. The fishbowl hadn't shattered into too many fragments. It was fairly easy for Vic and Perry to collect and dispose of the dangerous shards.

"What the hell happened, Arnie?" Helena Baxter asked, while anxiously checking on the status of Adam and Eve in their new residence.

"Just a freak accident. I wanted to move the fishbowl to a safer spot and it slipped out of my hands. I'm totally drenched. I've got to dry myself off in the bathroom. Excuse me." Engels quickly darted away in that direction.

"I think something startled him," said Bettie, as she dabbed at a few random wet areas of her dress with a cocktail napkin, "Arnie was looking down the hallway and seemed to be taken by surprise."

Ava remarked, "Thank goodness those idiot goldfish survived. The last thing Helena Baxter needs right now is another fatality at The Dakota."

Scene Eleven

Bettie arrived for work at Thompson & Co an hour earlier than usual on Monday morning. Marsha had just finished folding an oversized shopping bag and was settling into her desk chair. The receptionist looked startled when the elevator door opened with a metallic clang.

"Wow, you're here early, Bettie," she said.

"I have lots of work to catch up on. Where's Vito this morning?"

Marsha motioned with her head, "He's in the men's room."

The account executive walked briskly to her private office. It was too early to make business calls—no one in the theatre industry began their workday until close to ten o'clock. There were only a few scattered phone messages left over from Friday, so Bettie decided to attack the pile of papers stacked in her IN box. After a few minutes, she became aware of someone standing in the doorway. It was Vic, looking befuddled.

"Still recovering from another action-packed Dakota party?" Bettie asked.

Vic put out his hand, "Would you please come with me? I think I'm going mad."

With an invitation like that, thought Bettie, *how could she refuse?*

Senso hurriedly dragged her by the hand through the deserted production department. The door to the art archives room stood ajar. He pushed it open the rest of the way.

Bettie started to walk in and immediately saw it. She gasped.

"Oh, my god, the Chagall is back!" she uttered breathlessly.

The painting was once again propped up on the display poster rail and illuminated by the overhead canister light.

"Well, if you're crazy, I am as well," muttered Bettie.

Vic rubbed his eyes, "I'm not hallucinating then. It is *really* there?"

Bettie nodded her head, "We should phone Copcake right away. He'll be thrilled to hear about this."

"You make the call," said Vic, "I'm not leaving this room until Rodney gets here and sees this with his own eyes."

Bettie turned to walk back to her office. She called over her shoulder, "Maybe the lingering fragrance of Paco Rabanne will have evaporated by then."

Vic sniffed the air as he leaned up against one of the vertical storage racks to wait.

The Thompson & Co offices had come fully alive with arriving employees conducting the business of advertising Broadway by the time Officer Rodney Clements made his way to the Sardi building. Marsha nervously announced his arrival.

Rodney was awestruck looking at the canvas, "You say you just found it here again this morning? No explanation or idea where it's been or who put it back?"

Vic looked guiltily over at Bettie. He took a deep breath.

"Can we please go into the conference room to finish this conversation?" he asked gently, securely locking the door to the art archives.

Vic led the way through the bustling production department to the quiet conference room. Once Copcake was seated at the table and the door closed, Vic awkwardly began, "First, let me ask that what I'm about to tell you go no further than this room. Bettie and I are not exactly sure what's been going on, but we have a strong suspicion about who might have just brought the Chagall back."

"I'm listening," Rodney said patiently.

In turn, Bettie and Vic explained about their receptionist's boyfriend, Vito Lanzetta, whom they felt could possibly have ties to organized crime on a low level.

"Do you think that Mr. Lanzetta removed the painting on Friday? Possibly to show it to his...um... bosses?" Copcake asked.

"I think he may have taken it after eavesdropping on you and Bettie discussing the Chagall in our reception area last week. Vito might have become aware of its potential monetary value to his underworld network of petty Staten Island mobsters." Vic surmised.

"But then, I'm puzzled, Vic," Bettie asked, "Why would he return it?"

Rodney Clements listened most attentively before responding, "I think I may perhaps have an answer to that. As we told you, this Marc Chagall masterpiece was stolen in a bold art heist at the Neils van de Velde Museet in Oslo in 1957. There have been a number of leads over the years that have taken the investigation across the globe. Interpol agents have been tracking down its possible whereabouts from Cairo to Ireland and from Paris to Saudi Arabia. It was determined, a number of years ago, that the painting ended up here in the United States, with reported sightings at various times in Maine, Philadelphia, and New York City. That's when Special Investigator Volpe and his NYPD Art Theft Unit became involved."

Bettie and Vic listened with rapt attention as Rodney spoke.

"Experience has proven that when a painting by an artist as famous as Marc Chagall is stolen, it doesn't take terribly long for the thieves involved to realize that the merchandise they've robbed is too hot to handle. In other words, hoodlums that employ the traditional avenues of illegal sale and trading are too savvy to get themselves entangled with such highly volatile property."

Rodney leaned forward with his hands clasped on the table, "Even notorious private collectors would seriously think twice before purchasing a stolen Picasso or a Dali or, in this case, a Chagall.

"This led the Art Theft Detail to begin investigating another train of thought. Certain underworld characters in the United States became aware that sharing knowledge of a painting's location could often be viewed as collateral to bargain down the lengthy prison sentences being served by some of their more prominent members in institutions across the country.

"Helpful tips and information involving the whereabouts of stolen masterworks offered to Interpol, or to related agencies such as the World Customs Organization and World Intellectual Property Organization, can be used as another means of exchange. Working in conjunction with the FBI and other law enforcement agencies, not too long ago, the recovery of a lost Matisse canvas procured the release from prison of a prominent Boston mob leader. You can see the value to be had from obtaining inside information."

"At a considerable price—releasing a mobster," noted Bettie.

"It's a matter of weighing the value and gravity of one criminal offense against another, yes." Copcake assured his friend, "It's not an easy nor necessarily a pleasant thing to do. But, it's totally above board and legal."

Vic remained silent throughout Rodney's commentary, shifting in his seat from time to time.

"Now that the painting has been safely recovered, would we have to involve Vito, or mention his name at all? Clearly, he did nothing other than to 'borrow' the Chagall for the weekend. We may never know whatever happened for him to risk bringing it back here. Actually, none of us were even totally certain it was the original canvas and not an expert forgery," the art director said, "I certainly can't pretend to know the protocol for this type of thing. We just wouldn't want our receptionist's boyfriend to get into serious hot water. He's actually a nice guy."

Officer Rodney Clements rose from his seat and sighed, "First things first, Vic. Let's get the Chagall back in the hands of Special Investigator Volpe and the proper authorities. Then we can decide what we should do about involving or questioning Mr. Lanzetta."

Vic and Bettie traded knowing glances.

"Can we ask you to stay for just another minute?" Vic and Bettie appeared agitated enough to cause Rodney to again take his seat at the table.

"As you've no doubt have heard from your brother, there was a brutal murder committed the other day at the Helen Hayes Theatre involving some of our clients. The homicide occurred shortly after the poisoning at Helena Baxter's cocktail party, in which a book publisher died. Renny believes this series of awful events harken back to an accidental death from 1960." Although he was explaining it, Vic thought it all sounded so outlandish.

Bettie jumped in, "These incidents may be connected, or perhaps they may be a wild coincidence, but the man who was accidentally killed in 1960 was visiting here from Oslo. And he was in Manhattan to attend a conference for the International Council of Museums. His name was Mr. Magnus."

"Please allow me to regress a bit and quickly fill you in on the background as we know it," Vic began hurriedly.

The art director informed Copcake of The Dakota dumbbell incident back in 1960, as well as Helena Baxter's unpleasant involvement with Mr. Magnus and his widow.

Bettie, caught up in the intrigue, explained, "Obviously, because of his affiliation with the International Council of Museums, it's quite possible that Mr. Magnus was somehow closely connected to Oslo's Fine Art network. I realize it doesn't nearly begin to solve the mystery of how a stolen original Chagall painting ended up in our offices, but it strongly suggests there could be a viable connection between Mr. Magnus, Helena Baxter, the Neils van de Velde Museum, our art archives, and the recent homicides. Other than inadvertently eavesdropping on you and me in the reception area, I cannot imagine Vito's involvement in any of this business. It's possible that when he heard of its potential value, he attempted and failed to fence the painting through his low-level underworld network. At least, Vito was diligent enough to return the Chagall, which we had all assumed was most likely a masterful forgery at best."

"You say that Mr. Magnus worked at the museum in Oslo?" Rodney asked.

Vic responded, "We haven't a clue. Renny's waiting to receive the original police files from 1960. We're hoping they will contain some vital missing details."

"What was Mr. Magnus' first name?" Copcake asked.

"The conference name tag he was wearing simply read MAGNUS. Helena Baxter doesn't remember his first name. That's one of the pieces of information we're counting on the police files to supply. I realize Magnus is a common surname in Norway."

Rodney Clements sat completely nonplussed for a moment.

"This does appear altogether too bizarre to simply be coincidental. Volpe and some officers are on their way down here now. Let me talk with him about the situation when we get back to the precinct. I'll keep you in the loop concerning any relevant information we can uncover regarding Mr. Magnus' connection to the Neils van de Velde Museet in Oslo. I can fully understand why you suspect there might be some possible links between these two cases."

As a group, they walked soberly back to the art archives room where they waited for the man in charge of the Art Theft Detail. Upon his arrival, Special Investigator Volpe carefully collected and encased the lost Chagall.

Accompanied by another officer, Volpe took the elevator to the lobby along with the priceless canvas. They climbed into a waiting police car double-parked in front of the Sardi building.

Rodney, Bettie, and Vic stood silently in the Thompson & Co reception area.

Bettie breathlessly put her hands on her head, "My goodness, are we dreaming?"

Vic attempted a bit of levity in response, "I ask you, whoever said working in advertising was dull?"

Rodney unexpectedly leaned in and kissed Bettie.

"I cannot thank you enough for all you've done," he said as he entered the elevator.

After the lift had closed and the officer was safely out of range, Vic jokingly complained, as he shook his fist at the closed elevator door, "What am I—chopped liver? You owe me one, Copcake!"

When he stepped back into his office, Vic found a pink memo slip from Marsha with a beautifully rendered sketch depicting an unravelling roll of film. There was nothing else written on it. Obviously, Terry had called during Rodney's visit. The art director was beginning to grow fond of their receptionist's hieroglyphically oriented phone messages.

He dialed the photographer's phone number, and the young shutterbug picked up before the second ring.

"I just got back to my desk. What's doing?" Vic asked casually.

There was a long pause, during which Vic thought he could hear her sobbing uncontrollably.

"Are you alright, Terry?"

It took a few moments for the photographer to compose herself, "Oh, Vic, I feel like such a prize idiot. I was fairly drunk when I got home from the celebration last night. Pretty much, I'm always the last one to leave an event like that, and I love drinking champagne. When I got home, I know I placed the camera on my night table, undressed, and climbed into bed. I checked it this morning, and the roll of film was missing. I know I didn't unload it."

Vic felt a chill run through his body. "Was the film still in the camera when you got home from The Dakota?"

"I didn't notice, but I'm confident that nobody has broken into my studio overnight. I'm a very light sleeper, even when soused. Tu-tu would've made a racket if someone was sneaking around." Terry admitted.

"What do you think could have happened?"

"After the bulk of the guests left Helena Baxter's last night, I put my camera on a table in the entrance hall and sat to have a few drinks in the living room with her and some of the remaining diehard partiers. Other folks were still making their exits, and I guess there was a lot of activity. I can't imagine anybody would find the photos particularly captivating or even worth keeping as a souvenir. I'm also beginning to develop a bit of a persecution complex. Could somebody hate me that much?"

"Truth be told, if anything, whoever stole your film of Simone Caldwell's murder scene has made you a household name this week. You should be basking in your Andy Warhol fifteen-minutes-of-fame. It was obviously your turn to be in the spotlight, regardless of the circumstances."

Terry's mouth twisted into a deep frown, "Those pictures are so eerie and sordid."

Vic then logically asked, "Had you taken pictures of anything else on that roll of film last night before you got to The Dakota?"

"Just some candids at the theatre after the run-through. I had already given a canister to my assistant to process and send to Liz Smith for her column. There were just a few random shots from the Hayes on the new roll. Nothing special," she said.

Vic offered an assumption, "Maybe you have a genuine groupie. Now that your photos have been published on the front page of every paper on the east coast, you're a hot commodity. I once stole a Sardi's ashtray used by Elizabeth Taylor."

"Nice try, but I don't think that could be a rational explanation," Terry sighed.

"I wish I could offer another theory. I suspect we many never know what happened unless some of the photos you shot yesterday surface somewhere."

Terry shuddered, "It's what's making me so nervous. We all saw the gruesome results of the last Kodak film canister that vanished."

Vic had no sooner ended his conversation with Terry when his phone rang again. He had an uneasy feeling as he hesitantly picked up the call.

It was Ava. She started by shrieking hysterically that Helena Baxter had just discovered Caprice Fournier's dead body in the housekeeper's bedroom.

"I'm coming down to your office. Get Bettie and Tobin in there," she barked, slamming the receiver into the much-abused cradle.

The redheaded press agent was breathless when she reached Vic's desk minutes later, her hair a tangled nest of yellow pencils and random hair clips. She resembled a frenzied Madame Butterfly.

"When did this happen?" Tobin asked, as Ava threw herself into one of the guest chairs, fanning herself with an old *Playbill*.

"No one is actually sure." Ava said, "The police are on their way to The Dakota right now. It could've happened last evening while we were all there or, I suppose, sometime during the late night or early morning hours."

Arne Engels nervously entered the cramped room having just run down the fire stairs from his office on the floor above, "Can you believe it?"

"Does anybody know how she was killed?" Bettie asked.

"It almost sounds like a joke, but Rex told me that Caprice had a champagne cork lodged in her eye socket. The force of its trajectory shot clear through to her brain," the general manager announced in an excitedly hushed tone of voice, "Ordinarily, I'd question anything that pot head Rex thought he may have seen. But Detective Clements was on his way over to the Dakota apartment to question them. Perhaps we'll learn something from him later today."

"This'll definitely do Helena Baxter in," muttered Ava, "I don't know how anybody could survive this much bad publicity and negative press. Murder is about as bleak as it gets. Three murders will be perceived as hogging the limelight."

Arne needlessly reminded them, "It's been a string of seriously nasty incidents—all placed at Helena Baxter's doorstep."

Bettie reflected aloud, "A champagne cork lodged in her eye socket? Could it have been a terrible accident? Most everyone was taking turns opening bottles of bubbly throughout the evening. I happened to notice that people were being very responsible and careful."

"Helena Baxter told us that Caprice was horribly depressed and nervous. She was going to go directly to bed. I imagine that celebrating with a glass of champagne was the furthest thing from her mind," Ava snapped.

Vic said, "Let's wait to hear from Detective Clements. We were all at the party last night. I'm sure he's going to want to question us about it. Why don't we all try to get back to work until then?"

It was at that moment that a perfectly tousled Mark Rhodes ran into the crowded office holding up an early edition of The Post.

"Oh, my God, this is beyond awful!" he wheezed breathlessly, "I had to leave my desk to get away from the ringing telephones. Every line is lit up like a Christmas tree."

Ava burst into action, grabbed Mark's hand, pulled him out of Vic's office, and screeched as they sped down the hall, "Holy hell, let's see what we can do to subdue the vicious pack of media wolves."

As the publicists raced back to their offices, the others in the room craned their necks to read the newspaper headline left behind on Vic's drawing table by Mark.

"Celebrity's Chef's Corked Casualty!"

It was accompanied by a grotesque, close-up photograph of Caprice Fournier's corpse sprawled out on a rumpled bed, a champagne cork protruding from her left eye socket. The picture credit read, "Photo: Terry Hagen."

Detective Renny Clements spent the morning in Caprice Fournier's bedroom at The Dakota along with a proficient team of police officers, forensic investigators, fingerprint technicians, and homicide squad analysts. Medical examiner, Dr. Patrick Wheeler, was also on the scene studying the details of the brutal crime. He determined the obvious: that the housekeeper was killed when the force of the champagne cork shooting out of the bottle hit her directly in the eye and damaged her brain.

"As difficult as it is to believe, more people are killed this way every year than from poisonous spider bites." Wheeler said.

Renny raised a perfect eyebrow, "You're joking, right?"

"Not at all. It isn't the first time I've come across this sort of tragedy. Sometimes it's accidentally self-inflicted. In other instances, a drunken guest at a wedding or anniversary thinks they're being funny by aiming the lethal weapon at another partygoer. It's also a favorite misguided missile of frat boys everywhere," Dr. Wheeler said as he poked at the bloody wound with the tip of his pen and then jotted down a note on his clip-board report.

"Interestingly enough, when the cork is popped, it only leaves the bottle at around 25 miles per hour. However, the gases expelled from the bottleneck can reach twice the speed of sound. The cork wouldn't necessarily have had to hit Mademoiselle Fournier in the eye to have killed her. If the trajectory shot into her temple or forehead, it'd be just as deadly. But our killer apparently had great aim and was obviously out to make a statement." Dr. Wheeler looked up at Renny from over the rim of his reading glasses.

"Staged again. Like the trap door. Setting the scene to obviously humiliate the victim in death for some perverse reason," mused the detective.

Wheeler looked over at the forensic photographer who was solemnly going about his job of taking detailed pictures of the victim and the crime scene for further study afterwards, "I suspect our killer likes to have their work photographed for posterity. May I ask if the young lady whose camera was stolen the other day was in attendance last night?"

"Yes, I believe she was. But I cannot imagine Terry Hagen as a vicious killer."

Dr. Wheeler directed one of the fingerprint technicians to dust the side of the ornate mahogany headboard as he spoke, "There was also a bit of a struggle prior to the murder considering the condition of the bedroom and the fact that the contents of the champagne bottle spilled out everywhere. Mademoiselle Fournier's nightgown and the sheets are still damp from the bubbly."

"What was her time of death?" Renny asked.

"My guess would be between 8:00 and before midnight," determined the medical examiner.

Clements took out his worn notepad and jotted down that piece of information. "I believe that pretty much covers the duration of the cocktail party. I'm about to question the host and hostess. Perhaps they'll supply a more accurate timeline."

Dr. Wheeler adjusted his reading glasses as he muttered, "Somebody really has it in for Helena Baxter, don't they?"

With a nod of agreement, Renny exited the bedroom, which was becoming more and more crowded with police personnel. He walked into the living room.

Both Helena Baxter and her husband were sitting in stunned silence reading the newspaper headlines that had just been delivered by messenger from Ava Chasten's office. There were now several other early editions on the stands. All of them featured the grotesque photograph of Caprice Fournier's bizarre murder.

"Who took this picture?" a perplexed Helena Baxter asked, "How? When?"

Clements was at a loss for an answer. The detective was well aware that the police forensic photographer, who'd arrived first on the scene this morning, was currently still at work in the victim's bedroom. The only person who could have snapped the photo printed in the early editions was either the killer, or a guest with an extremely twisted sense of humor who failed to report the homicide. Renny took the publication from Helena Baxter's hand and squinted, his focus zeroing in on the photo credit in the lower right-hand corner.

"Terry Hagen."

"That's impossible," spat the actress.

Renny nodded his head and muttered, "I tend to agree with you."

"Any thoughts on who may have taken those monstrous pictures?" Rex asked belligerently.

"The likeliest suspect would be whoever murdered Caprice last night while the party was in progress. Either Terry is guilty and totally off her rocker, or the killer is trying to implicate the photographer in the crime for some reason. Her camera had already been stolen once before—sometime during Simone's murder at the theatre. We all saw the unfortunate results of that theft."

"Can my wife take a tranquilizer and go back to bed?" Rex asked while gripping Helena Baxter's hand, "She's hardly slept a wink."

The detective gazed into the actress's famously heavy-lidded eyes.

"Just a few quick questions first," Renny spoke in a soothingly calm tone of voice, "Do you recall if anything unusual happened during the celebration yesterday?"

Helena Baxter actually summoned a slight smile, "Well, we served pretzels and chips straight out of the box in order to avoid any incidents of food poisoning. Caprice was in a terrible state of anxiety while we were setting things up. I suggested she retire to her bedroom to get some rest. The guests arrived after the run-through, which I'm told was a great success," she patted her husband's hand for emphasis, "The rest of the party progressed as nicely as one could wish. The usual festivities, with actors, glitterati, and creative types getting tipsy on free champagne, taking turns showing off at the piano, and trading Broadway gossip. Oh, and my dear goldfish had a narrow escape. Arnie Engels dropped their bowl in an unsuccessful attempt to move it out of harm's way."

"Are the little ones okay?" asked Renny, "I'd made their acquaintances last time."

"Yes, thank goodness," sighed Helena Baxter, as she peered across the room at Adam and Eve swimming contentedly in their new home, "My husband, along with Earl, Vic, and Perry came to the rescue. Everything was cleaned up and fixed good as new in record time."

Renny stood, indicating his imminent departure, "My first order of business is to question Terry Hagen. May I use your telephone before I leave?"

Helena Baxter smirked and dramatically threw her hands up in the air, "Of course, my dear Detective Clements. You've been such a frequent visitor of late, I'm sure you could find the bloody instrument blindfolded."

Scene Twelve

Renny Clements had phoned Vic from The Dakota.

The detective casually filled him in on the details of the morning's bizarre events as well as Dr. Wheeler's startling statistics about champagne cork fatalities. As fair trade, Vic told Renny about his earlier call from Terry concerning the stolen film roll.

"Do you think you could set up a conference at your offices with Terry, yourself, Bettie, and your boss? I'd like to question all four of you together about last night."

"Would noon work for you?" Vic asked, "I could call Terry now."

"Let me know if there's a problem. You can leave a message for me at the precinct. Otherwise, I'll be at Thompson & Co at twelve o'clock," the ardent detective said authoritatively.

As the art director ended the call, Bettie walked into his office.

"Is there word, by any chance, on *Don't Hang Up* proceeding as scheduled? If so, we're going to need quote ad layouts prepared and ready for our post-opening Friday morning meeting." Bettie shivered, "I must admit, it does seem daft and totally callous to be concerned about advertising for a Broadway show when three people have been murdered."

"I'm guessing that as long as they're still selling tickets like gangbusters, nothing is going to stop that play from opening. Not even a few homicides."

Marsha appeared in the doorway waving a pink message slip. She placed it on Vic's desk and was about to quietly bolt when the art director asked her to take a seat for a moment. Marsha looked over at Bettie with a pained expression on her face equivalent to being ordered to report to the principal's office.

On the small sheet of tinted paper, the receptionist had drawn a beautifully detailed sketch of a detective's badge. Vic was once again impressed by her talent.

She said sheepishly, referring to the message, "He's been trying to get through for a while. Nice voice on him, that one. You were busy on another call."

Vic smiled, "It's okay. I just spoke with Detective Clements, thanks."

"Is Vito in serious trouble?" Marsha abruptly asked, almost in tears, chin trembling.

Bettie took the seat next to her, "Now, what makes you ask that? Has Vito done something wrong?"

"I don't know."

"Tell us, did Vito take the small painting from the art archives the other day?"

Marsha nodded her head, "Um…he borrowed it…but he put it back this morning."

"Any idea why he borrowed it in the first place?" Vic asked.

"Vito overheard Bettie and her friend talking about it. He wanted to show it to the other guys at his club."

Bettie smiled reassuringly, "And what club would that be?"

"He belongs to this social club on Staten Island. There's a whole group of regular neighborhood members."

Vic hesitantly asked, "They study art?"

Marsha briefly mulled that question over, "Well, they appreciate art for sure."

Bettie and Vic were both genuinely amused by her unexpected finesse.

"I got worried when I saw your police officer friend here again this morning," said Marsha, "It made me very nervous, I'll tell you."

"So, Vito showed the painting to the men at his club? What happened? Why did he decide to return it today?" Vic asked.

"Vito thought it was an expert forgery. He knew the other members would be interested in…um…seeing it. They sometimes handle merchandise like that."

"Do they deal in forgeries as a rule at this club?"

"I really don't know. You'd have to ask Vito."

Bettie attempted to calm Marsha down. She reached for the receptionist's visibly trembling hand and held onto it firmly,

"Rest assured, we're trying to keep Vito out of this messy business. Unless Rodney Clements has some further questions for him, we'll request that Vito's part in all this ends right here and now, okay?"

"That's good to hear. Thank you," said Marsha.

"Think you're feeling well enough to go back to your desk?" Vic asked.

The nervous young woman stood and maintained her grip on the back of the chair, "Yes, for sure. But…um…I never answered your question."

"Which question?"

"Why Vito returned the canvas this morning." Marsha emphasized, in a tone of voice she'd employ to explain a difficult concept to the learning challenged.

Vic leaned forward, "Oh, yes, so there *was* a reason?"

"What was it?" Bettie prodded.

As Marsha headed out the door, she replied, "Because Vito was told at his club that the painting was not a forgery, but actually the real thing."

The pedestrian walkway designated as Shubert Alley is a mecca for theatre lovers and is considered the pulsating central hub of Broadway. It was originally built as a fire exit between the Shubert Theatre on 44th Street and the Booth Theatre on 45th Street. At the time, the law required that sufficient space be allotted for fire vehicles and rescue equipment in case of an emergency.

Since the entrance to the prestigious Shubert Organization is located in the alley, the long passageway is now mainly used as a prime parking place for its chief executives whose offices it overlooks. Large, vibrant posters advertising current Broadway productions, known as three-sheets, are displayed on the wall between the stage doors of the two theaters. The alley poster gallery, which Vic often describes as one of his favorite places in Manhattan, serves as a great showcase for the creative output of theatrical ad agency Thompson & Co.

Detective Renny Clements wasn't fully aware of the alley's history, but was unquestionably an admirer of all things Broadway, nonetheless. Both he and his brother Rodney counted many friends among the theatre community due to its proximity to their workplace. It was an exciting industry—one in which Renny certainly never thought he'd become so intimately involved.

Murder has a way of swiftly forcing together certain handfuls of people surrounding the heinous crime, most of whom are labeled as suspects until proven innocent…or guilty. This homicide case possessed an amazingly colorful cast of characters that featured two glamorous Broadway actresses among its central participants.

"Are you anybody?" asked a slightly disheveled woman, so thin as to somewhat resemble a mop handle with eyes. She seemed to have appeared out of nowhere.

Renny blinked furiously, "Excuse me?"

The woman shoved what the detective quickly identified as an autograph book against his chest, "Well, are you an actor?" she asked, belligerently.

The mousey blonde lady was suddenly joined by an equally unkempt man, "Have we seen you in anything?" the wild-eyed stranger asked, autograph book in hand.

"No, I'm not an actor. I'm a police detective." Renny said ominously.

Clements recollected his brother Rodney mentioning two aggressive autograph hounds who trolled Shubert Alley, accosting anyone who looked remotely attractive or vaguely familiar. The detective's surprising response made the pair take pause and then scurry away as quickly as they'd appeared.

Renny looked up at the Sardi building as he approached it from the 44th Street egress of Shubert Alley. Entering the lobby, he flashed his credentials at sullen Guy Andersen, who was standing faithfully at his post.

"On which floor might I find Thompson & Co please?"

"Hey, you're Officer Rodney's twin brother, right? Are you here about the murders?" Guy asked, pointing to the headlines on the folded newspaper displayed on his desk.

"I'm here to visit Thompson & Co—which floor?"

"Seventh." Guy Andersen responded coldly.

At precisely noon on the dot, Renny Clements stepped off the elevator and into the advertising agency's reception area.

Marsha directed him through the office to the conference room, the entire time avoiding eye contact with the detective for fear of looking guilty. She was still shaken from her visit to Vic's workspace twenty minutes earlier.

Much to Renny's surprise, there were seven people sitting uneasily around the table when he arrived. Before he could even ask the question, Bettie volunteered sheepishly, "Word travels fast around here, detective."

"We wanted to know if we could be included in this pow-wow," Ava inquired defiantly, "After all, we were also witnesses at Helena Baxter's last night."

As the three anxious invaders stared in his direction, Renny Clements wondered aloud, "How did you know we were meeting here? I just set this up an hour ago."

"Oh, please!" Ava spat, ignoring the question, "You cannot deny counting us among the persons of interest in this case. We're definitely…um…interested."

"Actually," Renny conceded, "This does save time and makes things easier. Now, may I proceed?"

"Carry on, detective," urged the redheaded publicist.

Currently ensconced in the makeshift interrogation room were Bettie Balboa, who managed to look radiant as she drummed her lacquered nails against the cover of her notebook in a jittery rhythm…Vic was furiously doodling on one of the yellow pads, stacks of which were conveniently piled on the table…Terry was nervously keeping her red-rimmed eyes glued on the detective's every move…Arne restlessly lit up a cigarette and passed his Sardi's book of matches over to Mark Rhodes, who had a Marlboro already perched on his lips in anticipation of the first puff. The two men commenced filling the intimate room with a haze of smoke…Tobin was in the process of constructing an origami animal from a sheet of note pad paper…Ava was rummaging through her oversized Gucci tote bag and triumphantly fished out a thirteen-inch-long folding Chinese hand fan which she flipped open with a loud snap. She furiously began waving it in front of her face in an effort to somewhat curtail the rapidly accumulating cigarette fog.

Renny Clements remained standing with his fingertips resting on the highly polished mahogany table surface.

"You were all invited to Helena Baxter's apartment last evening along with thirty or so other guests. The medical examiner has determined that Mademoiselle Fournier was murdered during the champagne festivities between the hours of 8:00 and midnight. I want to know if any of you saw something suspicious, or someone acting strangely."

Clements focused his attention on the fragile blonde photographer, "Terry, you were taking candids at the party. Vic tells me that the film was mysteriously removed from your camera during the evening. I strongly suspect that whoever stole the canister also killed Mademoiselle Fournier and photographed her dead body."

"Even worse, the culprit later sent those horrible pictures to all of our newspaper and media outlets." Ava chimed in angrily.

"I feel like someone's out to ruin my career," sighed Terry.

"I'd hardly say that," Arne said, "Your work's appeared on the cover of every major print publication this week. I'll admit, it's totally humiliating for Helena Baxter, not to mention poor Simone and Caprice, who've been captured for posterity in those mortifying positions. That's how they'll always be remembered. A laughingstock."

Renny kept his voice steady and even toned as he peered closely at the seven anxious witnesses seated at the table, "I ask you all to seriously concentrate on what you can remember about last evening."

Terry began, "I think I've told you everything. It was a typical Helena Baxter gathering. People drinking lots of champagne and taking turns at the piano. There was certainly nothing extraordinary about it at all."

"Except for a murder happening under our noses!" Ava snapped.

The detective flashed an admonishing glance at the publicist, who shrugged insolently and accelerated her hand-fan speed in defiance.

"I was at the party only briefly," volunteered Tobin, "It all seemed to be a typical cocktail gathering. I noticed nothing remotely extraordinary or suspicious. I spent the short time I was there mainly talking with Venus and Rex."

Arne spoke next as he stubbed out his cigarette, "I was preoccupied with setting up and pitching in since Caprice was in a bad state of nerves. It was the intentional joke of the party that Helena was serving boxed pretzels and chips along with the champagne. It wasn't the type of evening that required a catering service staff. I didn't notice anyone acting any stranger than usual for Broadway types, myself included."

"Mr. Rhodes?" Clements prodded the clean-cut young press agent.

"It was a nice party. Early in the evening, I was chatting with Helena Baxter. She is about as charming as they come. I spent a lot of the time talking with Bettie. We were admiring the amazing view of Central Park and having a smoke. At one point, she was scolding me for tapping on the glass of the goldfish bowl. That's when Arnie came over to move it to a safer spot, away from me, and it slipped out of his hands," said Mark.

"Chalk it up to clumsiness." Arne sounded embarrassed, "Most of the water spilled out on me. Bettie and Mark were splashed a bit as well when the bowl hit the floor and shattered." He turned his head to sneeze.

Bettie raised her hand, "If I may, detective?"

Renny smiled, "This isn't a classroom, but I appreciate your politeness."

"I remember it a bit differently. A few minutes before that happened, I had turned to get a cigarette out of my handbag. My line of vision briefly faced the hallway leading to Caprice's bedroom. I noticed that her door was ajar, but there was no one around." Bettie continued nervously, "It was my impression that when Arnie picked up Adam and Eve...um...the goldfish, he glanced over my shoulder toward the hallway and saw something that surprised him. That's why he lost his grip on the bowl." She looked over at Arne with concern, "You definitely seemed startled by something."

"Or someone, perhaps," Detective Clements suggested, "Did you unexpectedly see someone leaving Caprice's bedroom who wouldn't ordinarily be there?"

Arne's eyes widened and he scoffed at the idea, "No, I didn't see anyone or notice anything unusual. I simply lost my grasp on the slippery fishbowl."

"This is a very serious business, Mr. Engels. Withholding information could prove to be dangerous for you." Renny said authoritatively, "There's already been three murders. If you've witnessed anything at all, now's the time to tell me."

"In my haste to move the fishbowl, I dropped it. Simple as that." Arne said sternly.

Mark interjected, "It all happened so fast. I can't say I noticed Arnie's attention focused anywhere in particular. I thought he looked startled because the fishbowl was capsizing and he'd lost control of it. All I know is, we all got drenched. Thankfully, everyone kicked into high gear to clean up the mess."

Tobin abruptly submitted a theory of his own, "You know, detective, one of the other guests could have used the accident as a perfect opportunity to slip unseen into her bedroom and murder Mademoiselle Fournier. For that brief amount of time, it seems all eyes were on Arnie and what was happening to the poor goldfish. It could very well have served as a convenient diversion. Our killer may well have taken advantage of it."

"I looked over just as it happened," said Vic, "It appeared to me as if Arnie was surprised by something that Bettie or Mark said. I was too far away to overhear any of their conversation, but that was my impression."

"We were talking about the goldfish. Nothing shocking about that," Bettie said.

Mark nodded in agreement.

Vic continued, "I cannot remember being struck by anything out of the ordinary. Perry and I ran into the kitchen to fetch a dustpan and broom to sweep up the broken glass. I believe Rex soaked up the water with paper towels while Earl Quick fetched a new fishbowl from one of the display shelves.

"I saw nothing," Ava remarked, "I didn't care about the stupid fish. The rest of the evening was actually quite pleasant. I watched and supervised as Terry was taking her candids. Celeste Farris and I had a lot of theatre gossip to catch up on. Her hunky bodyguards were getting a choice earful, I can tell you. It wasn't a particularly eventful party if you don't count the murder."

Renny refrained from an eye roll.

"I ask that if any one of you remembers something, no matter how inconsequential it may seem, please call me. In the event I'm not at the precinct, leave a message with the officer in charge. These homicides are definitely linked. Your entire circle of friends and co-workers are potentially in danger. I don't want to create a panic, but I do want you all to be aware of the gravity involved in keeping any information to yourself…for whatever reason."

The informal cross-examination came to an end. It seemed as if the group couldn't make an exit quickly enough to suit them. Vic, Tobin, and Bettie courteously escorted Terry to the elevator. Ava and Mark used the fire stairs to return to their offices one floor up. Arne was the last to leave the conference room. Renny Clements gripped the general manager's arm as he brushed past.

"I realize you probably think you're doing something noble, but I urge you to tell me if you saw someone leaving Mademoiselle Fournier's bedroom during the party. Your life could be in jeopardy."

It was obvious that Arne was riled, "I can take care of myself, detective. You don't have to worry about me. If I were you, I would hold with Tobin Klein's theory that a quick-thinking killer used the accident as a diversion. The art of misdirection, smoke, and mirrors, you know. Magicians use it all the time."

Vic crossed paths with Arne in the hallway as he returned to the conference room. Renny was purposely waiting for him there, perched on the edge of the highly polished mahogany table.

"He saw something. I just know it." Clements said, testily.

Vic shrugged, "I tend to agree based on his attitude, but he's a headstrong guy who's in great physical shape. I'm fairly sure Arnie could beat the shit out of anyone who confronts him looking for trouble. Also, there is definitely something to be said about the misdirection tactic. We were all preoccupied with cleaning up the broken glass, spilled water, and checking on the condition of Adam and Eve."

"I hope you're right." Renny didn't sound convinced.

Vic spent the rest of Monday working feverishly to create new quote ad layouts and advertising concepts for *Don't Hang Up*, now starring Celeste Farris. Terry sent him the full contact sheets plus several choice photo prints from their shoot at the St. Regis, which the art director was able to use in revising the advertising campaign for *The New York Times*. The work was progressing as smoothly as possible until he received a call from Ava Chasten.

"You realize that Celeste has photo approval, right, Rembrandt?" she reminded him.

Vic moaned, "We are so pressed for time already. There's bound to be retouching involved, not to mention having to send out for veloxes in order to meet the newspaper deadlines."

"Them's the rules." Ava sang flatly.

"I'll tell you what I'm going to do, Ava. I will choose the photos I think'll work best, send them to the retoucher tonight, and when I get them back tomorrow, I'll hustle over to the theatre to get Celeste Farris's approval on the already-retouched images. That will save us some valuable time."

"What if the great Miss Farris doesn't approve any of them?"

Vic sighed, "I'll tell the retoucher to make her look twenty years old. She's certain to approve something knowing what the circumstances are. She's a pro, she knows what's at stake. Jeez, Celeste Farris and her husband are co-producers now as well."

"Got that right, sweetie. I have the revised *Playbill* title page and bios to prove it." Ava laughed, "Now, get your nose back to the rhinestone."

"You mean grindstone…"

"This is glamorous, gaudy, glitzy Broadway, baby-cakes. I _did_ mean rhinestone."

While Vic and the art department were busy redesigning quote ads and new poster graphics incorporating Celeste Farris' image, changes to the theatre marquees, creating layouts for the front-of-house photographs, and the myriad other formats that now required updating, Bettie was attempting to write a :60 second radio spot that would highlight what everyone hoped would be good reviews from the newspaper and television critics.

It was always a joy to present the proposed radio commercials for the post-opening meeting since all of the quotes that Bettie would read to the clients were bogus rave reviews that she herself had concocted. The process generally bolstered everyone's egos and served to put the producers in a feel-good, hopeful mood, which lasted until the actual reviews were printed or aired. Now that *Don't Hang Up* was benefiting from an immense amount of publicity and word-of-mouth, be it good or bad, it'd be interesting to see if the dark cloud hanging over the play gives the reviewers a reason to be kind.

"Do you mind if I read you this radio copy I've written while you're working?" Bettie asked, as she suddenly appeared in Vic's office doorway.

"Only if you promise that we can run down to Sardi's for a quick bite to eat right afterward. It's almost eight o'clock, and I'm starving."

Bettie nodded. "The spot's meant to be read by a hard-nosed Winchell-type announcer who will make it sound more like a special report than a commercial. They'll be no music track at all, just the sound effects of tickertape and familiar hum of a newsroom." she explained.

"You have my undivided attention." Vic said, putting down his magic marker. "I can already tell you that if it's loaded with hyperbole and exclamation points, it'll be a sure winner!"

Bettie cleared her throat and began, "At the Helen Hayes Theatre, a new thriller just opened that has taken Broadway by storm. *Don't Hang Up* by Joseph Michaels is a bright and brilliant new play that provides chills and thrills galore!' exclaims Walter Kerr of *The New York Times*. 'Celeste Farris enchants us with her vivid characterization of a publicist in peril.' raves Douglas Watt in the *New York Daily News*. 'Broadway has a new hit! *Don't Hang Up* will keep you on the edge of your seat straight through to its exciting climax!' says Jack Kroll in *Newsweek*. Clive Barnes in *The New York Post* writes, 'Run, don't walk, to get your tickets for this new chiller-diller starring Celeste Farris. *Don't Hang Up* is brilliantly directed by Rex Merchant. The first-rate production team is topped by extraordinary scenery designed by Perry Chan.' 'Fasten your seat belts for the thrill of a lifetime!' says Pia Lindstrom on WNBC-TV, '*Don't Hang Up* is a marvelous new play.' Don't miss Celeste Farris starring in *Don't Hang Up*, a new mystery thriller, at the Helen Hayes Theatre. Call for tickets now!'"

"Where can I buy house seats?" Vic laughed as he leaned back in his chair, "All joking aside, it's an effective spot. We should only be so lucky to get reviews even close to those."

"I must remember to ask Arnie how ticket sales are going. Last I heard, it was a real standing-room-only scenario. Box office was selling like hot cakes." Bettie said.

"And all it took was an avalanche of front-page publicity, a mass poisoning, and several brutal murders. You can't buy coverage like that." Vic grimaced as he menacingly picked up his metal T-square, "Now, Ms. Balboa, if we don't leave my office right this minute to get something to eat downstairs, I'm going to slug you with this lethal twenty-pound art supply."

Both Bettie and Vic went back to work after their quick dinner. The night-shift operator squeezed in a few jokes as he commandeered their short ride from floors two to seven. He stopped the elevator and opened the doors with a loud thump, "Don't work too hard, you two. I think everyone else has gone home for the night."

Bettie began to revise the media plan to accommodate the new post-opening budget. Vic was still knee-deep in design revisions for print and outdoor advertising.

On impulse, Vic phoned Renny Clements as soon as he sat down at his drawing table.

The phone was picked up after only a half-ring on the other end of the line.

"Detective Clements speaking. How can I help you?"

"Renny, it's Vic. I just wanted to see how the rest of your day was going."

The officer sounded tired, "That's really nice of you. I was actually just thinking of doing the same. Still waiting on those police files to be delivered here, but I spent the latter part of the day questioning Celeste Farris, Earl Quick, and the secretary, Venus Pluto. None of them can recall anything unusual happening at the champagne party. It seems Engels' dropping the goldfish bowl was the height of excitement."

Vic smiled, "It was great seeing you at Thompson & Co this afternoon. What'd you think of our humble offices?"

"Incredibly impressive, I'll admit. What's going on with Helena Baxter's play?" the detective asked, "Are they considering closing?"

"Apparently, the show's forging full steam ahead. I believe they're going to resume previews tomorrow night. It'll be Celeste

Farris' first official performance in the role," said Vic, scribbling in bogus body copy on a rough quote ad layout as he spoke. "As far as I can tell, the producers are sticking to their originally announced opening night this Thursday. They're a brave lot."

"I wouldn't begin to know how your business works at all, but it's an extremely reckless decision," said Renny. "Your friends seem to be treating their situation very lightly. Dammit, there's already been one homicide actually committed on stage in the theatre. Somebody ought to remind these folks that this isn't a play. We can't flip through the script pages, reading ahead to find out what's in store, and revealing who the killer is. I wish we could."

"I guess you must be accustomed to dealing with murder in your daily work life, but Bettie and I are definitely starting to freak out about all of this." Vic said nervously.

Renny tried to calm him down, "All I ask is that you remain on the alert, keep your eyes wide open, and don't get yourself involved in any potentially dangerous situations."

"Are you getting any closer to a solution?" asked the art director.

"I'd like to think so, yes. But, unfortunately, without any proof, it's all considered circumstantial—or worse, conjecture." Clements quickly changed the subject. "On a happier note, would you like to meet for a drink tonight?"

Vic looked at his wristwatch and was stunned by the late hour.

"I still have an incredible amount of work to catch up on. Tell you what, how about we plan on doing something together tomorrow night? I've been wanting to catch the midnight show at The Elgin. Think you're up for that?"

"Sure. That'd be a refreshing change-of-pace. What's the movie?" Renny asked.

"It's called *Pink Flamingos*. I hear it's outrageous."

Scene Thirteen

Rain and wind were pounding against his window when the clock alarm jarred him awake the next morning. It was the kind of downpour that fell with such force, it created an ankle-high wall of mist on the sidewalks and rendered umbrellas totally useless. Vic usually walked to work—but that wasn't happening in this monsoon. It would be virtually impossible to hail a taxi. Even if he could snag one, the trip would take at least an hour to travel the distance from East 54th Street to West 44th Street. Manhattan traffic annoyingly remained at a standstill during storms of any kind. As adverse as he was to taking the subway, Vic had no choice but to hop on the local train for one station, change over to the crosstown shuttle, which then chugged and screeched its way to Times Square. During rainy weather, the subway system was particularly disgusting, dank, dirty, and delayed. Vic couldn't wait to surface back into the raging deluge.

As the art director stepped off the elevator, Marsha was fluffing out her somewhat damp hair as she handed Vic his messages. Vito Lanzetta was about ready to leave. The macho Italian avoided eye contact as he brushed past, nodding, and grunting a restrained good morning.

At least the office was dry and warm.

Vic shook out his umbrella before leaning it up against the corner wall behind his drawing table. He was unaware of Bettie's presence in the doorway until she began speaking. The sudden sound of her voice startled him.

"It's déja vu all over again!" Bettie announced loudly, "Tonight will mark the first preview of *Don't Hang Up*...for the second time. Instead of sitting through the performance, I thought we would stop backstage after the final curtain to extend our congratulations to Celeste Farris."

Vic answered enthusiastically, "That's a brilliant idea. I don't think I could face watching the play again this evening. It's depressing enough that the opening night requires mandatory attendance on Thursday. Which reminds me, have the producers mentioned anything about going through with the opening night party? Having a celebration reeks of total tastelessness given the unfortunate circumstances."

"No one's mentioned a word about it. I can phone Mark to find out if he's heard anything," said Bettie.

Vic nodded, took a deep breath, and began plowing through his workload. Aside from the various odds and ends he had to complete for *Don't Hang Up*, the art director was faced with designing the countdown-to-closing print ads for Edward Albee's new play, *Seascape,* which opened late January at the Shubert Theatre. The unusual drama received lackluster reviews despite the luminous presence of Deborah Kerr and Frank Langella featured among its stellar cast.

Premiering two-and-a-half weeks before *Seascape*, at the start of the New Year, *The Wiz* opened at the Majestic Theatre and, conversely, was doing gangbuster business at the box office. It was a spectacular musical version of L. Frank Baum's *The Wonderful Wizard of Oz*. The advertising was a pleasure on which to work, especially given that the sole producer, Ken Harper, was a dreamboat. Vic was charged with creating eye-catching, shallow two-column quote ads featuring the dazzling logo designed by Milton Glazer. They were scheduled to run weekly in *The New York Times* touting their rave notices. There were also early discussions about shooting a big-budget television spot. Bob Fosse's show, *Pippin,* had begun running a wildly successful commercial campaign just two years earlier to counteract his production's lukewarm critical reception.

The :60 second TV spot turned the tide, and the musical was still currently performing at the Imperial Theatre to enthusiastic, sold-out houses.

Meanwhile, facing a tight deadline, Vic ate a non-glamorous take-out deli salad at his drawing table as he revised the *Don't Hang Up* print layouts.

The next time he thought to check his wristwatch, it was nearing six o'clock. The torrential rain hadn't let up at all, but now added sporadic crashes of thunder and lightning as a reminder of the lousy weather raging outside. It was an auspicious night for Celeste Farris' first public performance in a new play. Wet weather has traditionally been a harbinger of good fortune for weddings and other major events. Maybe tonight, it'll include bringing luck to the second first preview of a show that has been plagued by three murders, bad publicity, and multiple poisonings. It could happen—but Vic didn't really think it would. It seemed that *Don't Hang Up* had a black cloud hanging over it. Closing the production might well be the only solution.

"How's about we grab a quick dinner before heading over to the theatre after the performance?" asked Bettie, abruptly appearing at his office door. "I totally skipped having lunch today. We could run down to Sardi's at eight o'clock for food and cocktails—and I stress the plural—cocktails. When we're done, it'll be time to show up at the Hayes just as the curtain's coming down. We'll pop backstage, express our heartfelt congratulations, and our tasks will be completed for the night. Then, it'll be, 'Finito la musica' as my Greek Aunt Helen says after a hectic day."

Vic agreed, "Sounds like a plan. I want to check in with Renny that we're still on for tonight. We're going to catch the midnight movie at The Elgin."

Bettie crossed her fingers, "Hopefully, by midnight, I'll be curled up in bed with a good book."

"I thought you'd like to know that we're on our way backstage at the Hayes to congratulate Celeste Farris," Bettie teasingly remarked to the gossip-collecting lobby attendant as she and Vic were about to exit the building, "Tonight was her first performance in *Don't Hang Up*."

The thunder, wind, and rain were swirling outside the front doors located just a few feet away from Guy Andersen's station which required Bettie and the somber guard to raise their voices in order to converse.

"Right," said Guy excitedly, "Jeez, what a flurry of publicity there's been about her replacing Helena Baxter in the starring role. Such a bad time for Miss Baxter and so much trouble brewing around that unfortunate lady. Three murders! There was even a police detective in our building yesterday snooping around— Officer Rodney's twin brother."

"I know. He spent some time at Thompson & Co."

Guy spoke earnestly. "I hope Miss Baxter continues to hold up under all this terrible press. It almost killed her last time around."

Vic and Bettie stood huddled in the lobby about to open the heavy glass doors.

"Are you sure you want to venture down to The Elgin tonight of all nights? It looks just awful out there." She shuddered at the thought. Bettie watched as random pedestrians entered Shubert Alley. The heavy winds whipped at their coats and turned their umbrellas inside out. It looked like typhoon territory. The walkway had a tendency to be breezy even in the mildest of weather.

"It shouldn't be too bad, I guess. Renny has a car, so we don't have to scramble for a taxi." said Vic, "He's meeting me outside the Helen Hayes."

Bettie took a deep breath, "Well, we have to get there first. Ready, Vic? Batten down the hatches and open the door."

"Be careful out there," warned Guy Andersen as Bettie and Vic braced themselves and stepped outside into the turbulent thunderstorm.

It was rough crossing through Shubert Alley. They walked close to the walls making their way to 45th Street, turned right at the Hotel Piccadilly, past the Morosco and Bijou Theatres, rounded the corner and headed uptown on Broadway. Vic and Bettie felt utterly bedraggled by the time they reached the Helen Hayes on West 46th Street.

Lester, the stage door man, waved them inside from the inclement weather. He gestured with his finger up to his lips and whispered, "The curtain will come down in five minutes. Quiet, please. This is the big climax of the play."

As if on cue, Vic and Bettie heard the entire audience gasp in fright and surprise. This was followed minutes later by wild, enthusiastic applause. It certainly sounded as though the performance went well.

They waited at the stage door in order to allow time for Celeste Farris to get to her dressing room and take a moment to catch her breath. Arne showed up drenched and windblown. "Umbrellas are useless tonight. Mine was last seen turned inside out and floating in midair around the Booth Theatre box office like a Doug Henning magic trick."

"You can head over there now, folks." Lester permitted them access.

Ava and Mark were already fending off members of the press when the dampened trio squeezed their way into the backstage area.

Both Johns—Sylvester and Elmo—were flanking the entrance to the star dressing room. Venus quickly answered their knock on the door. She was beaming.

"It was a triumph tonight! Her Majesty really brought down the house."

Celeste Farris was seated at her makeup table still wearing her costume from the finale. In the stage action, toward the end of the dramatic thriller, she's attacked by a crazed actor. Her designer dress was stylish but torn and bloodied in sections. Her wide smile curtailed any illusion that she was any the worse for wear from the ordeal.

Producers Quick and Merchant were grinning like proud parents, "Our girl did it. A marvelous performance! The audience adored her."

Congratulations were tossed all around until Ava burst in with three photographers.

"This won't take but a minute, kids. Just a few happy snaps for the press."

While the Broadway paparazzi were engrossed in their assignments, Earl Quick pulled the others aside as he spoke in hushed tones.

"As you're all aware, *Don't Hang Up* has pretty much decided to beg off any sort of opening night celebration. This morning, I received a call from the head of Magnum Pictures in Hollywood. We're in negotiations for a three-picture contract and he recognized an opportunity to sweeten the deal for me. He's generously offered his fully staffed residence on Washington Square as a place for us to congregate while waiting for the reviews after our opening night performance," the producer excitedly explained.

Arne, without a second's hesitation said, "That's ideal, Earl. Not indulging in an outright celebration is a great way to avoid any more bad publicity for the show."

Quick continued, "I explained to the entire company that everyone concerned thought it unseemly to have an official opening night party in light of the events surrounding our production. We're now arranging for the family and friends of the cast and crew to have a discreet celebratory dinner of their own at Sardi's, courtesy of *Don't Hang Up*. The rest of us will head downtown to Washington Square. I really wouldn't want to pass up an opportunity like this."

During Quick's sidebar, Celeste Farris enthusiastically struck pose after pose for the tabloid shutterbugs. It didn't take more than ten minutes before Ava and Mark politely ushered the press photographers out of the dressing room.

Celeste Farris gruffly sat at her table and muttered, "Not even a telegram!"

Venus gently put her hands on the star's shoulders, "Maybe he's out-of-town and got his dates mixed up. You know, Cal is sharp and charming, but conveniently forgetful at times."

"It's just not like him. For God's sake, the three of us are practically joined at the hip," fretted Celeste Farris as she carefully pulled off her wig.

Turning to the rest of the group, Venus added, "Her Majesty is right. It really isn't typical of Cal to ignore Celeste, especially when she's opening a new show."

Rex said, "Right now, we have notes to go through. The rest of the cast is waiting. I'm sure they're exhausted and want to get home."

Quick nodded in agreement and looked sadly at his concerned wife. "Why not check on Cal tomorrow morning? It's not as if he hasn't dropped out of sight before. We can have the car take us downtown before we get to rehearsal."

"I have a better idea," said Venus rummaging through her handbag, "Cal gave me a set of his keys so I could water his plants whenever he's away. I'll go to his place right now. He most likely left a note for us on his dining room table. He's been known to do that on several occasions. While you are all here dealing with the actors, JD can zip me downtown. I'll be back at the theatre before you've even had a chance to miss me."

Celeste took a deep breath, "Oh, Venus, would you? That'd be such a relief."

"I can't let you go there alone," Bettie said abruptly, "I recall that Cal lives on Varick Street near the entrance to the Holland Tunnel, right? You can drop me off at my place on your way back uptown."

Turning to the room, Venus sighed, "Well, ain't this something? She's beautiful *and* thoughtful. Thank you, I would appreciate the company."

Vic looked at his wristwatch. "Normally, I'd offer to join you, but Renny's waiting outside. We have a date with some *Pink Flamingos*. Once again, congratulations to all of you on a highly successful performance tonight."

"Bettie and I will walk out with you, Vic," Venus grabbed her pashmina.

The fierce wind and teeming rain seemed to have worsened. The crackling sounds of lightning and booming thunder filled the cool night air. Vic spotted Renny's car further up the street, closer to the 46th Street Theatre. He waved goodnight to the two women and bolted toward the somewhat battered Chevy Impala. Venus and Bettie made the short dash to Celeste Farris' Mercedes Benz which was parked directly in front of the stage door entrance. They didn't wait for JD the driver to extend any courtesies. The ladies quickly occupied the plush back seat before he'd even realized they were there.

"JD, this is our fabulous advertising executive, Bettie Balboa, and she is a real doll," Venus was fond of making introductions, "Bettie, this is JD, the coolest chauffeur on Broadway. Her Majesty and I both have secret crushes on him. JD, we're going to Cal Lockheed's place on Varick Street."

"Right away, Lady Vee," snapped the ginger driver with a wink.

Bettie observed Renny Clements' Chevy Impala about to merge into the congested street traffic ahead of them. The rain hammered noisily on the car roofs as the two vehicles pulled away from the Helen Hayes Theatre heading east, then downtown.

Once the Mercedes turned left and drove south on Ninth Avenue, the going was a bit easier. The storm continued to prove umbrellas futile. Both Bettie and Venus would share a guilty chuckle whenever one or the other would point out an unfortunate pedestrian in the street struggling with their uncooperative rain gear in the high winds.

"Oh my stars, I could do without all the thunder!" Venus barked at the night sky.

As the Mercedes revealed pothole after pothole, now veiled under the rising water level of the Manhattan streets, Bettie and Venus chatted, their voices pitched higher to enable them to be heard over the hammering rain.

"The show certainly seemed to go very well tonight judging from the enthusiastic audience response." Bettie remarked.

Venus nodded, "Her Majesty, bless her cagey little heart, wouldn't have offered to replace Helena Baxter in a dud role, believe me. Celeste can spot a good acting vehicle when she sees one."

"She must feel that she's put herself under a lot of undue pressure."

"Every show presents its own particular challenge. It usually doesn't involve being dragged into a real-life murder mystery."

"Who do you think is capable of all this insanity, Venus? None of the company seems deranged enough to actually kill anyone," Bettie noted.

"Honeygirl, we all go nuts at times. You never can tell with theatre people."

Bettie remembered the reason for their late-night errand. "The last time I saw Cal Lockheed was at the theatre the day that Simone Caldwell was murdered. I guess you haven't heard from him since then?"

"It's been radio silence since Thursday. The last time something like this happened, Cal had fallen in lust with another actor he'd met one day at an audition. The guy had flown in from Wyoming, Omaha, Nevada, or some such place, to try out for the same role in a new musical. His flight home was scheduled just a few hours after the tryout. On a crazy whim, Cal accompanied the guy to the airport, bought a ticket, and flew back to Bumfuckville with the new object of his affection. Cal hadn't even stopped to buy a toothbrush."

"Impulsive and impressive," sighed Bettie, "and insanely romantic."

"When Cal Lockheed gets a hard-on, honeygirl, best get out of his way. That thing can be dangerous when unleashed." Venus laughed raucously.

"How did you find out what had happened to him?"

"On that occasion, he sent Her Majesty a telegram backstage at the Billy Rose Theatre. It was about ten years ago, and she was due to open in a revival production of *The Threepenny Opera*. Western Union charges by the word, you know. It cost about sixty-five dollars for ten words. So Cal kept it short and sweet: *Kisses on your opening while I get kissed on mine.* The only clue to his whereabouts was the return address. Her Majesty was too busy laughing to get really angry at him. The three of us have shared wonderful times together. But he does sometimes have his head up his ass, to put it mildly. In the past, he has left handwritten notes for me propped up on his dining room table. He once sent me a *Congratulations on Your Holy Communion* greeting card with an explanation of his sudden disappearance. In another instance, he dispatched a singing telegram. You get the picture. Cal simply knows if we haven't heard from him, we're to be aware that his plants could very well require watering. This is the first time he's been gone for four days without making a phone call, express mailing a letter, or sending smoke signals."

"That's worrisome, but I'm sure there'll be a perfectly reasonable explanation," said Bettie, patting Venus' chilled hand, "You know, I've actually seen him on stage in a few Broadway plays over the years. He's always been a monumental presence."

"Oh, Cal's a scene stealer for sure. If you want to indulge in a star turn, it's a given fact to never act with children, animals, or Cal Lockheed. Did you ever happen to catch the one-man show he commissioned for himself? *The Legend of Sleepy Hollow*. Cal finally found the perfect showcase, got rave reviews around the country, and can tour with it until he drops dead from old age. In it, he portrays the entire cast of Washington Irving characters right down to a horse named Gunpowder. He refers to it as his retirement fund production. And make no mistake—Cal Lockheed, the theatre artiste extraordinaire, cannot be upstaged. One evening during his tour, performing *Sleepy Hollow* in an outdoor theatre somewhere in farm country, a stray cow actually wandered onto the stage area in the middle of Cal's performance. He did an expert double-take, stared directly at the creature and said, 'Excuse me, Bessie, but I believe this is *my* monologue.' It brought down the house."

Bettie laughed and offered Venus a smoke.

"Virginia Slims? Those skinny sticks are not even worthy to be identified as a cigarette," scoffed Venus, rummaging through her Valentino shoulder bag, "I wish they hadn't banned tobacco commercials on television, I'd have made a terrific Pall Mall spokeswoman for the brand. Smoking's such a glamorous way to kill yourself."

"I noticed that Cal constantly chain smokes."

"Oh, honeygirl, I once caught that man with two cigarettes in his mouth. It took him a few seconds to realize it. He laughed himself silly."

"He even attempted smoking while he was in the hospital," Bettie commented, "I thought the nurse was going to have apoplexy."

Venus flicked her gold lighter and took a long drag, "Cal phoned me from there. I could tell that he was happily puffing away. He said it was a more enjoyable means of being poisoned." She snorted heartily at the memory, "Now, that must've been one crazy experience for you folks—being served arsenic at Helena Baxter's cocktail party. I'm sure glad I left before all that madness started. I got the distinct impression, about that night from our conversation, that Cal knows something more than he's telling anybody. The man's always painfully coy when he's holding onto a secret."

JD pulled into a parking spot directly in front of Lockheed's stylish West Village apartment building. This part of town was akin to visiting a foreign country for Bettie. She often felt that she required a passport when venturing anywhere south of the Cherry Lane Theatre. The area felt unattractively industrial and the neighborhoods always appeared a little too desolate for her liking. Bettie was, admittedly, a bit of an uptown snob.

JD shouted to them over his shoulder, "I don't know if you ladies took notice during the drive here, but there's been a blackout on the west side below 4th Street. This area's been affected. It was just officially announced on WINS Radio. Nothing too serious, it seems, but the storm's causing lots of property damage. The newscaster said the power should be restored shortly. I have a flashlight in the glove compartment for you. It should help."

"Can this night become any more delightful? Venus seethed facetiously.

JD tested the torch by clicking it on and off several times. He handed it over to Venus just as she and Bettie made a mad dash from the Mercedes Benz to the entrance doors of Cal's Beaux-Arts building.

"It's lucky you've visited here a lot and know the lay of the land because I can't see a fucking thing." Bettie said uneasily as they started down the long corridor. She typically resorted to profanity when anxious.

Cal Lockheed had a duplex apartment. His front door was accessed from the ground floor of the building. The downstairs rooms were located below street level.

Bettie held the torch while Venus inserted the key in the tumbler and turned it part way. She reversed the motion when the lock resisted. It finally gave way with a crisp click and the door opened.

"I'm hoping that he left the note in the dining room. It's the closest area. We could grab it and leave. Screw watering his lousy plants." Venus said anxiously as she groped along the wall, "That flashlight doesn't exactly throw off much of a beam."

"Frankly, it sucks," said Bettie, "but it's better than the two of us stumbling around in total darkness."

From what Bettie could see of the apartment, it was quite tasteful and beautifully appointed. The lightning flashes occasionally afforded her a bit more of a complete image in brief fragments of time, like snapshots. There were large picture windows that looked out onto the sidewalk from the dining room. It was probably a breathtaking West Village view when the streetlights were on. Right now, there wasn't much she could discern in the pitch black. Bettie handed the torch back over to Venus.

"Dammit, I don't think he's left anything for me up here." Venus lamented. "As you can…uh…maybe…uh…see, on this level are the kitchen, dining room, powder room, and a bar area toward the back of the apartment that brings you out onto a lovely pocket garden. The staircase leading to the lower level is located over here. There are no windows since it's underground. Not that it'd make any difference tonight during a blackout. We can quickly search around his bedroom, master bath, and living room for some kind of note. Then, I promise, we'll scurry back up and scoot the hell out of here."

The torrential rain was beating against the picture windows, often accompanied by booming thunder and streaks of sudden lightning, as the women started to descend.

The actor's elegant duplex apartment featured a slightly rickety wrought iron spiral staircase making it a challenge to maneuver holding onto both the banister and the flashlight while wearing six-inch stilettos.

"Perhaps we should kick off our high heels." Bettie suggested.

Venus frowned, "With our luck, we'd probably never find them again in the dark. I don't know about you, honeygirl, but I'm not about to brave that monsoon in my bare feet if we have to suddenly bolt out of here."

Taking the lead, Venus first assured herself that Bettie was directly behind her, then guided their way slowly down the metal staircase until the two finally reached the bottom landing.

"It smells musty down here. Do you suppose water is leaking in from this awful rain? asked Venus, adding, "Now, I'm beginning to get creeped out."

Clutching the protective onyx talisman that hung around her neck, which her dear mother had given her to ward off *Mal De Ojo*, Bettie reached out for, and held on to, the other woman's hand for moral support. She was instantly put in mind of Catholic grade school fire drills and of Sister Mary Bernadette ordering the students to hold their partner's hand while filing two-by-two into the Church courtyard.

They entered directly into the living room. Sofa, television, divan, coffee table, all just as she remembered. "Oh, wait," said Venus in a hushed tone of voice, "the fancy chair is missing."

"You think there's been a robbery?" Bettie whispered nervously.

"His fancy prop chair from *Sleepy Hollow* isn't here. Cal loves that thing. It only leaves the apartment when he's on the road touring with it as part of his stage set."

"So it is possible he was booked for a last-minute gig." Bettie surmised as she felt Venus give her hand a tug, a signal for them both to move onto the next room.

A closet door was left open, and Venus cautiously focused her light inside the tiny space. "He keeps his show costumes in here. There's quite a collection. Looks as if Cal was looking for something in a hurry. Some clothes are on the floor. He generally treats his things with much more care."

In long, sweeping motions, Venus searched the bedroom using the flashlight and immediately noticed something odd. The bed was totally rumpled. It seemed as if someone had rolled all over the pristine linens after the bed had been carefully made. Cal was always fastidious in his housekeeping.

Then, she heard Bettie utter, "Look, that lamp's fallen over."

Training the focus of the torch to illuminate that portion of the room, both women could see broken ashtrays and cigarette butts scattered around the highly polished parquet floor next to the damaged light fixture. Venus followed the trail of the debris with the flashlight.

In a sudden panic, Bettie said, "Someone is in here with us. I can see his fucking shoes." She pointed nervously and shouted, "Quickly, turn the light over there."

Venus indeed saw the shoes, then the legs, as she moved the beam of the torch upward to reveal Cal Lockheed slumped in an ornate chair.

"Oh my stars, are you feeling alright?" breathed Venus as she reached for his arm. The sudden physical contact jarred Cal's motionless body. His head slid forward and fell at Venus' feet as she dropped the flashlight.

That's when Bettie first heard the sound. At first, she thought it was the crackling of distant lightning. Then she identified the sudden creaking as coming from upstairs. Somebody else had come into the apartment and was running along the floor above them. It was hard to hear very clearly because Venus was screaming. Bettie couldn't tell what frightened her the most—Cal's grimacing severed head on the floor in front of them, the heavy footsteps now clanking down the spiral staircase in their direction, or the fact that she'd involuntarily joined Venus in a scream that even drowned out the sound of the thunder and rain raging outside.

Finale

It was then that power was restored and the lights glared back on. Still screaming, Bettie and Venus were huddled together as JD ran toward them. He quickly checked that they were in one piece. Then, he ushered them away from the propped-up corpse in the throne-like chair. He tried to avert his eyes from the disembodied head still wobbling on the floor at his feet.

"Get hold of yourself, Lady Vee," whispered JD, attempting to maintain inner calm.

The three shaken people ran upstairs. Venus darted over to the kitchen wall phone and called the police.

"We shouldn't touch anything," said Bettie, "Let's wait for them in the Mercedes."

"Cal, poor Cal." Venus kept muttering as they walked the long corridor leading to the front door of the apartment building and to the vehicle parked outside.

JD started the car and immediately flicked on the heater. Bettie and Venus became aware that the sound of approaching sirens was now added to the deafening noise of the rain pounding on the vehicle's roof.

At the same time Venus was telephoning the police from Cal Lockheed's apartment, Vic and Renny stepped out of the storm and into a dive bar across the street from The Elgin for a quick drink before the midnight movie. It was a typical neighborhood hangout filled with an eclectic hodgepodge of downtown Manhattan locals.

The sleuth and the art director carried their ice-cold beers over to the quietest corner they could find.

"I had a call today from Rodney asking questions about Mr. Magnus," Renny began, "You hadn't told me about your office intrigue involving missing artwork. My brother and Special Investigator Volpe believe that there might possibly be a connection between the Chagall theft and my murder investigation. I gave him what scant information we'd uncovered about Magnus. I did share some theories that've been floating around in my head about the homicides. Rodney, in turn, told me certain suspicions he's had in respect to the stolen artwork from Oslo and how it might've ended up in your art archives." The detective took a healthy swig of his Budweiser.

Vic picked at a torn corner of his beer bottle label as he spoke, "Bettie and I told Rodney about Mr. Magnus, including his accidental death outside The Dakota and the terrible publicity it stirred up for Helena Baxter years ago. It seems like a jumbo jigsaw puzzle that doesn't make any sense because it has pieces from another box mixed into it."

"No doubt about it, Rodney and the Art Theft Detail do support your theory that the incidents are connected somehow. After speaking with him, I've come to the same conclusion. The big picture is starting to make a bit more sense to me." Renny said.

"Earl Quick has invited us down to Washington Square after the opening for a private celebration while waiting for the reviews." Vic prattled excitedly, "It's almost as if he's gathering all the glamorous suspects together—just like at the dramatic conclusion of an old Charlie Chan movie from Monogram Pictures."

Renny smiled, "Right. And yours truly is included among the list of guests."

"Say, are the two of you planning to do something wildly theatrical? Revealing the identity of our killer at the height of the evening and exposing the art thieves in one fell swoop?" Vic's eyes widened.

"I hadn't really thought about it, but you've given me a terrific idea," Renny's ice-blue eyes sparkled. "But I'd rather not discuss any of this right now if that's alright with you. The whole notion behind getting together tonight was to take our minds off murder and art heists for the time being. Tell me what you know about the film we're going to see."

Vic gave a muffled laugh, "I've heard that it's hilarious and disgusting. Just about everything you'd hope for from a midnight movie that has a 300-pound drag queen in the starring role."

"Vic Senso's still not at home and there's no pickup at the office," said Bettie hanging up the phone, "I've left several messages on his answering machine. I'm sure he'll call back as soon as he receives word."

Bettie was seated in Celeste Farris' suite at the St. Regis, which was shrouded in grief. Venus was totally devastated and could hardly speak. Both Celeste Farris and husband Earl were in a state of shock as they listened somberly to the details of the macabre turn-of-events. After dropping the two women off at the hotel, JD had driven back home to Brooklyn to soothe his frazzled nerves with a few stiff drinks.

"Thank goodness JD got bored with waiting in the car and decided to join us in Cal's apartment. He was carrying another flashlight. Venus dropped ours when we discovered the body. The light was shining on his…uh…face when the torch hit the floor and shattered." After a moment's hesitation, Bettie informed them, "The medical examiner believes that Cal was murdered sometime on Friday. It must've happened shortly after he was released from the hospital."

Celeste dabbed her reddened eyes, "I think I understand now what Helena Baxter's going through. This tragedy has hit a lot closer to home. We considered Cal a family member. It's so hard to fathom that he's actually dead."

"The police briefly questioned us. I think the officers realized that the three of us were somewhat in a state of shock. They said to expect a visit from Detective Clements, who will be in charge of the investigation," Bettie informed them.

"It seems wildly improbable that murder's been consuming so much of our lives recently," stated Celeste Farris taking a careful sip of her drink, "Normally, it's something we only see on the screen or in a stage play or read about in a book. Somehow, we never expect it to become a real-life experience. Homicides do not ordinarily occur among the circle of one's immediate friends. And suddenly, we're confronted with four of them. It all just seems so unreal. It makes me want to scream."

Venus was finally able to muster enough strength to say something, "I don't know much about Simone Caldwell, Oskar Lindqvist, or Caprice Fournier, but I cannot for the life of me understand why anyone would want to murder Cal Lockheed of all people."

"It's definitely puzzling, but I'm now beginning to wonder if Cal could very well have been the intended target the evening of the mass poisonings at The Dakota," noted Celeste, "He was one of the most severely stricken among the victims. This new tragedy seems to cement that theory."

"We must have faith that Detective Clements will eventually get to the bottom of it. Whoever's doing these awful things is likely to be leaving clues right and left." Quick surmised.

"The forensic technicians were in the process of taking fingerprint samples at Cal's apartment when we were released," Bettie sighed in hope, "Maybe they'll turn up something conclusive this time."

"There must've been quite a struggle because lamps were overturned and some end tables were knocked out of their usual positions. Cigarette butts and ashes were scattered all over the floor." Venus chattered, "Cal was a meticulous housekeeper. The rest of the apartment was in pristine condition. Whatever struggle or attack occurred was definitely confined to his bedroom."

Venus stood up and grimaced as she glanced down at her stylish outfit. "I've got to get out of this dress. There's blood all over it. Please excuse me." She bolted out of the room, tears welling up in her eyes.

Bettie noticed several dark red stains on her own blouse and skirt as well. She gave a noticeable shudder as she took another sip of her brandy.

"When was the last time you saw Cal?" the advertising executive asked to divert her own attention from her ruined Donna Karan outfit.

Celeste Farris and her husband answered and nodded in unison, "It was when we toured the Hayes on Friday."

"The day Simone Caldwell was murdered," added Quick.

"Do you think Cal could've accidentally seen something that might've threatened to expose the killer? We all pretty much stuck together except for a few random moments spent chatting with other cast and crew members backstage." Celeste said.

Bettie looked at the nearby phone, wishing it would ring.

"As you'll no doubt remember, Detective Clements had each of us account for our whereabouts in the theatre when we heard the commotion caused by Simone falling through the trap door. I would think, in the event that Cal'd witnessed anything suspicious, he would've spoken up then. If memory serves correctly, he was talking to Arnie when they both became aware of the horrible incident."

"Cal also said he could see Ava carping on the phone to her mother the entire time. They corroborated each other's story." Quick reminded them.

"I suppose we should phone Helena Baxter and Rex to tell them the news before they read about it on the front pages of every rag in town." Celeste spat anxiously.

Bettie shuddered, "Wouldn't it be horrible if pictures of Cal's murder suddenly surfaced? It happened in both instances with Simone and Caprice. The public exposure of humiliating photographic evidence seems to be another awful pattern with these crimes. Someone's maliciously adding insult to injury."

Celeste growled, "More like adding insult to fatality, you mean."

Looking gray around the edges, silver fox Earl Quick rose from his seat on the antique sofa just as Venus emerged from her bedroom wearing a fresh dress.

"Would anyone like some coffee?" the dutiful secretary asked, sedately. "I know I could use some. It might jolt me out of this stupor. This scotch doesn't seem to be working."

Celeste Farris grabbed Venus' hand, "You're in shock, Lady Vee, but a cup of strong coffee actually might help. Please, sit. I'll make it."

"I'm already up. Consider it done." Quick volunteered, "Coffee for four, *tout suite*."

Bettie once again glanced over at the nearby phone.

"It's nearly 2am," she breathed anxiously, "What the hell's keeping Vic?"

Although it only vaguely resembled the structure in style, the facade of the Elgin Theatre always reminded Vic of his favorite William Castle movie, *House on Haunted Hill*. The exterior of Frank Lloyd Wright's Ennis House was used in the Vincent Price horror flick as the idiosyncratic locale for a deadly gathering of disparate character types. Designer Simon Zelnik created the Elgin, on 19th Street and Eighth Avenue, which was equally cold and creepy looking, in the Art Moderne style. The dilapidated grind house had recently found a fresh life by running innovative, and in some cases highly artistic, oddball movies at their wildly popular cult midnight screenings.

Due to the violent storm outside, the place was already jam-packed with dampened but enthusiastic film goers. Vic and Renny were forced to settle for a pair of loge seats situated on the upper level of the cinema just as the house lights started to dim.

Every so often, Vic would glance over to monitor if Renny was enjoying the movie. The flickering screen reflected on Clement's classic features and highlighted the way his dampened hair curled around his perfect ears. Vic could just as easily have spent the ninety-minute running time of the picture staring at the detective's profile.

Pink Flamingos came to its cinematic conclusion hitting a high (or low, depending on your proclivities) standard of filth and total degenerate behavior. Vic loved every minute of it. He turned to hear Renny's opinion.

"I'm not absolutely positive, but I think we could all be arrested for watching that…um…piece of cinema." The sleuth laughed as he rose from his seat. "That sure was a carload of crazy, but it was a helluva lot of fun."

Vic stretched his way out of his cramped loge seat, "If I were putting a quote ad together, that would be a terrific headline. I'm glad you liked it. I wasn't really sure how you'd react."

The crowd at the Elgin was artistically bohemian. Typically, every fashion trend throughout the ages could be found in the audience from hippie chic to Halston couture at any given midnight showing. Vic was thoroughly entertained by the parade of hats galore, exotic boots, opera capes, even some fur, and rather unusual black vinyl rain gear, as the stylish patrons made their way towards the exit stairs. It could easily have been construed as a costume party by any innocent bystander watching the exodus on rainy Eighth Avenue.

Renny was walking directly in front of him as they reached the head of the steep staircase. People were jockeying to use the handrail, but Vic chose instead the center position with folks descending alongside him, two on either side, five across.

It all happened so fast.

Vic was suddenly aware that he must've tripped over his own feet walking down the rickety steps because he lost his balance and unsuccessfully reached out in front of him to lean on Renny's shoulder. The detective turned as Vic fell past him helplessly waving his hands in the air to gain equilibrium. The art director toppled down several steps and would have dangerously tumbled down the rest of the way, if Renny hadn't quickly grabbed hold of Vic's jacket, pulling him back onto his own two feet again. The staircase crowd was mostly drunk or high from smoking pot, causing some already unstable patrons to reach for nearby support as Vic flew by them.

Outside the Elgin, when they were once again seated safely inside the Chevy Impala, Renny said, "I hope you're alright, nothing sprained? Wow, two beers did you in? You're a cheap date. You could've broken your neck."

Vic was looking straight ahead through the rainy windshield, wrinkling his brow.

"Somebody pushed me," he said flatly.

Renny paused, "What?"

"At first, I thought I'd lost my footing, but now I distinctly remember being aware of the pressure of a pair of hands on my back shoving me forward. Maybe it's because of everything that's been going on. Am I being totally paranoid?"

"No, I don't think you're being paranoid." Renny said, "When you'd regained your balance on the stairs, I quickly looked at the crowd around us. With the variety of vinyl hats, rain gear, wigs, and turned-up collars, along with the pushing and shoving, it would've been difficult to recognize anyone. I probably would have been unable to identify my own brother in that mob. If you say someone pushed you, I believe you."

"You don't sound surprised." Vic was puzzled.

"In all honesty, I've been worried ever since you announced that you'd noticed something unusual involving the scenery at Helena Baxter's show. Something that had been changed or removed on the wall of headshots. Perry Chan insisted that nothing was different, but you've been adamant to the contrary and very vocal about it," the sleuth reported earnestly.

"Who the hell knew we were going to the Elgin tonight, anyway?" Vic nervously chewed on his lip. "Um…Renny…any suggestions on what I should do?"

"I don't mean to apply undue pressure, but you seriously need to figure out what bothered you on that stage set the day Simone Caldwell was murdered. You must've seen something that's threatening to expose our killer."

Vic sighed and shrugged his shoulders in utter frustration, "I've been trying."

Renny said authoritively, "Best be on your guard in the meantime, my friend. I strongly suspect that your life's in danger."

The yellow light on his telephone answering machine was flashing as they entered the art director's cozy studio apartment on East 54th Street. Renny was shaking off the rain from his jacket as Vic pressed the message retrieval button.

They listened in stunned silence as Bettie's halting, trembling voice filled the room. The two men immediately ran back out into the storm and climbed into the Impala. Renny sped and screeched through several red traffic lights as they anxiously made their way crosstown to the St. Regis.

Bettie threw herself into Vic's arms the moment he entered Celeste Farris' suite.

Renny Clements asked to use the phone to check in with police headquarters.

After everyone was settled, with cups of steaming coffee at the ready, the detective addressed himself to Venus and Bettie.

"Please tell me what happened tonight…um…in as much detail as possible," he said, taking out his notebook and pencil stub.

Both women took turns relating similar versions of the same story. They spoke as calmly and rationally as could be expected under the circumstances. Then, the detective posed some questions.

"You said it looked as though someone had rifled through Mr. Lockheed's costume collection?"

Venus took a careful sip from her cup before responding, "Most definitely. The closet was in complete disarray. Cal would never in a million years have left it in that condition."

"Offhand, could you determine what, if anything, was missing?"

Bettie offered some insight, "It was dark. The only light we had available was coming from a fairly weak torch bulb."

"I'm sure if I could return to his apartment, I'd be able to answer that question properly," Venus assured the detective, "I'm familiar with the closet's contents, and Cal keeps…um…kept…a catalogue listing everything he'd accumulated over the years from the various shows in which he'd performed."

Renny said, "If you're willing, I may ask you to do that once the crime scene's been thoroughly examined and given the all-clear."

"Provided someone comes along with me, of course." Venus said emphatically.

"Naturally." The detective stood, "It's been a long, long night. I appreciate your help. Everyone, please get some rest. You'll be hearing from me again tomorrow at some point, I'm sure."

Renny drove Bettie to her apartment, and then dropped Vic off at 54th Street. The rain was finally letting up as the Impala slid into a generous space directly in front of the brick apartment building.

"This is what I refer to as 'Doris Day parking'," Vic said with a grin.

Based on the mildly quizzical expression on the detective's sleepy face, Vic explained further, "In her 1960s films, whenever Doris Day arrived at her destination, a parking spot would be readily available right in front so she could maneuver her convertible directly into it with ease."

"Sounds as if Mamma Senso's little boy attended too many Saturday matinees."

The weary art director sighed, "Love those Doris Day pictures. We'll have to catch one soon. In the meantime, I'm going to phone Tobin in the morning. He shouldn't expect to see me at the office until later in the afternoon. I hope the police department allows you to sleep in for a bit tomorrow…um…today…as well." Vic said.

"Highly unlikely, but I'll give it a try," sighed the detective weakly.

Vic opened the car door, "Thanks again for grabbing my jacket on the Elgin Theatre staircase tonight. It was an altogether unnerving experience."

Renny smirked, "I could say the same thing about the John Waters movie."

Marsha dropped a healthy stack of pink message slips onto Vic's desk a few minutes after he'd finally settled in that Wednesday afternoon. Thompson & Co was a hive of activity as was typical for a day before the opening of a new Broadway play. More so, actually, since it involved strategizing all the media interest in the highly publicized and troubled production, *Don't Hang Up.*

The show, thus far, had racked up four violent murders and a fatal poisoning in its wake. Any dramatics happening on the stage of the Helen Hayes Theatre were certain to pale by comparison.

"All any of the columnists want to know is how poor, downtrodden Helena Baxter is coping with her plum starring role being usurped by her fiercest nemesis, Celeste Farris," carped Ava, who was draped on the corner of Vic's desk surrounded by a small coterie of fascinated secretaries and account assistants. "I've basically been running interference for the last few days. Even the homicides aren't enough of a distraction for God's sake. Further proof that show business is *mucho loco.* Maybe the reviewers will be softened by all the surrounding negative press. At least, I hope so. Being killed by the critics on top of everything else would be devastating."

"Not to be rude, Ava, but I have a ton of work to accomplish today," the art director announced in a huff, "Little of it will get done with you holding court in my office."

"But this *is* work, Rembrandt."

"Yes, *your* work. I need *my* desk and complete concentration for *my* work."

Ava snarled, "You don't have to get so pissy about it."

"Why don't you visit Bettie for a while?" Vic suggested with a forced smile.

"Bad idea. Bettie threw me out of her office fifteen minutes ago. Why the hell do you think I came in here—for your scintillating company?"

When Vic eventually came up for air, after plowing through a mountain of ad layouts and front-of-house display designs, a quick glance at his wristwatch alerted him that it was nearly 7:30. The workday activity at Thompson & Co. had noticeably quieted down as people from the art and production departments were leaving for the evening.

The other account executives were long since gone, except for Bettie, who was occupied with lining up her contacts at the various publications in order to collect the theatre critics' reviews the next evening before publication deadlines. The process entailed phoning each newspaper representative in order to secure a guaranteed connection to their journal's typesetting department after the *Don't Hang Up* review was submitted on opening night. Bettie would sit with pad and pencil jotting down any worthy quotes contained in the review, which was being laboriously dictated to her by the person who would be setting the type for publication.

The advance word allowed her some breathing room to rewrite the proposed radio commercials containing critics' authentic quotes. These would replace her bogus copy in the roughed-out announcer-read scripts. Bettie would then present the :60 second spots at the morning post-opening meeting for immediate client approval and release to the participating stations that would get them on the air during prime drive time.

"I believe I'm through for the night," she announced, throwing herself into one of Vic's guest chairs.

He looked up. "Well, you look like the cat who swallowed the canary. What's up?"

"The dreamy Mark Rhodes has just asked me out to dinner this evening. Finally."

Vic smiled from ear-to-ear, "Be still my heart. Took him long enough. I can't believe Ava is actually giving Mark a night off."

"She'll be busy at the theatre holding Celeste Farris' hand and fielding tabloid reporters through the final preview performance of *Don't Hang Up*."

"Any early indication on how the critics will react?" Vic reminded her, "Ava can sometimes ferret out top-secret information beforehand from attention-seeking, loose-lipped assistants."

"None that I've heard. Mark would've mentioned it."

Vic was drawing some straight lines on his tissue layout to indicate copy placement. He moved his heavy T-square incrementally as he drew parallel rows with his black permanent marker, making the process simple, requiring no thought whatsoever, and rendering conversation possible, welcome even.

"I wouldn't have expected you to be up to a romantic interlude after last night. I've never seen you as shaken and on edge."

Her lips twisted into a grimace, "It's not every day this girl finds a dead body in a darkened apartment. I still cannot believe that Cal Lockheed was murdered. Why would anyone want to kill him? He was practically a national treasure. If you think I'm a nervous wreck, Venus was totally devastated and somewhat in a state of shock. After all, she, Celeste, and Cal have been joined at the hip since their early show business days. They were featured in some legendary Broadway-bound flops."

"Cal had told me some wild stories about their antics over the years."

The account executive declared. "Anyway, I for one, cannot imagine a better diversion than getting lost in Mark Rhodes' smokey gray eyes."

"You'll get no arguments from me," Vic winked.

Bettie then burst into action, putting an end to her brief breather.

"I figure I have just enough time to get home, shower, and change before he comes a-calling. Mark made a nine-thirty reservation at one of my favorite neighborhood restaurants in Murray Hill. If things go well, I intend on inviting him up to my place for a nightcap afterwards."

Vic nodded, "That's my girl. Always thinking ahead. Oh-la-la, and about damn time!"

"It's eight-fifteen, I've got to dash. See you in the morning." She blew a kiss in his direction as she darted out the door and ran down the hall.

As Bettie breathlessly waited for the elevator, operator Mel Shapiro was closing down the other lift car, which was designated in the late evenings for freight. It was labeled out-of-service, and left inactive on the seventh floor, with switches off and door open, until early morning.

"Have a wonderful night, Miss Balboa," said Mel, tipping an imaginary cap.

"Thank you, Mr. Shapiro." Bettie vaguely curtsied, "Vic Senso is still hard at work and has coffee brewing in the conference room if you'd like a cup before heading home."

"It'd spoil my dinner, but I'll stop in to say goodnight when I'm through here," said the jovial day shift operator.

"Here's my ride," Bettie said as the doors clattered open and she stepped into the other elevator.

Vic was aware of distant sounds coming from the Thompson & Co lobby. He wasn't surprised when, moments later, Mel Shapiro poked his head into the office.

"Big opening tomorrow night?"

"Yessir. The new Joseph Michaels' play starring Celeste Farris at the Helen Hayes Theatre. By the way, if you and your wife would like to see it, I'll arrange for tickets."

"I'll ask the Missus, but I think she'd rather have seen it with Helena Baxter."

Vic laughed heartily, "Well, you be sure to let me know."

A while later, in the midst of designing a new poster incorporating quotes for ticket broker windows, Vic thought he heard the muffled closing of the metal door leading to the stairwell. The fire exit was located in the Thompson & Co reception area alongside the elevators. It was probably the cleaning crew, although it was a bit early for them. His watch read eight-forty.

He jumped slightly when his phone rang.

"How'd you know I'd still be working, detective?" Vic asked playfully.

"I'm beginning to suspect that you might be somewhat of a workaholic."

"And where, may I ask, are you?" inquired the art director.

Renny confessed, "Sitting at my desk, of course."

"This is clearly a case of birds of a feather."

"Or pot meets kettle. However, I have encouraging news. The

Helena Baxter case boxes from 1960 will be delivered here at the precinct first thing tomorrow morning."

"That's terrific. It certainly took long enough, but better late than never, I suppose." Vic put his T-square to rest at the top of his drawing board, "I'm seriously thinking of quitting for the night. Do you have any plans?"

"I could sure use a drink," the detective sighed.

There it was again. An unfamiliar noise coming from the hall.

"Make mine a double," said Vic, "I'm so jumpy, I'm imagining strange sounds in the office. But no one else is here. Would you mind holding on while I check it out?"

Thoughts of Cal Lockheed's murder popped into his mind, making Vic suddenly feel queasy. The charming actor's head was lopped off, for heaven's sake. Cal had been alone in his duplex apartment when it happened. Now Vic was aware of strange noises coming from outside his office. It took a few deep breaths and more courage than he thought possible to drop the phone and get up from his drawing table. He grabbed his heavy T-square for whatever protection it could provide under the circumstances.

"Hello? Who's there?" Vic called out in the deserted office.

He approached the doorway and looked to the left, down the dimly lit corridor. He didn't see anyone there but felt that there *was* indeed someone around the unseen corner of the hallway. There was a weird rustling sound.

It was then that Vic fully understood the expression his mom would sometimes use to describe fear: *Your blood runs cold.*

Stepping into his line of sight stood a shapeless figure concealed in a bulky black vinyl raincoat and fedora. The shiny hat was pulled down to cover most of the face which resembled a loosely hanging painted mask with a slash of red, indicating lips. The garment was ill-fitting and stiff, but perfect for disguising whoever was hidden underneath. With every step, the vinyl boots brushing against the coat created the creaking sound he'd heard earlier. And there was a bizarre whistling hissing noise. Vic couldn't really absorb more detail than that since he'd noticed the butcher knife.

Whoever it was—holding a long, sharp knife that somehow glistened in the shadowy corridor—was now moving menacingly toward him.

The frightened art director could hear Renny's voice, faint and frantic, coming from the telephone receiver, "Are you okay? What's going on over there?"

As if snapping out of a trance, Vic swung the heavy T-square in an arch in front of him as he spun around and ran down the corridor in the opposite direction. His unexpected visitor's heavy vinyl boots, fortunately, afforded limited mobility. With the awful squeaking sound of the stiff plastic fabric rubbing against itself with every movement, the masked assailant could only tread haltingly and mechanically following Vic down the corridor. Although hardly an athlete by any stretch of the imagination, Vic felt like an Olympic sprinter in comparison as he bolted toward the lobby and the door to the fire stairs. He turned once more to swing his lethal metal T-square, maintaining a secure distance from the ominous black vinyl figure with the raised butcher knife.

The inactive freight elevator stood open.

Vic hurled himself inside and reluctantly, dropping the T-square, pulled the heavy outer door closed with a loud clatter and thud. This plunged him into complete darkness. He was familiar enough with the manual elevator to feel for the handle of the metal gate and he slammed that shut as well. Through the two safety barriers, Vic could hear his would-be assailant on the other side of the door banging, kicking, and grunting in utter frustration.

It was pitch black inside the lift car. He was unable to find the buttons to activate the electricity or turn on the interior light.

He was safe.

And then, in a flash, it came to him. As Vic slowly slid down the elevator panel in breathless relief, he realized what he had seen at the theatre on the day that Simone Caldwell was murdered.

The stage scenery wall of actor headshots had neither been switched around nor changed. The steadfast Perry Chan had been correct all along.

When running up the rehearsal steps, Vic had glanced over, at just the perfect angle, to witness the killer's face reflected in the glass of one of the headshot frames. Hiding against the opposite wall, crouching stark still, the image of the murderer's face echoed on the glass acting as a mirror. At first, the impression was of a photographic double exposure—two images overlaying each other—but one clearly superseded the other due to the intense stage lighting.

Now, Vic knew the identity of the maniac who was violently banging against the metal door on the other side of the elevator car. It was the same person who'd killed Simone Caldwell, Oskar Linqvist, Caprice Fournier, and Cal Lockheed. The same person who'd tried to push him down the stairs at the Elgin Theatre.

The unnerving noise abruptly stopped. He could follow the sounds of retreating footsteps as they made tracks exiting via the doorway to the fire stairs. Vic knew that all he had to do now was to catch his breath and remain silently jittery in the pitch-dark cubicle. He was banking on the firm belief that help was on its way in the form of a speeding Chevy Impala. The art director was badly shaken, but anxious and eager to tell Renny what he'd finally remembered.

It took less than fifteen minutes for Clements and two assisting police officers to arrive at the Thompson & Co ad agency.

Vic could hear them running and shouting from behind the thick elevator panel. He called out as a precaution, to guarantee that it was indeed the detective and his men, before opening the gate and the metal sliding door.

Squinting at the harsh light after being in total darkness, Vic didn't attempt to move until his eyes fully adjusted.

"Just a typical day in the world of theatrical advertising," he announced to the handsome man standing over him, who was wearing a concerned expression.

"You left the phone off the hook," said Renny, relief written all over his face, "Do you have any idea how expensive that call is going to be?"

Vic felt a bit light-headed, "You can send the bill to Thompson & Co," he joked weakly as his friend helped him stand up on still-wobbly legs.

The detective pointed to the floor, "Careful when you walk out here. We need to photograph that weapon *in situ* before bagging it as evidence."

Vic followed the direction of Renny's gesture and shuddered at the sight of the butcher knife. It had been violently plunged into the plush lobby carpet outside the elevator door.

Curtain

Early that cloudless Thursday, producer Earl Quick was a bit taken aback when Detective Clements telephoned with his unusual request regarding the private celebration to be held on Washington Square after the opening night performance of *Don't Hang Up*.

"I'm eager to help and wholeheartedly agree to cooperate in whatever ways required," Quick responded enthusiastically. "Especially if it'll put an end to this nightmare for all of us. What do you want me to do?"

Ten minutes later, Renny was grinning from ear-to-ear as he winningly slung the battered phone receiver back into its cradle.

He just had a few more phone calls to make.

Vic unzipped the Paul Stuart garment bag hanging on a hook behind his office door to check on the condition of his tuxedo. Due to the abject lunacy of the last two weeks, he'd totally ignored his wardrobe requirements for this evening's opening night. It was a black-tie event, of course, as befitting any play penned by up-and-coming wunderkind Joseph Michaels and starring an actress possessing the legendary caliber of the one- and-only exquisite stage star, Celeste Farris.

The amount of press surrounding *Don't Hang Up* was staggering. The daily media coverage included front page photos and articles concerning both Miss Farris and her unfortunate predecessor in the role, Helena Baxter. Interviews with director Rex Merchant and the show's distinguished producer, Earl Quick, had appeared on

Page Six as well as on page one of every publication that reported 'exclusive' tidbits about the hottest story to hit Broadway in years.

Among the numerous tabloid articles narrating the ghastly details of the four violent homicides connected to the production, there'd be peppered several human-interest stories concerning "*A Glamorous Day in the Life of Celeste Farris*" and "*How Helena Baxter Maintains Calm Under Duress.*"

The Village Voice even featured a lengthy piece about 'sexy and shy' photographer Terry Hagen, who'd managed to document two grisly murders in as many weeks. The story was accompanied by a rare snapshot of the circumspect shutterbug herself. The picture had been taken surreptitiously at her studio with Hagen's beloved chihuahua, Tu-tu, sitting complacently on her lap.

Venus Pluto had been featured in a four-page *People Magazine* story about her intimate, friendly, long-time working relationship with Celeste Farris. She also spoke of the late, great actor Cal Lockheed. Venus related a few choice episodes from their time on the road together appearing in some notorious Broadway-bound disasters.

Publicists Ava Chasten and Mark Rhodes were often mentioned in the columns spouting quotes about the state of the production staff, the show's star, and supporting cast. Arne Engels was repeatedly approached for inside information for publication concerning box office numbers and advance ticket sales.

Variety and *The Hollywood Reporter* interviewed both ad executive Bettie Balboa and art director Vic Senso about the trauma of handling print and radio campaigns for a new play under such intense scrutiny.

Vic had shared a quick breakfast with Bettie at The Piccadilly Coffee House on 45th Street. Nearly every luminary attached to the world of the Broadway theatre could be seen in attendance feasting on Frances and Harry Edelstein's luscious, corned beef on rye sandwiches and creamy potato salad during any given lunchtime.

It was over early morning hot tea and blueberry danish that Vic relayed to Bettie the events of the evening before. 1) The figure in the black vinyl raincoat, 2) The threatening ten-inch-long butcher knife, 3) Vic's new-found fondness for his metal T-square.

He purposely failed to mention the fact that he'd remembered the familiar face he'd seen reflected in the headshot frame glass the day of Simone's murder. The detective had asked him to keep their intentions under wraps, even from Bettie.

"As crazy as this sounds, Renny told me that the butcher knife belonged to Caprice. It was missing from her expensive set of Wusthof gourmet cutlery. Helena Baxter reported it 'nowhere-to-be-found' after her arsenic cocktail party last week and happened to mention it to the police in passing. She thought one of the hired catering staff may have mistakenly taken it away." Vic whispered.

"Could the situation get any creepier?" Bettie asked.

"I shudder to think. On a lighter note, how was your date last night?"

"Mark was about thirty minutes late, but that's part and parcel with working for Ava. He seemed frazzled at first but calmed down after a cocktail. The restaurant honored our reservation and we had a lovely dinner. I really like him."

"Did you invite him over to your place for a nightcap afterwards?"

"Mark said he had some work to do. He tactfully asked for a rain check."

Now back at Thompson & Co, and peering into the unzipped Paul Stuart garment bag alongside the art director, Bettie asked, "Have you had this tuxedo dry-cleaned since our last Broadway opening?"

Vic shrugged, "I can't remember, but it's too late now. Besides, no one is going to be looking at me tonight. All eyes will be on Helena Baxter and Celeste Farris."

The opening night curtain rang down at nine-fifteen to enthusiastic applause.

It was obvious to Vic and Bettie, who were sitting with Tobin Klein in Row J on the aisle, that Celeste Farris was elated that the ordeal was over. During her solo curtain call, the actress was beaming and her carefree body language spoke volumes. In truth, everyone involved with *Don't Hang Up* breathed a collective sigh of relief. Celeste was graciously motioning toward someone in the wings to join her in the spotlight. Traditionally, this would be an honor afforded the playwright, in this case, young Joseph Michaels, who was currently away on a Transatlantic jaunt.

The opening night audience went wild when Helena Baxter made an enormously surprising entrance from stage right.

The two legendary Broadway actresses basked in the tumultuous applause generating from the adoring crowd. Celeste Farris and Helena Baxter embraced and joined hands in taking their bows as the tabloid paparazzi ran to the lip of the stage with flashbulbs furiously popping. It was electrifying.

Publicists Ava and Mark could scarcely contain the aggressive members of the press as the pushy photographers jockeyed to take the best pictures from the most advantageous angles. Broadway mainstay Terry Hagen was numbered among them but was the only one who would be attending the non-publicized after-party in the studio head's Washington Square mansion.

The guest list read as follows:

Miss Celeste Farris Miss Helena Baxter
Mr. Earl Quick Mr. Rex Merchant
Ms. Venus Pluto Mr. Arne Engels
Ms. Terry Hagen Mr. Perry Chan
Mr. Tobin Klein Ms. Bettie Balboa Mr. Vic Senso
Ms. Ava Chasten Mr. Mark Rhodes
Mr. John Elmo Mr. John Sylvester

The formally attired guests began to arrive at 10:00. A starched but jovial butler greeted them at the door as countless servants bustled and fussed behind him, taking coats, and escorting the impressive collection of theatrical types across the highly polished marble floor to a stately ballroom. As people entered, a subdued string quartet expertly played the compositions of Beethoven and Mozart as well as those of Rodgers and Hammerstein.

What came as a curious occurrence to some was the presence of Detective Renny Clements. Unlike the rest of the crowd, the staggeringly handsome man was wearing a plain brown suit—about one size too small, a tie, a crisp white shirt with an awkwardly oversized collar, and "looking like a billion dollars, regardless." This last observation was made by Bettie to Vic upon first catching sight of the sleuth standing in the center of the grand room.

"What an unexpected pleasure, detective," said Bettie, "However, I have a sneaking suspicion that Vic is not nearly as surprised as I am."

Tobin joined the intimate group and extended a welcome, "Evening, detective."

"I thought I was finally going to meet your lovely wife tonight, Mr. Klein," Renny said as he vigorously shook the creative director's hand.

Tobin reached for a champagne flute from a passing tray, "Olga doesn't particularly care for Broadway. She's much more of a foreign film buff. But, I keep trying."

"Hopefully, I'll have a chance some other time soon." Detective Clements said.

Perry Chan and Terry Hagen joined them, drinks in hand.

"Look, no camera!" Terry happily exclaimed.

"Amazing performance tonight," announced Perry, "The astonishing curtain call brought down the house, wouldn't you say? That's what theatre is all about."

"Congratulations on your clever set design," remarked Tobin, "It's like featuring an additional character in the play. Scenery rarely achieves that."

"Many thanks. It was a fun show to design. I'd never worked on a thriller before. It was a challenge." Perry bowed modestly, "Hey, here come our press agents. Any idea what time the reviews will be pouring in?"

Ava and Mark were attempting to relax a bit after their turbulent experience with the paparazzi. They were armed with brimming champagne flutes.

"Oh, it'll be a few hours yet, gang, so prepare yourselves for a long night," snapped Ava, who looked stunning in a low-cut silver evening dress, "Ordinarily, I would harangue a few critics for early word, but all anybody wants to talk about are the murders. I decided to steer clear of all that mishegoss."

"Reporter Stuart Klein, on Channel 5's Ten O'clock News, usually airs around 10:25. The rest of the television reviews generally follow at 11:20 or so." Mark said, "We usually cover a few television screens at once since the network news programs all seem to run their theatre critic spots about the same time. We've hired Anne Rose to monitor and transcribe the reviews as they come in. She'll type them up and send them along via messenger later tonight."

"The newspapers aren't expected to hit the streets until after midnight at the earliest." Ava added, taking a look around the ballroom. "Dazzling digs here, right? I mean, seriously."

Helena Baxter, radiant in a scarlet and black Halston creation, swept into the room. She entered arm-in-arm with her husband Rex, who appeared nervous and tongue-tied, still coming down from somewhat of a major marijuana high.

The couple's arrival was quickly followed by the star of the evening, Celeste Farris, brilliantly decked out in gold head-to-toe Givenchy.

The assembled party politely applauded as she elegantly drifted across the floor to be greeted by the others. Celeste Farris's entourage included her dashing husband Earl, who was clearly born to wear a tuxedo. He immediately took on the carefree task of playing host to the intimate gathering.

Venus radiated natural elegance in her blood-red evening gown. Even Arne's allergies were on their best behavior. The Johns discreetly stood on either side of the doorway after entering the ballroom.

"It seems as if everyone's here." Quick said graciously, "Thank you all so much for coming this evening. There's no doubt in my mind that my darling wife, Celeste Farris, gave one of the most luminous performances of this or any season. I extend my heartfelt congratulations to everyone involved with the show. It was not at all easy working under the constant glare of publicity. Please raise your glasses and toast a task well done under immense pressure. To all of you. Cheers."

Quick continued, "Traditionally, waiting for the critics' reviews is maddening. Tonight, we would like to offer a departure from hours of senseless anxiety with an unusual diversion. Please follow me into the library. The entrance is to your left."

Two stalwart servants opened the ornate mahogany doors to reveal another beautifully appointed chamber which served as a library. The shelves surrounding the room were filled with hundreds of books. An immense window offered a picture-perfect view of Washington Square. There were several plain wooden seats situated in one area. The centerpiece of the library was a rather large round table, composed of black obsidian crystal, circled by antique chairs. There was a stunning woman sitting facing them. She had a mane of shocking white hair that offset her rich, dark complexion and framed her remarkable saucer-shaped amber eyes.

"It's Mizz Mitzi." Bettie involuntarily shrieked, "What a thrilling surprise."

Silver fox Earl Quick smiled. "For those of you not familiar with this talented lady sitting before you, it's an honor to introduce Mizz Mitzi, one of the world's premiere psychics," he casually explained. "Her clairvoyant powers are renowned. She has communicated with many departed souls over the years. This great lady has provided answers to many difficult questions."

Quick extended his arms as he guided the various guests to their assigned seats at the imposing table. He turned to the discreet servants, "Please draw the drapes and switch off the lights. Thank you. We'll use the illumination from Mizz Mitzi's glass orbuculum, more commonly known to most of you as a crystal ball.

"Over the years, the press has had a field day concerning spiritualism and psychic phenomenon. In light of the recent tragedies suffered by our group, I felt Mizz Mitzi might be able to supply some insight, and perhaps comfort, regarding the untimely deaths of so many of our friends and colleagues in the theatre world these past weeks."

As Quick spoke, Renny and Vic sat in the wooden chairs situated behind the main table. The Johns were already settled there.

"Mizz Mitzi, our highly sensitive medium," Quick continued, "has proven time and again to be the genuine article amidst so many flam-flam posers. I ask you to assist her in obtaining communications from those no longer with us on this earthly plain. Please concentrate."

The gracious host then took a seat between his wife and Venus at the glistening black crystal table.

The clairvoyant gazed at the ceiling briefly before looking around at the twelve other participants. She'd been faintly humming the music to the song *On a Clear Day You Can See Forever*. She abruptly stopped and took a deep breath.

"Please join hands. I implore you all to never break the psychic connection, regardless of what may occur during this séance. Now, let us bow our heads in meditation," Mizz Mitzi began, her resonant voice filling the library, as she gazed into the glowing crystal ball, "Oh, Universe, please allow the spirits of understanding to descend upon the thirteen believers gathered here in the inner circle tonight. We are each, in our own way, seekers of the truth. Let your spirits guide us. All is in readiness. Permit one voice among your multitude to speak with us. We have so many questions. We are lately surrounded by so much mystery and puzzlement."

The mild tittering of the excited guests ended abruptly. The room fell utterly quiet and still. Anticipation of the unexpected was palpable. The light from crystal ball seemed to pulsate.

Shattering the total silence, a sudden intake of breath emanating from Mizz Mitzi was followed by the medium shouting out one bewildering word.

"Magnus," she said.

There were no reactions, neither physical nor vocal, from anyone at the table. The clairvoyant's amber saucer eyes scrutinized the hushed participants with concern as she continued, "Mizz Mitzi has a message from Magnus. Does anyone here know a Magnus? He is very distressed and desperate to apologize for all of the humiliation his unfortunate death has brought you. Magnus wants to tell you that he is sorry that, because of his premature passing, your mother slowly lost her mind, causing you further grief and degradation."

There was a stunned silence which lingered several moments.

From behind the cluster of thirteen seated at the circular table, Renny Clements whispered, "You may ask any questions of the spirits. I encourage you to do so while Magnus is within Mizz Mitzi's dimension. Quickly. Ask anything at all."

Celeste Farris shifted in her chair and spoke hesitantly. "Magnus, why have you come to us? To which of us are you apologizing?"

Mizz Mitzi closed her eyes as she communicated the spirit's response, "I am talking to my child. My poor innocent child who's been driven mad by grief and dishonor."

"Oh, brother." Ava sneered, rolling her eyes.

Perry reprimanded her, "Honestly, can't you take anything seriously?"

The psychic fiercely whipped her head from side-to-side, "I beg you to ignore the disturbance. Don't leave us yet, Magnus. We have so many more questions for you."

There was silence.

Mizz Mitzi attempted one more anxious plea, "Magnus, come back. I'm certain your child is here among us. I feel it as strongly as you do."

The library was noiseless and deathly still.

The silence was broken by the sound of a voice that seemed to emanate from every corner of the vast room. All eyes focused on

Helena Baxter as her body stiffened and her lips parted to give way to a disembodied cry, *"Pourquoi m'as-tu tué?"*

"Oh, my Lord, that's Caprice Fournier's voice." Bettie screamed.

"Please keep your hands linked and remain calm," warned Mizz Mitzi employing a soft, calm tone, "It seems we've contacted a second paranormal visitor. On occasion, another person is selected from the thirteen believers to serve as a conduit to the beyond. Miss Baxter appears to be highly susceptible. She's in a trance-state and not in control of her own senses. Any sudden movements or loud noises may be dangerous for her."

"Pardonne-moi. Je suis désolé pour ce que j'ai fait." Helena Baxter was trembling and her brow was glistening with perspiration. *"C'était toi!"* she bellowed as she stared across the black crystal table.

The actress was uncontrollably thrashing from side-to-side in her chair. Her dark eyes were filled with fright. Helena Baxter was trying to speak but only seemed capable of uttering guttural sounds and half-formed words. Throughout it all, she kept her eyes heatedly trained on the person seated across the table from her.

"Meurtriére!"

Helena Baxter again shrieked, "Murderer!"—only In English this time—as she released her right hand from the circle and dramatically pointed her lacquered red fingernails directly at stunned Arne Engels.

"Are you fucking crazy?" Arne sputtered as he violently threw back his chair, tipping it over in the process. He shook himself loose from both Bettie and Mark, sitting on either side of him during the séance, as he backed into the corner of the darkened library.

"I'd sit down again if I were you, Arnie," Renny Clements shouted as The Johns rose from their chairs and blocked the doors. "We have an awful lot to talk about."

The detective calmly approached the general manager, "About why you murdered Oskar Lundqvist, Simone Caldwell, Cal Lockheed, and Caprice Fournier. About how you poisoned the canapés at Helena Baxter's cocktail party. About why you attempted to kill Vic Senso twice in the last twenty-four hours. And lastly, about how you eventually came to stash a stolen original Marc Chagall canvas in the art archives at Thompson & Co."

"Bullshit. You're insane. You don't know what the hell you're talking about." Arne snarled. "I think you've gone over the edge. You're completely delusional."

Detective Clements countered, "I beg to differ. In the…um… spirit of full disclosure, between the opening night performance of the play, and our arrival here as Mr. Quick's guests, the police have thoroughly searched your office in the Sardi building and your apartment. They've uncovered some rather interesting evidence connecting you to all of our recent troubles. It's over, Arnie. You really should sit down."

Engels was in the process of catching his breath. He sneezed repeatedly, his allergies surfacing in full hyperdrive. Reluctantly, he returned to his seat between Bettie and Mark at the black crystal table.

"I must confess," Renny began, looking around the room, "I enjoy having a captive audience. The solitary exit from this library is now being blocked by The Johns—the human equivalents of a cement barricade. Naturally, in Arnie's case, if he attempts to make an escape by jumping out of the massive window facing Washington Square, let it be known that we're three stories up. Aside from probably not dying of a nosedive from this height, the spiked wrought iron fence surrounding the mansion no doubt may impale you and finish the job. Now, let's get down to business.

"I have rather a long story to relate. In the theatrical tradition of Grand Guignol, it will contain much blood, violence, and dramatic manipulation. We must go back in time to the year 1957 in Oslo, Norway when several masterpieces were stolen from the prestigious Neils van de Velde Museet. Among the paintings that were snatched, the most valuable was a canvas by Marc Chagall. As is often the case in robberies of this nature, some of the pinched artwork was so famous and so high-profile, it was impossible to fence or sell, even to private buyers, for fear of certain incrimination.

"So, the Chagall painting was passed around among the circle of thieves like a hot potato for a few years—each in turn hiding the canvas—until it fell into the hands of the only one of the culprits who was actually employed at the van de Velde Museet. He worked there as an archivist. This man was instrumental in supplying confidential museum information concerning alarm systems, guard changes, and security camera set-ups which eventually led to the successful art heist. His name was Magnus Engelstaad.

"It so happened that Mr. Engelstaad was planning a visit to The United States as part of the International Council of Museums convention being held in New York City. He saw it as an ideal opportunity to stash the hot Chagall overseas and perhaps unload it here. Somehow, he cleverly smuggled the canvas through airport customs. The painting, valued at over ten million dollars, was now hidden in Mr. Engelstaad's suite at The Plaza Hotel. That's how he came to be exploring the Upper West Side of Manhattan one sunny afternoon on lunch break from the ICOM conference. Still wearing his ID tag, on which he'd written his first name: Magnus, Mr. Engelstaad was instantly killed when a ten-pound dumbbell accidentally fell from Helena Baxter's window crushing his skull.

"The awful situation was heightened when Mr. Engelstaad's distraught widow and her fourteen-year-old son, Arne, were flown in to identify the body. Helena Baxter was branded a heartless killer until all of the facts about her actually being out-of-town at the time finally came to light a few days later. The entire incident was eventually written off as an unfortunate accident, not a homicide as originally reported.

"Ingrid Engelstaad was well aware of her husband's involvement in the museum robbery. Magnus informed her that he was taking the Chagall with him to America. She knew where he'd stashed the canvas in his hotel suite. After arriving in the U.S. to identify her husband's body, she retrieved it, quickly rented an apartment here, and never returned to Oslo. Her dashed dreams of a financial windfall now destroyed; Ingrid vowed to make Helena Baxter's life miserable.

She followed the actress relentlessly, until the legal system—plus a more realistic financial settlement—put an end to it.

"When his mother died a few years later, most likely due to intense mental anguish, young Engelstaad was now tasked with unloading the Chagall painting. By this time, Arne was already working in the theatrical arena. He secured employment straight out of college as a stage manager under an abbreviated name change. As Arnie Engels, most everyone assumed he was of Jewish heritage. He never claimed to be, but also never denied it. He maintained his first name, Arne, although almost everyone affectionately called him Arnie, assuming it short for Arnold.

"Under his new identity, he eventually established his own successful business in theatrical general management—distancing himself from his Norwegian roots and unsavory family history. Arnie's one driving ambition, throughout all of these years, was to take his revenge on the women who'd killed and made a laughingstock of his beloved father and drove his dear mother to the brink of insanity.

"Due to his proximity and access to Thompson & Co, Arnie became familiar with the art archives. What a perfect place to securely stash his priceless stolen artwork. It was a climate-controlled environment, rarely visited, except by Tobin Klein and Vic Senso. Arnie safely sheltered the small canvas among the hundreds of pieces of unpublished artwork in the ad agency's jam-packed vertical files—and was worry-free about it for years."

Unexpectedly, Arne gruffly interrupted the detective's narrative, "If I may ask, what are the whereabouts of the stolen Chagall painting that I've been accused of hiding?"

Renny signaled that undivided attention be transferred to Vic Senso.

"Fortunately, the priceless masterpiece is now in the capable hands of the NYPD Art Theft Detail." The art director exultantly informed the group, "They are working with the World Customs Organization in returning the Chagall to its proper home at the Neils van de Velde Museet in Oslo after almost eighteen years."

Detective Clements once again claimed the spotlight as he scanned the anxious faces in the library and continued, "The recovery of this most valued art treasure can be attributed to Bettie Balboa and Vic Senso of Thompson & Co. These events, just brought to light, serve as the background to our four homicides, not forgetting the mass poisonings at The Dakota, and the attempted murder of Vic Senso.

"Arnie Engelstaad spent most of his boyhood in abject humiliation. His father had been killed by a falling dumbbell. What could be more embarrassing? Whenever he was confronted with telling the story of his father's death, laughter typically followed. A dumbbell? Hilarious. It was an open wound that festered over time.

"This was the year you decided to murder Caprice Fournier and Simone Caldwell." Renny was laser-focused on Arne, "Not only would you kill them, but you'd humiliate and degrade them in the manner of their deaths. Oh, and, as a bonus, you could further hound Helena Baxter under a relentless black cloud of embarrassing publicity.

"After a lifetime of being teased and ridiculed whenever divulging the manner of his father's accidental death by dumbbell, Arne Engelstaad...um...now, Arnie Engels wanted payback. Working on the Broadway production, *Don't Hang Up*, afforded him the perfect opportunity.

"As general manager, he'd be working closely with Helena Baxter, whom he despised. He'd also have easy access to both Simone and Caprice without raising any undo suspicion. He so badly wanted to see those two women dead.

"When Arnie learned that Helena Baxter had secured a contract with Simon & Schuster for a cookbook featuring Mademoiselle Fournier's canapés, he saw it as an ideal time to take action. He set out to humiliate them both. At this point, Arnie didn't want Caprice to die, he simply wanted to embarrass her and make her life a living hell, dragging Helena Baxter along for the ride.

"Around this time, I suspect you started a rumor about Helena Baxter having an illicit affair. Confiding in the doorman at the Sardi building was a good place to start. Guy Andersen is known to spread gossip like wildfire with his blind items. It was a tailor-made smoke screen, as well as a red herring.

"Engels' next bit of ingenuity was taking full advantage of the chaos surrounding the cookbook announcement. With a multitude of curious party guests intruding on the kitchen during the canapé preparations, Arnie randomly coated some of the hors d'oeuvres with a dusting of arsenic to make a laughingstock out of Caprice Fournier's pretensions of being a master chef. How and when he was able to do it, I'm still not sure. But rest assured, I'll find out eventually."

"I sneezed." Arne Engels once again interrupted the detective, "Ever notice that everyone around you momentarily averts their eyes and moves away when someone sneezes? Oh, I'm not confessing to anything, I'm simply making an astute observation. Including the fact that any gracious photographer would avoid taking a shot of someone caught in the awkward act of sneezing. And, most important of all, no one would likely remember it. It's a non-event. Everyone sneezes at one time or another. A quick thinker would find it a perfect opportunity of which to take advantage of a few seconds' time. Pulling a handkerchief out of your pocket with one hand while using the other hand for some tomfoolery. You know, like a magician. Besides, I myself was counted among the poison victims, and I'm still here to tell about it. I really didn't intend the arsenic to kill anyone—just enough to embarrass Caprice and ruin her deal. What publisher in his right mind would move forward with a cookbook after the authors had poisoned a room full of people?"

"You murdered Oskar Lindqvist," Renny said.

"I'm not sure what went wrong there. It was a completely unplanned bit of luck for Caprice's editor to have swallowed a fatal amount of the poison. I suppose he ate too many of those ridiculous *White Monkeys*. Or perhaps he suffered from a delicate constitution. Whatever. His death was totally random."

"Which is more that I can say about your murder of Simone Caldwell." Renny said snidely as he turned to his audience.

"Arnie was quite busy earlier on the day of the scheduled advertising shoot at the Hayes Theatre. He, in effect, was getting ready for a photo session of his own. He needed to set up the pile of the noisy, sharp-edged musical instruments and metal trash bins under the trap door. As the general manager, anyone who might have seen him near the trap room would think nothing of it. Arnie could easily maneuver the trap door mechanism. All he required was to get Simone to be at the right place when he needed her to be. The orchestra section of the theatre was dimly lit. Arnie probably phoned Simone and asked her to meet him on stage before anyone else was scheduled to arrive. He most likely directed her to use the main front doors and to enter the theatre from the back of the house. I would imagine that Arnie had already begun talking to her, in order to divert her attention, as Simone walked up the rehearsal steps and started walking towards him across the stage. She was unaware that the trap door was open and she fell to her death just as he'd planned."

Renny Clements paused to catch his breath before continuing.

"What Arnie hadn't counted on was Vic Senso, Bettie Balboa, and Tobin Klein arriving just as Simone screamed and created a racket when crashing onto the piled up heap in the trap room down below. Arnie couldn't make his exit off stage fast enough, so he crouched against the scenery wall situated opposite the framed headshots. While Vic was racing up the rehearsal steps, by a fluke of lighting, he saw Arnie's face reflected in the glass of one of the frames. Vic later couldn't figure out how or why one of the pictures had been changed or removed from the scenery. Perry Chan, the set designer, was insistent that nothing had been switched because… nothing had. In all the ensuing chaos, Arnie easily blended in with the running crowd on stage who were anxious to find out what had caused the sudden commotion."

"Excuse me, detective," waved Celeste Farris from her seat at the séance table, "How do you explain his presence on the stage, supposedly killing Simone, when our dearly departed Cal Lockheed clearly told us that he was talking to Arnie behind the backdrop when all hell broke loose? Ava even swore she saw them conversing the entire time."

"That brings us to the third murder—that of Mr. Lockheed." Renny said.

"Wasn't Mademoiselle Fournier the third murder victim?" asked Venus, puzzled.

"No. Cal Lockheed was killed before Mademoiselle Fournier. Hear me out, please," the detective continued, "I strongly suspect that Lockheed witnessed Arnie's sleight-of-hand poisoning of the canapés with arsenic powder. Cal had a sharp eye—nothing usually escaped his attention. After all, he was the only person who caught sight of Ava Chasten swiping an hors d'oeuvre off one of the trays in full view of everyone in the kitchen."

"That's right. I'll attest to that!" the redheaded publicist squealed.

"Cal may not have realized at the time what he saw Arnie do but had ample opportunity while recuperating in the hospital to figure it out. I think he was planning on a bit of long-term blackmail. Mr. Engels was not about to fall victim to that," Renny said.

"After committing the murder in Lockheed's duplex, Arnie pinched a black vinyl raincoat, boots, and fedora from Cal's costume collection as a useful disguise."

Detective Clements turned his attention to the general manager, "Can you explain how those three items of clothing came to be rolled up in a trash bag stuffed at the back of your apartment closet?"

"Fuck you." Arne hissed.

A wicked smirk momentarily flashed over the detective's handsome face. He moved casually around the library as he delivered the rest of his case.

"I checked back in my trusty notebook to read what I'd written down concerning Cal Lockheed's statement of his whereabouts at the time Simone Caldwell was being murdered. He'd said, *"I could clearly see Ava from where I stood. Granted, she was across the stage standing behind the backdrop as Arnie and I were. Once or twice, depending on the angle, I'd lose sight of her as she paced while talking, but I could still hear her side of the telephone conversation."*

You could hear a pin drop in the Washington Square mansion library as Renny cleared his throat and said, "If one takes that statement from the other angle, one can surmise that, conversely, Ava could see Cal and Arnie across the stage standing behind the backdrop. That she, too, would lose sight of Arnie. Well, suppose Arnie was indeed there to begin with, but ran off to murder Simone while Cal was allegedly chatting with him. The actor would occasionally fake a sneeze to give an impression that Engels was there but could not be seen behind the backdrop. Lord knows, Cal could generate enough cigarette smoke for two. An expert actor such as Cal Lockheed could easily maintain the illusion of continually conversing with the man who was to become his guaranteed gravy train."

"You're saying, while Cal was talking, Arnie wasn't there?" Bettie reiterated.

"Not the entire time."

Venus was visibly upset, "Detective, that would imply that Cal was an accomplice to Simone's murder. He just couldn't be. Not dear, gentle Cal. I may be able to believe he was greedy for fame and fortune, but he'd never be a part of a cold-blooded homicide."

"I don't know that Arnie told Cal of his plans to murder Simone. He may have convinced him that he was setting up another awful prank to further embarrass Helena Baxter. Afterwards, Engels probably explained that the gag had taken a bad turn—as it had at The Dakota—and promised Cal a huge amount of hush money or had come to some other kind of generous arrangement.

"We may never know. Really, all Arnie had to accomplish for the moment was to keep his blackmailer quiet until we'd all left the theatre. He could've promised Cal anything to secure his silence. It's extremely likely that Arnie accompanied Lockheed back to his Varick Street duplex that very evening and killed him."

"You are so totally insane," shouted Arne, "I won't listen to anymore of this."

"You really have no choice in the matter," Renny seethed.

Helena Baxter stood while posing a question, "Detective, how in the world did Arnie have an opportunity to murder Caprice during the cocktail party? He spent most of his time fussing over the pretzels and potato chips table."

"I believe he killed Mademoiselle Fournier before the guests started to arrive. Miss Baxter, you told me Arnie'd made you a drink in the few relaxing moments prior to folks turning up. That you'd fallen asleep for about fifteen minutes when the Dakota sentry alerted you to the first visitors. Arnie even played some music on the stereo to cover up any noise. It was during that brief period of time that the murder took place. I suspect Arnie took the awful photos later in the evening, during the course of the party, when he noticed that Terry'd stopped taking pictures. It would only have taken a few minutes for Arnie to grab the camera, snap a few shots of his grizzly handiwork in the bedroom, remove the film, and put the camera back on the foyer table. Of course, it was risky, but we are dealing with an audacious personality. By the way, my team found the impressive makeshift darkroom equipment hidden in your apartment. Perfect for developing film and printing pictures from negatives."

"So, I have an interest in photography. Big deal." Arne spat.

"The whole point of sending the gruesome photographs to the media outlets was to permanently humiliate both of the women who'd publicly humiliated his father in death. Just as the stigma of being hit by a falling dumbbell plagued the memory of Magnus Engelstaad, Simone Caldwell would forever be remembered as the woman who fell through a trap door into a pile of garbage cans and snare drums. Caprice Fournier, oh right, the lady who caught a champagne cork in the eye. Hysterical, right?"

Renny walked over and stood behind Vic as he examined the sea of faces around the séance table. "Do you recall all of our speculative theories about the accident involving the goldfish bowl? We thought that perhaps Arnie had been startled having seen someone coming out of Mademoiselle Fournier's bedroom—

someone who shouldn't have been there? Was it the sudden surprise that led him to nervously drop Adam and Eve? Or, a second theory, one of advantageous misdirection taken advantage of by our mysterious killer?

"I suspect the actual explanation is much simpler. Arnie Engels was already soaking wet from having struggled with—and killing—Mademoiselle Fournier using the champagne bottle. He covered the spills down the front of his clothing with a bib apron for part of the evening. He came up with the clever idea of pouring water on himself, in the guise of losing his grip on the goldfish bowl, to explain the wet stains on his silk tie and shirtfront once the apron was removed."

Arne Engels crossed his arms petulantly, "You think you're so fucking brilliant."

Ignoring the remark entirely, Venus reasoned aloud, "Please explain why Cal Lockheed wasn't photographed after being killed, detective. Or humiliated. On the contrary, he was found regally sitting on a bejeweled throne from one of his stage plays. His death was certainly violent, but not embarrassing."

Renny circled the table as he spoke, "Arnie Engels genuinely liked Cal. He wasn't out to degrade him or place a permanent stain on his memory. I suspect your talented actor friend would be here among us today if he hadn't attempted a foolhardy spot of blackmail. I don't believe Cal considered how seriously unbalanced Arnie was until it was too late. That was really his undoing.

"Finally, we have Vic Senso, who'd caught a glimpse of Arnie's face reflected in one of the frames on the scenery wall of headshots. Only problem, he couldn't remember what he'd seen due to all the ensuing pandemonium. Engels overheard the art director mention his dilemma a number of times over the course of the next few days. He was determined that Vic must be stopped before his memory came back.

"Taking advantage of the Varick Street murder, Engels swiped a black vinyl raincoat, fedora, and boots from Lockheed's costume collection. After which, using the disguise, Arnie attempted to kill

Vic…twice. In the first instance, by pushing him down the stairs at the Elgin Theatre. Engels could have heard that Vic was going to the midnight show from Sardi building busybody, Guy Andersen. The second time, by blatantly threatening him with a butcher knife Arnie'd previously lifted from Helena Baxter's kitchen on one of his many visits to The Dakota apartment. Our killer here," Renny gestured toward the angry-looking general manager, "was prepared to commit murder number five at Thompson & Co when he knew the office was completely empty."

"You really should consider writing a play, detective. You've got quite a colorful imagination." Arnie Engels pompously sneered.

Renny smirked in return, "I don't need imagination. I have something even better. Evidence. Lots of it."

The detective gestured to The Johns who switched on the lights and swung open the library doors. Four armed policemen stood at attention, then swiftly muscled their way into the room.

"I think it's about time you left our party, asshole." Ava shouted across the séance table at Arnie Engels, as the officers pulled him to his feet. The outraged publicist turned to Perry, sitting next to her, and commented, "I cannot believe I allowed that psycho to put his hand down my panties."

"What panties?" Arnie yelled back at the redhead as the policemen escorted him out of the library.

"Ava, please, control yourself," said Perry, blushing.

Vic warmly embraced Renny Clements, patting him on the back.

"I'd say this handsome gentleman has earned a champagne cocktail. Also, all hail Helena Baxter for her superb performance at our bogus little séance."

The detective turned his attention to the stunning saucer-eyed lady seated at the head of the table.

"Mizz Mitzi, what can I say? I must apologize again for asking you to help us with our elaborate charade this evening. But it was for a worthy cause—to unmask a killer. You were absolutely wonderful."

The clairvoyant stood up from her chair, nodded graciously, and slowly looked around at the attractive group of elegantly dressed people in the library.

She said laughingly, "If Mizz Mitzi keeps hanging around with you theatre folk, she may have to apply for an Equity card."

Two Months Later

"This room is where it all started. Mizz Mitzi certainly caught the bad vibes early on," recollected Vic, "when she became physically ill at our *Blithe Spirit* presentation. She felt there was a potential killer sitting at our conference table but wasn't able to zero in on who it was."

"She did help immensely in filling in some of the gaps for me. I owe her much credit." Renny said, scanning the Thompson & Co conference room, which was bustling with exuberant animation. "I hope it's alright that I happened to conveniently stop by at lunchtime today."

"Feel free to do it a lot more often." Vic encouraged him.

"I have a surprise for you." The detective handed the art director his long-missing Canon F-1, "We were still holding your beloved camera in our evidence locker."

Vic embraced his prized possession and planted a kiss on it. "Actually, Renny, I just might award it to Terry Hagen. She certainly deserves it after her ordeal. Besides, I've wanted a reason to pay a repeat visit to her studio to have another gander at that psychopathic chihuahua of hers."

"Tu-tu? He's just an old sweetie," the detective said fondly.

"On the contrary, her dog is comparable to something you'd have nightmares about after eating too many *White Monkey* canapés." Vic snapped playfully.

Renny paused and widened his eyes for maximum effect as the volume in the room raised up a notch, "I must say, you theatre people always seem to be having a party of some kind. What're you celebrating now?"

The impromptu catered office lunch had been quickly organized in honor of the promotion of a Thompson & Co employee. Former receptionist Marsha was offered a permanent position in the art department. She would be tasked with creating the pictorial storyboards for proposed Broadway show television commercials. It was an undertaking that, quite frankly, Vic Senso was happy to pass on. He felt that he was developing into much more of a graphic designer than an illustrator, a talent in which Marsha excelled. The blonde bombshell was delighted.

"Vito was so excited when I called and told him the news," she squealed. "He wanted me to thank you again for…"

Bettie cut the former receptionist off mid-sentence since half the staff wouldn't grasp what she was talking about, not being privy to their intrigue involving the Marc Chagall canvas and Vito Lanzetta's part in its successful recovery by the NYPD Art Theft Detail.

"We're so thrilled for you, Marsha!" Bettie said excitedly.

From their offices on the floor above, Ava and Mark popped in to extend to Marsha their congratulations and to deliver unfortunate news.

"*Don't Hang Up* just posted their closing notice." Ava said sadly, her sharpened radar searching for roast beef among the various sandwich choices piled high upon the caterer's artistically arranged platters.

"I'd venture to guess that everyone involved in the production is relieved—Helena Baxter and Celeste Farris included. At least the play ran about a month. That's more than I'd have guessed after the lackluster reviews." Vic sighed. "When the flurry of publicity died down following the arrest, so did the action at the box office."

As Mark reached for a ham and turkey on rye, Bettie nudged him, "Remember, honey, we have dinner reservations before the theatre tonight."

"Yes, dear." Rhodes said, comically fluttering his thick eyelashes. "And *you* might remember, honey, we were running late this morning and had to skip breakfast."

Bettie giggled, "That wasn't entirely my fault if you'll recall."

"Get a room, you two," snarled Ava, "Oh, wait…it sounds as if you already have." The frenetic redhead rummaged around the room, "Hey, are there migraine remedies of any kind stashed in this verkakta ad agency?"

Arriving late to the party, Tobin Klein finally joined the celebration, kissed Marsha on the cheek, and tossed a leather-bound script at Vic. "This just came in. A new musical."

"A. New. Musical." Bettie waxed poetic, "Three of the most exciting words in the English language. What's it called?"

Vic scanned the gold embossed title. "*A Chorus Line.*"

Looking over their shoulder, while munching on her sandwich, Ava Chasten said, "Hm…sounds simply awful."

THE END

About the Author

Photography by Jon Bierman

Frank "Fraver" Verlizzo became synonymous with powerful and evocative storytelling through his poster designs. He designed the poster art for the original Broadway productions of Disney's *The Lion King;* Stephen Sondheim's *Sweeney Todd,* and *Sunday in the Park with George;* Ira Levin's *Deathtrap;* Stephen King's *Misery;* and the 50th Anniversary Celebration of Agatha Christie's *The Mousetrap* in London's West End.

His ability to capture the essence of a Broadway show in a single image earned him the prestigious Drama Desk Special Award in 1987. Playbill dubbed him, "the theatre poster legend." A collection of his work: *Fraver by Design—Five Decades of Theatre Poster Art from Broadway, Off-Broadway, and Beyond,* was published in 2017.

Frank's been a guest speaker at such venues as The NY Public Library for the Performing Arts at Lincoln Center, The Drama Book Shop; BroadwayCon, Pratt Institute and Yale University

Inspired by his mother, an avid life-long reader, Frank has been a devoted fan of books —specifically murder mysteries. In 2020, he began writing his own mystery series using his career in theatrical advertising as inspiration. The results of that labor are the books of the Retro Broadway Mystery Series.

www.ingramcontent.com/pod-product-compliance
Lightning Source LLC
Chambersburg PA
CBHW020407110726
47899CB00006B/1890